MELTING POINT
2040

MIKE BUSHMAN

www.meltingpoint2040.com

ISBN: 0988336901
ISBN 13: 9780988336902

Library of Congress Control Number: 2012917176
AltFuture Publishing

Printed in U.S.A.

Cover by Peri Poloni-Gabriel, Knockout Design, www.knockoutbooks.com

DEDICATION

My parents endured incredible sacrifices to provide all six of their children with the opportunity to define and build our lives. Without them, nothing I have achieved could have been possible. I am also grateful to my wife, family and friends for their patience during the many years I disappeared into work.

ACKNOWLEDGMENTS

A special thank you to friends and family who read early drafts of this book and provided guidance to help improve it, particularly Jennifer Marsh Ginder, Luisa Fernanda Cicero, Dan Cicero, Bill Bushman, Cathleen Bushman, Christine Hudzik and Lisa Ryder. I also need to thank hundreds of tremendous people I worked with during the past 25 years whose dedication, thoughtfulness and creativity enabled us to achieve success as a team.

Finally, my thanks to former Congressman Terry L. Bruce for inspiring my interest in policy and exposing me to the value of working across party lines to solve problems.

PROLOGUE

January 1, 2040

The most divisive issue since the 1960s, and perhaps even the 1860s, simmers throughout the United States.

Racial, ethnic and religious tensions have troubled the United States since its Declaration of Independence, and even earlier since Europeans first anchored along America's shoreline. All that's needed to again boil these issues over the sides of America's melting pot is the addition of a few more briquettes to the grill or the quick turn of a stovetop dial.

America's founding fathers wrote that "all men are created equal," but even they failed to recognize that "all men" rightly includes all men and all women regardless of race or other characteristic. So it's perhaps not surprising that America's multi-cultural society continues to battle the implications of its diversity 264 years later as the year 2040 starts. America's challenge is little different from the divides that have tested the world throughout its history.

Pockets of hate and intolerance have dotted the U.S. landscape in its less than three centuries of existence, though the objects of the greatest vitriol have changed repeatedly. Anti-black laws and sentiment lasted longest and resulted in the greatest cumulative violence. Italians were victims of the largest mass lynching in U.S. history. But many others have faced or still face discrimination as well. Irish. Hispanic. Arab. Asian. American Indian. Jew. Catholic. Mormon. Muslim. Women. Gays.

Conceptual truths embedded in the Constitution and the Bill of Rights helped shape the United States into a frequently positive global force. Failure to abide by these tenets has, at times, allowed others to surpass America as beacons of democracy, capitalism and freedom. Even on its best days, America must battle with demons of hate, fear and anger – confronting ignorance, narcissism and arrogance along the way.

At home, tensions erupt into violence when multiple failures overtake the nation's ability to solve problems. Failures to communicate, understand, tolerate and respect trigger these bursts of animosity.

Passage of civil rights laws in the 1960s moved America toward a period of integration that increased opportunities and requirements to work together. Then, after decades of progress, Americans started moving to live with people who shared their personal politics, values, religion, race and language. In doing so, the cross-fertilization of ideas and knowledge needed to reach consensus and solve important issues has become increasingly difficult.

Human rights and racial interest group advocates – supported by politicians elected in race-defined congressional and state legislative districts – accelerated this separation, sometimes unwittingly. In recent decades, efforts to help some immigrant communities catch up on standardized testing led many public schools to teach more subjects in each student's native language. As this trend took hold, parents often moved to place their children in schools where English is no longer the primary language.

The Depression of 2029-2035, brought on by government efforts to make debt payments without having to cede more land and resources to China, Japan, Germany and other large debt holders, further exacerbated racial tensions. Americans caught in years of deep unemployment sometimes looked for others to blame for their stagnation and despair. White supremacist groups saw startling membership increases, as did race-based hate groups organized by African Americans, Hispanics and others.

The addition of Puerto Rico as the 51st state created one of the most homogenous states in the nation and the second state after New Mexico to have Spanish as a legally required language. Then, in 2029, the U.S. Supreme Court approved the split of California into two states but only after redrawing the voter-approved boundaries to ensure a substantial

Hispanic majority in South California, or California del Sur. Race- and language-based separation accelerated nationally in the following decade.

Many other aspects of life have changed since the author's childhood as well. Cars reshape to the number of passengers and are driven by computer programs. People carry paper-thin, foldable Lifelink computers in sealed pockets requiring multiple security steps to open. Most U.S. citizens now work for foreign entities, partially a result of cheap currency from decades of excessive government debt. Only recently has Constitutional Amendment 29 cleaved inroads in excessively money- and party-focused political systems.

During this year, 2040, we follow the lives of dozens of individuals. The issues they face are complex. The challenge they battle threatens to divide a nation once united. While some know each other at the start of the year, most meet as the year progresses. This is the story of how their lives intersect.

CHAPTER 1

Important Note to Readers:

Quotes in italics are the author's best attempts at translating for meaning into English discussions that are taking place in Spanish and Mandarin.

January 3, 2040
West Nogales, Arizona

A parched, stale day greets Juan Gonzalez as he meanders toward FirstWal. He's decked out in Christmas gifts from Mama Gonzalez: shoes that fit with one pair of socks, hole-free black denim jeans and underwear from a sealed package. A button-down shirt borrowed from a neighbor billows to hide a thin, muscular frame, but these dressier clothes bolster Juan's confident stride. He smiles freely, even as he walks, just as he does most days.

While walking, Juan consumes two of the peanut butter, refried bean, brown rice and poblano balls he first made years ago when those ingredients were everything he could find at home. Now, he grabs them regularly for breakfast and late-night snacks. His walk to FirstWal takes him up and down gently rolling hills on the west side of the city. To his south, he has clear sight of shanties and small homes covering the hills on Mexico's side of the border wall. In front of him, he passes a mix of small apartments, mobile homes and middle-class fenced homes.

Border Patrol pick-up trucks pass routinely. During rush hour, he's also passed by automated school buses, parents chasing after kids to get to school on time, and trucks avoiding traffic delays on their way around massive distribution complexes sprawling west of I-19.

Now, days into 2040, Juan hopes to achieve the American dream. Though Mama Gonzalez often told him they moved here for opportunity, Juan only recently began believing he could live her dream. Tutoring wages help Juan buy food, clothes and anything else to help out at home, but aren't enough to also save for college. He needs more than tutoring pays to afford college.

As Juan walks to the West Nogales FirstWal store, a slight suction sound from his dress sneakers repeats like the ticking of an antique clock. Sticking to the flat black pavement. Popping on every move.

In just four years living in Arizona, Juan's achievements piled up. Starting varsity center mid. Holy Cross hospital volunteer of the year. President of the West Nogales High Mandarin Club and clearly the best Mandarin student in one of his only two classes not taught in Spanish. None of this success comes without work, but Juan's confident, casual demeanor in social settings makes it seem easy.

Nearing mid-day, temperatures are seasonally scorching. At nearly 90 degrees, it feels more like late spring. Coming after weeks of much colder weather, Juan's body reacts with more sweat than usual. Perhaps heat. Perhaps nerves. At FirstWal, he stops in the restroom to air-dry sweat from his head and torso before heading in for his interview.

"Pero, no necesito hablar inglés," Juan is forced to argue unexpectedly during his interview, before primarily switching to slowly delivered, but comprehensible English. "I know everyone here. Hablamos español. Anglos don't come here, except maybe to drink in México."

Store Manager Mike Sanchez understands Juan's frustration. Mike is also first generation American, his parents having moved to Nogales when he was a high school student. Twenty-four years later, the married father of two still speaks Spanish 90 percent of his day. In his corporate role, though, he relies on English perfected during four years of Jesuit education in Milwaukee.

Juan is one of three finalists for the West Nogales store's new personal shopping specialist job. Personal shopping is FirstWal's new offering designed to increase the share-of-wallet extracted from time-strapped customers. Mike knows from his nurse wife that Juan's personality is built for service. Juan adds warmth and brightness to the day of patients during his weekly volunteer shifts at Holy Cross, winning the Volunteer of the Year award last year. In the past two years, former patients posted hundreds of thank-you notes on his One World site. More than 3,000 people track his updates, including a large number of patients he helped and their extended families.

Mike also knows Juan could be a great asset if corporate management ever actually visits his store. Whether Mike's 15-year-old daughter is truly awed by Juan's command of Mandarin or just the victim of a terrible high-school crush isn't entirely clear, but Juan's regional Mandarin contest victories are even noted in the community updates Mike watches as his One Shot car takes him to work.

"If your English was as good as your Mandarin, Juan, I'd have hired you as soon as you walked in the door," Mike says, as Juan takes a few gulps from his refilled water bottle. "My wife can't say enough about how you are with people at the hospital. I double-checked with corporate management though, and our policy for all U.S. stores is employees must be fluent in English – no matter whether that matters here or not."

"I speak English . . . good enough," Juan replies before switching to a version of Spanglish where he blends English into his native tongue as he speaks faster than he can process his third language. "Como todo el mundo habla español aquí, I don't see how it matters. You know I'm good at Mandarin. Chino es el idioma más importante para los negocios. Es difícil to learn tres idiomas."

Taking a breath, Juan pulls out the multi-language translator he won in a Mandarin contest to be sure he says the next sentence correctly. "I just haven't focused on English, but I will if this is what you need," Juan tells Mike with a tone of resignation and a mix of Spanish and Mandarin accents to his English.

Mike adopts a more mentoring, fatherly tone. He's not rejecting Juan because he doesn't want him.

"You're making the right career decision focusing on Mandarin. It may not seem that way today, but with time, you'll see. Left up to me, I'd give you a job," Mike says, twitching intermittently to check the security screens on his wall panel to be sure the store is under control. "But our corporate team has to interview you and sign off before I hire anyone. Every corporate interview is in English, so even if I wanted to hire you, you can't survive that interview. Sorry. Your English needs to get better first and then you come back."

Juan stirs a bit in his chair, looking up from a seat noticeably closer to the floor than Mike's ergonomic black rolling chair, and faces into a stream of light from the glass brick windows behind Mike.

"FirstWal is a Chinese company," Juan says, saying "Chinese" with a Mandarin accent as he struggles to remember which language he is speaking. His fidgeting shows the first signs of any crack in his normal hard-earned confidence. He turns both palms up, bends his arms and lifts them slightly skyward with a shoulder shrug. Catching himself clenching his fists as he brings them down, he consciously opens them up. A long look at Mike tells him today isn't one of his good days.

"I thought Mandarin would . . . help . . . here, if anywhere," Juan says, aided by the translation program. "I need this job. I can't go to college without money. And I can't work my whole life . . . just to pay off college."

Mike understands Juan's dilemma – and admires his foresight. He contemplates ways to work around the corporate system to hire Juan – including have a double do the web interview – but realizes he can't risk his own career and family future.

"Our regional president wants people to succeed, but to him the highest level he cares about is people who report to him, so he can take credit for them. He only speaks English. He doesn't want anyone succeeding around him, and certainly not having a conversation he can't understand. He doesn't value Mandarin the way the Chinese do and he decides what we do here," Mike says as he reaches out to shake Juan's hand and then motions toward his door.

Juan couldn't know how much Mike wished he didn't have to follow policy.

For years, Mike's FirstWal store has been a top performer. Still, during the weeks Shanghai-based Executive Vice President Jia Lin spent with FirstWal in the United States each of the past three years, West Nogales had not made her agenda. Among the many possibilities, Mike thinks he may be blacklisted from corporate interaction because he isn't one of U.S President Chet Leach's vocal supporters.

Mike considers hiring Juan to personally listen to and translate FirstWal's corporate downloads, but realizes he won't know which of these are confidential until after they are translated. Again, too much risk.

The morning began with great hope for Juan. If hired into one of the largest global corporations, he could pay for college, strengthen language skills, gain business experience and build his resume. Only a few large companies around West Nogales are Chinese-owned. His options to make his high school job more than just a paycheck are limited. He can get work – the local economy is improving for some types of work, particularly south of the border – but none of these jobs help him really make it. Mama Gonzalez sacrificed too much for him to not do whatever it takes to succeed.

Stepping back outside FirstWal, Juan begins the two-mile walk back to his West Target Range apartment. The suction sound returns, now thoroughly irritating his eardrums. Juan struggles to control his indignation, talking out loud: "It's not fair. I've done everything right. I'm smart. I work hard. This doesn't make sense."

Walking with hands clasped behind his head, a habit when frustrated and trying to calm his temper, Juan considers how to get what he wants. "What side of the wall does he think I live on?" he screams. No one turns to look.

CHAPTER 2

January 3, 2040
Chicago

It's tough to call him a national hero, because the hatred felt by the old-guard political elite for University of Chicago Professor Paul Stark rages deeply. Seven years after a long campaign succeeded in imposing the most fundamental political reforms in U.S. history, many previously strident detractors now see the merit of his work.

His achievement came at great personal cost. In addition to the emotional torment of years spent trying to change the political order, he carries scars from a series of physical attacks police insist were robberies. Even today, he habitually looks for threats in any confined setting and around blind corners.

In 2033, Colorado became the 39th state to ratify a constitutional amendment Professor Stark helped champion that shook the political establishment to its core. The effort took five years from his life, beginning with the seed of an idea introduced in his now famous Integrated Culture and Policy course. After decades of U.S. political deterioration, his ideas built such strong popular momentum that politicians, most preparing to run in newly shaped districts during the second depression, felt compelled to support its passage in the 2032 elections. Since then, the amendment made way for a return of government to the constitutional promise of being "by the people, for the people." That progress, though, has not been a remedy for inherent national divisions built over the past century.

Improvement. Certainly. Panacea. By no means.

While Professor Stark helped foster political opportunities for Americans, many still sit on the sidelines, expecting others to create the America that best suits their needs. So while America is a better place with the Political Freedom Amendment, as Amendment 29 is now called in history classes, several of America's long-ignored issues remain unsolved.

Days before January classes, Professor Paul Stark sits in a small, comfortable restaurant several blocks south of the Hyde Park campus. Small puddles remain at his feet from snow long since melted off the soles of his shoes. Random piles of paper obscure the wrapper from an apple bran muffin consumed just as light started to make its way through the dense clouds encasing the city. He sits in the back corner facing toward the front door, looking impulsively at everyone who enters. His checkered flannel shirt is spotted with fresh coffee stains. He often misses his mouth as his concentration shifts to reading notes in mid-sip. Bran crumbs linger on top of his well-worn jeans.

Deep in thought as he finalizes preparations, he outlines his syllabus. Noting that whites will no longer be the majority of the U.S. population at the end of the year, 2040 is the perfect time to debate the roles of race, racial divides and racism on government.

"Excuse me Professor. It's 1:30. Are you interested in lunch today?" the owner says. Her thoughtfulness is one of many reasons Heart and Soul Café is one of Professor Stark's primary off-campus work locations.

"How many years do I have to ask you to call me Paul?" he says.

"How can I call you Paul when you're lost in Professor mode?" she says. "You haven't said 10 words to me or anyone else all day."

"I'm sorry. Just trying to make sure I'm prepared for a topic I haven't focused on in years," he says.

"What's that?"

"Racial politics and how it affects government."

"Interesting topic. Let me ask you: What do you see when you see me?" the owner asks.

"What do you mean?"

"Just answer the question."

"I see a friend, a caring, intelligent conversationalist and . . . and, uh, well your husband could snap my neck in two seconds, so I'll stop there," Professor Stark says, with a glimmer of a smile.

"Well if you don't see the color of my skin, you aren't ready to talk racial politics," she says.

"It's not that I don't see it. It's just that it doesn't matter to me, white, black, brown, yellow, red, whatever," he says.

"Well, honey, then you certainly aren't ready to teach that class. You have to acknowledge differences to appreciate and move past them. I'm not offended when someone recognizes I have dark chocolate skin. I love how I look, and I assume you love it too. And if you don't, well, then I'll say some prayers, maybe for you, or maybe just about you."

She smiles gently at him as a few seconds pass, holding out her notepad and pen. He stares back, though his eyes are glazed in a way that she knows he's back in his own world. Standing there, she waits for a response.

"You know. Maybe you're right. I need to be better prepared. I'll take the usual for lunch, but add in a sweet potato pie," Professor Stark says, refocusing on his Lifelink and notes. "I have a lot more thinking to do."

"Always happy to feed you Paul, and provide a little free lesson to the professor as well."

***

Fresno, California

Rachel Cruz hates this day for many reasons. The thought of leaving the relative warmth of Fresno, California for frigid, blustery Chicago is toughest at the start of each winter quarter. Challenging herself in one of the world's most intense academic environments made sense when Rachel finally picked Chicago over Yale. Now, doing this for the fourth year, she wonders what she was thinking.

Compounding the physical discomfort is the emotional detachment. Rachel and her Mom remain best friends, but they talk far less frequently without the intermittent, casual conversations that come from being physically close. Rachel is serious and driven when it comes to academics. Amiable and engaging, her few academic blemishes came when studying was pushed aside to help a close friend through a crisis. Her essays detailing the experience and explaining why she would make the same choices again helped win admissions to all of her stretch schools.

"Next time I see you, you'll be a University of Chicago graduate. I'm so proud of you sweetie," Rachel's mom tells her, holding on before letting her walk out the door to the Right Size adaptable car waiting with her dad to escort her to San Francisco's Pelosi International Airport.

The four-hour ride to the airport is quiet – even with congested traffic. Rachel messages dozens of friends to find out when they return to campus. She arranges the limited time she is allowing for a social calendar until she finds out if the Integrated Culture and Policy class rumors are for real. Rachel's relationship with her dad isn't as close as either would like. Long drives are much quieter than when her mom drives her, but Mrs. Cruz has to be back at work today.

Victor Cruz, Rachel calls him Papa, worked long hours through her youth, leaving little time to build as deep of a relationship as both would have liked. Rachel still cringes when arguing with her father, frequently the disciplinarian among her parents, fearing consequences she could typically avoid from her mother.

As they approach the terminal, Papa Cruz tries a bit of small talk, asking about Rachel's interests, friends and class schedule. A few short, cryptic answers later, they pull into the terminal's drop-and-dash.

Papa Cruz programs the car to reshape for one-passenger return. Air releases from the inflated central sections, small jacks drop to lift the right side and metal axles and undercarriages mechanically overlap to shrink the car. Papa hugs Rachel. "I'll miss you," he says. "I can't wait to watch you debate. Stay focused. You can set yourself up for a good life if you do well these next months. Don't let anything or anyone stand in your way now. This isn't the time to mess around."

As she walks inside, Rachel feels tears welling up. "Can't he just leave it? Why's he always pushing?" she says, louder than she intended.

Seconds later, she's checking in for her flight, thinking about the cold and ready to see her friends.

CHAPTER 3

January 17, 2040
Idaho Springs, Colorado

By 11 a.m. on this bright, cool morning, Pete Roote is desperate enough to step out of his Miner Street rented room and ride into dense urban congestion where jobs can be found.

Living just a short distance from fast-charging creeks sequestered amid serene, snow-capped mountains, Pete finds few daily distractions from his New Rite adventures. His sporadic social encounters are often cut short when he dwells on his biggest irritation – the large swaths of Denver where English is of little use. Lately, though, he focuses on his rapidly deteriorating financial circumstances. Despite a relatively frugal lifestyle, Pete is now faced with canceling his virtual war game competitions and treasured New Rite survival events. Losing these services would free up at least nine hours for Pete every day, but leaves him little motivation to move. For years, all of Pete's feelings of achievement have come from victories in war game competition settings.

With the state's extended unemployment and welfare limit coming to an end, Pete has no choice but to find work. Even if he can no longer abstain from paid employment, Pete's focus will remain on New Rite. He knows how long he needs to work before he does something to be fired and restart unemployment. Still, threatened with having to wait in charity food lines with people he has no interest in knowing, Pete is desperate enough to look for work.

Pete's spiral into poverty, with long periods of human connection coming largely through New Rite competitions, began early. An avid on-line war competition gamer early in high school, he deteriorated academically and socially from there.

During high school, Pete competed in on-line survival games while saving gift money to buy his New Rite competition pod. Pete's once promising academic record suffered from his game addiction. He was driven to succeed, just not academically.

During high school, teachers saw poor performance, but rarely understood the reason. Most assumed he drew the intellectual short straw at birth. Not a surprising reaction, given he had stopped making any effort to do well.

Pete wore glasses throughout high school that housed game screens. Combined with controls designed to look like they belonged in a school environment, Pete created illusions that he was listening and taking notes. As U.S. history was discussed during high school lectures, for example, Pete surveyed battle scenes, identified sniper locations, gathered supplies and even negotiated supply deals. Once in the heat of a battle, his eyeglass console allowed him to focus and click with movements of his eye. Adjustments on a pen-shaped controller and taps on a sheet mimicking a Lifelink keypad allowed him the rest of his control requirements at most game levels. While declining grades highlighted Pete's separation into an alternate reality, his growing insolence toward expectations beyond his war games strained his relationships – ultimately to the breaking point. Angered by his refusal to work or go to college, his parents kicked him out of the house. Pete moved west and only occasionally mentioned his "birth family."

Having long ago left the world of lectures, rules and obsolescent technology behind, Pete today is a top contender to win in-person, live-action New Rite battles in addition to his on-line victories. Now, survival weekends are the focus of his life. A certified New Rite ace virtual game fighter, Pete is also a highly ranked human competition survivalist.

While it talks about game players as "family," New Rite is very much a business; one of the largest based in the United States. Maintaining a family-oriented feel is increasingly challenging, but program managers live and breathe commitment to New Rite. The local Colorado chapter of New Rite meets monthly for three-day weekends in a group-owned compound encompassing Byers Peak and other areas formerly included in Arapaho National Forest.

New Rite gamers living outside the mountainous terrain quickly learn to arrive early on competition weekends to reduce the effects of altitude sickness. For those with jobs, vacation is synonymous with New Rite. Sometimes, those who can't escape work telecommute from New Rite training sites around the country. Encrypted communication at these sites allows New Rite members to appear to work from wherever they want to seem to be working.

Having lived now for seven years in an existence of online gaming combined with intense training weekends, Pete is in remarkable physical shape. New Rite's full-scale game – the one Pete starts up the minute he is functional each morning – puts participants in an air-injected, nearly room-sized pod. A harness system enables full-range motion over variable surfaces that continuously adapt to each competitor's movement. Participants run, jump, skydive, punch, shoot and compete in ways every bit as physically demanding as military training exercises.

As they move up the competitive ranks, New Rite fighters can spend hours in awkward positions in the unit, perfecting sniper and scouting techniques. Oxygen concentration units in the pods provide tiring participants energy boosts. Losers are punished – taking jet-speed air blasts from the pod that replicate feelings of being shot, sliced, hit and battered.

Health-monitoring systems New Rite participants wear during game play generally keep the harm from becoming too internally destructive to gamers, but bruises and welts are common.

Coming up to his last days with his game connections, Pete wonders how, with the coming loss of his New Rite access, he can maintain his competitive edge.

Several times a week now, Pete rolls out of bed, showers, drinks his breakfast protein mix and takes the Ultra Speed to Denver. His town has limited work potential, and Pete has irritated every employer there over the past three years as he made just enough contact in job searches to hold on to unemployment and then welfare payments. His remarkable ability to get caught up in competitions, missing interviews and even first days of work, had finished off bad impressions in town for those who hadn't found his strident, militaristic appearance and lack of experience a worrisome combination.

Realizing he has run the gamut on a long string of government support, Pete sets three alarms every interview morning and wears loose clothing to hide his chiseled frame. He can't think of any more tricks to stay on the government dole. He needs to get work so he can afford his war-game competitions.

TC Meatpacking has a Denver storefront designed specifically to recruit new employees for its slaughterhouses all around the state and region. In addition to being a majority Hispanic metro area, Denver is a stopping point for legal and illegal Mexican immigrants moving to Canada's continually burgeoning oil sands, the Dakota's gas fields, and mines around the U.S. and Canadian Rockies. TC Meatpacking needs to recruit enough of these travelers to pull them into TC operations. Decent wages and quicker returns home are selling points, offset by work often more physically demanding and aroma even tougher to take than the sticky oil substance extracted in Alberta.

TC wet meat facilities are nearly vomit inducing to the uninitiated, particularly sections focused on eviscerating offal – animal parts most people don't knowingly eat. The gutting of intestines, colons and other parts to be washed and ground into animal feed, sausages and fertilizer disturbs even hardened veterans. New TC employees wear scent packs for the first month of employment that gradually reduce in strength, helping ease employees into the world of ground meat, blood, bones and cartilage.

Pete needs income, but needs to be physically challenged at work to stay in shape. He can't go soft and hope to maintain dominant standing in New Rite's competition hierarchy – let alone become champion of the Rites of Passage national survival competition. He hasn't worked this hard to become one of the dominant competitors in the country only to have a soft-serve job eat away at his physique and stamina.

Walking into the TC storefront, Pete knows he's the ideal candidate for anything in meatpacking and is sure this is the right job for him – at least until he can re-qualify for unemployment and refocus on New Rite.

"I'd like to work for TC as long as you're flexible around my monthly weekends," Pete says. TC has a long policy of prioritizing reservists because of the discipline and proven ability to endure physical hardship they bring to the role. Pete looks like he is in the military.

"We fully support the reserves and National Guard. As long as you work with us the rest of the time, we can work with you on military duties," the recruiting officer said. "But before I waste your time, or mine, you're speaking to me in English. Hablas español?"

"What? Is that some Spanish crap?"

"Sí, hablas español?" the recruiter repeats.

"I don't speak no freakin' Spanish. This is America, in case you can't tell," Pete says.

"I'm afraid there's no point applying then," the recruiter says. "Our entire workforce speaks Spanish, including our management team. You wouldn't be able to understand any of the directions, read the safety warnings, talk with anyone."

"I don't need to talk at work. I'm perfectly comfortable on my own. I'll just read what I need and be fine," Pete says.

"Sorry, it's not even worth discussing. We only hire Spanish-speaking employees, and you clearly don't fit. Thanks for coming in though," the recruiter states as he returns back toward his desk.

Pete shatters the cheap pressed-wood desktop with a slam of his fist and forearm. Glaring at the recruiter, who has turned at the startling noise, Pete walks out.

"We're not done here," Pete says with enough menace to make his point, and nearly enough to incite the recruiter into calling police.

Pete gets off the Ultra Speed 10 miles short of his stop, having decided to run the rest of the way home along the highway. After a long run, he hopes he'll be in a less destructive mood when he gets home.

CHAPTER 4

January 26, 2040
Dallas, Texas

The open-air ice rink in the recently revived Dallas Galleria warms in 60-degree outdoor temperatures, but the firm ice attracts hundreds on this afternoon break. Ramon Mantle is dazzled watching his 10-year-old sister as she spins, skates backwards and does toe loops, axels and other jumps that all look the same to him.

Despite calling her an "accident" since she was born nearly 17 years after him, Ramon takes his responsibility for her seriously.

"How's my little angel?" he asks.

She reaches up, grabs Ramon around the neck and hugs him. Ramon begins to lift her until the front of her skate taps dangerously close to an area of tremendous potential pain.

"Let's get those skates off before you end our family name," he says.

Celia Mantle carefully unlaces and places her custom-made skates in a black leather cases emblazoned with white, red and green stones – all gifts from Ramon. Transported quickly back to their Shady Shores estate by his private service, Ramon is followed as usual by his full-time security team. That team still uses an antique gas-powered car Ramon modified to respond quickly if trouble develops.

Ramon is an important figure in Dallas business and political circles. Though only 27, he turns out thousands to work political campaigns. His favorite candidates always seem well funded. Ramon has a reputation among those he supports of never asking for favors – just asking them to do what's right for the community. Despite this almost altruistic support, politicians don't quite know whether the young upstart is a supporter or a future competitor.

Ramon is a local hero to many who believe he forced drug dealers out of town. He uses his public reputation as an anti-drug campaigner to great advantage. To keep his surrounding communities clean, he personally starts some of the worst rumors. Thanks to the rumors, young kids in the area fear that experimenting with drugs will get them tortured or worse. A local legend spread years ago graphically detailed how he ordered the serrated knife torturing and partial skinning of teens pushing younger neighbors into the drug world. No public evidence ever linked him to any tortures or killings. But rumors continue.

Local police and prosecutors, well aware of these suspicions, never found anyone who admitted suffering abuse from Ramon or his men. More importantly, they like that drug use in the area is declining, and aren't about to do anything to reverse that trend.

Ramon's intimidating image is bolstered when anyone sees his security team. Though paid through the logistic systems company famous for his Easy Ride operating system invention, Ramon doesn't select the ex-military agents who follow him everywhere.

Ramon is even more feared by those few aware of his side work as Cesar Castillo's de facto Chief Technology Officer. Mexico-based Castillo is known to almost everyone as Caskillo. Ramon does none of the dirty work with Castillo's business and personally knows little of the violent work that happens – though he is not naïve about what Castillo uses his technology to deliver.

When competitive threats emerge, Castillo's elite Protection Corps travel quietly to permanently settle scores. Made up largely of ex-Mexican and ex-U.S. military personnel, the Protection Corps is the best-armed and best-run private military in the world, aided by the quiet cooperation of many in the Mexican military who earn handsome additional income providing training, technology and information. In large stretches of Mexico, the Protection Corps acts as police, judge, jury and military defense.

Ramon long ago had a miniature camera and microphone implanted in his left ear lobe, looking every bit like an oversized diamond stud.

Thanks to a five-point welding job between the front and the back of the stud that signals if ever disconnected, he can remove it without notice only by severing his ear lobe from behind the camera view. From this surveillance stud, Castillo's team sees and hears nearly all that Ramon does. He trusts Ramon as much as anyone in his organization, but told Ramon the electronic surveillance is standard business practice to ensure employees don't try working around him. He sometimes quotes long-ago U.S. President Ronald Reagan in explaining the studs to Ramon: "Trust, but verify."

The extra margin Castillo earns on each kilo with Ramon's technology support allowed him over the past decade to become the sole U.S. and Canadian distribution service for any drugs brought north from Mexico. Each delivery earns a 10 percent commission from drug pushers who voluntarily turned shipping over to Castillo in return for being allowed to run street sales networks unabated in select markets.

More importantly, Castillo's profit advantage on his own sales enables him to expand his share by buying or forcing his primary rivals out of business. If remaining or new competitors acquired Ramon's technology independently, Castillo would need to return his operation to the days of competing for superiority through extensive on-street violence, beheadings and decimation of entire communities.

Castillo won't shy from killing if that's what's needed. As a younger man, he personally gutted a few people, severed some limbs and beheaded several who he thought betrayed him. But his real thrills are money and control. His vast wealth and strong alliance with his host government are made possible by the substantial largesse he shares with its leaders. Peaceful, well-supported local communities make these relationships easy for politicians. This support could be strained again if violent confrontations flare up.

Castillo's far-reaching finance arm takes his excess drug wealth, launders it and invests in legitimate businesses. Through these controlled companies, Castillo has both enriched himself and gathered wide-ranging economic and political influence.

Ramon came to the drug world accidently, having been discovered at an early age after building what continues to be a state-of-the art logistics program. At first, he only tapped into Texas police systems and conducted real-time satellite tracking of police vehicles. Ramon built his first program at 15 so he could drag race illegal cars without running into police interference. Driving off-grid cars at high speeds remains one of his favorite leisure activities. The ability to evade detection enabled by Ramon's program allows Castillo to optimize delivery routes in real-time to avoid lost cargo and prosecuted employees. As a side benefit, it saves fuel costs and distribution fleet capital.

Little sister Celia is Ramon's greatest treasure. He guards her with the passion of an over-protective father. That intrusive behavior comes at a cost to Celia. Boys fear hanging out with her. Girls at school are superficially nice, but Celia faces a larger dose of the behind-their-back nastiness that dominates interaction among middle-school girls. The wealthy lifestyle enabled by Ramon drives envy from her friends. Ramon's rumored tortures generate fear from students and teachers alike. Celia's flirtatious style with older boys upsets boys her age and girls of many ages. All of this adds to the typically tortuous way middle-school girls treat each other – alternating between best friends and mortal enemies within hours and even minutes.

"I'm sleeping over at Raquel's tonight. Mom said it's okay," Celia announces on the drive home.

"Who's Raquel? She's not in your class and she's not on your skating team," Ramon replies as he drives the two home.

"She's in sixth grade and we met on the playground. I get to be friends with whoever I want," Celia contends.

"You can play at school. But I don't know about sleeping over," Ramon says, being sure to provide the stern look he imagined his father would deliver if he could be there.

"You're not my father. You can't tell me what to do," Celia tells him.

"I sure as hell will tell you what to do and what not to do. You need to listen to me – for your own protection. I'll check out Raquel," he says as he sends a quick note to his security team.

Thirty seconds later, the answer comes back. Raquel checks out. Her father works for Ramon and would know not to let harm come to his little sister.

"You're fine to sleep at Raquel's. You know I'm just trying to protect you," Ramon says in now-calm voice.

"I'm not an idiot. I wish you would stop treating me like one," Celia screams, pounding her feet on the steps up to her room. *"I'm not doing anything stupid."*

Ramon fights off an angry reaction as he chases after her. *"Look, Celia, it's not what you do I'm worried about. Someone has to look out for you and Dad would kill me if I let anything happen to you,"* Ramon tells her.

CHAPTER 5

January 31, 2040
Chicago

The grey color accenting Professor Paul Stark's slightly receding hairline provides an aura of distinction and respectability that makes him more appealing than in his younger years. A decade earlier, he was sometimes referred to derisively as "youthful, inexperienced and naïve." Then, during rise to national prominence working to stamp out the excess influence of money on national politics, these charges carried some truth.

With a nose more prominent than his chin and skin sagging under eyes that need the magnification of his glasses to not appear undersized, 43-year-old Professor Stark isn't physically a head turner. Yet, a decade after his major political battle, heads still swivel with an obligatory "don't we know him?" question exchanged between passersby. He generally pretends to have not heard, but searches the area for threats before dropping his head and slowly unleashing a slight, wry smile.

Professor Stark, the David Laitin Distinguished Professor of Political Science at the University of Chicago, finds it interesting to study the quirks of his students. Professor Stark helps the University attract a diverse group of students who think at an early age that Congress or the Supreme Court is on their career path. A recognized expert on the interaction of culture and politics, Professor Stark is noted for inciting intense debate in his classes and demanding thorough preparation. These debates attract media coverage, in turn attracting better students.

"Explain to me what is racist about requiring that everyone in a political system share a common language," Professor Stark says.

"The concept itself is inherently racist," says Rachel Cruz, an engaging social wanderer when not intensely focused on her next achievement target. Professor Stark's reputation attracted her here and she took great pride in winning acceptance into his course. She's not about to let this opportunity slide, not after preparing through winter break with notes on points she thought might earn his respect.

"Tell me why," he says.

"Clearly, it shows a lack of respect for diversity. You teach about the importance of cultural diversity in America's growth and the dominant role immigrants played in 20th century politics and economics," notes Rachel, the half-Mexican, half-white native from the south end of the State of North California. She reflexively twists the back of her long, dark hair into a hand-held ponytail.

Rachel was raised in a modest Fresno, California home. Her Mexican American father, Papa Cruz, had worked full time while struggling to earn his college degree; then worked even harder to create financial stability for his family. Rachel's mother was raised in a far more privileged upper-middle class Monterey home until divorce left Rachel's mother and grandmother struggling to get by. The randomness of child support payments sent from overseas added to a tough childhood for Rachel's mother. With appreciation for the difficulties life brings, both of Rachel's parents instilled a sense of hard work and self-reliance. As language skills went, Rachel also began with a tremendous advantage. Until high school, her father spoke to her only in Spanish. Her mother spoke to her only in English.

Rachel continues, "So language is just an extension of culture and you can't respect a culture if you don't respect its language. In fact, you can't even truly understand a culture without knowing its language because mastery of a language helps explain a culture."

"So people who don't master their own language can't understand their own culture. Is that what you mean to say?" Professor Stark says.

"I don't know that I said that. I meant people learning a new culture can only truly understand that culture if they also master the language."

"So, if cultural diversity is so important and language diversity is the same as cultural diversity," Professor Stark inquires, "why do you think the Supreme Court decided in *Sanchez v. the United States* to re-split California in a way different from the manner originally designed. The Court ruled that the initially approved new borders to split California into two states violated the Voting Rights Act by 'confining a large Hispanic population to minority political status in both states when this population could obtain clear majority status in one state with more thoughtfully aligned boundaries.'"

The Voting Rights Act of 1965 was originally intended to ensure that disenfranchised African Americans in southern states could register and vote. Soon, interest group advocates, some federal judges and the U.S. Justice Department charged with protecting these voting rights, began pushing the creation of majority-minority legislative districts. When passed in the 1960s, racism was far more overt than it is today. Then, the majority white population was largely unwilling to vote for candidates of any other race. In much of the country, even sharing a water fountain across racial boundaries was either tacitly or legally forbidden.

Only a few years before the Voting Rights Act passage, the election of President John F. Kennedy shattered one cultural divide many did not think America was prepared to handle – the election of a Catholic. The idea that America would, in the lifetime of those born that year, elect three women, two African Americans, two Hispanics, a Mormon and an Asian to the top two offices of the nation would have generated scorn and perhaps even fear among some in the 1960s.

The evolution in American views about race continues to swing as wildly as Supreme Court decisions on Voting Rights Act implementation. The Court regularly adjusts its view of the proper balance between creating majority-minority districts and keeping political districts contiguous. At least every decade, a new battle erupts nationally, with U.S. House control often in the balance. State elections this year will shape the Supreme Court's new political geography challenges for 2042 elections.

The 5-4 Supreme Court vote in the 2029 *Sanchez* case remains controversial more than a decade later. In that case, the Supreme Court reset negotiated borders after Californians decided to split into two states. The *Sanchez* decision ensured Hispanics dominated political control of California del Sur, or South California.

Rachel, again running her hand through the ends of her hair, is confident she can articulate an incontrovertible truth. "Clearly, the Supreme Court understood the Hispanic population – while thoroughly dominant in southern California – wasn't large enough to consistently overcome the North's Anglo-Asian-black coalition to maintain political control," she tells the class. "Today, California del Sur has Spanish as one of two official languages and North California continues to operate in English. The Court understood the importance of respecting different cultures and allowed the different cultures to thrive by creating two states with more reasoned borders."

Professor Stark surveys the class and sees no one prepared to immediately debate Rachel's point.

"So if I hear you properly," he says, "your argument is that we all need to respect cultural diversity and the best way to respect cultural diversity is to allow cultures to operate separately, up to and including using a different language. Did I capture your position accurately?"

"I think that's right," Rachel says. "We've proven this works in North California and California del Sur. The division of the state allows people to live where they fit better."

"And where do you best fit Rachel?" Professor Stark asks. "You come from mixed heritage. By quirk of map lines set under court order, you're part of North California. Is that the right answer for you? Within the U.S, should political and economic opportunities be determined by geography?"

Thinking for a brief moment to be sure she understands, Rachel looks around the room to see if facial expressions give her any hint at the right answer.

"In reality, we all have the right to choose the situation best for ourselves. If we had wanted, my family could have moved south. In fact, I very well may move there when I finish here," she replies, looking toward a large pane of windows streaming in natural light and views of Midway Plaisance Park. "It'll certainly be nice never to have to trudge through 10 inches of snow in below-zero weather with 30-mile-an-hour winds burning my cheeks."

Professor Stark leaves his elevated speaking platform, stepping to the windows as if he is searching for something new outside. Leafless trees and several evergreens dot the open space as he looks south to a tougher part of the City.

"Okay. So, keeping your circumstances in mind, let's talk about another important Supreme Court case, *Brown vs. Board of Education*. Who can tell me about this case and why it matters on this topic?"

Tamika, a Chicago public school system product who lives nearby and attends with help from an academic scholarship, sees an opening to get the professor's attention. An intense competitor – she was captain of both her debate and basketball teams in high school – Tamika wants to make a positive early impression as the new quarter starts. *"Brown vs. Board of Ed* is an important 100-year-old case in which the Supreme Court ruled it's unconstitutional for a state to keep blacks and whites separated in schools. Basically, they said separation by race inherently creates inequality," Tamika's says with a confidence that had helped her overcome innumerable barriers to success.

"That's a fair summary Tamika. Now tell me what that has to do with Rachel's argument," Professor Stark says.

Tamika looks at Rachel and takes what seems a protracted time to think about it and consider what she is about to say. No one else in class offers to save her from the silence. Professor Stark stares at Tamika until she is ready to answer.

"Well, she's arguing that respecting cultural diversity means some cultures must have government-sanctioned opportunity to function independently. In the *Brown* case, the Court argued that keeping races – and really different cultures – separate by law inherently creates inequality," Tamika says, confident she understands what the Professor wants her to say.

"Someone else jump in here," Professor Stark pleads. "So if separation inherently creates inequality, how do we justify the Supreme Court's *Sanchez* decision to ensure Hispanics can operate independently of what Rachel calls the Anglo-Asian-black coalition in North California? Or for that matter, how do we justify seven decades of creating majority-minority congressional districts under the assumption that race is more important than many other attributes as the primary determinant of a political community's shape."

Jeremy hadn't thought about the contrast in how the Voting Rights Act and education system requirements were enforced by the Supreme Court before, but he could see discrepancies in the concepts now. Raising his hand, the Milwaukee native gets Professor Stark's attention. Professor Stark nods for him to go ahead.

"I have a lot of Irish in me, so I spent time studying Irish history in high school," Jeremy says. Professor Stark looks at him quizzically – not really knowing whether Jeremy will speak to the question being asked or show himself as one of the mistakes Stark makes every year accepting a student more interested in speaking than thinking.

"When the Irish came to America during and following the Great Famine, they were ostracized and segregated. Others had been here for more than 100 years already and largely spoke English with each other, though there were big sections of the country where German was the common language and many places where other languages were important. America might have viewed itself as an open society, but the Irish were unwelcome for a long time, especially the Catholics," Jeremy says, looking toward Professor Stark for assurance it's okay to continue. Jeremy is tall, gangly and wears clothes more likely to be seen at Easter mass than in the classroom. Professor Stark reminds himself that you can't tell intellect by appearance and motions for Jeremy to keep going.

"It took literally decades for Irish Catholics to escape Know Nothing and KKK target status and achieve integration into mainstream America. They did this by speaking English outside the home and, over generations, marrying other religions and other races until there were enough cross-culture Irish people doing lots of different types of jobs so Irish were no longer a mystery to everyone else," Jeremy continues. "Ironically, the creation of Catholic-only schools and colleges slowed Irish integration into mainstream society."

"We have only a minute left in class, Jeremy, so get to the point," Professor Stark says.

"If the Irish had been given a separate state and allowed to make Gaelic the separate language of the state when they first arrived, the lack of focus on learning English would have kept the Irish separate from the rest of the country for generations and perhaps forever. It was the need to learn

English and work with people of different ethnicities to achieve their economic dreams that allowed the Irish to integrate and stop being victimized by No Irish Need Apply discrimination," Jeremy concludes.

"Good close," Professor Stark says. "We'll come back to this next quarter, so consider yourself warned I'll expect a 3,000-word essay on your view of how the *Brown* and *Sanchez* decisions affect the cultural direction of our country. I suggest you start working on this now."

CHAPTER 6

Summer, 2032
Dallas, Texas

The relationship between Ramon Mantle and Cesar Castillo formed by happenstance.

A Texas-based Castillo delivery driver known as Speed supplemented his income by drag racing, competing against Ramon frequently for cash or cars.

The results of a destination battle in which he lost his fastest car to Ramon infuriated Speed. Three miles into the roughly 10-mile race, both were travelling near 190 miles per hour on a highway that should have taken them 80 percent of the way to the finish line. When Ramon sharply braked and exited the highway early, Speed was sure Ramon's car would be his to take home. His certainty was erased one mile later when he spotted a police speed trap.

Speed braked hard and slammed his car down the exit ramp, with police taking chase. Speed drove furiously through side streets, damaging his car repeatedly as he pushed to reach the pre-arranged escape traps on the other side of the finish line. As he drove past the finish line, he saw Ramon at the line – waving and smiling.

Speed escaped a closing collection of police by getting into a pre-arranged street maze in which puncture strips were popped up behind him. When multiple police cars chasing him skidded with blown tires, he safely pulled unseen into a waiting garage. It was then his fury grew that he must have been played.

Days later, when Ramon came to collect his winnings, Speed and his friends grabbed him, beat him enough to make clear they were serious, tied him to a pole and threatened his life if he didn't explain how he knew to get off the highway. Speed assumed that Ramon had told police where to set up. Recognizing the futility of lying, Ramon told Speed how he used law enforcement's own tracking systems against them.

Not believing Ramon, Speed raced with him through the heart of Dallas for two hours using Ramon's detection system. Following that success, Speed realized the detector could be used to protect his cargo while working for Castillo. He also knew Castillo would kill him if he hid this advantage. Speed kidnapped Ramon, taking him to a remote desert in Mexico to explain his technology to Castillo's security team and later to Castillo.

Castillo invested in Ramon's technology, including providing Ramon with access to satellite tracking through one of Castillo's legitimate companies. The private version of the program Castillo uses today scours police computers, satellite and other electronic data to create a real-time map of police locations, phone connections, air traffic and other signals that allow his drivers to evade travelling near anyone in law enforcement. The private program Ramon provides only to Castillo allows drivers to find side streets, country roads, and even secure stop points to minimize arrest and cargo capture risk.

In the six years since Castillo's drivers started using Ramon's programs, arrests in the U.S. dropped more than 90 percent – increasing Castillo's profitability by billions each year. This allowed him to buy out his primary rivals. When several refused to be bought, Castillo either hired away their teams or used his fast-growing Protection Corps to send them to permanent retirement.

Castillo rewarded Ramon with enormous wealth, but requires Ramon's father to work at a secure facility in Mexico. Much of Ramon's wealth comes from having adapted his original program into Easy Ride operating software now used to run almost all U.S. vehicles with optimal fuel efficiency. Castillo's legitimate businesses were the first to run their distribution fleets on the software. Other companies followed and the federal government has since mandated that all vehicles operate on the software in order to use federally funded roads. Ramon's Perfect Logistics business, where he is Chairman and Chief Executive Officer, employs several thousand Dallas-area residents at great wages, creating a local economy booming out of the last depression.

Ramon's commercial Easy Ride logistics program, introduced when he was only 21, is used by the makers of One Shot, Right Size and other similar vehicles to optimize guest delivery to each location. Easy Ride software adjusts course mapping in real time for traffic delays, weather and other variable conditions such as congestion- and ticket-based traffic delays. Ramon – as clearly instructed – carefully protects knowledge of his capability to know where every police car is at all times.

Within months of launching his national system for Castillo, Ramon's software using Castillo-owned satellites had identified and was tracking well more than 99 percent of law enforcement vehicles nationally on a continuous basis – including unmarked cars. All traffic coming in and out of police stations is tracked, and only when an unmarked police car goes into heavily trafficked underground parking does Ramon's system briefly lose the vehicle.

CHAPTER 7

February 20, 2040
West Nogales, Arizona

At a few minutes before 7 a.m., Juan Gonzalez arrives in front of the First-Wal store. In the trunk of a friend's car are 100 wood sticks about three feet long, each with one end sharpened. Posters with hand-written protest messages are stapled to the sticks.

Last night, Juan launched his plan with video notes to friends detailing his rejection from FirstWal. His contact list covers more than 3,000 friends, family and former patients. He scrubbed the hospital staff from his distribution, knowing that Store Manager Mike's wife would alert him to the pickets. Juan also made sure Mike's daughter Amber and her friends didn't get the note.

Juan told people of his frustration, and found writers, One World show hosts and connected activists interested in taking up his cause. Parents of several friends active in the Honor to Mexico (H2M) movement redistributed the message through H2M channels. Juan's initial note had gone to more than 2,000 people. Twelve hours after his first message, more than 20 times that number have seen his story.

"Mis amigos," his video message began, *"FirstWal rejected me for a job simply because my English is not good enough. I've worked hard at school and learned Mandarin that would make FirstWal a perfect fit for a career. I need your help. Our silent, non-violent protest is aimed at letting FirstWal leaders know what language we speak here. They don't have the right to force us to use a language we*

don't need. Spanish is our language. If we allow it to be taken from us, we risk hav-
ing our heritage destroyed."

As 7 a.m. nears, more cars than usual pack into the FirstWal lot. Hundreds of friends, family and those who want a change from daily drudgery walk from nearby communities. Public transport buses drops loads full of protestors. Central dispatch reroutes even more buses as riders send start and end locations to the Perfect Ride reservation and real-time routing system created by Ramon Mantle's Perfect Logistics Company.

By 7:30 a.m., nearly 1,000 people are at the FirstWal entrance. Juan organizes friends, family and new activist allies in a sit-down that thoroughly blocks every public entrance and exit. His bright smile, easy laugh, strong eye-to-eye connection with each person and chiseled features make people want to follow him. As the protest develops, Store Manager Mike contacts local police. He asks police to disband the protestors, but the duty captain puts him off while he checks policy.

Juan's 100 sticks and signs had since been attached, largely written in English as Juan had asked:

"FirstWal. Last Barrier."

"Español? Sí. Ingles? Aquí no."

"No habla español? You must be lost."

"Our home. Our language."

"Why do you want signs in English, Juan," one friend asks.

"Our message is for Anglos who don't know us. Our problem isn't Mexicans. We need English speakers to understand we need to be respected."

"If we want respect, shouldn't we use our language?" his friend asks.

"It's easier to ignore us if they don't know what we want," Juan responds.

As Juan requests, the protest is quiet, signs are raised and the few customers who aren't here for the protest stay outside. Some take photos and send messages to their friends – helping to attract a steady stream of new onlookers, including a growing number of students skipping school. Most join the protestors. From everything they hear, they agree with the goal.

After spotting Juan leading the organizational efforts, Mike realizes why this is happening. Though he knows he's supposed to soon review quarterly results with FirstWal U.S. President Chet Leach, he also knows he can't leave the problem unaddressed. He steps outside and finds Juan walking around the closely seated protestors, talking to everyone and thanking them for their support.

"Juan, how can you do this to me? If people think we're anti-Mexican and the business here falls apart, I lose my job and the store could be closed. You'll put people on the street," Mike pleads. "Even just creating an issue could cost my job. There has to be a more productive way to express your frustration. You know there's nothing I can do."

"*Look, Mr. Sanchez, this isn't against you. We need to get corporate attention. It's not like I'm going to drive all the way to another state to march outside a fence around a headquarters building,*" Juan says. "*Your big-shot executives need to see Arizona for who we are. We aren't a bunch of Anglos here, so applying Anglo rules to us makes no sense.*"

Mike looks at the growing crowd of protestors, who all watch him speak to Juan, wondering how the discussion is going. "How can I get you to stop this? I told you I respect and admire what you've already accomplished. I can even see you ultimately having a great career here once your English is better. But if you keep up what you're doing, there is no way FirstWal would ever let me hire you."

"*I obviously need the job, but this is about doing what's right for West Nogales and for these people,*" he says loudly, pointing and spreading his arms to make a virtual circle around everyone who joined him. "*These people aren't here to put money in my pocket. They came because they're tired of trying to fit white America's definition of what's right. And it hurts, Mr. Sanchez, that one of us is doing what the Anglos want, even when you know it's wrong.*"

Taken aback by the charge that Mike is enforcing a racist policy, he nevertheless knows he needs this problem to go away and go away quickly.

"Juan, I need you off the property by 8 a.m. I have my quarterly call with corporate and he always scans the property during the call," Mike says. As he finishes the statement, Mike realizes he has just assured that Juan and the protesters won't go anywhere.

"*All the more reason to stay,*" Juan replies. "*I'll tell you what. Once I know he understands what we can do to you and the media have covered the story, we'll leave. After all, most of us have other things to do than sit around protesting.*"

CHAPTER 8

February 20, 2040
Spring Valley, Illinois

On the outskirts of the Chicago metropolitan area, Chet Leach lives within 15 minutes of the last Ultra Speed train stop to Chicago and just as close to the new regional air hub. Every decent morning he takes a six-mile walk through Starved Rock State Park, stopping only when he spots a bald eagle patrolling its territory to see if he can watch it make a kill.

Chet lives in a 10,000-square-foot home overlooking the Illinois River just west of Spring Valley. Estate homes like Chet's sprang up over the past 20 years after farmland at the Southeast corner of I-80 and I-39 was converted into an integrated regional transport hub. The massive airport, Ultra Speed train center, truck depot and Right Size conversion centers made it an extraordinarily convenient location for business executives with regional, national and international travel responsibilities.

Chet is the highest-ranking executive to stay with the company after helping to sell WalCo to an immensely successful Chinese retailer. First Empire, seeing the need for on-the-ground continuity, rewarded Chet by naming him to run U.S. operations. To protect his family from daily attack for his role in selling out, Chet moved a small headquarters staff to this area, convincing his new bosses the move was justified by travel efficiencies.

First Empire is the only company that could have technically "merged" with but in every other way acquired WalCo. First Empire combines WalCo's distribution and product selection savvy with upscale service offerings to make personal shopping affordable for the middle and upper middle class. For 23 straight years, First Empire's rapid expansion attracted primarily homeland attention. The chain increased its existing customer share of wallet by understanding each person better than any other retailer. Coming out of WalCo, Chet's predisposition is to focus on product and operations – which he has said WalCo did better than First Empire. He struggles to adapt to the more service-oriented focus he now must lead, but by squeezing suppliers and employees harder each year, he continues to meet his post-acquisition financial performance targets even as service percentage objectives continue to be missed.

Chet knows his ultimate career ambitions were killed three years earlier when he helped sell WalCo, but the personal financial rewards were too great for him to do anything except make it happen. Called Bai by leaders in China, Chet speaks no Mandarin and thinks it too late in life to learn enough to have promotion potential to Shanghai. Besides, he's not sure he can afford to live in one of the world's most expensive cities in the luxury he expects.

Most high-level foreigners in FirstWal adopt Chinese names to fit in the new culture. Chet bristles when called Bai, a name selected by First Empire's HR department after he refused to pick one.

Despite this annoyance, Chet enjoys his new life. He dedicates himself to being successful enough that First Empire managers won't interfere in FirstWal until after he retires. He has two children in university already and twins just a year away. Of course, he can afford to retire today, but not with the level of extraordinary luxury with which he intends to live the remainder of his life.

Today, Chet is scheduled to participate in eight store reviews including West Nogales. Chet opens his full-wall analytic panel, which he personally designed to look like a mix of financial market and movie studio displays. He taps to open a dialogue with Mike only to see an empty chair; a transgression that causes Chet to punch the boxing body bag hung in his office. He opens the West Nogales store security views, scanning across his wall-sized console system until something unusual catches his eye.

That Mike is not where he is supposed to be is no longer his source of anger. He steps back and punches the large body bag again. Sitting down, he starts to slam his fist down on the console. Catching himself before he breaks the expensive equipment, he gets up and hits the body bag again.

After failing to convince Juan to end the protest immediately, Mike realizes he can't make it through the crowd fast enough to be in front of the video eye for his call with Chet. He still tries to make it through – playing what in his mind is a version of an old Frogger arcade game – except with sit-down protest bodies and marching sign holders to evade.

As Chet, a hierarchical command-and-control executive, scans through store security cameras, he continues looking at an empty interior contrasted with a jam-packed parking lot and a huge crowd outside. Blowing up the outdoor views, he quickly realizes the West Nogales store is losing sales to a devastatingly effective protest. His real-time sales monitor shows the only sales in the last 45 minutes are of water refills.

Mike knew Chet could see what was happening as the electric buzzer ID he is required to wear on his wrist 24/7/365 goes off. Under Chet's policy, he has two minutes to call in without excuse. This policy has crazed his wife, but Mike's pay is hard to replace without disrupting every aspect of their extended family life. Mike has it relatively easy by FirstWal stand-ards. One of Chet's direct reports is either divorced or hospitalized annually from buzzer-induced stress.

In less than a minute, Mike crashes into his glass-enclosed office and taps in to talk to Chet. Though just after 8 a.m., Mike is already sweat-ing from the anxiety of knowing this day and many more to come will be miserable.

"What the hell is going on there?" Chet yells, pounding the desk and standing with his best bear-in-the-woods routine that had been his trade-mark for years. Chet's strength as a leader is delivering the appearance of leadership to his superiors. To those under him, he acts just crazy and mali-cious enough to generate fear that he will turn irrational on anyone he thinks isn't making him look good. "Better be a damn good answer, and damn quick end to this," he says, pursing his lips and turning a shade of red Mike has learned he wants to avoid.

Mike feels the sweat start to accumulate on his brow and isn't sure whether it is triggered by his personal Frogger race or fear he has collected his last paycheck.

"Mr. Leach. What you see is a protest started by a kid we didn't hire because his English wasn't good enough. We had no warning of the protest, and certainly are shocked and outraged at the turnout given all we do to support the community," Mike says. "We're working with local authorities and every friend we have in the community to try to end this right away."

"I better not see this appear nationally," Chet says.

"Unfortunately, sir, I believe it's too late to keep that from happening. The organization of this protest was very sophisticated. The group outside includes news people and local Honor to Mexico activists. I'll get a written update to you in 30 minutes that you can forward to Shanghai to head off any undue concern. We'll do everything we can to keep this to a local issue and resolve it quickly."

Chet pauses for just a second before responding.

"In your note, make it clear this is your problem, but that I am sending in support to fix it. I'll have HR, Communications, Security and Operations teams there in five hours or less. We need to kill this fast," Chet says. "Also, no references in your note to the English policy. That's not the real issue here."

***

Sinaloa Province, Mexico

Cesar Castillo's Nogales drug distribution operations are stalled by the heavy police presence at FirstWal. Getting his drugs across the border isn't the problem. His underground tunnel system starts in a warehouse miles south of the U.S. border. An artificial floor opens to drop containers 50 feet. From there, the containers are mechanically pushed sideways to reach the elevators that take them down another 950 feet. Once at the bottom, each container is hauled 12 miles to a massive elevator below a Border Flooring manufacturing and distribution center on the U.S. side.

Normally, the company's flooring products attract little attention. Ramon's logistics system allows the trucks to escape police notice once on the road. With most of the West Nogales force now at FirstWal, the system can't identify a path that evades law enforcement notice. Castillo's security team tracks deliveries carefully. They see NG-14 sitting still.

"What's going on with Nogales 14?" Castillo's security head asks Ramon after he connects. Ramon's sleep ended instantly when buzzed by his most demanding customer.

"I'll check. Give me 35 seconds to get down to the console." Ramon steps behind a secure, hidden door, and quickly drops down to his deep ground console room. The room serves to provide both secure communications and access to a secure escape route for Ramon and his family in an adjoining house.

Tapping the console map open to West Nogales, his satellite view quickly shows that all of West Nogales' on-duty police are at the FirstWal store. He shares visuals with the security team and pulls up on-line searches that tell the story, including playing Juan's video. *"You can pull this garbage up yourself,"* he grumbles. *"Stop wasting my time."*

"We know, but Señor Castillo always asks what you think," the director responds.

"Find whoever is running this thing and let them know it will end by 9 a.m. or everyone in their family will find the sharp end of a drill bit through their ear," Castillo tells his security team when alerted to delays in Nogales-based shipments.

The security director then traces Castillo's employees and finds three are on site at FirstWal. He patches through to one long-time associate who normally works the cross-border underground tunnel. He had stopped at FirstWal to pick up his personal shopping order.

The director alerts his long-time ally, a captain in the local police force on duty during the protest. "At 9 a.m., the protest ends. By 9:15, I want your cars redeployed away from our path," he tells him. The Captain normally can keep police vehicles out of the floor replacement truck paths, but the action at FirstWal is too unusual to avoid.

After Mike's call with Chet ends at 8:25 sharp, he returns outside to find the protest breaking up.

"Juan, I hope this made your point and we won't see a protest like this again. I understand your frustration, but you can't do this to me," Mike pleads again.

"We'll see. It's not you I'm after," Juan says. *"Fix the policy and I'll be your most vocal supporter."*

CHAPTER 9

April 5, 2040
Chicago

"Papers in," Professor Stark calls as everyone's ID buzzes at the start of class. Satellite tracking of student IDs tells Professor Stark instantly that only one student is missing. His screen quickly tells him who turned in papers and met word requirements, as well as which papers may have been plagiarized.

Professor Stark studies students for any signs of weakness and uses what he learns to shred students whose primary interest is using his class as a resume item. He particularly enjoys putting students on the spot when they try to game the system by stealing others' work. Inevitably, some foolish student each quarter is verbally gutted when Professor Stark's grilling makes clear a student doesn't understand his own arguments.

"Okay, Jeremy. You've seemed passionate on this topic when we've covered it before, so I'm giving you the first spot today," Professor Stark says to kick off the second session of the spring for this two-quarter course.

"Great. I reviewed the cases carefully. To me there's no question *Brown vs. Board of Education* was a proper, thoughtful decision. The California del Sur, or *Sanchez*, case was a politically motivated decision that I believe could lead to the ultimate destruction of the United States," Jeremy started.

"I appreciate the subtlety of your argument," Professor Stark says, smiling. "So tell us your basis?"

"I actually based my argument on research of someone you might recognize," the Milwaukee native said, causing Professor Stark to look at him
with eyebrows furrowed.

"When I petitioned for this class, I was curious what the named
Professorship you have is based on. So I looked up Professor Laitin's research to
understand what bias you might have. If you read Professor Laitin's research,
you discover his belief that the abundance of civil wars in the world – 127 of
them in the 50-year period he looked at in one study – are related to diversity
in languages and cultures inside national borders. In his research, he found
that, 'The world accommodates to cultural differences then not because of
a growing recognition of the rights of minorities, but rather because weak
states are not fully able to exert domination over their own peripheries.'"

"So the United States is a weak state?"

"What do you mean?" Jeremy asks.

"If you don't know what I mean, you don't understand his conclusions.
Regardless, tie that quote back for us to *Brown vs. Board of Ed*," Professor
Stark says as he circles the room, checking the expressions of students strug-
gling to hold their tongues until they can argue with Jeremy.

"Countries have to create a united culture, or at least a fused culture, so
everyone believes they have the same rights and opportunities as everyone
else. Countries divided by language and/or culture move toward disintegration or, even worse, civil wars. In these cases, the question is when and how
a country will be destroyed, not whether it will be ruined."

"If it is a weak state," Professor Stark states.

"Oh, I see what you are saying. My belief is that even nations that
survive for centuries have periods of weakness over time," Jeremy says. "So
allowing separate languages to dominate regions can ultimately come back
to hurt a country during those times of weakness."

"Interesting argument. Okay, tie this to *Brown*," Professor Stark says.

"*Brown* said that there's no such thing as separate but equal, and I think
that decision has merit. If we want a united country, we have to stop any
effort that gives legitimacy to the concept of groups operating separately.
The *Sanchez* California del Sur decision supported separation of the races,
while the *Brown* decision clearly and rightly focused our education system
on the integration we need for our people and country."

Tamika couldn't hold herself back any longer.

"Any lovers of old movies here? If you watch some really old B movies, you sometimes see a mist come across the screen when a bad character is entering. What we just saw was the mist of stupidity, no offense Jeremy, blasting through the room with each word you spoke. I grew up in the Chicago Public Schools and let me tell you what getting rid of separate but equal did for me. I grew up in what was supposedly a mixed race school," she says.

"You want to know what we had for diversity. We had two white teachers, one Asian and one Puerto Rican teacher. We had one Mexican student whose parents clearly made a mistake when they rented their apartment. He bolted as soon as he could find another relative to live with. We got to enjoy metal detectors every day and at least 200 cameras that tracked our movement, even in restrooms. We got to watch the police enter the building 20 times a month to haul students off. We had 18-year-old freshmen spending school days scouting new clients so they could close drug deals the minute kids left the school perimeter. We watched teachers get spit at, pushed, ignored and then we got to be ridiculed if we displayed any act of public intelligence. So don't tell me that Brown did anything but make people feel righteous while continuing to sentence us to a life of hidden failure," Tamika says, with anger evident in her voice and expressions.

Professor Stark interjects. "So, Tamika, did you read the case or are you responding to the impact of how failure to follow it has affected your life?"

"I read it. Conceptually, it makes sense. But this is Chicago. And I know Chicago isn't the only city where segregation is the reality of day-to-day life," she says.

"Okay, let me pick on someone who hasn't had the chance to participate." Professor Stark looks at Jeremy to let him know he isn't getting a chance to respond yet, and then looks down at his screen. "Ric, was the court right in *Brown* or was it right in *Sanchez*? Or do you think the court was right in both cases?"

"I think the *Sanchez* decision was right. The First Amendment guarantees people the right of free speech and the right to assemble, which is the right to freely associate in public with anyone we want. So in *Sanchez*, the court decided that the Mexican Americans in California del Sur did not have to associate with people who didn't share their culture and gave them their own state so they could stay together."

Professor Stark shakes his head for several seconds. It seems like an eternity to Ric, and others who begin to feel uncomfortable.

"So you equate the right to assembly with the right to have elected officials who look and sound like you. I can't wait to read your paper to see what other stunning insights you're able to deliver," he concludes, then waves the class to head out. "Everyone. Please be sure to filter what you say and what you write through your brain. Just because a thought crosses your mind does not mean it makes sense or should be expressed."

CHAPTER 10

April 11, 2040
Near Arapaho National Forest, Colorado

Pete Roote contemplates his next step. He won't move further away from the New Rite compound to take a hard labor job. But few of the hard labor jobs in the area want English speakers.

After his blow-up, he can't take direct retribution at the recruiting center and probably not even at TC Meatpacking. His desk destruction ensured that surveillance tape of his visit would be saved.

Pete desperately needs income, just weeks away from having to stand in soup lines with the weak failures he despises. He hates the thought of not being able to compete in New Rite battles. His victories there are his greatest achievements. New Rite is where he defines himself.

This weekend's battle gives him a last chance to network and get help from New Rite friends in finding a job. Perhaps a few will have surreptitious ideas to pay TC back for its rude rejection.

It's time for Pete to get to higher elevation to prepare for the first Colorado site weekend New Rite battle of the year. At high ground, it's still winter, so he needs to fully acclimate to both elevation and temperature. He takes public transportation to the nearest station, hops on a tourist bus that regularly traverses the area and hikes to his final destination near Byers Peak.

The hike is rugged, intense and potentially life threatening during mid-winter but is easy enough for Pete in April. He prepares by climbing to the tree line at 11,500 feet, adjusting to the least oxygen-infused air he will move in during the weekend battle.

His 70-pound pack carries everything he needs for the hike and weekend competition, including portable electric stakes he uses to protect campsites from predators and competitors. Pete also carries camouflage materials to help him hide in lingering snow packs, evergreen forests and rock formation crevices.

Pete always checks in for battles 12 hours early to recover from his inbound hike. Battles start one hour after the last participant checks in, but no later than 10 p.m. Friday night. The battle zone adjusts each game, with up to 100 acres per participant. With the maximum 100 participants in most battles, games can sprawl up to 10,000 acres. Combatants are required to wear equipment that sends back video feeds to fuel rapidly expanding New Rite pay-per-view programming. Pete's early check-in allows him to get to the game zone perimeter to start his attacks, his preferred starting point.

Each battle participant carries a high-power rifle containing fluorescent dye pack bullets. These rifles can be used only to fire from 300 meters or farther – any closer shots risk serious injury to competitors. Even at 300 meters, the fluorescent bullet leaves bruises that take a week of recovery, but New Rite competitions are not for the physically or mentally weak. Along with rifles, participants carry mid-range guns and blowguns for "kills" inside 25 feet. For hand-to-hand battles, they carry sticks that go limp and trigger a kill when swung at aggressive speed near a combatant's headgear or upon contact on the rest of the body. Broken bones below the neck are more common than publicly acknowledged from hits in the heat of battle.

Strength and speed are important in these games, but cunning, stealth and accuracy differentiate mere survivors from winners. The object of each competition is simple; generate the most kills in 40 hours of competition without being killed. Combatants can survive entire weekends hiding, but can never win unless they either get mobile, or encounter a large number of first timers as easy prey.

As the battle starts, Pete is just over two miles from the game center. A beep tells him he has reached the edge of the game zone. Starting from outside in, Pete's advantage is at least temporarily sealing off one direction of potential attack. Rather than attacking toward the middle, Pete's combat strategy this weekend is to circle the zone, seek out clear sniper spots and catch people with three or fewer escape directions.

Seeing a single lane path less than 400 meters away that anyone in the area would need to use, Pete climbs 60 feet up a Douglas Fir, high enough to be tough to spot from the ground, but not so high to risk clear exposure from the ridge. Once properly positioned, he ties his torso against the trunk. A hole between branches will allow his shots to clear. It's well past midnight already, and the four hours of rest he allows himself the first night will be crucial to his sharpness the next two days.

First night kills are rare. Night vision goggles are prohibited for kill use. New competitors might slip into a competitor's lap, but most combatants use the dark to prepare attacks for the morning. Since the safest movement comes with faint light, Pete prepares to shoot as soon as first light appears. Full moons change the strategy, but cloud cover tonight means this is the most sensible approach.

An owl swoops off a limb below, finding this the perfect time to stalk prey. As Pete begins to doze, he hears the faint whir of wings, the bustle of needles, and the piercing scream of death – a sound equally eerie coming from small prey as he imagines it sounds coming from a human.

Pete smiles. This won't be the only sound of writhing death pains he hears this weekend. Be patient, he tells himself. Your time is hours away.

CHAPTER 11

April 13, 2040
Detroit, Michigan

Castillo's legitimate business network has expanded dramatically in recent years, but still contains many long-held favorites. One such company, Phoenix Mining, continues growing rapidly and is achieving success with Castillo-directed purchases of the previously abandoned Detroit Salt Mine and several other mines on the northern border of the United States.

Detroit Salt Mine Manager Rich Dore follows simple, but aggressive instructions. When hired, he was directed to extend and construct the mine to find new and richer salt seams, while also exploring below the salt seams for other minerals Phoenix believes can support the mine. Starting further down than the Empire State Building is up, Rich's digging efforts have taken him east from the newly expanded lift area. To date, Rich has made sure mine inspectors only saw the room and pillar salt mine area, blocking off view and access to the deep ground tunnel work going on well below the salt seam. Rich operates from two sets of plans – one submitted for permit approval and the real plan he uses to set daily work orders.

Rich knows his new deep tunnel will soon cross under Canada. He is equally confident, though, that no one in Canada will ever know at these depths if he doesn't tell them. To do the deep mine work, he uses a hand-picked crew he had worked with for more than a decade, and pays wages 50 percent above anywhere else in the industry.

Phoenix Mining – the company that purchased Detroit Salt and hired Rich to reopen and work it – has expanded its mining business on both sides of the U.S./Mexico border for more than two decades. Mining is dangerous work, with environments physically and psychologically challenging. While difficult, salt mining provides a stable work environment. Every day, the mine at salt level is a pleasant 65 degrees, though temperatures crank up for the small crew working the deep dig. No sun. But no rain, no snow and no pests at these depths either. Machines do most of the heavy digging. Giant haulers carry containers of salt, with those containers being lifted and driven away for sale.

The expansion work has gone on for several years when Phoenix Mining executive Max Herta arrives with a team of 20 people and a camera crew.

"Rich, we have a surprise for you," Herta starts as a camera lights the area and starts taping. "I want to congratulate you and your team on your outstanding work this year. You far surpassed every expectation we have and I know you couldn't do this alone. Call up your crew for a general announcement. I think you'll be thrilled at what we have for you."

Rich is a bit nervous. Herta seems like a good guy, but Rich has heard rumors about Phoenix ownership. Nothing he has seen makes him think the rumors are true. But he can't understand why 20 people need to be here to say thank you. Bonus checks aren't that heavy.

Still, he has no choice but to follow instructions. If the rumors are true and it's going to be bad, it's going to be bad no matter what he does now. He needs Herta to see him as a loyal lieutenant. Not listening to an order like this is a sure sign of insubordination and at the very least will cost him his job.

So Rich sends out an ID alert. Each employee is buzzed on the mobile device that serves as employment credentials, mobile communicator and tracking system. The buzz normally happens only at quitting time.

"I want to congratulate each and every one of you for surpassing every goal set for us last year," Rich tells the now-assembled team. "Mr. Herta, Phoenix's Vice President of Special Projects, wants us to take a few moments to celebrate."

Everyone watches the cameraman move to shoot a better view of the team until he finally stops 10 feet behind Herta. Herta glares as he moves.

"Thank you. As Rich said, Phoenix Mining shareholders and I are thrilled with your work. I came here to personally congratulate each of you and thank you for your extraordinary performance. Now, you might wonder why I brought along 19 of my friends to just say thank you. Well, our appreciation runs a bit deeper than just saying thank you," Herta says.

Rich looks around for any sign of unusual movement by the Phoenix team. Seeing none, he refocuses on Herta.

"In recognition of your performance, each of you will go with your families on a Caribbean cruise. Your spouses already know and your families are in limos upstairs waiting to join you to the airport. From there, you'll fly to Ft. Lauderdale, board the luxurious Queen Kate, drink and dance to your hearts content and make stops in Cuba, Grand Cayman and Cancun before returning to Ft. Lauderdale. The team here will do your work for the week, so we won't miss a beat and you'll get paid on top of having the trip covered," Herta says.

As everyone applauds and cheers, Rich grows even more concerned. Won't miss a beat. Deep underground salt mine with plenty of time to destroy the bodies in an acid bath before anyone knows they are missing. This isn't sounding good. But what about the camera? Surely, they don't keep records of things like this – and bring in audiences.

Team members don't give the circumstances a second thought. They celebrate the recognition. The vacation is welcome – even for those who might not have taken their families if given the choice of guests. Before leaving the topside mine facilities for limos, all shower and change into fresh clothes bought by Herta's team for them to wear as they travel. It appears Herta has thought of everything. Each miner is handed a bag that contains gifts personally tailored to each spouse or live-in.

Walking into the sun, Rich exhales deeply. He sees limos and looks around the perimeter. Nothing. Then he spots his wife of 25 years walking a bit faster than usual toward him with arms open. "Isn't this a great surprise?" she says. "Our flight is in two hours. Let's get moving."

***

Dallas, Texas

As Chairman and CEO of Perfect Logistics, Ramon uses substantial amounts of corporate money to support Honor to Mexico (H2M as it is more commonly known). H2M is a long established and fast-growing organization focused on helping descendants of Mexico in the United States, while also helping Hispanics from other countries. H2M accelerated its expansion after the last white governor of Texas had the Texas National Guard join local police in breaking up student demonstrations at UT, A&M and other universities.

Thousands of student protesters demanded that more courses and degrees be offered fully in Spanish. The A&M demonstration turned violent when students damaged local businesses and then fought arrest attempts. When one student started shooting at local police, Guard and police forces returned fire, killing seven students and wounding dozens more. While local police were using rubber bullets, some Guard troops had not switched from live ammunition.

H2M was founded on the principle of ending U.S. oppression of and creating opportunities for Mexican immigrants, but over time had increasingly advocated the return of Mexico to pre-1835 borders. Early 19th Century Mexico borders included Mexican territories called Texas, Nuevo Mexico and Alta California. During the Texian War of the 1830s, Texans violently reacted to efforts by then Mexican President and General Antonio López de Santa Anna to expand central power at the expense of the states. Today, similar anger is directed at a Congress and White House that increasingly dictates daily life in Texas.

Tonight is H2M's big Dallas fundraising gala, held at FC Dallas Stadium. More than 5,000 people arrive to start a gala dinner at 6 p.m. Later, the stadium doors open for a three-hour sold-out concert.

Ramon enters early for a private meeting with tonight's honoree U.S. Senator Manny Jones, a well-respected Democrat from Texas whom many consider a potential future presidential candidate. The meeting was arranged by H2M as appreciation for Ramon's generous support of the organization.

"Manny, great to see you again. Congrats on your well-earned recognition," Ramon says. Ramon hates the pretense of titles. He asks everyone to call him Ramon and he calls everyone by first name, regardless of stature or preference. Senator Jones finds this particular habit annoying, but isn't about to let it interfere with a relationship that requires him to do little beyond suffer a lack of respect in return for campaign ground troops and cash.

"It's great to see you too," the Senator says. "In addition to being a good friend to me, I understand you're one of H2M's most generous friends." The two shake hands and walk toward the pre-dinner photo session arranged for the biggest of the large contributors. *"Before we go to pictures, I want you to know that tonight will be one of the most memorable nights of any of our lives,"* Senator Jones says to Ramon.

"It certainly is nice to see you honored. My sister will join me for the concert. She might even like me for a few days after seeing her favorite stars, so I'm looking forward to this," Ramon replies.

"Better than that, mi amigo. Our state leaders have agreed to call the legislature into emergency session tomorrow to pass Spanish language requirements for all state and state-supported institutions. We'll announce it during the concert tonight. I'm returning to D.C. as soon as the announcement is made to ensure no one in Congress tries to interfere in our State."

"Can you do this?"

"We've been very quietly testing the waters the last few months – ever since the Arizona incident kicked up attention to the issue. We believe we have the votes to pass both bodies with more than 65 percent," says Senator Jones, who despite his last name is three quarters Mexican heritage.

"This is exciting. I can cut costs if I can make ours a single-language operation. It makes no sense that the majority needs to adapt to a small group of people who refuse to learn our language," Ramon said emphatically.

"Ah, I think you've hit on the argument I'm worried about," the Senator says, switching to English. "Nationally, English is still the dominant language and everything we do in Texas could be ruined if Congress were to pass English-only language requirements. Any one Senator can stall these efforts for months and maybe even years, thanks to our traditions. Longer-term, we need 43 of the 104 votes to prevent cloture from being invoked on any bill to mandate English. We guarantee 12 votes from Florida, Texas, New Mexico, Arizona, Puerto Rico and South California. I believe we can get support from other states where Spanish and other languages are important constituencies."

"This really is great news." Ramon walks over to the gala organizer as she checks last minute logistics. *"I want to bring my sister and mother in early to hear Manny speak and share this excitement. How do I get them in?"*

CHAPTER 12

April 14, 2040
New Rite Compound, Colorado

As he wakes, Pete's breath billows in front of him. Frightened of visibility, his eyes quickly dart, searching for signs his exhale is attracting interest from the ridgeline or the ground below. He looks to be sure that no telltale signs point to his path. It's still too dark to be sure.

In the distance, three figures appear to move in lockstep along the ridgeline. They alternate movement between objects. Dawn is barely cracking and the ridge is far enough away that Pete needs his targets in full view to hit them. Since the three may be working as a team, he knows his first kill will open a firefight. It's critical to remain still after the first kill to avoid being spotted.

Boulder to boulder, the first of the trio sprints. Pete sees the second team member edging toward the end of the boulder. He's going to make the same sprint, Pete thinks. Can I take him before he goes? No, the angle is still too sharp for an accurate shot. Patience. After the boulder-to-boulder sprint, a group of tall pines will block Pete's view for 100 meters. If the three are continuing along the ridgeline, all three will soon enter his kill zone. Take the leader? No, wait for the rear. The others might retreat if he hits the leader and never get in his kill zone. If he waits for the third, will the first two abandon or return for his weapons?

The quick sprint of the leader begins. It isn't clear where the spotters are hiding, but Pete sees his kill zone. Enough light has crested the mountaintops behind him to make night vision goggles unnecessary. He can't use them to kill in this month's contest in any case. Live action in visible light makes for better at-home viewing.

New Rite remote camera operators track Pete as he turns off his safety, and the pay-per-view live feed switches to his perspective. They track as he watches the runner, while announcers speculate why he isn't shooting. "Maybe we had a better view than Pete did."

"He clearly sees a better kill zone. That's in range for a shooter with Pete's skill," the second announcer states.

Another figure flashes through the ridgeline, this one a bit larger. A hawk leaves a nest close to Pete and begins his patrol, searching for morsels to feed its family.

Where is target three? Pete questions whether he has missed a runner. He adjusts his scope, searching north to south again. Maybe one of the three had been a loner tracking his prey – only to be taken out already. Was it a bad decision to wait?

Don't give up. Keep an eye on the ridgeline. Pan north to south. South to north. North to south.

The light continues to grow. Then Pete spots him. "A crawler," he catches himself mumbling audibly. Three was crawling the line – perhaps fearful the first two had attracted notice.

Almost there. Almost there. Wait for the sight line. Wait.

Tap. He hits the trigger.

"Kill for Pete Roote," the announcers proclaim. The electronic signature in Pete's bullet registers to credit him with the kill. "Less than 10 minutes of visible light and we have our first kill of the day. This should be a great day, so stay with us for an action-packed battle. Oh, oh, watch this."

Just as suspected, target two instinctively scrambles back to check if his teammate is hit. He's only three feet out of tree cover when he realizes the error and turns back to the tree line. Too late. Kill number two for Pete.

As her teammates drop, target one searches from her cover perch. She takes aim in a direction that caught her eye. It appears opposite of the angle both dropped. No visible light to aim at, she takes a couple of shots in the direction she estimates the shots came from. Bullets in the game aren't real, but still pack a punch before the electronically controlled packages disintegrate.

As target one moves to shoot, Pete spins around the trunk, minimizing the amount of body available to be hit, but with enough caution to avoid shaking the 25 feet of tree from his head up. He is high enough and weighs enough that one slip will shake the tree and give away his position.

After what seems an eternity, but is probably only 20 minutes, Pete comfortably and methodically descends the trunk. No one will dare cross that ridgeline for the next several hours as the killed combatants have now marked kill spots with flags and started the frustrating journey back to base with other flags on top of their helmets. Pete needs to add to his kill total to win this month. Target one has probably scooted by now, having not shot for more than 10 minutes.

New Rite contestants sign up alone or in teams. A three-person group needs at least three times the kills as Pete needs alone to win. If Pete has five kills over the weekend and survives, a three-person team would beat him with 16. However, if the three-person group has a team member killed, they need 21 kills to win. Any team member death has to be offset with double the kills. No reason to chase target one. There's almost no chance of her winning with two teammates dead.

Pete sees no benefit from being part of a group. Teams have the advantage of secure communication allowing them to move as a unit and run prey into traps. But they are also more likely to be distracted by fast-paced target pursuit. Moving too quickly means Pete or other loners can pick them off from well-concealed static positions.

Nearing the bottom limbs of the tree that had been his bed and kill perch, Pete moves cautiously. It's an eight-foot jump to ground, with very little cover from the last branch. Pete weighs noise versus speed and decides to worry about noise. He wraps a small rope around one hand, reaches under the branch with his other, wraps his hand on that side and then slides his body slowly over the branch and down. His feet are now just two feet above ground, and he slowly releases rope from his left hand to softly step to ground.

Avoiding any trail, Pete makes his way deeper into the tree line. Pine needles rustle in the distance. Stepping slowly and softly, he crouches as he moves toward the sound. More rustling. More steps. A quick burst of rustling, Pete releases his safety and holds his finger to the trigger of his mid-range weapon. Damn. A squirrel. Being chased . . . by . . . a squirrel. At least he didn't get between a mother bear and her cub or a mother moose and her calf. If that happens, this is no longer a game.

Knowing the noise attracted him, Pete searches for signs of movement, or signs someone has been in the area and left a trail.

Not seeing, hearing or smelling anyone, Pete moves to his next spot – a lower-level and heavily covered area he expects others may try using to spot prey. He straps the rifle to his pack, pulling his knife and blowgun into his hands.

More noise.

Pete crouches into a crevice of a rock formation. The rocks protect his body from three sides and the shadow of the crevice makes him hard to spot even from his exposed front and top. Looking up, he can't see anyone at angles to get at him. But he hears enough noise to be sure this is a large target. A couple of small bush branches crack slightly as they snap back to place. Pete has to trust his instincts on this one. This time it is Pete's knife that does the trick. At one inch from his target's throat, Pete's knife is starting a raking motion across the throat when the kill registers and the knife goes limp. Pete has his third kill.

"I didn't even see you," his victim says.

"Shhh." Pete's eyes survey the area, looking to see who else is around. He waits a few minutes, and then turns quickly as the victim marks his kill site.

"See you next month," Pete softly whispers.

New Rite Founder JT Alton started New Rite as a survival preparation movement before seeing the potential to extend into a broad line of businesses. He created innovative game technology to spread his survivalist mantra in electronic combat, then built enough popularity to charge competitors to enter contests, for which he also sells subscription video rights. JT ensures he has cutting-edge game technology by continually reinvesting profits into advanced weapons and systems research that is now gaining New Rite a reputation among elite tactical military units. New Rite's military sales are much smaller than they would be if JT turned New Rite into a publicly traded company. JT is very selective about his customers and just as selective about what technologies he lets the outside world know he has created.

In addition to weapons and systems development, JT invested in building out New Rite compounds. He is now one of the single largest landholders in the United States by acreage. In nearly every state with interesting and challenging topography, JT has established competition sites. Often, he buys formerly protected state and federal lands at cheap prices as governments scramble to make debt payments.

The best game participants win their way in to battles, as Pete has done for years. Still, even winning their way in requires monthly on-line competition fees, creating a steady stream of cash for New Rite that most business owners envy. Pete looks at those who pay their way into the in-person games as easy kills, and they often are just that for experienced New Rite gamers. Pete particularly enjoys the rich father/spoiled son pairs that pay $25,000 for training and a weekend bonding experience. It's Pete's joy to make that bonding as short as possible, whether it's hitting the overweight Marine-wannabe dads or the easily distracted 18-year-olds who thought they would have fun.

Just watching a dad see his son squeal from the pain of a hit is delightful to Pete. It always takes them a few seconds to remember their kid isn't really dying. By then, Pete makes sure dad's game is over too.

***

April 15, 2040

As Sunday afternoon begins, Pete has nine kills. He decides to test a trick he thinks may work in the last hours of a contest. Less than a mile removed from being melting snow, the mountain creek water temperature is barely above freezing. Much time in the water causes hypothermia. Pete's heated gear and strong will allow him to withstand the cold in a way few will even consider.

It's a continuing surprise to Pete that as the official end of a weekend's game approaches, contestants move – albeit cautiously – toward the central camp. They move carefully, slowly searching their surrounding before each motion. But contestants don't want to be too far from camp at game end and risk being stuck in the wild for an extra night. For most this meant they could miss a day's work, and winning the game wasn't worth losing their income. Pete has no such concern.

At this time of year, melting snow expands creeks. But in shaded areas, ice that coats these creeks through the winter first melts from water level up. Pete finds a crossing where thick ice still covers the creek, with water flowing rapidly below. Under that ice, though, is enough space for Pete to back in, lay prone and breathe comfortably. No one will see him until he has a shot. He hides most of his pack under several trees taken down by winter winds, wrapping the pack in his tree camouflage tarp.

As Pete backs into the creek so the ice sheet extends three feet past his head, he finds enough of an air pocket between water and ice that he can keep his head out of water and his mid-range pistol on a relatively dry rock top. His head is above water, but the part of his body in constant contact with the recently thawed water must adjust to the frigid temperature. While his warming clothes help keep him from shock, every part of his body that can withdraw from the cold does just that. It's not just his bellybutton that's an "innie" now.

From here, Pete can hit targets crossing the creek narrows. The felled tree and collection of rocks 30 yards downstream provides the driest crossing in sight. There are other crossing points, but this one has an advantage Pete is convinced others won't skip. Entrance to the crossing is obscured by high, curving rock walls. At the center of the crossing, every sight line in the water is protected by rock. Every normal sight line anyway, as Pete has a clear angle from his prone position in the creek.

Pete saved this technique for a competition he is sure he can win. Each target coming to the pass approaches the same way. Carefully and slowly, they leave the protection of the tree line to sprint to rock cover. Following the rock cover, they move to the relative safety of the curved rock walls. They look up to make sure no snipers attack from up top, but don't have to keep their heads on a swivel. Then, after checking one last time, they stand to walk across the tree trunk and rocks before heading back to camp. That's when Pete hits them. He nails four final kills.

All of Pete's victims have the decency after being hit to walk away and leave no trace a kill has taken place. They can't push the kill flags into rock or trees above the water so they put them in the creek, where they are quickly swept downstream. Soggy footprints in the dirt where victims walked away made it seem as if the crossing was still safe and the only threat could be where those footprints headed. Only during his second hour under the ice sheet does Pete realize he's trapped if he hits someone with team members behind. Fortunately, few teams travel close together if they have even survived this far in the competition.

As time expires, Pete pulls himself out of the water and undresses, moving to mid-afternoon sunlight to absorb warmth until his body returns to more normal appearance. Pulling his pack out from under the trees, he puts on dry clothes and hiking boots for the return to camp.

With 11 kills, Pete easily wins the weekend: a free year of New Rite gaming and automatic entry into national Rites of Passage preliminary contests.

JT greets Pete at the camp central arena accompanied by 5,000 weekend survival trainees and more than 30 million viewers globally watching the conclusion of the competition.

"Ladies and Gentleman, our Champion Pete Roote," JT says. The live audience gives Pete a standing ovation, having watched highlights of the contest during its final hour.

As studio announcers make their final comments for the weekend, JT turns to Pete and asks to walk with him. Several minutes later, with both men well away from the rest of the group, JT reaches up to put his hand on Pete's shoulder.

"How would you like to test your skill in something a bit more real?" JT asks very quietly.

"What do you have in mind?"

"Let's head to my cabin. We can talk there."

Pete is thrilled. Despite his long association with New Rite and admiration for JT, he has never really done more than shake JT's hand. Given his financial desperation, he hopes "more real" translates into "paid job."

JT's cabin home at this site has beautiful floor-to-ceiling views across the terrain. The view is nearly panoramic from the main home, and for the part that isn't, a tunnel had been dug to the other side of the mountain to a guest cabin.

A small path takes the men up to the house.

Once inside, JT shows Pete his home. Stopping to check out the panoramic views now aided by moonlight, JT hands Pete a beer, a hefeweizen he has grown fond enough of to have mini-barrels imported monthly. As they sip and walk, JT realizes his guest must be exhausted.

"Do you need to be at work tomorrow?"

"No sir. Unfortunately, I'm out of work and this was the last game I could enter. If I hadn't won, I wouldn't be able to afford to stay with New Rite," Pete says.

"Pressure worked well for you then. This may be your day. Why don't you head through the tunnel and spend the night at the guest cabin. We can talk tomorrow when you're a little less exhausted. The offer I have is too important to consider with less than a clear mind," JT says, nearly assuring that Pete's sleep will be more restless than his exhaustion requires.

CHAPTER 13

April 16, 2040
Shanghai

At 5 a.m. on Shanghai's Tianjin Road, twelve red-clad teens jog in near lockstep past high-end Chinese stores mixed with the occasional McDonald's and Baskin Robbins outlets. Eleven of the twelve glide in perfect pace, with the 12th stretched to keep up and no one looking back to bring him forward. Catch up or be dropped is the less-than-subtle message.

First signs of life in Shanghai begin at this hour, only a few hours after the last motions of the prior day. Some men and women walk their assortment of tiny dogs, the only size pets that make sense in this city of nearly 40 million. Some, mainly the young, jog. Others start their walking or in place exercise routines, moving their limbs and torsos in smooth, flowing motions.

At dawn, shimmers of red and yellow light the sky, providing a backdrop to small puffs of white on this clear, brisk morning. A few rituals remain unchanged over hundreds of years. Early dawn exercises open the day at elite high schools that prepare the best of the best in China for university entrance exams. These exams disproportionately influence who will join the nation's intertwined corporate and government elite.

As the 12th of the young men returns to school premises to start his day, Shanghai's corporate world awakes. Early risers dominate success in this corporate world, where late starts often mean extensive traffic congestion and pre-work travel migraines.

"We need to decide if Bai is the right person for where we want to go in the U.S.," First Empire Executive Vice President of International Operations Jia Lin, or Lin Jia as said in China, notes during the monthly management committee review. *"His old school ways limit his usefulness to us in a world increasingly driven by collaborative management."*

Jia translates to beautiful in English and she is neither shy about nor vulgar in using her beauty to captivate men. She dresses to get her way; showing just enough cleavage and leg to attract attention, but not so much to be treated as art or worse by the male-dominated leadership. She is particularly adept at knowing when a male superior or colleague is about to disagree – showing the graceful ability to close in physically and put her hands on them as if saying, "I know what I'm doing here." Or perhaps a less subtle, "If you like my touch, you'll shut up now."

With the most obstinate colleagues, she stands next to them and draws diagrams or other visuals that show a particular point, standing bent over at an angle. This forces her colleagues to concentrate their eyes on her drawing or her face to avoid staring at the now noticeably exposed smooth-skinned rounded cleavage. By the time she finishes, most forget their objection. When truly struggling to win an argument, she turns her head toward the ceiling long enough to give her male colleagues the idea she isn't looking at them. As soon as she thinks their eyes are moving toward her chest, she quickly glances down. As if to say it's okay that you looked, she puts her arm on their shoulder as she stands back up. She hates that she needs to use this weapon, but loves the power of controlling men so easily.

While her beauty and cunning softens up those who can help or hurt her career, those working under Jia know her as Sparrow. Sparrows were one of the four pests the Chinese government sought to eliminate in the Great Leap Forward, part of Mao Zedong's hygiene effort. Sparrows ate grain seeds, robbing the people of the fruits of their labor. To those beneath her, Jia is skilled at doing the same, taking credit for every success.

First Empire Chairman and CEO Chang Chen listens to Jia as much as the rest of the leadership, but knows Jia's game. A mistress had played him the same way, displaying enough sensuality to be impossible to ignore. Knowing the game and with better self-control as he ages, Chang still tolerates and even promotes Jia's role on the leadership team because she keeps the team unsettled. Years after joining his Chairman's Council, she is still the first to share information on anyone back-stabbing him. He carefully avoids giving away his information source, but doesn't take long before demoralizing those disloyal to him with assignments to lead less-than-special projects. Over time, his skill at identifying and crushing internal dissension allowed him to create an aura of omnipresence. Underlings quickly learned that those who consider acting against Chen found their way to distasteful roles.

Chairman Chen is one of the most revered business figures in the country, creating a retail juggernaut named First Empire in honor of *Qin Shi Huangdi*. First Empire is noted for the extraordinary service levels provided to upper-middle and middle-class customers, and for developing technology to drive service efficiency. Chairman Chen knows Jia is interested in placing an ally loyal to her in Chet "Bai" Leach's role. He won't approve until he is sure it is the right decision for the business.

"Whatever his failings, and I know he has them, Bai transitioned to First Empire without losing a step. You and I both know more than 80 percent of acquisitions fail, usually because of mismatched cultures. Bai helped WalCo people see us as sharing the same culture and qualities. In my mind, this made the deal far better than it would have been under poor leadership that exposed differences before people were prepared to handle them. We owe him a great deal for that work," Chairman Chen says.

"Understood," Jia says, *"and I agree he has been an asset, though I would argue that the reason he doesn't talk about our differences is he isn't smart enough to see them. What I don't know is whether his protecting the old ways is going to keep us from expanding WalCo, I mean FirstWal, with our services. He's not a change leader from what I've seen."*

"Explain."

"Earlier this year, I woke to find out a U.S. Southwest store was shut by a protest for almost two hours, during which the only thing we sold was water. If that isn't disturbing enough, the reason for the protest is a policy Bai maintains that we never authorized," Jia says.

"What policy?"

"Bai's policy is that all employees need to speak English, even though Spanish is the main language in many states and French is the primary language in parts of

Canada. A kid started the protest because we turned him away for poor English," Jia says, seeing her opening to tie this customer protest around Chet's neck. *"In this store, and actually in many stores in the Southwest, most guests speak Spanish. What makes this more interesting is the kid we refused to hire is one of the top Mandarin students in the state. Question is, would we turn away a good, low-level employee for speaking Cantonese and not Mandarin in Guangzhou if he didn't need Mandarin for the customers he serves?"*

Chairman Chen motions to Jia to join him away from the rest of his executive team for a private discussion. *"We'll return to issue resolution in 15 minutes,"* he says to the others.

From First Empire's 95th floor executive terrace overlooking Changfeng Park, thousands of skyscrapers span the horizon. Shanghai is among the most modern, beautiful and overcrowded cities in the world. Chen moved to Shanghai from Wuhan as a young child as his parents chased dreams of better life than industrial labor. Chen was old enough when they moved to recall what it felt like to scrape dirty air off his tongue. In his youth, blue skies were an aberration. Today, air here is as clean as other modern cities.

After 25 years laboring for others, Chen founded and built First Empire through the combination of quality products, leading service and reputation as an environmental activist. He plowed one percent of First Empire's profits into environmental programs to help dramatically improve the quality of water and air his grandchildren now drink and breathe.

Most thought Chairman Chen, a billionaire many times over after selling large chunks of First Empire in multiple stock offerings, did this out of charity. While true he believed in the cause, he saw environmentalism as good business: nothing wrong with making money and a difference at the same time.

The skies are clear and he sees thousands of office buildings, condo and apartment complexes and urban integration centers that combine mass traffic stops with all the recreational amenities the Shanghainese could want. He breathes deeply the clean air he loves and turns to Jia.

"So if we don't like the English policy, just change it. This doesn't mean we need to fire Bai. He is useful and has been a good soldier. Allow him to save face by letting him change the policy and then redefine his role," Chairman Chen says.

"What do I do if he resists either on the language or on his role," Jia asks.

"There's no point spending time discussing an outcome that will not happen," he responds, making it clear it is her job to make sure it works.

Knowing Jia is disappointed at not having her way, Chairman Chen decides to help her understand.

"There are worse things you can do to a powerful man than fire him," he says. *"You can kill a man by slitting his throat. But that is merciful and lets him move quickly to his next life. If you really want to hurt a powerful man, you skin him a layer at a time and let him die a slow, painful death in front of everyone. Our global management team will more powerfully learn with the skinning victim still visible that First Empire's reputation must be protected at all costs. That way, all will see the pain and agony in Bai's eyes, in his movement and in his decimated heart,"* Chairman Chen says.

Jia feels a rush of vindication and renews her admiration for Chairman Chen, whom she sometimes worries is too old and soft to lead his global empire. *"I'm sorry I did not understand. I will make him squirm until he is willing to pay us to leave,"* she says, trying to stop a smile to not give away how happy this approach makes her.

"If you want to lead this company, you must have the capacity to use cruelty strategically – to serve the business, of course. Not to serve yourself," Chen says.

Walking back toward her office, Jia tries to wipe the visual Chairman Chen just provided out of her mind. She moves from thinking about a skinned Chet to conjuring new methods of business torture.

Later in the evening, walking inside of Hong Qiao River Park, Chairman Chen admires the white marble carvings of people working in industrial China. Those with the broadest smiles seem engaged in the most manual labor. The curved metal fencing around the park adds a beautiful edge to traditional park fencing, but conjures up a more introspective reaction. Beautiful confinement, the fencing appears to signal.

The Putuo District of Western Shanghai is a most sought-after corporate location – with the more central People's Square long-ago having succumbed to exorbitant rents and extremely difficult commutes. While Suzhou Creek is Putuo's only natural waterway, Changfeng Park houses numerous small lakes and ponds that attract the area's senior citizens for early morning stretch walks. When humidity is not overwhelming, business leaders often seek solace there to ponder the next strategic move.

At the end of another long day, Chen enjoys his walk, planning for the next day's achievements.

***

New Rite Compound, Colorado

Pete wakes to a stirring sunrise making its way over nearby mountain ranges – wisps of crimson red and golden yellow melding into the predominantly burnt-orange sky. The breeze of the cool morning blows in through the cracked door to the modest balcony. The blending aromas of western omelet, sliced berries, carrot cake muffin and dark-roasted hazelnut coffee sift in through the screen, delivering the inspiration Pete needs to move more rapidly than he might otherwise consider.

Pete isn't sure how breakfast had been delivered without his notice but, at the moment, he doesn't care. Placing on a warm robe and comfortable slippers, he steps outside. The aromas aren't misleading. Even the hot sauce he had grown to enjoy was on the tray, with a simple note under it. "Let me know when you're ready to talk."

The muffin brings back memories. Soft, moist and full of walnut, carrots, raisins with just the right cream cheese frosting – tasting almost exactly like the muffins his dad used to bake. As he consumes it, his mind wanders to why his family forced him out. Watching the sunrise dull and the sky brighten as dawn breaks, he decides he needs to at least reach out to his sister. Maybe they watch his competitions and saw his win yesterday.

Pouring a second cup of coffee, he steps inside to throw back on his clothes, then returns, presses the call button and ponders what offer could come his way.

After less than 10 minutes, JT knocks and walks in.

"Morning Pete. Congratulations again on your victory. I hope you enjoyed a great night's rest. I can see you enjoyed Ally's home cooking."

"Breakfast was wonderful. I don't know how you got it in here without me noticing, but I enjoyed every bit of it. Would you like some coffee?"

"Certainly." A spare coffee cup had been included on the tray.

"Is Ally your wife?" Pete asks.

"No. No. No. A wonderful woman, certainly, but Ally's role here is quite challenging without worrying about someone like me. Ally runs the show here. She takes care of everything. Only rarely have I been fortunate to get a meal from her so consider yourself special," JT says.

Turning his chair to face Pete, JT starts on the real purpose of inviting Pete to stay in the cabin.

"Pete. I'm going to be very blunt with you, and I need you to understand that this conversation never happened," JT says, waiting for Pete to nod that he understands before proceeding. "We have a problem in America and I need your help to fix it."

"We've got lots of problems here," Pete says, "Which one do you want me to fix? What do you need me to do? You really think I can help?"

"Whoa, whoa, whoa. No need to hurry unless you're on a deadline, Pete. Let's slow down and take our time," JT says, walking over to look out over the surrounding mountains. "So your first question, which problem? My biggest concern is people who are destroying the very fabric of America, selling the idea of drugs as the way to happiness. These people don't care what happens to us. If they want to do this type of stuff, whatever. But stay away from our families."

Pete stands next to JT, with only railing as high as his mid-section between him and at least a 500-foot fall.

"Agree with you on that. I've seen it even more since I moved here. These Mexicans control everything. I've been turned down for work so many times because I'm not Mexican. I can't even get an interview for a meat-cleaning job because I don't speak Spanish. Last I checked, this is America," Pete says.

JT looks at Pete. The seriousness on his face starts to ease as he realizes he has found someone who will share his enemy, even if it's not clear Pete understands his purpose.

"So what do you want to do about it?" JT asks.

"If they didn't have my face on security, I'd have beaten the last breath out of the guy who threw me out of that meat company," Pete says, "if that's what you mean."

Sipping on a refilled cup of coffee, JT puts his arm on Pete's shoulder. "I think we may have found each other at the right time. I have a job to be done. You need work. And the work I'm asking you to do will make a difference – more than I think you can imagine," JT says.

Over the next hour, JT and Pete talk on the balcony of a cabin far enough away from the nearest neighbor that they can't be overheard. Just to be sure, JT's security system includes soundproofed walls and glass. As added protection, JT turned on a sound distorter as he entered the room, and plays music to empty space around the balcony. If distance doesn't keep government sound spies away, Dan Fogelberg and Yanni should eliminate outside worries of anything criminal happening here.

"So," JT says as he stands to walk out, "I'll be back in touch after you get settled. Ally can give you a ride to the RTD if you need one."

***

Cancun, Mexico

Not long after Rich Dore and his Detroit Salt team headed for the airport, Herta and his team began detoured digging in the deep mine path below the salt seam. They work nearly around the clock for seven days – taking the tunnel even further off path from plans submitted to dozens of government departments and from the seams Rich was working. Salt is just one intended income stream from the mine, though few in Phoenix Mining understand this. Eliminating interference for Castillo's products in and out of Canada is the revenue source justifying this particular investment. Canada has stepped up border searches to protect itself from porous U.S. borders.

Not only does Herta's team need to complete a tunnel and conveyor system while Rich and team cruise the Caribbean, they also need to create a protected, sealed entrance that only Herta's team can enter. Herta considers taking out Rich, his team and their families now that they are in the last stage of tunnel development: a few car bombs, a plane crash, a series of unfortunate accidents. Many ways exist to make people disappear.

But the common link of these deaths could draw attention to the salt mine, attracting government inspectors Phoenix doesn't own. Herta learned over the years that nobody cares about basic industries like mining until something goes wrong. Police are bound to poke around if too many people disappear from one place. So the mine will operate with two shifts.

Herta's handpicked team, all with families in Mexico, works the night shift. Day shift delivery trucks will return at night from the distribution center with bags of powders and pills. Once transported in the sub-mine to Canada, these bags are elevated to a warehouse. From there, Castillo's drugs are shipped under commodity agricultural products to final distribution points.

As the final tunneling work proceeds at feverish pace, Rich and his nearly grown family relax on board the floating cities common in island cruising – complete with surfing machines, wave pools, swim-up bars and every other amenity found in the best water park resorts. Laying poolside with a fruity drink he would shun back home, Rich considers what awaits his return.

While he respects Herta's mining expertise, he worries Herta's family and those of the other second shift miners continue to live in Mexico despite wealth that should allow them to move here. Of course, Herta's endless ridicule of his second wife might explain his willingness to always be away from his family. "My wife tells everyone she's my trophy wife. If this were a wife contest, I'd be lucky to win a participation ribbon," Herta says whenever asked to explain how it feels being away from her.

The lavish vacation week for Rich and his team also concerns him. No company just does this.

With the cash envelopes each worker received, Rich and his family decide to take a side trip to Cozumel – a small, peaceful island just a catamaran ride away from Cancun. Boarding the catamaran, they briefly meet the crew, stow their dry clothes below board and take spots on the front tarps where they can feel the breeze and relax in salty mist bouncing up as waves crest and fall below.

"I want everyone to put on life jackets," Rich says to his wife and kids.

His teenagers protest, as does his wife, who wants to be sure her first tanning efforts of the year leave as few lines as possible. "We'll be fine on the boat, nothing to worry about," she says.

"We don't know how strong the waves will be. Put life jackets on," Rich repeats.

Rich's caution might require explanation, but he fears sharing any concerns. His wife would likely say something to her friends. Any risk, if there is a risk, will be multiplied if Herta thinks they can't keep their mouths shut.

As the boat pulls out into the Gulf of Mexico, waves get choppy and everyone bounces up and down a bit. Not so much they get sick, but enough for everyone to laugh and bounce on the tarp. The sun reflects off the waves and reflections from metal rings occasionally blind Rich.

One of the crew comes around to everyone on the Catamaran – passing out juice cocktails with and without rum. Steel drum music blasts over the speakers, every song sounding the same. "Ole, Ole. Ole, Ole." Blasts of salty mist jump off the Gulf, with everyone up front shutting their eyes to avoid the splash. Shore is just three miles away. Rich closes his eyes, relaxing to enjoy the sun and thinking about the shoreline snorkeling he plans to do just minutes after docking.

CHAPTER 14

April 23, 2040
Detroit, Michigan

As Rich and team return to the Detroit Salt mine, they feel renewed pride in their work and appreciation for an employer who gave them such an unexpected vacation.

Detroit is a long way from the shores of Cozumel. Snorkeling in Cozumel, Rich relished the ability to hear only his breath and heartbeat. Though the water was just four or five feet deep in places above the beach-front reef, he wore a life vest to help avoid stepping on the coral below. This amplified his relaxation – allowing him to focus on beautiful colors, smooth movement and carefree relaxation.

Detroit is a shell of a once-vibrant city, now attempting to remake itself again as an international business hub with an intense focus on developing Arabic, Russian and several African language skills among its youth. But few meander aimlessly through the city. Sights, sounds and smells are alerts to risks that must be avoided.

No amount of human invention replaces the warmth of glistening sunlight and reflection off waters below once Rich returns to the salt mine. At least Rich controls his environment inside the mine. Pulling up to the parking lot, he suspects something is different, and hopes it is only poorly created room and pillar areas.

Driven by cart to the east mine face, Rich is happy to find progress. Even more startling, Herta's relief team, and now night shift, has built an enclosed and reinforced recreation room for the crews to use during breaks. The room blocks off the deep tunnel his small team was building. Herta tells Rich that corporate concluded the few minerals discovered to date in the deep shaft don't warrant continued digging.

As he watches his crew walk around the rec room, finding stocked beverage and snacks, Herta walks up, puts his arm on Rich's shoulders and asks: "Did my man find you on the boat in Cozumel?"

Rich looks, not sure what to say. Turning ashen and sullen, he slowly nods, recalling how he was jolted from rest on the return catamaran to Cancun.

"I hope he put the fear of God into you," Herta says, squeezing the top of the shoulder, and with a smile that seems entirely out of place for the message.

"Uhh, yes sir. If fear was your goal, mission accomplished," Rich says.

"Good. I hope you see by the way we treat you and your boys that we are serious about staying union free," Herta says.

Rich looks at Herta, closes his eyes, and looks again.

"Union free?" Rich says. "Is that what the warning was about?"

"Of course. We pride ourselves on results," Herta says. "Staffing our team with the best makes that work. Your work has earned the respect of your men. That's why we hired you in the first place. What we learned last week is that my men could only make a fraction of the progress your team achieves. You outperformed my best team."

Rich noticeably exhaled, his torso dropping nearer to the floor. He took a few more deep breaths as the men walked back to the wall. "So the warning was about not being a union shop?"

"We're in Detroit, so I can't take anything for granted." A few strides later, Herta asks: "What did you think he was telling you?"

"I'm not really sure, but my mind went many directions," Rich responds, shaking his head from side to side. "I've been in a union before, but long ago lost my love of everyone getting paid the same regardless of talent or effort. I take a lot of pride in what I do, and so do my men."

"We see that," Herta says.

"It's a risk to not have union protection, but I've been in the salt business long enough to know unions don't protect you from bankruptcy. My dad was a union autoworker and my mom a union flight attendant. They had great benefits until their companies disappeared, and they were left with almost nothing. Union or non-union, it doesn't matter if the company disappears. So my goal is to be better than anyone else. I take care of my own future."

Herta pats him on the shoulder. "Glad to hear you say that. As seriously as I take union independence, my boss thinks far worse of leaders who let their businesses become unionized. I can't take any chances not being clear." After a short pause, walking out of Rich's office, he adds, "I'm sorry the message wasn't clearer. I was pretty explicit on what he was supposed to say. I wanted you to think about the message so you could decide not to come back if you didn't like my rules."

"Don't worry about that," Rich says. "I'm just glad I agree with what you want."

Rich stands up and walks toward the rec room where he barks out: "Okay boys. Time to prove the manicures and body waxes haven't turned you into cubicle clowns."

Walking back to the wall, Rich notices a small pile of dust outside the rec room. Looking back he realizes the surface area in front of the rec room has been swept.

Wow, they really went all out to make this nice for the boys, he thought. Headset back on, he goes back to directing that day's production. That was all about being non-union?

CHAPTER 15

May 5, 2040
Phoenix, Arizona

It's hard to believe Juan Gonzalez is still weeks away from June high school graduation when he, H2M leaders and state officials lead 50,000 people in a prolonged march from the U.S. Airways Center in Phoenix, past the Maricopa County Court on Jefferson Street, crossing Carnegie Library Park to Washington Street and up to the Arizona State Capital. At a pre-set stage in Bolin Park, most of the state's elected officials join Juan. A two-mile stretch of road is closed for the march, but even advance preparations by state, city and county officials had not anticipated the enormous turnout for the march in support of Spanish language requirements, timed to match the Saturday Cinco de Mayo festival.

"Sólo en español."

"Sólo en español."

"Sólo en español."

The chants grow increasingly loud, broken only on the walk by Mariachi-led sing-alongs. Mariachi groups from throughout Arizona brought their violins, trumpets, vihuelas and guitarrón; creating a festi-val-like feel as the marchers celebrate through the streets. More than a thousand live video streams follow the marchers with lenses embedded in protester glasses, shirt buttons, belt buckles and pen tops. Marchers range from babies in strollers to more than a handful of 90-year-olds who long dreamt of this day.

Governor Jesús Muñoz, a third-generation American of primarily Mexican heritage, takes the stage: *"A young man — one of our young men — has been shamed for speaking Spanish. We cannot simply sit and watch this happen. Juan Gonzalez is one of the finest young men in our state. An academic star. A volunteer who helps heal the sick with his charm. An athlete, both skilled and intense. Juan is an example of the youth we must celebrate. He is the pride of West Nogales, but because he only speaks two languages fluently and English probably better than most Anglos, he's not good enough for the racist FirstWal."*

Hoots, boos and hollering interrupt the Governor.

"No más."

"Not in our house."

"It's not your rules."

As the noise starts to die down, the Governor returns to the microphone. *"This is your state. This is our state. And you put me here to create and enforce rules that respect Arizona. So it is time to take a stand. A tough stand. A fighting stand. A stand for Latinos of any heritage, but particularly for Mexicans whose ancestral home is blocked from us by an insulting wall. A foolish wall alone cannot keep us from our rightful place, no matter which direction we choose to go. For those old people among us, perhaps we learned nothing from Berlin so, today, we start teaching America a lesson. Today, I am introducing the Juan Gonzalez Freedom Act."*

Juan beams and joins the crowd in loudly applauding the Governor. But the Governor has only given him an overview of the law he wants to pass, so he is as curious as the crowd to know all that the Governor is planning.

"We have way more than half of the State House and much more than half of the State Senate up here on stage. If they agree . . ., if you agree . . ., we will march to the House, and then march to the Senate, and then come back here to sign into law the Juan Gonzalez Freedom Act . . . to make español *the official language of the State of Arizona and ban any discrimination against any citizen who speaks Spanish."*

The crowd erupts, surging forward and pressing bodies tightly against the stage – now fully surrounding the stage.

After being implored to back up, the crowd gives the governor time to finish.

"Viva México. Viva Arizona," he starts chanting, quickly joined by the crowd.

"Now, Senators. Representatives. We've heard from the people that they want this law. Are you ready to walk to the Capitol and do our job? We will give Arizona back to our people," the Governor says.

Every legislator on stage raises a fist. As a group, they march to their respective buildings and begin the process.

CHAPTER 16

May 6, 2040
Shanghai

At 3 a.m., Jia's face flushes a brighter red than the makeup she always wears publicly to accentuate well-defined Han ancestry features. In the midst of a sound sleep, her best friend from university wakes her to say the Arizona government is verbally attacking FirstWal. While traveling in the United States, Jia's friend is angered to hear a Chinese company being attacked as racist. She realizes Lin Jia, as she is called in China, is a high-level executive at First Empire. Quickly tuning into a livestream of the Arizona event, and checking news reports on her 12-screen home console, Jia knows the coming days will be rough. FirstWal openly debased by U.S. government officials. This is unacceptable.

Only weeks removed from her 95th floor terrace discussion with Chairman Chen, she hasn't fully implemented his instructions. First Empire is paying a price for her failing. Chairman Chen is certain to question not only his wisdom in putting the company's financial future on the line with the WalCo acquisition, but also his decision to have her lead international operations and bring WalCo into the fold. Seeing the protest live and early in the morning her time meant she would have a head start in formulating a plan. But that head start might be only 15 minutes if Chairman Chen is awake. One of her competitors to replace Chang Chen when the 69-year-old chairman retires will surely hear about the protest and rush to be the first to let him know what is happening.

If he is still sleeping, her competition will be reluctant to enter the sleep override code Chen entrusts to just six executives, his wife, his children and his assistant. If entered, the triggered alarm will wake him from the deepest of sleeps, but every executive knows it better be crucial.

If he is awake, though, they will happily destroy her reputation with all the tact of a high-speed train crashing through a construction barrier. Back and forth, multiple deep slices at a time explaining how this political attack displays all the reasons Lin Jia can't be trusted running the company. Of course, the context they present, if they beat her to the messaging, will be highly distorted. Blame is quickly assigned. Responses are ordered before emotions can be removed from decision-making processes.

What's my plan? What's my plan?

She calls Chet.

"Are you listening to Arizona?" He is surprised to hear from her in the middle of Shanghai's night, as he typically enjoys a full day of solving any problem before being confronted by her. "What's your solution?"

"We have to isolate the problem," Chet says. "I've already talked to HR and we agreed to say we made clear that store managers have discretion to make exceptions to our language policy when in the best interests of WalCo. Uh, FirstWal. We can easily hang this on the store manager and make it an isolated incident."

Jia is surprised to hear the language policy is discretionary. "I didn't realize you gave store managers that option," she says.

"We had talked about giving them the option, and I've already lined up five people who will say they clearly knew they had the discretion to override policy if it helped serve our customers," Chet says. "It's all about protecting FirstWal, and if we have to sacrifice someone to protect a century-old brand, that's a no-brainer. Once you give the okay, we'll put out a release announcing the store manager's resignation and his apology for not fulfilling his responsibilities," Chet says.

"It sounds like this was a policy change under consideration, not actually implemented. Why would the store manager take the fall?" Jia responds. "We'll take a huge chance not being honest here if he does anything to counter our statements. Did you review the interview video files? If he contests anything in court here, those are certain to be discovered."

"Not yet, but we pay our HR and legal teams well to take care of problems," Chet says. "They've already erased any records of concern we can get away with erasing. With our systems, it's easy to track these issues and make 'em disappear, along with any similar types of documents so nothing seems unusual."

"I'm having trouble seeing how this is a good idea," Jia says after reflecting for a few seconds. "Can't we fix the policy, apologize for past transgressions and move on? If we make the store manager a victim, he could bite us, can't he?"

"We could do it your way," Chet responds, "but my gut feel is that admitting we're wrong could be used by competitors here against us. Then our chance of making our earnings targets this year would be slim."

Strongly built, dark-haired and attractive, Chet is used to charming his way out of any difficulty, and can't believe this woman hasn't quickly jumped on his plan. Over the years Chet mastered the corporate art of taking credit for successes that he had only marginally participated in, while always ensuring he had a co-partner on any high-risk project he could sell out the instant any concerns were raised by superiors. Now, as the lone top executive, he has had to refine his art. He systematically blames holdover managers as mistakes are discovered, while paying those he elevates onto his executive team so much above market that they do and say whatever it takes to protect their elevated income stream.

With Jia, he isn't sure if it is the physical distance or racial divide that interferes with his ability to charm her. "Mike, the store manager, has been one of our top performers for many years. I'm sure that once we let him know a resignation will allow him to keep stock, options and retirement while a firing would cost him much of all three and a hefty severance – he will see clearly to do the right thing by his family," Chet says.

"So let me get this right. He's a top performer. He followed company policy. He speaks the language of the people who are angry with us. And your recommendation is we make him the sacrificial lamb," Jia says.

"He's the perfect foil to get us out of this debate, with no harm done," Chet responds. "And if we need to pay him a little extra to be a good boy, it's money well spent."

"Okay, I understand," Jia says, even though she clearly thinks Chet should be the sacrificial lamb. "Give me three hours to get approvals, but get the wheels in motion."

Jia has no intent of following through on Chet's plan, but as he moves to implement his plan, he will clearly display his willingness to sacrifice any of his team to protect his personal interests. That clear view of his moral code may break loyalty bonds some could otherwise feel. By telling him to work the plan, but not pull the trigger, his team will see him selling out one of his long-time top performers for short-term political expediency.

Making Chet the fall guy will help Jia get someone loyal to her in place and get FirstWal off the hook by making short work of the person who established the now unpopular policy.

Chairman Chen may still be asleep, but Jia knows she needs to wake him up now that she has a solution. She sends a message and types in the override to send an alarm. Now that she is on top of the problem, she wants to be sure the Chairman hears her version of the story.

CHAPTER 17

May 23, 2040
West Nogales, Arizona

Honor to Mexico Founder Ángel Herrera is in his 70s but sees a path to his dream for the first time. Riding along Interstate 10 and Route 83, he peers out over sandy and increasingly hilly terrain, passing cacti, nearly bone-dry grasses and four-foot wire fences around ranches so desolate that miles sometimes separate roaming deer, cattle and horses. Patches of small towns dot the landscape on the long drive from Las Cruces, New Mexico, where local officials honored Ángel last night for his dedication to Mexican immigrants. After waking just south of Sonoita from a nap that filled in a short night's rest, Ángel drifts mentally to mapping next steps in his effort to reunite Mexico.

High school senior Juan Gonzalez has quickly achieved stardom among Mexican Americans well beyond his West Nogales hometown. As Ángel told his H2M Board, Juan's leadership talent and personal appeal make him an ideal face of hope to his people. His schoolboy good looks and charm are disarming – generating momentum for H2M's causes without stirring anti-Hispanic sentiment.

After studying past race-based movement successes, Ángel decides that an inspirational, non-violent leader is necessary to win a human rights issue like freeing Mexicans in America's Southwest from U.S. control. To succeed, the leader needs a passionate following. Violence could either help or hurt, Ángel has concluded. When a government uses violence ruthlessly against its own people, a movement can be repressed for years, decades and even generations. However, violent incidents against his people could galvanize followers. Carefully targeted violence against an incumbent regime and its supporters can push a government to fold quickly to the initiator's demands, particularly in a democracy.

In freedom movements Ángel studied – South Africa, India, Cuba, Eastern Europe, Egypt and numerous colonial revolts – Ángel saw that outbreaks of violence catalyzed attention to issues but rarely provided the full solution.

Since using violence as a tool carries substantial danger, he needs to protect H2M from backlash. Violence needs to be used strategically, providing the barking of dogs that pushes the American sheep to the waiting pen where H2M provides the soothing comfort of rational solutions. Juan can be the publicity agent for H2M's secession solution.

Ángel considers whether U.S. leaders would embark on a concentrated campaign to kill large numbers of its prior citizens to avert secession. Certainly, the Civil War showed whites would kill each other over the right to control non-whites. But Ángel believes slave owners were driven in the Civil War primarily by greed and power, and President Lincoln by fear of being known primarily for the unraveling of the United States. Leaders won't give up their ability to dominate others unless the consequences of not doing so are so painful as to outweigh their shame.

Ángel decides he can't be direct. H2M will initiate demonstrations to force federal government response, creating the campfire of violence that turns into a forest fire. When violence is needed, Ángel's friends can make sure to create relentless fear.

H2M and Juan need to be seen as the Mexican equivalent of Martin Luther King Jr. in this civil rights battle. But, to succeed, Ángel decides a Mexican version of the Black Panther movement must be created. The Pumas. Why not? But who becomes the Malcolm X? Malcolm X and the Black Panther movement were so threatening that whites ultimately accepted King's vision and unshackled blacks from the long post-slavery economic handcuffs just so Malcolm X and his kind would leave them alone.

Ángel tells a small handful of allies that independence will never come without fear of what will happen if they aren't allowed to leave. A peaceful, service-based movement is foolish without a parallel violent track, Ángel told these select few.

Still, even H2M's non-violent approach has lacked focus. Non-violence needs a leader to inspire tens of thousands, even millions, to endure pain and hope for a better future. Juan is younger than other successful leaders, but has already shown incredible poise and resourcefulness in making Arizona the fifth official Spanish-language state, and with stricter requirements than in South California, Texas, New Mexico or Puerto Rico. He has the passion of the aggrieved combined with the naïve, unbridled optimism of youth. He can galvanize Mexicans to retake their homeland.

Though Ángel believes his movement needs a villain, his courtship of Juan to be the non-violent leader reaches a critical juncture today. As Ángel makes his way to surprise Juan with the H2M Medal of Honor in a packed audience of West Nogales High soccer fans, he thinks carefully about how much Juan needs to know to be interested and successful.

As the 80th minute approaches, Ángel makes his way toward the center of the sideline, shaking hands with substitutes from both teams who recognize him. West Nogales is winning handily on senior night. Juan has contributed a beautiful half-volley goal from just outside the 18, along with a back heel assist that left the goalie dumbfounded and one of Juan's teammates with a nearly empty net to pass the ball into.

As the game concludes, the announcer interrupts the cheering: "I ask everyone to stay for a very special surprise award ceremony recognizing one of our very own."

It doesn't take too long for people in the stands to realize Juan will be recognized, but Juan is oblivious and is heading off the field before being stopped by the school principal. Not knowing what is going on, Juan is nervous about what he may have done, even more so than speaking in front of 50,000 people at the Capitol. He hasn't worked so hard to have something hurt his reputation so close to the end.

"Señores y señoras," the principal says as he stands on the hastily constructed stage in front of what made do for home stands. *"Honor to Mexico has brought families together, helped educate our children, fed our homeless and created economic opportunities for millions of our friends and family. Today, I have the great pleasure of introducing the founder and leader of the H2M movement, a man who has done so much to help Mexicans improve our quality of life for 30 years — Señor Ángel Herrera."*

A tremendous standing ovation erupts. H2M began as a social service organization and is one of the most critical social service agencies in the Southwest, with branches in other parts of the country as well. Over the decades Ángel ran the group, H2M has helped tens of millions of Mexican descendants build better lives, including many in the crowd today.

"Thank you all very much for the warm welcome. On behalf of H2M and our hard-working staff, I appreciate your recognition for the efforts we have undertaken on behalf of you — my family and friends," Ángel says.

Another round of applause. Ángel extends his arms and waves them downward to quiet the crowd.

"I am here today to honor one of your own here at West Nogales and I will do this in English for the cameras to capture for all of the nation to see. The local radio station is airing a translation live in Spanish for those who prefer to hear in our native tongue."

Ángel waits several seconds to allow people to turn on their Lifelinks and connect to the station before proceeding.

"Rarely in life do we have the opportunity to see a hero start his journey. For those in West Nogales, you've been able to see this hero enter the community and grow quickly as a student, athlete and leader," Ángel says. "But for the rest of H2M, we saw the birth of our newest hero over the past few months with the extraordinary, inspirational efforts of Mr. Juan Gonzalez."

The crowd interrupts Ángel again with applause. This time, he does not try to quiet the crowd. He wants Juan to soak in the adulation before continuing.

"Juan has played a critical role in delivering this community from the requirements of people who speak different languages, listen to different music, eat different food – or, to be fair, perhaps Anglo versions of our food. This part of America fears our heritage, fears our culture, and, most of all, fears our power."

The crowd listens intently, some nodding their heads, but many just listening.

"In a shorter time than I ever imagined," Ángel continues, "Juan has taken the issue of our language and elevated the rights of Spanish speakers.

More than almost any other measure taken by H2M and any other organization, Juan is leading the movement to open up economic opportunity for all. So, on behalf of the H2M Board of Directors and our Executive Committee, I am pleased to present tonight to Mr. Juan Gonzalez the 2040 Honor to Mexico Medal of Honor."

Juan's lips quiver as he tries to maintain his composure. He and his mother had received assistance from the local H2M chapter when she moved to West Nogales years earlier. To be honored by this same group is overwhelming if the tears falling are any indication.

Juan's mother joins in walking to the makeshift stage, holding his hand and trembling with such forceful pride that Juan turns his attention from his own sense of gratitude to helping his mother manage her emotions.

The crowd's cheers are accentuated by the school band, which strikes up a rendition of "Our Time," Antonio Perez's Latino-pop hit that speaks to the needs of young Latinos to seize their place in the world. Juan's teammates and friends stand to the side – ready to engulf him in a group hug as soon as he walks off stage. A broadcast of the event is beamed nationally and captured to play at the formal award ceremony Juan is asked to attend in Washington, D.C. later in the summer. As he moves to the center of the stage, Juan composes himself and begins to speak.

"I am so deeply honored, but I fear you may have made a mistake. My name is Juan Ángel Gonzalez. In my life, I have studied, played games and tried to be a responsible part of this community. Most importantly, I am the son of a loving mother who has sacrificed all of her dreams in this world to provide me an opportunity to pursue my dreams. My mother is my hero and if you believe I have done something worth honoring, I would ask that you honor her."

Juan takes the H2M medal and ribbon off his neck and places it on her, as she and other mothers in the audience cry and the rest of the crowd applauds. *"So I thank you for this medal because today you have given me the chance to make my mother proud – to give her a moment that I can see she will cherish,"* Juan says, stepping back from the microphone and wiping away tears with the sleeves of his dust-crusted shirt.

"If you honor me because of what we have accomplished at the Capitol, you must also honor everyone here. It's people in the stands who stood beside me at FirstWal when I was told that speaking Spanish was not good enough – that I could not work

there because I had chosen the 'wrong' second language to focus on in a country where so many people speak only one language. It is the people here who led the way to the Capitol and whose passion and enthusiasm helped build statewide support for the Spanish-only movement. So I thank you for this surprise, this honor . . . this extraordinary honor . . . on behalf of everyone here in West Nogales. And I thank you, most of all, on behalf of my mother."

Ángel smiles in a way he had not for years. Such maturity. Such humility. Such composure. He really is the one.

CHAPTER 18

May 23, 2040
Chicago

Near the end of the University of Chicago's spring quarter, windows are cracked to allow temperate air to displace air dulled by continuous recycling. Students anxiously wait for even fresher air to breathe on the last weekend that won't see them fully focused on finals.

"It has been many years since current events have been this interesting," Professor Paul Stark begins his lecture. "So the discussion today, and your assignment for next week, is all about developments in Arizona and the other Southwest states." Audible groans, driven by an unexpected paper just ahead of finals, echo around the acoustically designed classroom.

Professor Stark's two-quarter Culture and Policy class is known for its interdisciplinary approach to topics. Students are asked to combine perspectives of history, politics, business, economics, law, psychology, sociology, theology and just about every other "ology" into a unique blend of study that forces students outside traditional academic silos. More than anything, Professor Stark focuses on translating academic theory into real-world public policy implications.

Entering Barack Obama Hall, most students are more focused on how much skinny caramel latte they have left – and, at least for the guys, the first spotting of bare legs in more than six months – than on the topics of the class they are entering. While every new class enters viewing Professor Stark as a mythical figure, they find all too quickly that he can be disorganized or meticulous and temperamental or warm-hearted depending on the day. His primary constant is his pursuit of achievement, with developing students to achieve as his primary mission. He stopped wearing business dress in public years earlier to better blend with his surroundings. Having sacrificed so much personally – he had wanted to have a family before being absorbed by the Political Freedom Amendment battle – he has no patience for people who won't put in the work needed to succeed. Students can be wrong in his class and perhaps receive only mild rebuke. But unprepared students, or those showing they don't care, are subjected to verbal ridicule they rarely fully comprehend.

"So, who can tell me about Arizona," Professor Stark asks, scanning for someone new to tackle the topic. Finding no volunteers, he turns his back, grabs the tattered Nerf combo rocket and football he played with as a child, turns away from the class and tosses the ball behind him into the crowd to determine who will kick off today's debate.

"Jeremy, much as I would like to have someone else take this, the ball did hit you on the head while you were gawking, so tell us what is happening in Arizona," Professor Stark says.

As Jeremy speaks, the microphone sensors hone in on his voice and amplify it throughout the room.

"I haven't followed this that closely," Jeremy said, "but it seems pretty simple. A company discriminates because a guy doesn't speak English. The Spanish-speaking community protests. They get elected officials all riled up. These people pass a Spanish-only language law for the State. Last week, everyone gets in a tizzy when the law takes effect. Everyone is mad at someone else," Jeremy says. "That about sums it up."

"So why is everyone upset?" Professor Stark asks.

"The new law bans discrimination against Spanish speakers. This means that even someone who doesn't speak Spanish has to serve the Spanish speaker as if they understand what's being said. Since this isn't possible if you don't know the language, it really requires everyone working for the State to speak Spanish. People who don't speak Spanish are mad about the law, and people who do speak Spanish are mad that people are mad about the law," Jeremy responds.

Professor Stark paces up the aisle and down the row. He is standing next to Jeremy by the time he finishes. "Does this matter to anyone here?"

Tamika enters the conversation. "I'm all for it. Why should someone be discriminated against just for the language they speak, especially when it has no impact on their ability to succeed in a job?"

"That's a good question, Tamika," Professor Stark said. "Does anyone want to answer it?"

Davi, a junior economics major, jumps in.

"Let me make sure I understand this. So all state operations in Arizona are done in Spanish? This, I assume, includes the police, the courts?"

"It's a spectacular day when students make arguments based on assumptions. I assume you agree Davi?" Professor Stark interrupts.

A few blank stares are traded as the class looks around for someone to clarify whether Davi's assumption has a basis. "Really, you know what pop music stars eat for breakfast, but you don't know the contents of the most crucial laws being imposed in our country?" Professor Stark says. "All state operations includes police, the courts, and every private operation that uses any state-supported funds or service – which is another way of saying just about everybody. So now that we are hopefully done making assumptions for the day, continue Davi."

"If I drive through Arizona on my way to South California, and I get pulled over for speeding, how will I communicate with the police officer?" Davi asks.

"With respect, I presume," Professor Stark interjects.

"That's a great question," Jeremy says. "If he speaks Spanish to me, I won't know what he's saying. What if I think he wants me to display my license and I reach for my wallet and he thinks I'm pulling a weapon?"

"We would get shot just for not knowing Spanish. That makes absolutely no sense in America," Davi says. "This shouldn't be allowed. Won't Congress pass something to make English the only language we require?"

"I will assume – since you like assumptions – that you understand you've identified an important implication of the new Arizona law and congratulate you on the thought. Unless, of course, you want to tell me this assumption is wrong and you have no idea what I just said," Professor Stark says. After pausing for a few seconds and hearing no response, he adds, "Any other implications stand out?"

Rachel, raised by a Spanish-speaking father and an English-speaking mother, adds her thoughts.

"It seems like Arizona responded to discrimination against Spanish speakers in one company by imposing discrimination against all other languages statewide. Wouldn't a better answer be to prevent discrimination on the basis of any language?" she asks rhetorically. "I suspect Congress now will want to counter this law since it goes beyond the other Spanish language equality states. And many other English-speaking states could impose English-only requirements, expanding discrimination against Spanish speakers."

A fully engaged debate ensues, with students defending, opposing and even ridiculing the Arizona law on the type of scant knowledge that so frequently drives political debates.

"So, if other states respond with English-only requirements," Professor Stark says as the class draws near to an end, "let's consider what this means. For Spanish-speaking residents of states like Indiana or Illinois, what happens if they get stopped by the police – to go back to Davi's earlier question? Will these people understand what they are being ordered to do any more than Davi would understand what he is told in Arizona when he wildly flaunts state law, treats their highways as his personal race track and automatically assumes the officer is a man?"

"We're only touching the surface of this topic, and it's too important to treat superficially. So, I want a 5,000-word essay posted by Sunday at 11:59 p.m. Every essay will be public and, next week, I'll open our class to 10 journalists interested in scoping the implications of the Arizona law. So be unique. Be clear. Be thoughtful. And be prepared to defend what you write," Professor Stark says as he hears groans around the room. "You have nearly 50 hours to complete your essays. That's just 100 words an hour, so I know it's within your skill set. Many of you will babble that many words between your seat and the doorway."

As the class starts to walk out, a few forget that Obama Hall was developed for acoustic clarity.

"What a prick. Would one of you ladies please just do him so he stops taking his misery out on us?" Davi says.

"After you, Mr. Ass . . . sss . . . umption," one of the women responds to Davi as she walks out the door.

***

West Nogales, Arizona

After leaving the West Nogales soccer field, Ángel Herrera boards public transportation taking him to the FirstWal store that started the Juan Gonzalez controversy. Ángel tells his son Gabriel, heir apparent to his leadership, and the H2M security team that he will take public transportation and walk to the store to see firsthand how irrelevant English is in West Nogales.

And he does just that, at least for a while. He walks up and down the aisles, talks to the store's service specialist team about a custom-shopping program, and checks out with mandarin flavored soda without ever having to utter a word of English. It's always good to check facts personally. Ángel learned from personal experience that bad early reporting creates lingering inaccuracies. After walking inside and then leaving the store, Ángel heads away from the bus stop. Turning the building corner and seeing he is away from exterior surveillance cameras, he looks for his ride.

Ángel moves slowly up to the cab of the truck, checking to avoid being seen. Entering, he quickly slumps out of sight. His driver takes him several miles down the road to the Border Flooring manufacturing and distribution center. After entering the facility, the driver leaves Ángel alone – following clear instructions to leave the building and set the security system. Neither man speaks. Ángel wants to avoid recognition and his driver prefers not knowing who this guy is, or perhaps was. Once the system is set, and it's clear no one else is in the building, a well-dressed, imposing figure walks over to Ángel, looks him over carefully, and then gives him a strong hug. For his best friends, the hugs are always the same – strong enough for Cesar Castillo to show his power, but gentle enough to show affection.

Neither man speaks, knowing their voices might be traceable even inside this building. After a long walk to the concealed entrance and 15 minutes of a slow, quiet ride down the elevator shaft, any concern with surveillance is behind them.

"*It's been so long since I've seen you,*" Castillo says, putting his arm around the shoulder of his friend, as they drive back to more comfortable surroundings under the other side of the border. "*Why would you take such a chance to see me after so many years. Our arrangement continues to be beneficial I presume.*"

Ángel smiles. "*I can never express how grateful I am – not only for your support, but also for the help you direct to us. I always feel your presence and support,*" Ángel says, making clear immediately that he understands his place in this relationship with the same submissive behaviors displayed to an alpha animal.

"*So I came for two reasons,*" Ángel continues. "*First, I'm getting old and I don't want to miss any chance to tell you how important you are to me and the people I serve. On its own, this would be reason enough. But, as you might suspect, I have a request. It is part of achieving an objective we share, but which before now I thought was beyond my lifetime.*"

Once reaching the south entrance to the tunnel, the two men pace underground along the tunnel road. Castillo is certain he knows Ángel's plan. "*I dreamt that someday you would come with such news, but truly believed it was a dream for my sons. What makes you believe the time has come to bring Mexico together,*" Castillo asks.

"*I don't know if you have followed the Nogales boy,*" Ángel says, "*but this young man may be the Zapata of our times. He gives life to the idea that 'it is better to die on your feet than live on your knees.' I just came from meeting him in person for the first time. His humility, his strength, his integrity make him ideal to speak to our ambitions.*"

"*I have followed this boy with great interest. Clearly, he's a young man of remarkable courage, though I fear he may have his mother's stubbornness,*" Castillo says.

"*From what I saw, truly a wonderful, inspirational woman,*" Ángel says. "*How do you know of her?*"

"*Few know of this, so this is for you only. Juan's father left Juan and his mother in my territory while he accomplished his assignments – most of which took him away from home for many months at a time. He supported them until he was killed. I'm not sure Juan remembers his father. From what we know, he tells people he never met his father. After her husband died, we offered to support Mrs. Gonzalez until Juan was 18 – a great gesture of goodwill on my part. Instead, she asked to be released and to move to America to make it on her own. I was concerned this would risk exposure, but approved her request, as long as she lived within my easy reach,"* Castillo said. *"She has remained silent, but she must be quite a stubborn woman to refuse my generosity and live such a hard life."*

Ángel delays for a moment as he tries to think through the implications of what he has just heard. After quickly concluding it has no effect on his plan's chances of success, he continues.

"Now, I hate to do this after benefitting from so much generosity, but I need to request your help with something I cannot do on my own," Ángel continues. *"I need someone to create the equivalent of the Zapatistas or perhaps something more like the American Black Panthers. We need to create a violent threat that makes it easier for America to turn to H2M when we propose a sensible end to the confrontation between Mexicans and whites in America."* A student of war history, terrorism and particularly guerrilla warfare, Castillo fully understands what is being asked.

Founded in 1966, the Black Panthers created fear in American society with carefully selected killings and well-documented shows of force. The Zapatistas began pushing for land reforms early in the 20th Century, and were quelled when the movement's demands for large landowners to give land back to the state drew fear from the wealthy elite. Both movements sought the overthrow of those who tried to control their communities, creating enough turmoil that many communities were constantly one match flick away from explosive confrontation.

"Just to be clear, it is just the Anglos we go after, correct?" Castillo asks. Seeing a nod, he continues: *"Mi amigo, in six months America will run to you, begging you to take their land and go away."*

Castillo works quickly.

The Puma party is founded in just days by Castillo allies who he believes cannot be traced to him. They immediately create a manifesto modeled after the Black Panthers that circulates through public and private networks.

We demand FREEDOM and POWER to determine the destiny of oppressed sons and daughters of Mexico.

We seek full access to employment – free from those who attempt to dominate us.

We require an end to the racism that has robbed Mexico's children of their rightful place as leaders of our government and economy.

We want guaranteed education in the language of our choice that enables success of the impoverished, unveils the decadence of America and teaches the truth about our history.

We demand an end to racist laws that steal true freedom from the sons and daughters of Mexico.

We insist on full political control of our land.

CHAPTER 19

June 5, 2040
New Rite Camp, Utah

Nearly two months after Pete's Colorado survival victory, Pete works as Utah training commander for donors who buy their way in to New Rite's monthly battles. The New Rite Utah camp northeast of Kanab includes terrain ranging from stark desert and rock environments to forested highlands, some of which had been national lands.

Pete's Colorado win made him eligible for the job, but JT's endorsement gained him quick approval. JT still is consulted on hires for state camp trainers and compound directors. Pete arrived weeks ahead of his start date to gain familiarity with the terrain and devise appropriate combat and training strategies.

The gallon canteens allowed in battle packs contain only enough water to survive one day before dehydration and its debilitating effects start to set in. Pete quickly decides the first day of training must be water survival – how to find it in a desert environment, how to ensure it is safe to drink and strategies to minimize perspiration loss. On his first day, Pete follows three hours of classroom water instruction with a cramping, water-less three-hour workout. Once fully drained, he drives and hikes trainees to open rock and desert with everything except water they need to survive until the next afternoon.

Twenty hours later, Pete returns to find one of the 18 trainees had been too drained to secure water the day before and fell asleep immediately.

Waking up disoriented today, that trainee begs to go home. He'll be an easy kill in competition. The water-drain test is dangerous, but medical monitoring equipment worn by each trainee helps medical staff know when trainees are crossing into medical threat. While this badly dehydrated trainee slowly recovers function after Pete shares his water, the others are ready to delve into six hours of camouflage training. After training, everyone has to be camouflaged and hidden by 4 a.m. for a game of hide-and-seek in which those who are found have to repeat the Day One workout.

Pete finds this game great fun – a chance to hone his camouflage detection skills and stay in shape. By noon, Pete finds every trainee – hitting each with a blowgun blast for added sting. Knowing a repeat workout is coming, trainees are delighted at the second chance Pete offers. If they can find him, everyone gets to skip the training. With a two-hour head start to secure his position and camouflage, Pete is confident he will not be found. At 5 p.m., the deadline for trainees to find him passes, and Pete comes out of hiding just 500 meters from the starting point of the hunt. Pete left visible footprints taking him to a rocky area where his prints would be hard to track, then walked backward on his first set of prints to reach a rock ledge. From there, he dropped into a shaded crevice that his students could only spot from right on top of him. Once they passed him at the beginning of the hunt, Pete knew he would not be found.

The training regimen for these wannabe warriors is challenging each day, with focus on long-distance marksmanship, hand-to-hand combat, human tracking, night survival, food identification and wild animal attack survival.

At the end of the week, JT meets with Pete to review his performance.

"I'm impressed with your knowledge of competitive combat," JT starts, with a wood fire crackling nearby, and both men drinking HS hefeweizen – a JT favorite. "It's clear to me you can adapt to different physical environments, in addition to handling tough situations."

"Thank you JT. I came early to scout the area and make sure I knew what I was doing. I know New Rite's reputation can be hurt if I don't live up to your trust."

"That preparation and dedication tells me you will succeed in any challenge. I'm going to take a risk here in asking you to do something. Can I trust you to think about it before you react?"

"Of course, anything," Pete says.

"Tell me what you know about the Honor to Mexico movement."

"Well, I think I already told you that I couldn't get jobs even in Colorado because I don't speak Spanish. So, it sounds like Arizona is making this the law and that group is behind it," Pete says. "Honor to Mexico only cares about Mexicans. Seriously, if they love Mexico so much, why are they even here? And I know they want to take our borders back with Mexico to the way it was before we defeated them at the Alamo."

"Okay, so maybe history's not your strength, but I don't know whether to blame the school system or my own game scenarios for that. I'll have to work on historical accuracy," JT says. "But, anyway, I think you get the gist of the issue. So what do you think about the language laws and this Honor movement?"

"Pull up all the nasty words I've ever said when I got shot in a game and you'll start to get an idea of what I think. If someone wants to live in Mexico, they should just leave," Pete says.

"I thought you were angry about this, but I wanted to be sure," JT says. "So, the question I have is how interested are you in doing what it takes to stop the United States from becoming a colony of Mexico?"

Pete nods quickly: "I'm all in."

"Are you willing to risk spending time in jail, at least until I can get you out? And when you get out, you still probably need to keep everything you did to yourself," JT says.

"I'm not quite sure what you're asking, but there's nothing I won't do to make America the way it should be," Pete says.

JT asks Pete to stand up with him and walk toward a nearby cabin. As they get inside, he closes the door, and turns on the exterior sound system. "This is the ideal partnership then. I can help you figure out how you can make the world a better place, and support you financially while you do this work. You have the skills to pull this off. But, so we're clear, if you succeed, no one can know. And if you fail, it's your reputation and maybe your life that takes the fall. I won't abandon you if you get caught, but no one can know I seeded these ideas with you," JT says.

"Look, JT, I guess there's something I'm not willing to do. I'm not willing to kill people just for fun, but I realize we're at war here, so I understand I may have to hurt people who are trying to take away our country. I'm okay with that," Pete says. "So what do I do?"

"Have you heard about the kid who convinced Arizona to ban English?" JT asks.

"You don't want me to go after him, do you?" Pete asks.

"The Honor to Mexico group gave him their medal of honor, and they're bringing him in for their national event to recognize him in just a few weeks," JT says. "They're trying to push Spanish language requirements nationally."

Pete starts to turn a brighter shade of the red he has picked up from his outdoor training. "That's as stupid as when my dad walked around with his pants hanging down. That's embarrassing," Pete says, his knee rattling up and down enough that the floor is shaking. "How can I stop this?"

"It's simple. We send a message to H2M that we won't tolerate their destruction of America," JT pleads.

"Like I asked, do you want me to hurt the kid?" Pete says. A few moments of silence follow as JT looks around and Pete waits for a response. "Or what?"

CHAPTER 20

June 5, 2040
Chicago

Professor Stark selects a group of livestream video services, influential political commentators and a few mainstream reporters to cover his in-class debate. From a small, elevated stage at the front of the room, the cameras follow presentations and debates anywhere in the raised, theater-style classroom.

Professor Stark's public course debates generally attract external coverage. He long ago realized that unexposed good ideas are as useful as highly exposed dumb ideas.

Opening his Lifelink, Professor Stark sets the in-room environment. Shades drop to darken the long row of 10-foot high windows. Professor Stark long ago raised money to make his classroom as visually and acoustically stimulating as the best news studio sets, helping to attract media coverage.

"I would like to thank our students for producing largely well-constructed and well-researched papers. Even better, the conclusions vary widely on the impact of language on public policy. We have 75 minutes for this session – 25 minutes of hearing summaries of papers I've selected as the best. After this, we'll open up to roundtable, followed by my favorite part of the session – random grilling. In appreciation for their interest, we reserve the last 15 minutes for the media to badger any students as they see fit, something I also enjoy."

On any given day, regardless of weather, Professor Stark is as likely to show up in flannel or a bizarre t-shirt as in the more conservative clothes he wears when he knows cameras are on in the classroom. If caught by media unexpectedly, he turns to the blue blazer, button-down shirt and tie he keeps in his office, or the tweed sport coat, shirt and tie permanently stashed in his car trunk.

"The topic at hand," Professor Stark says. "What role should language play in politics and public policy? A number of events transpired recently to elevate this national issue. Let's get started. Tamika. Introduce your thesis, your reasoning, and what you see as the optimal outcome from your policy recommendation."

Tamika looks around the room at her classmates, glances at the media panel, turns back to Professor Stark and tries to hide the glow of knowing hers is a top paper.

"America is a multi-cultural country, founded on the idea that people of various races, religions, cultures and languages can live together by respecting, tolerating and growing through exposure to different people. That idea was taught when I was a child and there's no time better than today to actually start living this concept," she says.

"Over the years, we've seen countless examples where society failed to tolerate differences. My ancestors were enslaved, beaten, humiliated, tortured – and worse than almost all of this – purposely left uneducated so many thought they had it good if their children weren't sold away. Jews, Mormons, Muslims and Catholics were considered vulgar religious bastards and marginalized, ignored or ridiculed for generations – openly by hate groups, but in less obvious and more cynical ways by the rest of America," Tamika adds, looking around the room, focusing on making eye and camera contact as she speaks.

"Get to your primary point," Professor Stark urges.

"Okay. Many people could not learn English when they came here, either because they were illegal immigrants without access to education or because supporting their family meant working every day to the point of exhaustion just to survive. In most of the United States, these people were stuck on the periphery of society, obtaining only menial work. So, America is a multi-cultural society, and yet fostering tolerance remains our greatest challenge."

As she continues, Stark types a quick note into his Lifelink.

"Our politicians established laws to punish people harshly when crimes are based on race-based hatred. Leaders from Abe Lincoln to JFK and Dr. King to Barack Obama helped promote tolerance. But today too many lives remain defined by hate. One visible sign of intolerance is our failure to embrace people who speak other languages. So, in considering whether a Spanish-only language requirement makes sense in Arizona, we need to determine if this stops intolerant behavior or makes things worse," she says, pausing in part to catch her breath and in part for dramatic effect.

"Again, good background Tamika, but I need you to get to the conclusion," Professor Stark interrupts.

"It's not an easy call," Tamika says. "Clearly, the decision by FirstWal to refuse a job to someone because he doesn't know English well enough when he won't even need it is a sign of intolerance. Spanish is the primary language in that whole region and should be respected. So, to the extent the law corrects an inequity in respect, it appears on its face to side with creating a culture of tolerance. However, the law passed in Arizona makes Spanish really the only language that has to be used and gives employees only six months to be fluent. Ironically, many second, third and forth generation Mexican Americans aren't fluent. That means people need to choose between spending six months trying to become fluent in Spanish or looking for work in another state."

"Tamika, your conclusion please," Professor Stark says.

"My conclusion. The reaction of the legislature in Arizona identified a legitimate issue, but passed an illegitimate law to fix the problem."

As several students begin to applaud and others start to boo, Professor Stark waves his arms to shush the crowd. "No applause. And when we disagree, let's try using words. This is a discussion, not a Blackhawks game." After a pause, "Okay Jeremy, you're next up and please don't save your thesis for the last line."

Jeremy stands and paces as he talks, stopping to linger in front of several female classmates.

"Ladies. Gentlemen. Everyone else. Passage of a Spanish-only requirement will accelerate the flames of disintegration of our nation if left in place." Pausing to let his rehearsed opening sink in to the class, Jeremy walks to the front of the class and looks for reaction.

"You've heard me talk about civil wars being fostered by separations of religion, race and language. Just in the past hundred years, we've seen the disintegration of the Soviet Union, the violence and massacres of the Baltic wars, slaughters in Africa along tribal and religious lines, and conflicts too numerous to cover elsewhere. These atrocities represent the price these nations paid for being built on separate cultures and languages. For generations, we've seen attempts by factions in Canada, Spain and other countries to separate from their countries based on language differences, and Quebec appears about to succeed," Jeremy says.

"We've been heading toward the disintegration of our country for generations. This is disturbing because as Tamika said we spent the first two centuries of national existence trying to keep our races separate. When we finally began to integrate across racial and ethnic lines – something our founders may not have envisioned but which was clearly inspired by the concept that 'all men are created equal' – our progress was derailed by development of regionally isolated cultures and economies. Because of all of this, I believe the Arizona law needs to be superseded by a national law requiring English as our common national language."

"Okay, Jeremy. Interesting points. And on behalf of those people here who are neither ladies nor gentlemen, let me thank you for being inclusive in addressing non-human life forms attending class today," Professor Stark says.

"I didn't mean . . . "

"Jeremy, just having fun," Professor Stark says. "One more point. You've made great progress in not fixating your attention on just one or two women as you speak. But I still haven't seen you recognize there are any males in this class."

As Jeremy walks back to his seat, with a smattering of laughter and applause, a male voice shouts, "You can stare in my eyes Jeremy." Professor Stark introduces the next presenter. Karina presents a cogent argument that the abilities of China and India to sustain their existence over the centuries despite each being aggregations of dozens of different ethnic groups and local languages is based on establishing common languages used by citizens with the aptitude and desire to be part of the national economic and political elite. "By creating a separate language for the elites in Arizona from the elites in most other states, you exclude people outside Arizona from succeeding there, but you also create a culture inside Arizona that could deter leaders there from venturing out to other roles in broader American society," she concludes.

Aracelli argues that the First Amendment right to Free Speech ensures the rights of every citizen to speak the language they want to speak, and only the language they want to speak, without any discrimination. "Any entity that impacts an individual's ability to function effectively in society, to earn an income, raise their family and exercise their rights as citizens – must have their ability to effectively participate protected by government. Given how inexpensive it is to have real-time translation, I believe government's responsibility is to protect native language interactions at all times. If that means translation systems need to be installed in every classroom, every business and every workspace, so be it."

Rachel Cruz concludes the opening presentations.

"We've heard some great arguments on multiple sides of the debate today. My perspective is different. I am the first generation in half of my family to be born American, and had the wonderful advantage of being raised in English by my mother and in Spanish by my father. Until Fresno became part of North California when the state split, a lot of my education was in Spanish. As I headed to middle school, I started thinking about what else besides a movie star I wanted to be. It struck me that if I wanted to be President or a CEO, or even a big enough movie star to be popular everywhere in America, I needed to better learn English," Rachel says.

"In my part of Fresno, I could be successful with Spanish alone. With classes often taught in Spanish, that was my primary language. So I had to go out of my way to learn English. Obviously, my mom helped. Without this, I don't know whether I would have even been able to make it here. This is clearly unfair," Rachel says, again twisting her hair as she does whenever she gets nervous.

"Tolerance and fairness are not the same. We can be tolerant and still unfair. I think this will always be true. Some people are born with advantages. Sometimes the advantages are inheritances or famous parents. In other cases, advantages are talents, or a willingness to work hard. No one is owed anything. There is nothing in the Arizona law that prohibits people from speaking English. There is nothing in the law that prevents people from learning Spanish. To make it fairer, there is a transition time for people to learn. So, I fully support the rights of the people of Arizona to make Spanish the state language. As I've thought about it, I don't believe that the law discriminates, because anyone who wants to participate in the state can learn Spanish, and they get time, just as I had time to get better at English. No one made it easy on me. Yet, I've been able to achieve my goals," Rachel says as she finishes her argument.

As the end of class nears, Professor Stark thanks the class and media attendees for an interesting and productive debate.

"As you can see, there are strong feelings and interesting arguments on multiple sides of this debate," Professor Stark says. "So let me raise concepts that I have been thinking about as this debate proceeded. Tamika's test is a good one: Would such a law promote tolerance or facilitate intolerance? So, the question is, are we a more tolerant America in future generations if we all speak the same language, or a less tolerant America? Can we resolve conflicts more effectively when we communicate effectively?"

Stark pulls open his tie and unbuttons the top button on his shirt. Though he knows the cameras are still running, his end-of-quarter added weight makes his top button too tight.

"We live in a global economy. English is not the dominant business language it once was. We depend on foreign tourism to support our economies in many parts of the country and we depend on exporting products and services in many other parts. So if we all speak English only, we will not understand the languages of business in many parts of the world, and will not be able to communicate effectively with visitors. That is the risk of an English-only requirement, and one that can be overcome only through education," Professor Stark says.

"Do we need to take notes on this?" Jeremy whispers to a classmate, forgetting that he can still be heard. Professor Stark looks at him and decides to ignore the question.

"Good discussion today and interesting concepts from a lot of you. Here's another take I would like you all to consider. Should our education system require that all Americans learn a second language and, with that, gain understanding of at least a second culture? One thought I haven't heard yet is the idea that every student should receive foreign language and culture training throughout their formal education, starting in kindergarten. If we better understand the world, we better fit into it," Professor Stark says. He projects photos and video clips of failed empires on the walls behind him, with the projections moving to follow him as he paces the room.

"How do we avoid the arrogances of empires?" he continues. "Whether it's the Greeks, Romans, Persians, Mongolians, Spanish, Egyptians, Germans, Brits or literally hundreds of other societies over world history, those who have tried to control peoples of a different language and culture have only succeeded as long as they succeeded in either terrifying them into submission or in enlisting the ambitious among these minorities to become part of the controlling culture. If the United States becomes a nation where we all can speak together and coexist across sub-cultures in relative peace, would our place in the world be less threatening and more inviting to those wanting to come here?"

Another click and the projections switch to pie charts showing the racial, ethnic, religious and language make-ups of the world and the United States.

"So, with the caveat that we all need to speak other languages, I would question whether the right answer isn't to move toward being a multi-cultural, multi-lingual America aided by one shared language. The America my gut tells me we need is a melting pot where we all behave like ingredients seeking to blend our flavors together to create the best nation in the world," Professor Stark concludes as the projection switches to various stews, soups and chili dishes from around the world.

A loud stomach grumble from a student punctuates his last comment.

"Okay class," Professor Stark interjects. "I get that you're ready to get out of here. I'm hungry too."

Before Professor Stark dismisses class for the day, fifty Lifelink devices vibrate at once with an alert. Lifelinks are thin, collapsible personal connection centers containing everything needed to write, talk, watch, listen, pay and prove identity in daily life. Most students carry them in inside pockets that are sealed and code-locked. Professor Stark prohibits students from keeping anything except the recording and writing components on during class, but all Lifelinks have emergency override alarms that now sound in unison.

"Explosion at Northwestern. Cause and injuries unknown. Everyone, please be alert."

Seconds later, another alarm.

"Explosion at New York University. Cause and injuries not yet known."

As students read the second alert, a third comes. "Explosions at Georgetown University and Georgia State University."

Mobile device and overhead system announcements quickly follow. "Please evacuate all buildings calmly and swiftly."

Faces tensed, a few with tears as some start to turn hysterical, students evacuate each building. Most run toward the Midway Plaisance and Washington Park. A few arrive to the open areas bloodied and hurt after tripping or being shoved into walls. Several professors and administrators lag behind as they lock their areas and sweep buildings for students. Campus police frantically communicate assignments to sweep buildings.

University police are well drilled in evacuating multiple buildings, drills built into police training regimens ever since senseless shooting attacks at Columbine, Virginia Tech, Northern Illinois and countless other schools and venues.

But no one expected simultaneous, full-campus evacuations at all education institutions, leaving police thinly spread in their search and empty efforts. A mobile command center is set up in the skating rink area of Midway Plaisance Park. The duty commander climbs to the top to identify evacuation problems and deploy teams to assist in minimizing injury risks.

"Oh my God, what's going on?" Rachel asks Tamika as they huddle in the light spring drizzle. "This is crazy. Are we under attack?"

"I'm not waiting to find out," Tamika replies. "We're not going back to class today so if you want to escape your apartment, come with me."

Wanting to feel the comfort of a home, Rachel agrees and the two walk toward the 59th Street Metra Electric station. The view is surreal. Neither had ever seen so many people outside the Hyde Park campus at once, with everyone just standing and waiting. A few seemed shocked or were crying, but some saw the gathering as a social opportunity.

As they walk toward the Metra station, Rachel and Tamika walk past Jeremy. They stop to watch for a few minutes, knowing he is likely to be entertaining. It doesn't take long for them to start joking about how it looks like he is scanning the crowd for every cute redhead – or maybe just every girl who will talk to him. In a ten-minute period, they watch him introduce himself to three girls before breaking out his Lifelink to either send his phone number, set a date on his calendar or do something else that looks completely out of place in an emergency.

"He'd be a lot smarter if he could get more blood flowing above his neck," Rachel comments as the two laugh and start walking again, happy to have had their tension temporarily relieved. Nearing the underpass to the electric line, they hear screaming start and see several students start running in their direction as they receive the next alert on their Lifelinks.

"Evacuated students under machine gun fire on Harvard campus. Dozens killed and injured," the message reads.

As implications of the announcement strike people over the coming seconds, the massive crowd starts to run in all directions, with escaping the same potential outcome the only objective. Blinded by speed and fear, students and faculty knock each other over. Rachel and Tamika had a head start on the crowd and are determined now to maintain that advantage. At full pace, they run to the Metra Electric line's crumbling stairwell and are fortunate to catch a train just prior to its departure.

Professor Stark responds to the first alert by walking to his office and pulling his desk in front of the door. Glancing outside his window with a mirror, he spots several students seeking to shelter themselves from sniper vantage points. Not sure whether it is worse to be bombed or shot, many students hedge their bets, finding concrete and brick walls just inside buildings to hide behind. Hundreds of students run into Rockefeller Chapel and do something many had not done in recent years – pray.

Around the country, police units scramble toward educational institutions to prevent shootings or bombs in their areas. That the university bombing attacks are coordinated is now clear. The motive, however, is unknown. Torn between keeping students outside to avoid bomb impacts and inside to minimize sniper threats, university administrators alert students to head home. Elementary and secondary schools bring students into windowless gyms while teachers and police race around buildings searching for signs of a bomb.

Tamika and Rachel follow the attacks while on the train. As they reach Tamika's empty home, they quickly close and lock the doors and gates behind them. After minutes watching the nine-station simulcast news channel, they flip to CNN.

CNN's anchor begins, "In what appears to be one of the most significant terrorist attacks in the past 40 years, America's enemies have targeted our youth. Bombs at Georgetown, Northwestern, Georgia State and New York University injured or killed hundreds and sent millions of students scrambling outdoors to safety. At Harvard University, students congregating in Harvard Square to avoid bomb attacks became victims of an open slaughter. Eyewitnesses have told CNN that at least five Arabic looking men in full Islamic garb opened fire from rooftop sites, but disappeared into the crowd before being apprehended. Though we do not have a formal count, it appears at least dozens of these students were killed and hundreds injured. A massive manhunt is underway for the men who launched this terror attack."

Hearing the news, parents leave work in droves, congesting highways and creating traffic flare-ups across the country that no amount of Easy Ride optimization software can keep moving smoothly. Video from Harvard Square shows ambulance personnel and university medical staff treating what looks to be hundreds of students strewn around the grounds. Live reports show students at the NYU, Northwestern, Georgia State and Georgetown universities bloodied and dazed.

Rachel and Tamika begin deep sobs, composing themselves only after realizing they need to find out if family and friends are okay.

CHAPTER 21

June 20, 2040
Washington, D.C.

Ramon Mantle enjoys his newfound freedom from the overbearing security team Cesar Castillo had assigned to protect and watch him. After years of Ramon suggesting that ear-stud surveillance and holding of his father should be enough, Castillo finally relented last week.

As summer arrives with all the hair-mangling, sweat-dripping thickness of swampy Washington, Ramon is one of 8,000 guests at the largest ever H2M Celebration fundraising event. Held at the Washington Convention Center, it has again attracted a who's who of Mexican American and other Hispanic leaders. Founded to support Mexican immigrants, whether legal or otherwise, the group has long served any Hispanic in need of its service.

With tonight's audience made up of nearly 100 members of the Congressional Hispanic Caucus, all three Supreme Court judges of Hispanic heritage, U.S. Defense Secretary Xavier Mendoza, and numerous Hispanic business leaders, the gathering is now the premier place to see and be seen among the Hispanic elite.

Extensive security surrounds the event, even more so now that it occurs just days after the Harvard massacre, as Wednesday's events have been quickly labeled. D.C. and Capitol Police, joined by the Secret Service and FBI, scour the site for bombs, then block off the streets and force participants to walk the last two blocks to the event.

D.C. traffic has long been congested enough that the only cars allowed to drive in the city are One Shot individual cars, Size Right adaptable vehicles and knock-offs of these designs. Developed specifically to resize the car to only transport the number of passengers and amount of cargo inside, Size Right vehicles also require each passenger to insert a government identification strip at the beginning of each trip. The vehicles then adjust automatically – folding up unneeded seats, redistributing weight and collapsing or expanding the external vehicle cage for ideal aerodynamic driving. Most vehicles also adapt to multiple fuel types, changing from oil to gas to electric to biofuels so the owners can optimize trade-offs between fuel costs and air emission standards. Engines even adapt to fuel changes in mid-drive. Wind streams passing around the cars drive miniature turbines to charge each vehicle's ample electronic package, further improving fuel efficiency.

To police and other law enforcement agencies, the greatest benefit of these cars are the electronic signatures needed for the Easy Ride operating software to work. This software, developed by Ramon Mantle's Perfect Logistics Company, ensures that vehicle occupants are identifiable and traceable. Each occupant inserts Lifelink-encased identification and alternating eye, fingerprint, dental and DNA scans. Vehicles approaching anywhere near the White House, Supreme Court or Capitol are searched against every terror and criminal database to assess potential threats. Vehicles entering the security zone with unidentified drivers or passengers are stopped automatically. The technology enabling this system means the H2M gala stands little risk from a mobile, on-the-ground bomber. Air security is even tighter, so once the bomb sweep clears the venue, the largest remaining threat is what walks in.

Bombings at the four universities other than Harvard turned out largely to be diversions, creating loud noises and setting off extensive smoke and fire in crowded areas. Hundreds of students were hurt, but few died at these diversion schools. Harvard Square, however, was a slaughter field and now appears to have been the real target.

Initial reports of what happened were inaccurate. Several people in clothes typically identified with the local Arab population had been spotted on campus that day, but several turned out to be students with full alibis.

The snipers who witnesses spotted from several areas turned out to be noise and light machines. Only days later did CNN acknowledge on air that it had released uncorroborated information about the attacks. In the race to be first, the general news media has long lost focus on accuracy. Most viewers discount the truth of their reporting but can't help turning to them in a crisis. Viewer impatience fuels media focus on being first with any potential news that might attract viewers.

The 123 students killed Wednesday died from the explosion of improvised explosion devices (IEDs). Security cameras later showed two people dressed as students set down backpacks containing the IEDs. Extensive security reviews have not yet identified either backpack dropper. Both made it well outside the kill zone before the IEDs exploded.

In the mass scramble following the Harvard Yard explosions, it was easy for the backpack droppers to be lost. That these bombs were developed to maximize death and maiming is clear. Each device contained hundreds of small titanium spiked arrows that shot into victims, shredding organs and opening gaping holes in other body parts.

The reason for the attack is still unclear, though news reports have leaked partial contents of a note taped to one of the flash machines on a Harvard Square rooftop. "Respect the will of our majority. The elites who try to stop us will suffer," the leaked part of the note read. No signature. No claimed responsibility. No clear lead.

At his H2M Gala table, Ramon is joined by his mother, sister, the CEO of the nation's largest freight company and her husband, Texas Senator Manny Jones and his wife, a Supreme Court justice and her husband and Juan Gonzalez's mother. From their table, they have the best view of the dais to watch Juan be honored. In the meantime, Ramon mixes his two passions – selling his company's logistics capabilities to the biggest account in the country and building his political network.

The irony of the Washington Convention Center dinner being adjacent to D.C.'s Chinatown is not lost on Ramon, who had a preview from Ángel of the surprise that was to be delivered to Juan that night. As the cocktail hour ends, Ramon escorts his mother and sister to their table before continuing his networking.

It takes 10 minutes after H2M Founder Ángel attempts to call the dinner to order to get table talkers quieted to a low enough level to proceed. The world of Washington is known for its insatiable appetite for chatter. Even tight tuxedos and gala dresses don't restrict lung capacity enough to modify this behavior among the political elite.

Archbishop Jesus Marino, leader of a fast-growing part of the Catholic Church pushing for rigid enforcement of church doctrine, stands in front of the dais and begins with a blessing.

"I would ask everyone to kneel with me and honor our Lord Jesus Christ," the Archbishop says, ignoring D.C. custom of making any such prayers non-denominational. He pulls the microphone down as he kneels, making the sign of the cross in exaggerated motions with fingers fully extended to the sky.

"Dear Lord, you honor us daily with gifts you provide, asking only that we follow your simple laws in return. We work each day to be moral and to honor your faith in us. We ask for your help in understanding the tragedy that befell our nation with the Harvard massacre and university bombings, and pray to you to help heal the families and friends of the victims while saving from permanent evil the perpetrators of this catastrophe. We thank you for the blessings you bestow on us, blessings such as your children Ángel Herrera and Juan Gonzalez. We ask you to bless the nourishment we are about to eat. We pray in the name of the Father, the Son and the Holy Spirit."

As the Archbishop concludes his prayer, 800 waiters descend on the dinner, each bringing trays of nopales cactus salad mixed with jicama, cilantro, avocado, tomato and onion in a lime and olive oil dressing.

Fifteen minutes later, the main meal sets even more mouths watering, with filets coated in a chipotle steak sauce, a bass and halibut ceviche and grilled corn with queso anejo, cream, and powdered chile.

Finally, Ángel begins his opening remarks.

"In one of the ironies of our global world, I would like to thank FirstWal President of International Operations Jia Lin for joining us tonight. What makes this a great irony is that FirstWal's initial contributions to our cause were to play the role of our villain. Tonight they join us to help correct this error and set a better path forward for everyone in this room."

FirstWal's contribution and inclusion weren't pre-announced except to a handful of key contributors like Ramon, so the crowd had been stunned to see a Chinese woman on the dais.

"I probably don't have to explain FirstWal's involvement," Ángel continues, "but this is too important an event to gloss over. The young man we honor tonight, Juan Gonzalez, achieved a great victory for our culture and language – spurred on by discrimination. In responding to that discrimination, Juan not only changed his life, but changed his State and, God-willing, will change the fate of many of our children of Mexico and other Latinos even more dramatically over the coming years. As you will hear, Juan is in every way the best of our people, and he would not take rejection he knew to be unfair.

"Because of Juan's activism, Ms. Lin became aware of what was really happening in FirstWal's U.S. operations. Tonight, she will finish rectifying the wrong Juan endured," Ángel says to polite applause.

"I commend Ms. Lin for fixing FirstWal's policy. Juan endured the pain of rejection, but that pain inspired a new surge of activism and now gives us the opportunity of a lifetime. Before we honor Juan, I would like to bring Ms. Lin up for an announcement," Ángel says.

Jia walks from the end of the dais to the microphone. Despite short stature, she strikes a figure equal parts imposing and engaging. Walking with a confidence and energy necessary among women in China's business leadership, she steps to the podium, hits her pre-set to elevate the podium and looks over to Juan.

"When First Empire acquired WalCo several years ago, we worried substantially about ensuring that our company cultures melded effectively. Most acquisitions fail because previously competing cultures continue to compete. We were determined to move cautiously because few companies are more storied for their culture than WalCo. The drive for productivity and low-cost, high-quality products is embedded through the organization. Stories of the company's founders still shape the culture many decades after their departures," Jia starts, speaking slowly to allow translation staff to do its work and to be certain she doesn't step on her opportunity to plug FirstWal.

"One cultural element that appeared entrenched was an expectation that all U.S. employees needed to communicate in English. The ability to speak a common language, I was told by U.S. leadership, was critical to the organization's cost-efficiency. Alerted to this inequity by Juan, we investigated and found the policy was unnecessary and sometimes even counterproductive. For accepting prior management's view of the world without question, I apologize to each of you and to the Honor to Mexico organization."

Looking around the audience, she continues, "It is now clear that my lack of understanding of America led FirstWal to continue a misguided policy that is clearly irrelevant and counterproductive. That error has caused great pain to Juan, and I believe must have similarly led to discrimination against many others," she says, as many lawyers in the room gasp.

"Speaking to Juan earlier, I learned he is a positive community leader already today and the type of leader I can see shaping FirstWal at some point. Juan, after much discussion, has agreed to delay his university studies for at least one year to be a spokesman for H2M and its important causes. We wanted to assure Juan and Mrs. Gonzalez that this year is only a delay to a promising future. I see Mrs. Gonzalez waving one finger to make clear that this is one year. I can assure you, Juan and Mrs. Gonzalez, that his service will not deter Juan from his long-term ambitions. So on behalf of FirstWal, I am proud to present Juan with a scholarship to the university of his choice in the amount of $1 million dollars to cover a full four years at even the priciest university," Jia concludes.

Mrs. Gonzalez, until now concerned that Juan was making a mistake taking a year off, tears up noticeably. Juan looks at her and wells up himself, at moments turning his head away from the crowd to wipe the corners of his eyes. The crowd delivers a long, standing ovation.

After gathering himself, Juan walks to the podium. As soon as he stands on the podium, he grasps at his neck, feeling a sharp sting. Shaking his head, he begins to look flushed and turns pale. The audience takes his reaction as a sense of shock at having his dream fulfilled. His story is a sensation, particularly in the Mexican American community. H2M members doubled their contributions this year for the chance to get pictures taken with Juan at a pre-event special reception.

As Juan collapses moments later, a physician and board member rush to his side. Others on the dais gather around him, assuming Juan is overwhelmed and needs a bit of bracing to give his remarks.

"There's no pulse. Get the heart kit," the first doctor yells methodically. Ramon catches Juan's mother as her legs give out on realizing her son isn't breathing. "He's been shot," they hear someone on the dais yell.

Celia, Ramon's little sister, breaks down as her mother grabs her. "Get under the table Mom. Under the table Celia," Ramon yells, while helping Juan's mother to her chair.

"Get me to my son," she says as she regains physical control. "I need to hold his hand. I need to hold his hand. Let me hold his hand."

Ramon takes Mrs. Gonzalez behind the dais, pushing people out of the way as they go. They quickly follow the group carrying Juan on a stretcher.

"I have Juan's mother. Get her with her son," Ramon shouts at the group ahead, pushing aside security personnel who initially try to keep them from following.

Loud explosions sparking from centerpieces on each table send the rest of the H2M gala audience scattering.

Police recognize the explosions as an attempt by the assassin to cover his escape. They try holding attendees inside the Convention Center, but quickly realize the crowd pressure to escape is overwhelming their ability to send everyone back through security screens. The on-site commander orders everyone released through the barriers. "We'll add trampling deaths to the tragedy tonight if we hold everyone here, but make sure every recording device is on," he bellows into every police earpiece. "Let people out, but make it orderly."

Screaming through bullhorns, police and security leads at each perimeter yell instructions. "No trampling." "Slow Down." Though many continue to run, the attendees become more compliant once they feel comfortably away from the building.

With thousands now moving between the Convention Center and their vehicles, the Commander has a horrifying thought that turns his face ashen as the concept flushes down from his brain.

"Bomb alert. Damn it, search immediately for snipers and bombs. Look for backpacks being dropped. This could be a Harvard. . . . Search anyone even remotely suspicious with anything bigger than a tiny purse," he bellows, before calling for immediate backup from every available unit.

Those who took their own vehicles that night quickly find their cars and begin the tedious process of escaping the Center. Several walk or jog, moving faster than traffic in many spots. Chauffeured participants wait for drivers to return hours before initially required. It doesn't take long after the Commander's revelation for some of those frantic contributors and politicians to recall the Harvard massacre either. Suddenly, some start running back to the convention center, narrowly missing being run over by those still running out. The chaotic scene differs from Harvard only in attire and ground surface.

Inside, police officials try to identify where the shooter must have been, led by Sergeant Rey Moore.

"Juan was facing straight out to the crowd," he says to no one in particular, but within earshot of three patrol officers protecting the stage exits. "He grabbed at his neck, slamming his hand like he was swatting a wasp. The shooter had to be in this direction, but at what angle?"

Sgt. Moore messages the officer riding in the ambulatory Mobile Care Unit (MCU), accompanying Juan, Juan's mother and two paramedics. "Any idea what angle the bullet entered at?" he wrote. The on-board officer reads the message, and jots back his response.

"Not a normal bullet. Thin entry wound. No exit wound. Hard to guess angle."

"No exit wound? What the hell is it?" Sergeant Moore types back.

"No idea but kid is alive. Not responsive though," comes the message back.

A 20-year veteran of the D.C. Police, Sergeant Moore thought he had seen everything, but was puzzled. "No help on the angle boys. Even worse, we don't know the weapon type. No exit wound, so could have been shot from a very small weapon. Search around the stage, in the front rows, and start rounding up everyone who was within 100 feet of the podium to get statements," Moore orders.

Teams of officers begin a visual search. Though Sgt. Moore knows surveillance for heat signals is too late, he tries everything else he can think of to find the shooter. Searches are conducted underneath the stage, in front and behind the dais and all around the podium.

No luck.

As the MCU races to the hospital, a display screen projects video of Juan's stage collapse to everyone inside it. The video informs all on board that Juan was shot with Belcher's Sea Snake venom and immediately needs an antidote injected to avoid death. As Juan's mother begs the paramedic in back to listen, the paramedic locates the filled syringe labeled "for Juan" and injects it into him.

As Juan's heartbeat and breathing slowly return, the paramedics realize they made the right call, but now wonder if the reaction was quick enough to avoid brain damage to the kid. "How did this stuff get in here?" one asks the other.

As they race to the medical center, a new video message begins, appearing as if it is being broadcast live by someone who can see what is going on in the vehicle.

"Mrs. Gonzalez," the substantially distorted voice and face says. "Your son is trying to destroy America and our values. I think we've proven to you that we can kill Juan any time and any place we want. There is nothing you can do to stop us and nothing the police can do to find us if killing your son is what we want to do."

At this point, the on-board officer realizes the criminals have a camera on board and he begins searching for it.

"Had we not provided the antidote to you in this ambulance, your son's brain activity would be stopping now and he would soon be dead. If you do not want to hold his dead body in your arms, you will convince him to go to school, get a job and leave American politics to Americans."

As the MCU pulls up to the medical center, the projector begins burning. Juan is rushed into the emergency room. By the time the MCU driver returns to put out the fire, the tiny projector is essentially a melted, mangled plastic rod.

"Poisoning," the mobile care paramedic shouts to the hospital emergency team. "But the antidote was on board and it seems like it worked."

Belcher's Sea Snake is one of the most toxic snakes on earth, but largely found in waterways in the Pacific. Under normal circumstances, the arrow in Juan's neck contained enough venom to kill him in 30 minutes or less. The antidote was clearly marked in the MCU that took Juan to the hospital. Police quickly demand that everyone maintain strict silence about the poisoning and antidote.

The emergency room doctor checks Juan's vitals and finds them weak. "Let's give him adrenaline to get his heart moving," the doctor shouts, setting off the robot arm to prepare an adrenaline shot and move it toward Juan's arm.

"Stop it," one paramedic screams. "Do you know how that interacts with this antidote? I've never heard of this kind of snake. He's improved dramatically from the shot we gave him. Give him time."

"You give him a shot with no idea what's in it, and have the audacity to tell me not to give a shot I've given 1,000 times to help people like this. Take your tiny little degree and stuff it up your overstretched backside," the doctor yells back.

"You shove it, you arrogant bastard. My patient was dying. Your patient is healing, which you would know if you listened before getting on your hero horse," she continues, glad she isn't a hospital employee.

The doctor fumes, but sees the point: "I'll wait 60 seconds. Now unless you have something else vital to tell me that you didn't communicate in the handoff, get out."

The paramedic steams that the doctor won't take responsibility for not thinking through the injection, but he won't be the first or last person to blame others for their mistakes.

CHAPTER 22

June 21, 2040
Washington, D.C.

As Juan regains consciousness, he struggles to feel his limbs and use his voice. The ER nurse stands in the room watching his vitals. His mother sits by his bed, continuing to hold his hand. She caresses his hair with her left hand, much as she has done since infancy. With her right hand, she moves her thumb and forefinger from bead to bead on the rosary she wears on her neck.

"Our father, who art in heaven, hallowed by thy name," Juan hears his mother say in Spanish. "Thy Kingdom come, thy will be done on earth as it is in heaven. Give us this day our daily bread; and forgive us our trespasses as we forgive those who trespass against us; and lead us not into temptation, but deliver us from evil."

As she moves to the Hail Mary, Juan's consciousness is far enough along to allow him to speak. "I'm here Mother. God heard your prayers."

More tears.

The nurse steps outside the room to let the officer stationed at the door know what just happened. Sgt. Moore receives the first call from the officer.

"I've never seen anything like this. This appeared to be an assassination, but the killer didn't want the victim to die. The kid might even be out of danger now. I thought he was dead. Without the antidote, he never would have made it. The good news is whoever did this touched so many places, we're bound to track them down," the officer reports.

"We're searching the Center, but we need to check how they got everything on the MCU," Sgt. Moore says.

When the officer walks back in the room, Juan asks him who did this. After recounting the video message, the officer shares his speculation. "I think this was done by the same people who massacred those kids at Harvard. A message was left at Harvard to say we needed to respect the majority or the elites would die," the officer says.

"I'm hardly the elite," Juan says.

"Maybe not, but you're all over the media so to a kook or a white supremacist or someone like that, you're a threat now," the officer responds.

"So you think these are racists?" Mrs. Gonzalez asks.

"This is because I am Mexican?" Juan says.

"We have a great deal of police work to do but the links to your work and the massacre are too obvious to ignore," the officer tells him.

"I can't let them scare me away from doing this," Juan says emphatically.

He asks to see newfound benefactor Ángel Herrera. Ángel is leading a vigil outside the hospital with more than a thousand H2M supporters; some still dressed in tuxedos and long dresses. Sergeant Moore has since arrived at the hospital and now waves to Ángel to come to the side of a temporary stage set up on a blocked-off street beside the medical center.

"Mr. Herrera," Sgt. Moore whispers in his ear, as media cameras and sound microphones push in on the discussion and try to pick up the exchange. "Juan is conscious and speaking and wants to see you if you can come with me."

A tear drops down from Ángel's right eye as he smiles. He drops to the ground on one knee and makes the sign of the cross while looking to the sky, now clenching his mouth together to try to avoid breaking down from both relief and exhaustion. Gathering himself, Ángel walks to the media podium. National and local media break in with Ángel's remarks.

"I have just been informed that Juan Gonzalez is alive, conscious and speaking. Praise be to God for giving our hero life to continue his mission. I'm leaving to speak with Juan, but ask the Archbishop to lead the group in prayer. After that prayer, I would ask that you all go home and pray with your families. Thank you for being here for Juan. God has answered us."

CHAPTER 23

June 24, 2040
Washington, D.C.

After a three-day investigation at the Convention Center, one so detailed that two events were cancelled, the police finally release the Center to resume operations. Sgt. Moore supervises a final search for clues as stage structures are removed.

As a laborer prepares the podium to be carted away, he notices something unusual under the riser that adjusts the platform height for each speaker.

"Officer, something strange here," he calls out to Sgt. Moore. "There's a piece attached that doesn't belong."

Sgt. Moore runs up to the stage. "Thanks. Take a break so we can look at this," Sgt. Moore says as he calls in the forensics team. The Gonzalez shooting is a high-profile case that will make Moore's career if handled properly, and will destroy many careers if mistakes are made. Sgt. Moore has explicit orders to be meticulous in his investigation. The speed at which the lead detective and forensics team respond to his call attests to the importance of the case.

The forensics team carefully scans the riser for prints and any DNA. Hair and skin residues on the riser come from dozens of different individuals but none of the on-site tests conducted turn up anyone in criminal databases.

Now, Sgt. Moore sees what the laborer must have been saying was unusual. A modification to the riser has turned it into an electronic scale. "Does this scale have a purpose?" Sgt. Moore asks the facilities man.

"None I know."

The lead detective turns to Sgt. Moore. "Can you think of any way a weight scale on the platform riser could be linked to the shooting?"

Moore and the detective look around what remains of the stage, then the podium, the riser, the nearly vacant hall.

"Give me some gloves," Sgt. Moore says to the forensics team. As he suspects, there is a small hole in the top of the old wooden podium that is large enough for the miniature arrow to have fit through.

"I need a dummy that's Juan's height, size and weight and I need it right away," Sergeant Moore says before explaining his theory to the detective. "Until we have that, we need to keep this area sealed and guarded."

Later that evening, the forensics team comes back with a dummy carefully shaped to Juan's height, weight and size. The team sets up high-speed cameras at multiple angles around the podium and arranges for a hoist to mechanically place the dummy on the riser and release it.

As the dummy is remotely released on the riser, everyone stands back from the podium, watching carefully and quietly. A minute passes. Nothing. Two minutes. Still nothing. After five minutes, the detective calls off the experiment.

"With the scale attachment, I thought a shot might have been triggered by weight. Let's tear apart the podium to see if a shooting device is built in. It probably had only one arrow."

As the robot picks up the dummy, one of the forensic team members speaks.

"There's something in the dummy's neck."

"Did anyone hear or see that," Sergeant Moore says.

"No, sir."

"Okay, put the video feeds up on the screen."

Sergeant Moore flips open his mobile projector and syncs up simultaneous video feeds from the four high-speed recorders. A large screen is dropped behind the dais – providing three-dimensional views fed from a device no bigger than his pen.

"Drop the lights. Show front, back and left feeds. Display at 1/10th speed."

The projector display auto-corrects for Sgt. Moore's instructions, then starts projecting from his Lifelink, continuously rebalancing the display to offset the shake in his hand.

Exactly one minute into viewing the display, Moore and the others catch sight of the front edge of the arrow.

"Stop. Slow to 1/100th speed. Rewind 20 seconds. Begin." As the arrow-like metal object enters the picture, it clearly travels at a downward angle. "Calculate angle of moving object," the lead detective calls. The projector takes control of the display, moves the arrow in and out, and backs the display out to a broader view.

Printed on the screen, the projector answers the detective's question. "Object came from 63 degree angle up from entry point, at exactly 270 degree angle from front center. Object entry at 1200 kilometers per hour."

"Okay, we know where the shooter was now," Sgt. Moore says. "It wasn't the podium. Let's pull every video feed we can from anyone who attended the event and see if we can identify our shooter. I'll start searching that angle from here."

The detective and Sgt. Moore carefully trace the arrow's origins, then set Sgt. Moore's Lifelink to record everything from podium to ceiling at that angle. The recording displays on the screen as it is taken.

An on-scene officer sends the data to headquarters, so the video detection team can search the nearly 1,000 Lifelink recordings collected of the shooting for a visual of the shooter. In less than an hour, the team finds its answer. A long, tube-like object is attached to a rafter beam at exactly the angle where the shooter would have been. Behind it is a device containing an automated trigger mechanism.

"This was a remote hit. I'm going to bet the shot was triggered by the kid's weight and there's some type of electronic relay in the scale and the mechanism. Whoever did this may not have even been here," Sgt. Moore speculates, with the lead detective agreeing someone smart enough to pull this off would be smart enough not to be there. As they reach the conclusion, a message from headquarters confirms: "Remotely fired device spotted in rafters. Sending team to recover device."

At one Sinaloa province compound, Cesar Castillo pumps his fists in the air when he hears Juan's recovery is the lead news story everywhere in the United States.

In Washington, D.C., Phoenix Mining's Max Herta scans his daily news feed service and sees an article on the oldest living Mexican American to serve as a tunnel rat in the Vietnam War. Seeing the tunnel rat article, he knows where he needs to be exactly 48 hours from the article's posting.

Herta was scheduled to return to Detroit from Washington, D.C. where he had attended International Mining Association meetings and the H2M fundraiser. It's only three days after the eventful H2M dinner and his curiosity is now elevated by the demand that could only come from Castillo that Herta meet him at the bottom of a tunnel outside McAllen, Texas.

Meetings between Herta and Castillo are infrequent. Herta first proved his mining expertise 30 years earlier working on the deep tunnel project for Castillo he must get to now. Originally transported to the site with no ability to see the outdoors during a 20-hour drive from Golden, the group of single 20-somethings then worked 14 hour shifts 7 days a week through an entire summer on a mining "internship" program that proved far more lucrative and educational than any had expected.

Castillo made sure the same group was hired post-graduation by Phoenix Mining, were they have all worked since. Herta is the primary contact the group has to senior management, and the only one who knows his ultimate employer. Castillo met Herta personally just 10 times in the interim, following a code established at the beginning of their relationship to stay out of sight and avoid any patterns that could be tracked. Herta's value to Castillo is dependent on there being no evidence of a relationship.

Herta's role at Phoenix Mining as head of special projects reporting directly to the CEO was carefully selected so most in the organization would have no idea where to expect him or what he was doing. Herta and team recently designed a new vibration-free, low noise drill and seamless seal technology. The operating plan connected an underground municipal water pipe to a concrete floor at a width big enough for a person to get through. Herta's design conveniently used the water pipe to haul away debris left after the ground-squeeze drilling effort.

Though he hadn't gone to the basement of the Washington Convention Center, he suspects a Castillo team used his latest design to get into the Convention Center unnoticed. He can't understand, though, why Castillo wants Juan Gonzalez dead or why he was told to be in DC when the shooting was happening.

After arriving in Dallas, Herta takes an off-grid vehicle equipped with Ramon's drag-racing evasion technology and drives south. Carefully avoiding police, border patrol and military vehicles, he travels untraced to near the Mexico border. Once there, he heads to the Border Flooring manufacturing and distribution center.

In the tunnel, Herta and Castillo embrace. Herta fears Castillo, but has been well rewarded for his loyalty. Castillo demands dedication and Herta has delivered throughout his life, often at great personal sacrifice. Never once has Castillo sensed any police pressure that could have originated from Herta or anything he touched.

"Mi amigo," Castillo says, giving Herta a handshake and tight hug, "so good to see you."

"Of course. I am always available for you."

"I want you to know how much I value your loyalty," Castillo says, putting his right arm around Herta's shoulders and squeezing firmly. "Loyalty is important to our success, don't you agree?" Not waiting for a response, Castillo continues: "It's good to work with men who support me whenever I need them, without question. But even the best have questions, temptations, so I watch carefully. I pride myself on paying attention to my people."

Herta looks around to see if anyone is coming after him. He looks to see if Castillo has a weapon in his free hand, but sees his left hand is moving in support as Castillo speaks.

"Don't worry," Castillo says. "You've done nothing wrong. We're approaching a great time for our people and I need you again. Since I was a child, I dreamed of returning Mexico to its borders before the gringos stole from us. Everything I've done – including some, shall we call them, unfriendly encounters – will be redeemed in God's eyes and in the eyes of all Mexican people if we free ourselves from America's enslavement."

Herta is taken aback. Castillo always struck him as rigidly profit focused. While Castillo considers Herta a long-standing friend, Herta considers it an association based more on fear than friendship.

"That's a greater goal than any I ever imagined," Herta says, knowing his own goals mainly consist of staying alive, protecting his families and enjoying a few personal pleasures. *"I'll be honored to assist with whatever work you want me to do."*

Castillo puts his arm on Herta's shoulders. "Let's walk together, because we will want to think back to this time together when we have achieved our goals. Besides. This will take some time to explain."

The two begin walking up and down the broad tunnel floor as Castillo explains his plans.

"The week brought us extraordinary opportunity far faster than even I had imagined. First, some lunatics created a radical diversion with the Harvard massacre. Second, your latest engineering feat proved so effective we drilled a tunnel in the heart of D.C. completely undetected. Third, we helped to turn a fine young man into the new Messiah for our movement. You, and everyone else at the H2M dinner, thought that Juan had been assassinated. Right?"

"I did, and, and, and . . . I must admit I was tortured to think I had played a part in killing this young man. I hoped that such a thing, if I had played a role, would have a purpose," Herta says.

"Of course you knew. I can't ask you to be brilliant most of the time while hoping you will be selectively stupid," Castillo says. *"I knew you would be troubled since your youngest son is the same age as Juan. After 30 years together, I want you to know everything you sacrificed is for a cause greater than you could imagine. This Gonzalez kid is a good young man, but we do not have time for him to gain popularity a little each day. So the poisoning and resurrection provide him with an instant national audience, and a following larger and more loyal than he ever could have achieved alone. He'll be the Messiah of our cause. Sleep well at night knowing you played a part in this."*

Castillo's McAllen tunnel is more than 25 miles long, and drops down three-quarters of a mile at its low point. Constructed over the years by teams that included Herta and his men, the tunnel is reinforced with cross-layered plastic and steel beams. In his early years, Castillo pumped a substantial amount of his profits into deep tunnel and other projects to improve his distribution efficiency. Loans taken by his more legitimate businesses were skimmed to further fund these efforts, then repaid with drug profits to avoid inciting any investigations. When Castillo became worried the site was under surveillance, the McAllen tunnel was converted to only special delivery and Protection Corps transport use.

"I may ask you to do some more work for me, so I want you to know what I'm hoping to accomplish so you sleep well," Castillo says. *"I started in the drug business for the sex and power."*

Herta's eyes widen. He tries to keep his smile from offending Castillo.

"I can see you are surprised by this admission," Castillo continues in a tone that makes clear he finds it humorous as well. *"But as I have aged, I saw that this was part of God's plan for me. I want to hurt those who hurt my people, so I tell my people now to sell to everyone except Mexicans."*

Castillo unbuttons his sport coat, and Herta glances to be sure nothing is being pulled from inside.

"Ultimately, I realized we need to pose a threat to the U.S. if we want to restore our nation. The government has learned we can't grow a military big enough just by taxing our people. So, I use American money to fund Mexico's military. Our military looks aside while we sell drugs to America, and I give money to the military to make Mexico stronger. Today, I am the greatest benefactor of Mexico."

"That's truly honorable," Herta says, knowing Castillo sees himself as living by a self-defined code of honor.

"I am the true leader of Mexico, and of Mexicans living under U.S. control as my people," Castillo continues. *"I have an obligation to achieve our goal. So now you know more than almost anyone about what I'm doing."*

Herta is not quite sure why he is being told this. He has known for his entire adult life that Castillo is one of the world's most feared criminals. Knowing too much about a dangerous man is rarely a good thing.

"You know Juan is alive and well. What you don't know is he was told the shooter wanted him out of U.S. political life – to tell the Mexican to go home. I suspected, and it appears I'm right as usual, that he would react with anger to this intimidation. He has confirmed he will be spokesman for our movement to have the Southwest secede and align with Mexico, and perhaps more importantly, with me for protection."

Herta's eyes open wide. *"Won't the U.S. military clamp down hard? Or the FBI at least arrest everyone as traitors? If it's okay that I ask, of course."*

"I don't worry about them. I am in the United States many days every year. They never find me. So how good can they be? Besides, these are free speech issues

in America. Once it's clear the people support freedom, we'll pounce before anyone in Washington knows what happened to their country," Castillo says. *"Besides, American politicians are as likely to think beyond the next election as you are to think with your brain inside a whore house. Am I right?"*

Both men laugh loudly.

"So American politicians will spend this year begging Mexicans for votes so they can win this year and then they can start begging for Mexicans to vote for them again the next time. I love democracy."

Among the important tactics Castillo long ago mastered, his security team watches his key people like a hawk to make sure there's no risk to his safety or his business. Because of this, he learns employee weaknesses and uses this knowledge to build loyalty and create control. Herta has spent so much time away from his two families over the years that he has developed a taste for playing around. Castillo sometimes supplies him with his "rewards" after a job well done, and enjoys the chance to tease him about his hobby.

"I know. I know. Two women should be enough for me. But if I relied on them for my needs, evolution would eliminate manhood from my descendants because those parts have so little use with them," Herta says before turning back to more serious topics. *"I assume I have no reason to worry about the police. No one found the tunnel, have they?"*

"Of course not. My friends tell me the Feds are focusing on a white supremacist group for the Harvard bomb. You had nothing to do with this, and no one thinks we did. But the bombing helps our cause. People are going to be so afraid to say anything that can be taken as racist now. We'll spread our message while accusing anyone who disagrees with us of racism that ultimately kills people," Castillo says, with a slight shrug of the shoulder. *"My political friends in America are talking to every minority interest group, asking them to make sure the media understand that anyone speaking against one race is condemning the country to more violence like the Harvard bomb, or Juan's shooting."*

Herta looks around and sees no guards or product shipments in the tunnel. Watching his back is a physical reaction from years of wondering if his next step would be his last, a fear that heightens in Castillo's presence and anytime he does something he thinks Castillo might want to hide.

"I'm honored to help you however you wish," Herta says, still coming to grips with the risks he knows are likely coming. It was easier to ignore the risks as a younger man, when he thought he was invincible. *"And I am honored that you would take your time to help me understand your goal. You know I will keep this to myself. But what can I do to help?"*

"I need you and your team to tell your salt mine friends you need to be away in Australia on multiple trips over the next several months," Castillo says. *"We need new tunnels built, and I have some special work for many of your men."*

CHAPTER 24

June 27, 2040
Washington, D.C.

Bipartisan groups of 15 senators and 78 U.S. House members introduce Senate Joint Resolution 58 and House Joint Resolution 118 to substantial media attention. The Joint Resolutions seek to amend the United States Constitution to require that "no business by any unit of government or entity funded by the government within the boundaries of the United States and its territories may be conducted, unless that business will also be conducted in English at anyone's request."

Several networks lead off their next news segments with the story.

"For the first time in recent memory, a bipartisan group of elected members of the U.S. Congress has joined together to propose a constitutional amendment that would institutionalize racism," CNN anchor Brody Maguire opens his hour-long personal viewpoint show. "In a stunning display of intolerance, 93 members of Congress, largely from northern and Midwestern states, are proposing to amend the United States Constitution to ban the use of Spanish, Mandarin, Hindi, Yoruba, Indonesian and every other language spoken here.

"CNN has mapped out these racially insensitive elected officials for you, and compared them to the most recent census data showing the ethnic and language demographics of their districts. As you can see, the bulk of these intolerant legislators represent rural and far-suburban areas where ethnic, cultural and language diversity is less prevalent. However, as you can see on this map," Maguire continues, pointing, "several represent large groups of people who speak languages other than English."

"While it would be nice to treat these proposals as the sabotage to America's tolerance that they appear to be, I want to expose our viewers to all sides of this debate. To discuss the topic with me, I'm joined by Congresswoman Jill Carlson, a conservative independent from Indiana and lead House sponsor of the proposal; Juan Gonzalez, the brave young man who fought language discrimination in Arizona and turned FirstWal's previously racist policies on its head; and Professor Paul Stark of the University of Chicago, whose culture and politics class has engaged in extensive debate on this topic and who is well known for his work to reduce political corruption. Thank you all for joining me," Maguire says.

"Juan, let's start with you. While your English has clearly improved dramatically since this battle began almost six months ago, we have a translator here to assist if you prefer to listen or respond in Spanish."

"Thank you for inviting me. I appreciate the translator but will do my best to speak in English," Juan says.

"So Juan, how does it make you feel to be part of a nation that wants to ban your language from the halls of government? To treat you as a second-class citizen because of the language you learned as a child?" Maguire says.

"How does it feel was the question? Well, Mr. Maguire," Juan says.

"Please call me Brody," the anchor interrupts.

"Well Brody, it feels like a stab to the heart to hear people who run the U.S. government want to wipe our culture away. The constitutional amendment would permanently put in the idea that people who speak English are more important than people speaking other languages. This is complete opposite of what I think America stands for," Juan says as Maguire nods his head in agreement.

Turning to Congresswoman Jill Carlson, Maguire asks, "Given this destructive impact on America's youth and our core value of tolerance, why are you moving ahead with this proposal?"

In her late 30s, Jill is serving her third term and is frequently mentioned as a potential future presidential contender. Tall, thin, brunette and single – she is the perfect muse for men who had glommed onto her Republic Network News show prior to her run for office. RNN was founded 10 years earlier when Republican Party officials decided they needed more voices covering news without a liberal bias, having given up hope of fair treatment by the general news media after the Hancock Park scandal. Despite her RNN background, Jill ran for office as an independent believing her personal views crossed party lines. After winning, she decided to caucus with Republicans and is considered a reliable conservative vote on economic issues.

A natural beauty, Jill as most called her, is as deep intellectually as she is attractive on the surface. Many of the men she encounters struggle to focus when they first meet her, but her casual conversation style quickly disarms them and draws more attention to her thoughts. Modest in dress, Jill neither hides nor flaunts her beauty. But she won't hesitate to take on a fight, learning to battle as a child watching her mother fight cervical cancer for more than five years before finally succumbing when Jill was a high school sophomore. As one of two girls raised on a dairy farm, Jill knows hard work, and understands the persistence and sacrifice required to overcome obstacles.

"Brody, thank you for inviting me to join your entertainment program. I appreciate the chance to have what I hope will be a fair debate," she says.

Brody didn't invite her for fair debate, but whatever convinced her to come was fine with him.

"Can we get to the question?" he says. "Why would you support an inherently racist policy?"

Jill smiles, as she often does before taking her opponents for a ridicule ride they don't see coming. "Brody, your facts are as wrong as your interpretation. The constitutional amendment proposal does not ban the use of any language for use in government. It simply says that if a government body in the United States is going to conduct business in any language – it must also offer to conduct that same business in English. So nothing here prevents Arizona, for example, from allowing government business to take place in Spanish as long as they allow English to be used on the same forms, in the same booth or in the same issue discussion."

Juan starts to raise his hand. Realizing that he isn't in class, he asks to respond and is encouraged to do so.

"Congresswoman Carlson is technically right. I read the joint resolution before I came on the show. I like to be sure I understand the facts before . . .," he says, causing Jill to smile and stopping himself before completing the thought. "But what the Congresswoman is missing is that by saying English speakers always can be accommodated, and not affording that same requirement for every other language, she is saying that English speakers are more important. I think that's wrong."

Brody looks to Professor Stark, but isn't able to invite him into the conversation before Jill responds.

"Juan, I certainly appreciate that you took time to read what we are doing before commenting on it. That's a commendable habit and one I recommend for others," Jill says, looking at Brody. "I think what's missing is perspective. I understand that in your hometown of West Nogales, more than 95 percent of the people living there speak Spanish – most exclusively so. From what I understand, you are fairly fluent in Mandarin, extraordinarily bright and obviously are almost fluent in English as well. What you may not know is that Americans today speak more than 100 native languages. Applying this same requirement to every language we propose to apply to English would be simply impossible and unaffordable, even with available technology."

Brody interrupts: "If we can't accommodate all languages then, the non-discriminatory approach is to not mandate that any single language get preferential treatment. Isn't that right Professor Stark?"

Professor Stark straightens up in his chair, pulls the back of his sport coat down behind him and clasps his hands just below his face. "Brody, we – with your audience – have had a number of conversations over the years about diversity, the importance of respecting various cultures and the critical need to increase tolerance in society. So my opinion here may surprise you."

Jill had not studied Professor Stark's few statements on the issue, so came to the debate thinking she was being tag-teamed in a three on one.

"I think the proposal by the Congresswoman is fine as far as it goes, but when it comes to the topic of language, it may not go far enough," Professor Stark continues.

"Whoa, whoa, whoa," Brody blurts, clearly taken aback as he had also not understood Professor Stark's position. "Did you say doesn't go far enough?"

Juan looks a bit ashen. He'd been told Professor Stark was a political reformer and was certain to support any reforms that helped people take more control of their government – just as Juan had succeeded in doing in Arizona.

Pulling Brody's attention away from the camera, Professor Stark looks at Brody as he continues, "Every year, there are civil wars and political dissolutions started somewhere in countries where people don't speak the same language. For as long as the civilized world has existed, people ruled by those who do not share their language, culture and values tolerate that rule only until they have enough power to take it back."

Brody jumps in. "That's exactly my point."

"If that's your point," Professor Stark says, "then you must have thought through the long-term ramifications of leaving the nation's policies as they stand or even following the path of multiple government languages the Congresswoman and others would allow."

"Those are very different paths, as you know professor, so the ramifications as you say are vastly different depending on which of the paths we follow," Brody says.

"I believe either letting states choose their own language or making English just an option that must be available both lead to the same long-term outcome," Professor Stark says. "When people don't speak the same language, communication fails. Throughout history, nations operating with multiple languages and divergent cultures ultimately decide they can no longer coexist whenever the central government weakens. The only real question in allowing the United States to further develop into multiple conjoined, but not integrated societies is whether the split of the country will be violent – a civil war – or whether we will allow parts of the country to secede without a fight because we no longer share anything in common."

Brody clearly is not expecting the debate to take this direction and stares at Professor Stark for an uncomfortable moment of silence before Jill comments.

"I think our constitutional amendment addresses the issue Professor Stark just raised in the least confrontational and difficult way possible," Jill says, looking between Professor Stark and Brody. "To be frank, we did discuss a constitutional amendment to require English only to be used in any government entity. But we're concerned this would make it that much more difficult to attract the immigrants we need to come here to keep our social systems viable."

Brody raises and extends his palm outward. "I'm afraid we're running out of time so would ask Juan a final yes or no question. Juan, do you think this constitutional amendment should be adopted?"

"Clearly no. Each of us has the right to speak the language of our choice," Juan says.

"We'll see you back here after the break," Brody concludes.

Jill shakes hands with Professor Stark and Juan after the discussion, and waves at Brody, who is back fixing his hair and reading producer notes for his upcoming segment.

"I don't have approval to make this offer, but I'll do it anyway," she says to Juan and Professor Stark, after their microphones are removed. "I'd like to invite you both to testify to the House Judiciary Committee right after the Fourth. We're pulling together a hearing on this topic, mostly with constitutional scholars. I'm going to speak to the Chairman about a panel focused on real-world implications of the constitutional amendment. I believe both of you could represent your opinions well in that venue," she says, reaching out and putting her right hand on Juan's shoulder and left on Professor Stark's elbow. What she doesn't say is that her hope is to position Professor Stark on the right and Juan on the left in the debate, allowing her proposal to be viewed as the proper centrist position.

Fidgeting and looking around as he often does when his thoughts take him on multiple paths at the same time, Professor Stark says, "Uhm, Uh. Well. I guess the simple answer is yes. My only commitment next week is finishing a book, and I can do that from anywhere."

Jill smiles a bit at Professor Stark as he keeps talking, "I wish I could say that our political system fixes had eliminated all our issues, but I think this debate is too important to leave alone."

Jill nods at Professor Stark and then looks to Juan. "I guess the good news about not getting the job at FirstWal is I'm free of any commitments other than H2M," Juan says. "I suppose they would support me testifying in Congress. Can Congress pay for my trip, or do I need to see if H2M can get me back here? I'm not exactly rich enough to afford flying around on my own savings, which I just exhausted buying gum this morning."

"I suspect H2M will want you to testify and get you here. Do you need money for Metro or a cab, or for food?" Jill asks Juan.

"No thank you Congresswoman. I'm walking back to H2M's offices."

As they walk outside the studios, the three wave politely. Jill walks to the curb to catch a ride back to the Longworth House Office Building. Professor Stark and Juan both subconsciously walk slowly behind her, neither making eye contact with each other as Juan asks, "If we do get asked to testify together, can I spend some time talking to you about your ideas. I hadn't thought about the issue that way and I just want to understand your perspective."

"Happy to do it, although I'd like to hear your views as well. I never learn anything when I'm talking," Professor Stark says.

CHAPTER 25

July 11, 2040
Washington, D.C.

Cong. Jill Carlson succeeds in convincing Judiciary Committee Chairman Will Henry, already an announced amendment opponent, to add an early afternoon panel to his agenda. The new panel features Professor Stark along with Juan Gonzalez as the official spokesman for H2M. Also on the panel are representatives of a Hollywood-linked liberal advocacy group People for Freedom and a representative of a neo-Nazi hate group that supports the constitutional amendment. The final panel roster isn't publicly announced until the night before the hearing.

As Professor Stark finishes preparing for the session, he sees the panel roster and senses an ambush linking his views to those of a hate group. On the opposite side, Juan Gonzalez is paired with the Hollywood-funded group that ostensibly promotes liberty and freedom.

Though he hadn't predicted this particular strategy, Professor Stark isn't entirely surprised. Chairman Henry was an ardent opponent of the Political Freedom Amendment Professor Stark led into implementation many years ago. Although Chairman Henry's opposition was publicly framed as concern with Constitutional tinkering, he had never hesitated pushing prior Constitutional amendments that fit his own views. When the Political Freedom Amendment was launched, Chairman Henry had served 24 successful years in the U.S. House and liked the way the game was played. Now, the risks inherent in a short campaign cycle with no ability to pre-stock massive war chests forces him to stay aligned with his congressional district. That has meant more relationship building at home and more travel back to the district.

Prior to the Political Freedom Amendment, the financial advantages of incumbency were so overwhelming that Henry rarely attracted more than token opposition. This year, with the short campaign cycle, several local leaders recently launched campaigns against him. For that, including the wear and tear on his body of traveling regularly to what is no longer his real home, he maintains a strong disdain for Professor Stark.

Outside the House Rayburn Office Building, Professor Stark sits on an Independence Avenue step facing the U.S. Capitol building. Realizing his hard-won reputation as a thoughtful, fair advocate for what is best for America is at stake, he quickly reworks his opening remarks before entering the hearing room.

As the session opens, the other three panelists quickly complete opening statements. Professor Stark is cut off before he can begin his opening remarks as legislators are called to vote.

After a nearly 20-minute voting delay, giving him time to consider his remarks, Professor Stark begins his opening statement.

"Thank you, Mr. Chairman and members of the Committee, for the opportunity to testify. I have provided my prepared remarks electronically and ask for permission that these be entered into the record."

"So moved," the Chairman approves.

"Before I get into the substance of the issue, let me address the elephant, or perhaps more descriptively, the male donkey in the room. On this panel, you have two groups opposing this effort who are represented by thoughtful, intelligent people who I believe are clearly well intended in their views despite failing to recognize the long-term consequences to the country of such views."

"Supporting strengthening the amendment, you have me paired with an avowed white racist who would like to see nearly 50 percent of this panel forcibly removed from the country, and who refers to himself as 'commander.' I must say, this is extremely uncomfortable company for me, and I don't doubt for a moment Mr. Chairman that you hope audiences will be left with the impression that the amendment being proposed and those supporting any aspect of it are inherently racist. Given your long history and experience, I don't find this particularly surprising, though I do find it disturbing."

Chairman Henry bangs his gavel and interrupts angrily: "This is a ridiculous assertion on the part of the gentleman and I demand that you apologize for the inference that this is a staged event. This issue is essential to the fabric of our nation and that is why we have devoted much of the day to hearing testimony on the issue, much beyond the views of this panel."

"Mr. Chairman, I do apologize," Professor Stark says, at which point Chairman Henry stops listening and takes on the snide smile that appears whenever he feels he got the better of a witness. "I apologize if it was my mistake in suggesting you would have thought through the implications of the panel line-up."

"Apology accepted," the Chairman responds, as a staffer rushed to let him know Professor Stark had not really actually apologized for his earlier remark. As Chairman Henry grunts and snarls toward his staffer, Professor Stark continues.

"Mr. Chairman and ladies and gentlemen of the Committee. I wish the issue of whether government business should be conducted in English could be a matter of pitting the racist versus the tolerant. That simplistic view, though, misses the point about what kind of America we are as a country.

"There was a time when, despite our many failings as a country, America was more culturally interested in being a melting pot – though many times a reluctant stew to be sure. In most of the United States, real economic opportunity was reserved for a subset of English speakers. In most of the 19th Century and the first 75 years of the 20th Century, we generally respected the rule of law when it came to immigration. People who came to America did so legally or were sent home. Of course, through most of this time, the nation was wise enough to allow a large enough pool of immigrants into the country to maintain and support economic growth.

"In addition, because back then we provided newcomers with the opportunity to create a better life for their families without excessive government interference, we tended to attract freedom-oriented people who had been prevented at home from seeking a better life for their families because of lineage, ethnicity, politics, religion or perhaps even a physical attribute. Over the past 70 years, the flavor of our melting pot has changed, as has the expectation of new people to effectively blend into an integrated society. When my great grandfather moved here, first generation immigrants would often stick to people from the same culture with the same language, but the next generation would start to integrate into the rest of society. By the third generation, marriage of people from other backgrounds was common. This is not so today with some recently arrived immigrant communities."

"More recently, we've failed to allow for enough legal immigration to ensure we have a steady flow of new people ready to work hard to live the American dream and to support a tax system that relies on a growing economy to finance our social programs. Instead, we now have entire cultures formed here that operate outside our legal system. Many, if not most, of these immigrants come for economic reasons rather than shared interests in our political system. Because many believe the constitutional rights of American citizens are really universal rights available to anyone who can get here, legally or otherwise, we've created whole sections of the country where it is possible and in fact encouraged to discriminate against generations-long Americans whose primary or only language is English."

Chairman Henry clearly grows frustrated and cuts off Professor Stark during his statement. "Your comments suggest that somehow people who are born in the United States have God-given rights over others who want to be here," Chairman Henry says.

"No sir. But the U.S. Constitution provides different rights. What I'm saying is that any country should want the people who live in that country to have a vested interest in its survival. Civil wars are brutal, horrific experiences. Nations survive when people share values, elements of culture, language and a shared belief in a political system that balances freedoms and responsibilities. Getting that to happen without resorting to internal use of force takes hard work and clear expectations," Professor Stark says. "When immigrants break the law to get here, that very act shows a disdain for our system. I certainly understand this disdain because the current immigration system is broken. But do we really want an America where those who break the law succeed and those who follow the law suffer? That isn't my view of how a nation gains lasting strength."

"Look, Professor Stark, with all due respect for your view of right and wrong, I think you see this issue as clearly as a coyote outside a 12-foot fence at a miniature dog kennel. You smell an issue you want to go after, but don't have the foggiest idea of the right way to address the issue," Chairman Henry says. "So let me ask you this fundamental question. We have children born in America of parents who are citizens of other countries. When that child is born here, he or she becomes a citizen of the United States. Is it your desire that we should immediately separate that infant from his or her parents and kick them out of the country?"

Neo-Nazi Commander Kirk Park tries to turn on his microphone, but is waved off by Chairman Henry.

"Mr. Chairman, what would any of us think of parents who would abandon an infant?" Professor Stark says. "Not much, I'd suggest, unless it's clearly in the child's best interest. Once we have the right policies in place, parents will put in the work to be here legally, which includes gaining an understanding of and appreciation for our system of government and culture and language. In the meantime, we have all these people here illegally today. Many are working and we need them. So we put a streamlined process in place with rules that allow them to earn the right to be here legally. Culturally, it is never a good idea for people who ignore the law to gain advantage over those who follow it, and we need to stop systematically enabling this with our immigration process. The vast majority of illegal immigrants are very good people who come here to build a better life for their families. Who can blame them for that desire? I find it hard to believe that an improved immigration process won't make it possible for hard-working people to join us legally and help create a rich, integrated culture," Professor Stark says.

Chairman Henry looks down from his perch at the top of the Rayburn committee room dais. "Before I turn questioning over to members of the panel, let me just ask one question directly to Congresswoman Carlson, the chief House sponsor of the proposal we are debating. If we proceed with enacting this constitutional amendment as you have proposed, what do you see as the costs to government and the consequences to people who don't speak English in this country?"

"Those are fair and critically important questions," Jill responds, trying to hide her surprise that Henry was asking a question devoid of political rhetoric. "The costs to various government bodies are clear. They will need to either hire bilingual employees for the various roles that interact with the public, provide English language training programs in areas where English is uncommon, or buy excellent translation equipment for each potential encounter location. It's quite possible that in some parts of the country, bilingual employees will be more expensive to recruit and harder to retain because they have useful private sector skills. I believe these costs to be fairly minimal over the long-term, but acknowledge there would be meaningful start-up costs."

"On the more critical question of what this means to people who do not speak English in the United States," Jill continues. "Well, for one, it means that if they do learn English, they have the ability to obtain government support no matter where in the United States they choose to live. Municipalities with large groups of Mandarin, Vietnamese, Spanish or other language speakers will have to provide any services they provide in these languages in English as well. It also means that if they learn English, they will better have the ability to pursue economic opportunity anywhere in America and not be confined to a set geography."

The red light at the table comes on, letting Chairman Henry know his question time has ended. "I'm afraid my time has expired," Chairman Henry says. "But I'm sure others on the panel will have questions as well. Before I turn it over, Professor Stark, I suggest that if you ever testify to this panel again, you not act like a squirrel spotting a nut in the snow. You're so hungry to get your point across that you ignore common decency. I will not be so gentle in my response should this happen again."

Professor Stark stares ahead at the Chairman, making no motion nor offering any response.

As Chairman Henry chastises Professor Stark, Juan furiously tries to interject.

"Since the ranking member is not here, I'll turn to Congresswoman Carlson, lead sponsor of the constitutional amendment, to ask her questions," Chairman Henry says.

"Thank you, Mr. Chairman. I appreciate your willingness to convene this discussion. Mr. Gonzalez, you clearly have a point to make so my first question is a simple one. What do you want to say?"

"Thank you Congresswoman," Juan says, at time looking down to check word translations. "I still don't understand how selecting one language over another doesn't turn Spanish speakers, or the speakers of any other language for that matter, into second-class citizens here? That's my biggest concern with a government in Washington deciding what language is appropriate rather than having such a critical decision made by the people in each place." Juan had been coached by H2M lawyers for the two days leading up to the session, including a half-day spent in mock question-and-answer session with experts on the Judiciary Committee predicting what questions would likely be asked by which members.

Jill responds, "I know my answer, but I'll ask each of the panel members to quickly respond, starting with Mr. Patel from People for Freedom."

"We don't agree that the federal government or any other government should impose a preferred language," Patel says, over-stretching the organization's perspective to incorporate his view.

"Does that mean," Jill asks, "that you are opposed to the Arizona law requiring that all government business in that State be conducted in Spanish?"

"I don't know that I meant that," Patel says. "In Arizona, it was the people who demanded to have a common language."

"All people, Mr. Patel," Jill asks, "or just the majority, in this case at the expense of a minority? The difference between our constitutional amendment and what has happened in Arizona is that we don't prevent governments from communicating in languages other than English, we simply require that English be one of the options. And we don't make English the official language, whereas Arizona makes Spanish its official language."

Jill hesitates as she looks at neo-Nazi Commander Park, but knows she should ask. "Mr. Park, your response."

"It's Commander, Ms. Jill, and I appreciate you not treating me like a big bowl of eye candy and giving me the chance to say something here," Park says, to giggling in the crowd. Park is anything but eye candy. Nonetheless, he is known to speak highly of every aspect of himself. "Frankly, if people don't want to speak English and don't want to act like us, they should just get the hell out," Park adds.

Jill drops her head in disgust and turns around. She mutters to her staff something that sounds like "racist trash" before turning back to the panel: "I believe Mr. Gonzalez's question is most clearly directed at you Professor."

"Thank you Congresswoman. It's a pleasure to see you again today," Professor Stark says. "The issue of language to me is not an issue of feelings. It's an issue of fact. The fact is that, over the course of history, nations built on common languages and cultures survive, while nations in which strong minority populations live, work and raise families isolated from the rest of a country eventually get restless. That restlessness leads to isolation, which leads to a desire for separation, which leads to the dissolution of the nation as soon as it weakens. For the United States, the fundamental choice is either remaining one country or splitting into separate ethnic- or language-based countries at some point. If we don't take action today to stay united, we'll be asking only about the timing of our separation and whether or not it will be violent."

Jill thinks Professor Stark is getting a bit too dramatic: "I don't see this issue as being about whether we want to be separate countries, but instead whether we want this country to be accessible to everyone."

"I'm sorry, Congresswoman," Professor Stark retorts. "We disagree on this point. It's hard enough for countries that share the same language to stay together – take Korea for example until that dictatorship was overthrown, Ireland for many generations or greater Germany over many centuries. So when you add in the additional complexity of language and cultural differences, you create an environment in which separation becomes nearly inevitable if you take a multi-century view.

"Look at Sudan, the Soviet Union, Yugoslavia, the former colonies of the Europeans. It simply doesn't work to have a ruling class and a ruled class where those in the latter see no hope of joining the former no matter how hard they work or how good they are. We're at a point in the Southwest today very similar to the conditions that existed in many nations when they dissolved. What does the Southwest share with these examples? We have a dissatisfied populace looking for more direct control over their lives. The only thing missing from creating the circumstances for separation has been the absence of a truly charismatic leader. I fear for what these coming years will bring."

Chairman Henry taps his gavel. "On that happy note, the gentlewoman's time has expired. The Chair recognizes the Honorable Ricardo Estrada from Texas for two minutes."

Congressman Estrada is only in his second term, serving one of the few contested districts in the State, and hoping to secure a better Democratic base in the upcoming round of redistricting. Logistics systems entrepreneur Ramon Mantle was one of his most meaningful supporters, helping him get into a run-off and upending one of the state's last veteran Republican congressmen in the general election.

Ramon supported Estrada financially and helped generate 500 campaign workers for him. For the first time yesterday, Ramon called in a favor, requesting that the Congressman ask a question at the hearing if he had a chance.

"My question is for Mr. Gonzalez, but I'll provide a bit of historical context first. When the now Southwest states were taken from Mexico in 1848, the U.S. had the opportunity to take much of what is Mexico today into the United States. After the U.S. victory in the Mexican-American War, while voting on the treaty to settle the war, the U.S. Senate voted against taking in as U.S. territory a large part of what is now Northeastern Mexico by a 44 to 11 vote. This vote was overwhelming largely because of the view that the Mexican culture was too different from the rest of America. So America's racist culture didn't want non-Europeans as anything but slaves. Conflict between the U.S. and Mexico began earlier. By 1829, descendants of Europe outnumbered Mexicans in Texas. Texas sought its independence as a nation just seven years later, and became part of the United States in 1845, triggering the full-scale war. Today, Texas is nearly three-quarters composed of people with Mexican heritage, a higher percent aligned with one race and culture than when Texas last sought independence. So, Mr. Gonzalez, given these facts, my question is does this make it clear to you that politically, Texas is at a point again today where independence is the appropriate step for the people there and for several states with cultures better aligned with Mexico?"

A loud ruckus starts immediately as Estrada finishes his question. "Even asking this question is an act of treason," a Montana Republican congressman shouts and members along the dais engage in heated debate on whether the topic should be discussed. Chairman Henry quickly calls for a recess to discuss the question with the parliamentarian and his staff.

During the break, Jill finds Professor Stark and invites him back to the Republican anteroom, where she pulls him into a glass-enclosed office. She shakes the Professor's hand and thanks him again for taking part in the panel. She also apologizes for his being paired with Commander Park, making clear she had nothing to do with this move.

Then she gets to the point.

"Look, I have a lot of respect for you, but you could kill my hope of passing this constitutional amendment by making the proclamation that this is about preventing civil war. The media will make you out to be a kook. Thank goodness Estrada trumped you by suggesting that Texas secede from the union. Histrionics are not helpful to the process and frankly, Professor, I'm surprised you went this direction," she says in the kind of whispered yell clearly intended to get the message across that she was angry while avoiding having her comments heard by staffers and other members through the windows and door.

I guess this is not the time to ask for a date, Professor Stark thinks as he struggles to understand where this outrage is coming from. He looks at her for several seconds, tilting his head a bit as he thinks about how to respond. Jill just continues to glare. Clearly she was practiced at controlling a conversation with her eyes as well.

"Here's the problem with your plan," Professor Stark finally says. "Juan is a charismatic leader who could take this nation toward dangerous conflict. He's smart, attractive, hardworking and most of all real. What scares me is the hold H2M has on him. I'm not worried about your constitutional amendment right now, because as I said, it doesn't go far enough to solve the problem in any case. I'm worried about getting a message planted in Juan's head that he needs to think independently of where H2M is trying to take him, in a way he clearly hears."

Jill at least sees his point; even as she disagrees with the way he is raising the issue. "I guess the good news is the media will focus on Estrada's proposition about Texas independence and the cries of treason. We'll have a chance to recover," she says, still making the supposition or perhaps the assertion that she and Professor Stark are driving for the same outcome.

After a contentious backroom discussion with Estrada, the parliamentarian and a hastily placed call to the U.S. Attorney General, during which exaggerated media reports of the break-up of the United States begin circulating nationally and globally, Chairman Henry calls the session back to order. The panel is now aired live by most major news media.

As Chairman Henry calls the room back to order, he bangs his gavel repeatedly to regain quiet.

"The calls that the gentleman's question are an act of treason are out of order. Treason is acting in concert with a foreign government against the United States, or giving aid and comfort to a foreign government during a time of war. The gentlemen assures me that he asks the question on behalf of the people of his district and with the best interests of the healthy functioning of the United States as his purpose," Henry says. "Mr. Gonzalez, you may respond to Congressman Estrada's question."

Juan had come into the day fairly comfortable and confident in the answers he intended to give. But the preparation sessions with the H2M teams had neither gone over this question nor anticipated the raised voices in the debate. He is now taking his own counsel.

"I think the Congressman asks a very important question, one I believe is too important to answer without deep study and reflection. So I'll answer the part of the question I'm prepared to answer at this point. In seeking to require that all government actions in Arizona be conducted in Spanish, and to prevent discrimination against those of us whose primary language is Spanish in a state where that is the case for the majority of the people, my focus is on protecting the rights of people. One of the most important rights of all mankind is the right to self-government, the ability to decide how we want to be governed and not to have government imposed on us against our will. So, my answer, Mr. Chairman and Congressman, is that if the people of Texas want independence in order to better protect their rights and their culture, I think I support that decision. I also believe the rest of the U.S. should see this as in their best interests and support such a decision as well."

Chairman Henry bangs his gavel. "Thank you Mr. Gonzalez, and the rest of the panel, for participating today. While this debate can and should continue for a very, very, very long time, I believe we have covered as much ground as we can in the time allotted to this panel today. The committee is in recess until the call of the Chair."

CHAPTER 26

July 18, 2040
Washington, D.C.

In the many weeks since Juan Gonzalez's shooting and widely proclaimed "miracle" recovery, Juan has become a prominent national leader. His performance at last month's Judiciary Committee hearing only bolstered his status as the new public spokesman for Hispanic rights. This elevated profile has, in turn, heightened media attention on slow progress in finding his shooter.

With pressure bearing down on the lead detective on the case, who further pushes Sgt. Moore, Sgt. Moore increasingly isolates himself to focus on his work. While tucked away in a suspect interview room, absent any suspect to interview, he receives an unusual message. "We need to trace a message I just received. It's clearly from the killer," Sgt. Moore says as he shuts the detective's office door behind him. "Not only do the shooters want us to know they can pull off a sophisticated assassination, now they want us to know that they know who's in on the investigation," Sgt. Moore says.

"The game takes a twist," the lead detective says. "What's the message say?"

Moore reads from his Lifelink: "In the new America, our rites will be protected from all intruders on our soil. Juan knows this now. You now know we know you know we can succeed. Soon, everyone will know."

"What the hell does that mean?" the detective asks.

The multi-agency task force investigating the shooting starts a trace. After multiple attempts, no return contact information is found.

While the detective focuses on electronic surveillance, Moore looks into the message content. He launches several keyword searches, individually and in every combination, hoping to spot anything that should trigger further investigation. Words that strike him as worth exploring include rites, protected, foreigners, intrude, and soil. Criminals often speak in repetitive terms, using language familiar to them in everyday life.

On the rare occasion written notes are involved in a crime, language experts look for patterns. They routinely search public and private electronic interaction sites for unusual words or sentence structures in postings. One World's interaction web forum and its dozens of variants can provide interesting clues to criminal identities. Sgt. Moore then crosschecks identified criminals against people using identified words and sentence structures in on-line communications. From there, he and the task force narrow the list to only those with the intelligence for the Convention Center attack. A probability sort narrows the list to nearly 10,000 potential people around the country. Then, the hard work begins.

***

New Rite Compound, Utah

Local police contact survival gaming champion Pete Roote. Pete lists witnesses to verify he was in Colorado and Utah in the weeks leading up to the Convention Center attack. A check of his car rental driving records and several interviews confirming his presence quickly takes Pete off the suspect list.

As police leave, Pete wonders how fortunate he must be that someone else already took a shot at part of H2M. As importantly, he has a clear alibi. Still, this is the first time he's been stopped for anything more consequential than a few anger management issues. The timing strikes him as too coincidental to ignore. Pete asks, but isn't told how he turned up on the suspect list. A possibility he considers is that his New Rite success identifies him as a skilled shooter and tactician. Pete is largely right. The U.S. military buys user lists from many war game sites to identify potential recruits. With New Rite games the most physically demanding of the elite war game sites, the correlation between good New Rite competitors and good soldiers is higher than for any other site. A small FBI unit also accesses these lists from the military. While initially used for FBI recruiting, the lists now are used to search for criminal suspects. When New Rite gamers start buying real or dual-purpose weapons, FBI officials add them to criminal suspect lists. They then trace gamers on this narrower list for purchases, vehicle travel and state ID movement – and share this information with local police in tough-to-solve cases that appear to have required combat skill or techniques. Several of Pete's weapons are dual-purpose New Rite game and lethal use weapons.

Pete uses a contact device JT provided. "Sir, this is Pete. I need to talk, but in person," he says after JT says hello.

"The transponder I gave you is secure," JT assures him. "But I suspect discomfort from the tremor in your voice. I have a few things to finish up here and then will be there in a couple of hours."

"I can come to you," Pete responds, "if you let me know where you want to meet."

"It's alright. I'm not too far away and I expected your call after today's busy day. I'll meet you at the camp, but we'll take a hike before we talk," JT says.

Less than three hours later, JT meets Pete at the Utah camp headquarters and game center. The two men set off on a hike. Pete grabs a canteen of water, his hunting knife, a medical kit and a stun gun he's able to easily fit in his backpack. While he trusts JT, he isn't quite sure why they need to hike before talking. JT grabs a canteen and the two take off outside the camp and start hiking into a canyon. Along the way, they engage in casual conversation about game challenges and the recruits Pete recently trained.

JT directs Pete to an overhang that Pete instantly recognizes as covered by the same unusual coated mesh that is over JT's Colorado mountain balcony.

"We can talk here Pete. The cover distorts our noise waves, so even if a satellite is tracking our conversation, they won't be able to tell what we're saying," JT starts. "So, you must be a bit spooked. I hear the local police paid you a visit."

"Yes, sir."

"And I suppose they asked your whereabouts on the night the Gonzalez kid was shot," JT says.

"That's right," Pete responds, a bit surprised JT would know this, even if it's clear at this point that he shouldn't be amazed by what JT knows.

"Whoever did the Gonzalez shooting may be trying to frame New Rite or our people," JT says. "Some in the media have attacked me for years as a right winger because of my weapons business. Still, the coincidence of this coming so soon after our recent conversation has me concerned. I need to know that you haven't spoken to anyone about our prior discussion. If you've said anything, the only thing saving you is lots of people know you weren't in DC."

Pete doesn't feel physically threatened. JT is standing a couple of feet away and his hands are in plain view. But he instinctively reaches to check that he has his knife.

"Pete, I'm not going to hurt you," JT says, having seen Pete's facial tension combine with a check for one of the weapons JT is sure he has with him. "I just need to know if you talked to anyone. If you have, we'll pull away now."

Pete relaxes a bit, though he's a bit spooked that his fear is so obvious to JT. "I haven't mentioned this to anybody. I'm not about to say anything linking me to what I'm doing," Pete says.

"Very few people have heard me talk about my issues with H2M. You're one of them, so Pete, I'm asking you again, have you talked to anyone, even in passing at a bar, about our discussion," JT says, eyebrows furrowed and bottom lip jutting in front of his top lip.

"Absolutely no one," Pete responds. "I need total op security to succeed. But I need help knowing what to do now. With the attack on the kid, security is bound to get tighter around H2M. That makes my mission much more difficult, and requires extra caution. The last thing I need to worry about is anyone else knowing what I'm doing."

"So, no discussion with friends, family, the hot bartender at the pub, anyone?"

"No. No. No one," Pete says, turning palms up and spreading them out. "But I have some questions, if that's alright?"

"Shoot," JT replies. Both men watch a rattlesnake spring out from cover just 40 feet away and bite a lizard, injecting its venom to leave it stunned, and quickly lifeless. "Of course I mean that in the verbal sense."

"Why would the police check on me?" Pete asks, both men still watching as the snake starts to slowly pull the lizard into its body.

"Good question I couldn't have answered yesterday. This morning, about 200 top New Rite gamers had police break into their homes. Several were pulled out of games at gunpoint. Our camera feeds were still tracking fighter body movements to drive game response, so we could replay the police taking down game players," JT says, shaking his head slightly back and forth, but still watching the rattlesnake slowly absorb the lizard.

"We started sending out alerts to members, but the raid timing was coordinated. A member filled us in on what happened making his first jail call to us. He's being charged with resisting arrest because he thought being yanked out was part of the game and fought like hell to get away. A lot of these guys were smashed up pretty hard. Then, the FBI raided our data centers and tried to shut down our network. Fortunately, I don't trust any government enough to put my company at its mercy so we transferred feeds to other countries," JT says.

The snake slithers back to its hole with several days of lazy digestion ahead.

"Oh damn. So they must be watching you closely," Pete says.

"I'm sure you're right and that's why we're talking here," JT says. "What I've learned is they've been tracking our players for a long time. I didn't know it, but a now ex-manager sold player lists to the U.S. military for years. I'm sure the government used this list to track you all. What's even more interesting is, from the questions they were asked, our players believe the government knows where they drive and what they do on a routine basis. So if the feds didn't think you were anywhere near the operation, they simply asked for the names of five people you encountered leading up to the shooting. But everyone within a quick drive to D.C. was attacked by armed SWAT units, thrown to the ground, handcuffed and hauled away for interviews."

"Whewww," Pete exhales. "Glad I wasn't one of them. I might have fought back before they could tell me what was going on and been sitting in jail with the other guys."

"And women," JT adds.

JT nods his head, wrinkles his eyebrows upward and shakes his head back and forth in a slow, repetitive motion. The pit of Pete's stomach begins to ache as he realizes how lucky he is to have not chosen DC for his shot.

Pete grabs some of the dusty sand off the ground and rubs it between his hands. Seconds later, he speaks again: "Given what's going on, shouldn't we call this off?"

JT looks at Pete and puts his arm on his shoulder. "Actually, Pete, this is the perfect time to attack, 'cuz now we know how to fool them and keep you clean," JT says.

"What do you mean?"

"I mean we know they track our game, not just the list. They are hacking into the system and tracking players in real time. I can show you as playing on-line and make sure the location of where they think you are playing from is nowhere near where you are. We also know they are tracking driving, so we can't use an on-grid vehicle, and I suspect they have tracers in almost anything you might wear or carry that requires any sort of government approval."

"Okay," Pete says. "What does that mean?"

"It means you'll need to get in and out of the kill zone the old-fashioned way. On foot. On a horse. On a bike. Doesn't matter. Just so your face isn't seen in the area and no evidence puts you near the scene – no money cards, licenses, cars, or anything else. We'll need to be sure your face isn't identifiable anywhere close to where the action takes place."

"I'm still not entirely getting this," Pete says. "I need to be seen in places other than where I am? I'm good at camouflage, but I don't know how to make that happen."

JT walks away from the overhang, but catches himself and steps back under. "I can show you how to do your part, and I can do the other part for you. But I'll need some voice tapings, and I'll need measurements to use creating a dummy for my part. You'll need to get to the location in a way no one sees you coming or going – masks, camouflage, night cover, whatever."

"I know you can pull this off. So let's talk about how," JT says.

CHAPTER 27

August 22, 2040
New Rite Compound, Utah

After weeks of preparation, Pete stows a bag packed with his Lifelink and other traceable equipment behind the seats of JT's Advanced Propulsion Blend (APB) transporter. That night, Pete and JT walk out to the helicopter-inspired APB. As Pete opens the undercarriage, JT remotely opens the ground panel at his landing strip. Pete drops down onto the metal ladder, climbs 10 feet below, and then walks through a tunnel that takes him back to either a remote shed exit or JT's personal room. This time, he'll climb up through the room flooring.

As Pete descends to the tunnel, JT pulls a string to inflate a life-size mannequin of Pete; dressing it in the sweatshirt and hat Pete wore when he entered the APB.

JT sets course to return to the Colorado New Rite compound after ensuring that only Ally will be on hand when he lands.

Once back at the Colorado camp, JT programs the New Rite on-line game in the guest cabin so government hackers will believe Pete is playing from JT's mountain retreat. JT uses the camp home as his work base for the month, dropping over to the guest cabin early and late each day dressed in the kind of competitive clothing Pete would wear. With his face covered enough to be unclear, he climbs in and out of the New Rite competition pod and exits through a second opening outside of any external view. JT has long worried his camps are being watched by means other than just satellite.

Back at the Utah compound, Pete waits until three hours after dark before heading back below ground and to the remote shed exit. Outside, he walks briskly and quietly – wearing multi-directional night vision goggles one of JT's researchers developed. Pete is now a beta tester for the new equipment, which has far more capability than current military fare. The goggles offer more than enhanced sight, helping to identify optimal paths over viewable terrain. An enhanced version that links to satellite is also available for testing, but JT is concerned the satellite links needed could later be used to track Pete's path.

Though the goggles are used at night, the multi-directional views created by the headgear's high-speed computer uses stored images to color in the views for Pete. In addition to improving his sight, the daylight-strength views minimize the strain on Pete's eyes, aiding his progress compared to common night vision.

The majority of Pete's view frame is what he sees in front of him, but small panels along the top of the goggle panels display rear, right and left views. He sets movement alerts for all humans and animals that pose a physical risk. With physical health risks and the risk of being spotted both equal threats to Pete's mission, he takes few chances. To be safe, he darkens his face and wears dental implants to distort his identity even during primarily nighttime travel. Setting the alerts allows Pete to keep the majority of his attention focused on his path.

To further help Pete avoid human and animal contact, the hat from JT contains his latest invention: sound detection and analysis that works in 360 degrees for up to two miles. Software embedded in the hat sorts for noises and estimates its source based on extensive sound maps JT created from tens of thousands of live competition New Rite gamer feeds. Using this data, JT's developers' linked sounds to actions so clearly that the software can tell whether a squirrel, raccoon or mountain lion is stepping through a pine needle pile 500 yards behind a thick, sight-restricting spruce grove.

Even with the sophisticated equipment assistance, Pete stays in the most isolated parts of the path he and JT outlined, hiking at pace through

desert, dry grassland and deep forest environments. Armed with a full snip-
ing set with missile-launch bullets, a knife, water cleansing tablets, a gallon of water and dehydrated meals to supplement juniper berries, pine nuts
and other natural foods he can gather along the way, Pete is moving briskly
under the barely moonlit sky. Covering 20 miles of challenging rock and
desert terrain the first night, he knows he is in for many long, lonely nights
of hiking. All of this leads to a tree-nestled spot in a hill east of Flagstaff
with clear view of the new Walnut Canyon concert arena.

Ninety minutes before daybreak, Pete finds a location with no visibility from the sky and crawls in for somewhat restless sleep from which sound
alerts will wake him repeatedly. As he wakes fully in early afternoon, he
pours cleansed water from his canteen into a plastic, multi-pocketed container into which he has also deposited today's rations of dehydrated food.
Fresh food is hard to find on this barren part of his journey. In no hurry
since he can't go anywhere anyway, he lets the rations soak for an hour to
fully rehydrate before enjoying a relatively decent meal of gazpacho with
chicken and brown rice. He puts aside the fruit and nut bar to eat at sunset.

After sleeping for five hours and spending 30 minutes preparing and
consuming his first meal, Pete's confinement in order to avoid being spotted is even more isolating than he normally feels. In this desolate mix of dry
prairie and hard rock, his biggest challenge for the first few days is refilling
his canteen until his path nears the Colorado River. Soon, he'll be able to
take short, but demanding side trips down to the river to refresh his water.
He struggles against daytime boredom. No games since he can't be connected electronically or risk being found. No music. No entertainment. No
people contact, even with his camouflage to protect his identity.

To fill his time during the flat, open parts of his hike where jumping
four-foot wire fences, evading the occasional wandering cow and avoiding
ankle sprains provide the primary challenges, Pete considers and recon-
siders how he will get a shot off and escape unseen by man, camera and
satellite. So after hiking for anywhere from eight to 25 miles every night,
Pete spends every day, for several hours, going over in his head how he'll
succeed. He thinks about sending the shot off from tremendous distance,
maintaining the missile bullet's aim through the multi-mile kill zone,
and how far into the shot the bullet needs to be before he can release the

guidance system for the bullet's final journey. JT has made clear the missile guidance system is so sophisticated that police may identify JT's military weapons group as one of a dozen potential global sources. So getting the right release point may be as important as hitting the shot.

More importantly, if the guidance system is spotted too soon after Ángel goes down, police could broaden their search area beyond normal sniper range. If the search is too expansive, Pete may not be able to slip away – even in the dark with Pete's equipment advantages.

After he thinks about taking out the man he now recognizes as more threatening than even his race-based politics would suggest, Pete thinks about how he'll get away with it. As soon as the shot connects, he needs to drop from his tree view and get around the ridgeline. From the back of the hill, he needs to grab his pack and bolt as quickly as possible without being spotted. In 10 minutes, the time he estimates it will take for response vehicles to start blocking the surrounding area, he wants to add another mile of separation from his shot location. He'll need sound detection technology to alert him to anyone getting close. He'll need to prepare hiding holes in case anyone searches the area, and cover his scent and tracks as he moves.

Most importantly, he'll need patience to get back to New Rite's Utah camp without being spotted, from which he can go into JT's APB as baggage, escape to the Colorado compound and replace JT's computers as his own game player. If he succeeds. No, no, when he succeeds. When he succeeds, he gets to sleep at night knowing he helped eradicate a terrible societal plague. It doesn't hurt that he's sure he can get a lifetime of New Rite gaming on top of the year he won in April.

As night five of his solo hike nears an end, Pete is mentally and physically drained. New Rite games hadn't prepared him for the discomfort of sleeping with animals in the area that pose a threat. This makes his daytime sleep restless. At least traversing the Grand Canyon is now an interesting challenge, particularly trekking up and down narrow paths barely safe for daytime travel. Fearing a wrong step using his goggles here, he travels at night using just the moonlight to stay on path. Most importantly, he studies the terrain to identify potential escape paths, hiding spots and food sources for his return trip, when roads and normal human walking paths will likely be monitored.

Pete controls against the feeling of exhaustion that starts kicking in at 3 a.m. every night – concentrating as hard as he had to do in countless New Rite contests. On his best days, Pete competed in New Rite games for as much as the one-day limit of 12 hours with only the game-mandated 30-minute break. Pete hadn't been aware the game panels filtered concentrated oxygen into his breathing area when he showed signs of fatigue. These panels were one of JT's creations that helped him addict his players in the same way retail coffee shops blend extra caffeine in their coffees and fast food restaurants stuff their menus with sugary and starchy items that drive quick insulin responses.

Without concentrated oxygen and particularly in sub-alpine elevations for parts of this hike, Pete finds exhaustion isn't so easily offset. A week in, Pete's body isn't set on his new schedule. His efforts to force it there through concentrated focus leave him more than a bit constipated. On top of this, he's already had two occasions where the daylight spaces he found to hide from satellites and people were so confined that the bodily contortions to fit in the areas left him cramped. Inconveniences, he tells himself.

Having just finished a difficult river cross, the terrain is at its most challenging. Pete climbs up a trail to leave the south side of the Grand Canyon and head into the dense forests that cover much of his remaining path to Flagstaff. Not every location he maps to get water is as easy to access as he had hoped. No matter what the mission, water is essential to survival. As Pete and JT planned this hike, they made sure water capture was not left to the last hour before daybreak. So far, Pete is keeping his thirst quenched. Still, with only a one-gallon water container, he can't afford any mistakes even moving primarily at far cooler nighttime temperatures. At this pace, he'll reach the outskirts of Flagstaff in just a few more nights. This gives him time to build his last holes and rest ahead of his mission and fast-paced return plans.

The small forest water hole Pete thought he would draw from tonight is too dry. What remains is filled with elk, deer and other dung too thick to be fixed by his cleansing tablets. Though he learned outdoor survival to compete in New Rite game challenges, Pete is glad he refreshed his desert survival knowledge training with some of New Rite's contributors at the Utah camp. Maybe that's why JT wanted him to be a trainer there.

He pulls up his map on his goggles to search for alternatives. A small lake is six miles off course round trip, but he can't afford a day without water and he's a bit ahead of schedule.

The rapid pace he moves at leaves him bruised by continuous branch hits. His ankles and legs are strained, though the pain is less than during the last rush up the Grand Canyon trail to get to forest cover and away from tourists before daybreak. The snakes that occasionally sprung near him with no warning at the early part of his journey seem a thing of the past. But now nearby howls and yips of coyotes are getting Pete's attention.

CHAPTER 28

August 24, 2040
Austin, Texas

As Pete makes his way toward Flagstaff, the real reason for the late-August H2M concert series is publicly announced with just about everyone except Pete hearing the news. In Texas, Arizona, New Mexico and South California, H2M launches campaigns aimed at getting those states to secede from the United States – forming an independent republic. H2M statements suggest its objectives include creating a close post-secession alignment with Mexico. Ballot wording is carefully managed to reduce the risk of treason charges. Ángel Herrera also expressly orders H2M staff to avoid contact with Mexican government officials.

In Texas, the ballot initiative reads in part:

"We, the people of Texas request that our elected officials seek release of the State from the United States of America in order to form a new national union to be known as the Republic of Alta Texas. Alta Texas is envisioned to consist of whichever of several states approve of joining this union, and will seek national identity under the approval and protection of the United Nations."

When the ballot initiatives launch at massive rallies in Los Angeles, Phoenix, Santa Fe and Austin, H2M founder Ángel Herrera, spokesman Juan Gonzalez and other leaders attend every rally. The day begins with a 7 a.m. CDT rally in Austin and ends with a 7 p.m. PDT rally in Los Angeles.

More than 20,000 people attend the Austin rally, despite having been alerted to the rally only two hours earlier through H2M's messaging network. Trucks that unfold with large screen and speaker systems are spread out around each Capitol's grounds to be sure attendees are directly connected to the presenters. Local police chiefs in each city had pre-approved the gatherings, but follow Ángel's request to not alert their departments until early that morning.

Trucked-in stages at each city fold out with bulletproof glass between the speakers and the crowd. At this stage of his life, Ángel intends to live to see his legacy's creation.

"Buenos días señores y señoras," Ángel begins his talk in Spanish. English subtitles track at the bottom of the screen for the many attendees who had let their language skills suffer or hadn't bothered to learn Spanish at all. *Today begins a great day for each of us and I argue an important day in world history. No country that tries to dominate other peoples can expect to maintain that domination. Through world history, empires come and go. Only a select few survive for a thousand years. Most disintegrate far sooner. Those nations that survive must change shape, adjusting borders to include only those people who want to be governed together.*

"More than 200 years ago, Texas was overtaken by a rush of Europeans. These people bristled under the rule of an ever-changing Mexican nation and sought independence. Despite joining the United States, Texans have maintained their independent spirit. While the spirit remains, much of what makes up Texas has changed. Today, more than 70 percent of Texans are really Mexicans by blood. These people, our people, you and me, have more in common with our brothers and sisters to our South and West than with our cousins to the North and East. The United States served its purpose for the people of this land for many years. I believe that purpose is now one of the past."

The blue portions of the red, white and blue decorations around the front of the stage are torn down, replaced by green to display the red, white and green colors of Mexico. The Texas and Mexican flags are raised at the same height as, but in front of the American flag.

"Today, our values, our families and our economy are more intertwined with Mexico than with the United States. I have no ill will toward the people of New York, the people of Wisconsin, the people of Oregon or any other state. Many of our

friends and family live in these states. So while I call on you to join me in a revolution today, it is a revolution of peaceful change and renewed hope we so desperately seek. I long for the opportunity to create a new nation that better represents our hopes and aspirations as a people. I believe the best way to achieve our goal is if we pursue our dreams in a way that does not threaten war on our brethren," Ángel concludes.

Some in the crowd chant for Juan; others for pop star Perez. Instead, they hear next from Gabriel Herrera, Ángel's son and planned successor.

"H2M has worked for 25 years to help Mexicans stay connected to our language, . . . our culture, . . . each other. For as long as I've been alive, my father has been the real inspiration of our movement. For years that movement focused on the basics of social justice. We helped feed our hungry, house our homeless, protect our families and pursue our belief in Jesus Christ. Today, I'm proud to be part of H2M in launching our pursuit of the ultimate social justice: the right to self-determination."

Gabriel's remarks are interrupted by applause before he is able to quiet the crowd enough to be heard.

"We stand before you to ask your support. We ask you to approve a referendum in Texas in favor of reestablishing our independence. With this new independence, it's our hope we will rejoin with our families in New Mexico, Arizona and South California – and any other states that want to join us – to create a new nation that better represents people living in these states," Gabriel says to a loud and continuous ovation that goes on for several minutes. Chants of "Texas, Texas" and "Viva Mexico" spring through the crowd. Many pump their fists in the air and hold their children above their heads. The most boisterous sing and dance.

Ángel returns to the stage.

"Before we go any further, I want to again say that we are pursuing this effort peacefully. This is an emotional topic. But we must be calm to make it happen. We want our Anglo and Asian and black cousins to recognize that allowing us to leave is right for them, as well as for us. We want to help 'em understand that by letting us form a new nation, they'll save lifetimes of grief and anguish. It we do not succeed peacefully, we all know that many of our people will seek to achieve this outcome in more violent ways. But before we pursue this dream of independence, I need to be sure that you, my brothers and sisters, agree that secession is the right path forward."

A prolonged, loud and raucous cheer builds throughout the crowd. Many yell out their impatience with government control. If independence means regaining their lives, some chants make clear they are all in just for that reason.

"All around the park, you see volunteers wearing red, green and white vests holding petitions I need you to sign and then I ask each of you to personally gather 1,000 signatures around the State. Our goal is to have more signatures on these petitions than the number of votes we need to win the referendum. Our goals are simple. Seek independence. Then align in a new nation with other states that want to join us. With independence, we'll establish a true brotherhood with Mexico and finally tear down the physical walls that separate us," Ángel says, again to massive cheers and crowd celebration.

"Now as you read these petitions, you'll see the proposed name of the new nation is Alta Texas. The name of the nation can be changed once we have independence, but our thought in proposing the name is to merge parts of the Alta California, Nuevo Mexico and Texas lands that were taken from Mexico, helping to honor the history of our people and our land."

Emotions begin to overwhelm many in the crowd, with weeping now heard amidst cheers and jubilation. Balloons set up around the square are released overhead as cheers continue. It takes several minutes for the crowd to calm enough that Ángel can again be heard. *"Now, I want to introduce a man whose greatness we are only beginning to see, Mr. Juan Gonzalez."*

"Hola," Juan says. The piercing scream of schoolgirls adds to the chorus of cheers for Juan. *"My mother moved me to America for opportunity. Together, we can pursue the opportunity my mother hoped for in a way few of us could foresee even as little as a year ago. In our excitement for freedom, we need to be calm. Be honorable and humble in how we seek power. Three of the greatest men of the 20th century – Mahatma, Martin and Mandela – taught us that lasting change is best achieved peacefully. Each of these men achieved their objectives using the righteousness of their message, the steadfastness of their resolve, and the strength of their souls to create fundamental change for people so dear to them. While no one here pretends to belong in the company of such great men, my hope for you today is we will honor each other and show belief in the truth of our goal to pursue our dream of independence the right way. In peace. In truth. In honor. With each other. For independence."*

Juan steps back from the podium and surveys the wildly cheering crowd. Just nine months ago, the largest audience he had been in front of was at the high school soccer stadium in West Nogales. The Mandarin competitions he entered typically attracted only judges and relatives of the participants as audiences. Though new at speaking to such audiences, he grows increasingly comfortable with each event. Teleprompters scattered in front contain his approved script, but now he steps around the bulletproof glass barriers so he can eliminate separation from the audience.

Ángel and others on the stage motion at Juan to get behind the protective shields. In his earpiece, the producer yells at Juan that no one was checked for weapons. *"Get back behind the shield. You are putting yourself and everyone in the crowd at risk,"* the producer yells feverishly. Distracted by these instructions, Juan removes the earpiece and steps to the front of the stage. Cameras continue to follow his movements. He paces from end to end along the front of the stage as he continues to speak.

"This is an enormous group and I applaud each of you for being here. The coming months and perhaps even years will not be easy as many in the U.S. will not understand our desires. They may feel spurned – creating the animosity of a broken-hearted girlfriend you never wanted to hurt but no longer love. Personally, I've seen a little of this anger and it is not always rational," Juan says to nods of agreement from most in the crowd, and some light-hearted laughter.

"Our friends up north may feel entitled; entitled to control our lives through government we do not ask for and do not want. Some may feel relieved; relieved at the idea of getting rid of a people they don't embrace. Whatever others feel, they need to understand we seek only justice. The right to govern ourselves. Our laws. Our courts. Our culture. And, the issue that first connected me to this movement, our language."

An H2M security team member takes to the stage to physically prod Juan behind the security glass.

"The organizers of this event, the security team from Honor to Mexico, are telling me to get behind the bulletproof shield because we need to protect ourselves from those who hate," Juan says, pausing dramatically as he looks around the crowd. *"But I don't see any hate here today. I see love. I see hope. I see a future that fulfills our destiny."*

The throngs continue to cheer and chant, as Juan bends over to slap hands and exchange handshakes with those in the crowd.

"I will come back here later this year, after we have travelled to Los Angeles, Phoenix, Santa Fe today and the cities in our fundraising concert tour to thank you personally for creating brighter futures for my Mother, for me, and for all of us."

Several politicians make comments after Juan, but the jostling to avoid following Juan the rest of the day makes clear that his message is the one that resonates. For the rest of the day's events in Los Angeles, Phoenix and Santa Fe, Ángel makes sure to have the politicians go in front of Juan so the event ends with Juan firing up the crowd.

As Juan and the rest of the H2M travel team are driven to a private jet waiting to fly to Santa Fe, Mama Gonzalez grabs Juan by the bicep and squeezes tightly.

"Mama, what are you doing? That hurts," he says.

"That hurts. You think a little squeeze hurts. How about the hurt of fearing your son will be lost to you forever. You have any idea what that pain feels like?" she says, lips quivering and in an angry tone Juan hasn't heard since his mother saw him climbing under the ropes and down a side of the Grand Canyon with no path, no rope or anything else to save him from even a single slip.

"Mama, mama. Stop it. I'm not trying to hurt you. You raised me to not be afraid to do what's right. I know now that creating freedom for our people is why I was brought to this earth, and why I was fortunate to have you as my mother. God has now blessed me with the opportunity to fix injustices in the world and I would let him down if I did not do everything in my power to succeed."

She relaxes her grip and hugs him with her remaining strength. *"Just promise me you won't be stupid. Please don't risk your life and safety for needless publicity stunts. I have already thought I lost you once. My heart cannot bear this pain, and nearly collapses at even the thought."*

"I understand. I'm not trying to hurt you. I want to make you proud. I want the father who abandoned us to see he was wrong. I want the world to be somewhere I belong, where I make a difference."

Sitting quietly in the car the rest of the way to the airport, she reaches down to hold his hand. As they near the airport, she speaks again. *"You may be important now to many people, but you are everything to me,"* she says. *"I want you to remember one very important thing so you don't lose sight of who you are. You don't have to save everyone in this world to matter. Before this year, no one but our family, friends and people I work with had ever heard of me. I could have lived the rest of my life this way and still known that I had made the world better by being here and loving you."*

As the flight lifts off for the short travel to Santa Fe, news of the ballot initiatives goes global, setting off a tempest of activity in Washington,

D.C. The crowd in Santa Fe had five hours from when they received message alerts to gather. With the enormous publicity from Austin, more than 100,000 people line the streets and parks of Santa Fe. H2M and local police are nowhere near prepared to handle this size of a crowd. The Governor calls in state police to help. Local bar, restaurant and other merchant owners quickly open live event broadcasts to provide places for people to gather. With too few formal sites to watch the event, small group Lifelink huddles allow those wanting to take part to physically connect to the rally.

Police escorts work feverishly to get Ángel, Juan and the remaining speakers to the main stage for the start of the rally. Juan's speech draws even wilder reaction; this time including dozens of bras and panties on the stage. As Juan shakes hands, a number of teenage girls and even older women try to jump on the stage to hug and kiss him, prompting stage security to intervene.

On the flight to Phoenix, Mama Gonzalez starts another admonishment. *"Juan, you see the crazy way the girls react to you. They are practically falling over themselves to be part of your life – even if only temporarily,"* she says. *"And you know what I mean by temporarily so don't make me say it."*

"I know. It's crazy," Juan says, smiling, but a bit sheepish over the extreme reaction.

"I know you want to rest," Mama Gonzalez continues. *"So I'll keep this short. Keep your pants on. There are so many girls who will throw themselves at you right now, but none of them even know you. You get them pregnant, and you will right away if you are anything like your father, they will be proud to have Juan Gonzalez's baby. But your life will change forever and you'll no longer control your destiny. So you be polite to these girls and let them down gently. But if I find out you are having sex with these girls, I will castrate you myself."*

Juan's mouth drops open as he hears his mother scold him like she hasn't in years.

"Jesus Christ, Mama."

"Don't you dare take the Lord's name in vain with me."

"Mama. Some girls throw their bras at me and you leap right away to wanting me castrated. You're getting a little crazy here," Juan says. *"I'm not stupid enough to put this opportunity at risk. Besides, I know how tough it was for you so I am not going to be a dad until I'm ready to be a father."*

Mrs. Gonzalez knows this isn't the time to stress the issue. Juan is on an emotional high right now, but is also physically drained from playing such a major role in what is destined to be one of the most highly contentious issues of their life. That this role comes to Juan as an 18-year-old makes it that much more challenging to handle.

CHAPTER 29

August 24, 2040
Washington, D.C.

As the H2M team flies to Phoenix, U.S. President Marc Phillipi convenes an emergency cabinet meeting to explore response options to the secession initiative. The secession referenda could not come at a worse time from the President's perspective. It adds a politically volatile variable that neither he nor his staff anticipated to a short campaign cycle.

President Phillipi is the first true independent elected to the Presidency since George Washington, having benefitted from the Stark-led reforms that took full effect in the 2036 elections. Phillipi, a Tennessee native, amassed reasonable personal wealth from building two businesses. His minimalist-government views alienate people in both major political parties, but the open primary system resulting from Stark's reforms let him energize people who felt disconnected from both party structures. While some in the media declared Phillipi's election evidence of the end of the two-party system that dominated U.S. politics for more than 100 years, Phillipi fully expects a fight.

With open primary campaigning well underway, Phillipi is fighting off efforts from the Republican and Democratic parties to reassert dominance. Fortunately for Phillipi, both main parties have more than one candidate in each state's open primary. New rules are beginning to fundamentally change who runs for office, how they campaign, and what they focus on in governing. The effort to circumvent the new rules is also well underway and, in this cycle, several candidates are running with no intent of winning so they can advertise during the last 30 days of contentious primary campaigns, when only candidates are allowed to name themselves or opponents in advertising.

As the Political Freedom Amendment first gained momentum, the political establishment dismissed Professor Stark as simply a naïve, juvenile, elitist trying to impose ivory tower ideas on the American public.

For decades, elected officials put interests of the Republican and Democratic parties ahead of the long-term future of the United States. When not focusing on winning the next election, even the large number of politicians who ran for the right reasons spent too much time confined to a city almost entirely built around taking and redistributing what others earn. The rules and spending political elites advocate too often focus on the self-interest of a select view.

To these elites, Professor Stark was the political Grinch.

In the beginning, media organizations also decried his ideas as ill conceived; never mentioning their own extraordinary financial interest in maintaining a political system of nearly continuous campaigning. The constant stream of dollars that came with political advertising lined media pockets for generations.

Professor Stark's ideas were simple enough. The U.S. Supreme Court had long ruled that interfering with the right to fund political campaigns impeded free speech, and a *Citizens United* court decision sent the system on a downward spiral into excess. A free speech advocate in principal, Professor Stark decided it best to use the structure of the political process to curb the corrupting influence of money on America's government. So he proposed, and with the help of a variety of highly unlikely partners, helped secure Amendment Number 29 (the Political Freedom Amendment) to the Constitution.

By shortening the election cycle, opening campaign fundraising activities to public scrutiny and ensuring candidates are fully responsible for political communication during the final weeks of election seasons, Professor Stark accurately predicted that America's leaders today could now spend more time actually governing than they had in at least 60 years.

The Political Freedom Amendment had been feared by unions, trade associations, trial lawyers, government-feeding corporations, billionaire interest group founders and others used to dominating the time and attention of law-makers. Freed from a constant need to raise money, House members can now focus on substance for 20 of every 24 months and the proportion of time spent on policy is even greater for Senators and the President. Freed from hours every day raising money from the Capitol Hill Club, DCCC headquarters, senatorial party headquarters or elsewhere, legislators increased substance-based connections to their constituents and cross-party relationship building.

Prior to these reforms, lengthy political campaigns were so costly that elected officials held fundraisers for their next campaign almost two months before taking office for the race just won. The most aggressive politicians started even sooner, not letting even a weekend pass after an election before imploring for more cash.

In the past, real policy debates rarely survived the first 90 days of a new term. Even in those first months, congressional leaders focused on framing debates to create issues aimed at winning seats in the next election cycle. Solving substantive problems was a secondary consideration. Media outlets facilitated this focus by rarely investigating the complexities of real issues. Even today, conscientious reporters who would like to explore issues are hamstrung by tight budgets and tighter story deadlines. Professor Stark was drawn out of his comfortable academic shell by frustration with policy failures borne in this system.

In the cabinet meeting as the Santa Fe H2M event gets under way, President Phillipi explores his options, asking for idea exploration before anyone starts advocating favored solutions.

Secretary of Defense Xavier Mendoza suggests the military be put on immediate alert and recommends that the Department of Homeland Security be put on the same heightened level of alert: "We should also start closing military bases in states that pass these resolutions – hit 'em in the pocket book so they understand the benefits of being part of the U.S. of A. and get our weapons out of their reach."

"That's the most idiotic idea I've heard out of a sober adult," responds Secretary of Homeland Security Ray Peyton. "You can't honestly believe this is a financial issue."

"Whoa, whoa," the President steps in. "We're not debating the merits right now. I want options, even if you think the option is asinine."

"But you know the media will hear every aspect of our debate. We'll sound like a bunch of loonies if anyone hears ideas like that," Peyton says.

"Not if you all recognize the seriousness of this time in the history of our country and keep your mouths shut," Phillipi adds. "So, back to generating ideas? What are the options?" He looks at his assistant.

In two hours of discussions, the ideas listed are extensive, contradictory and subject to discussion even as the President tries to quell early debate. Some of the ideas include:

Banning votes on any initiative that seeks to break up the country.

Injunctions against including the ballot proposal in November's elections.

Letting the votes go ahead, but cutting federal funds to the states if they pass.

Arresting everyone involved for treason.

Kicking the referenda states out.

Threatening military action against Mexico.

Suspending habeas corpus, allowing the government to arrest anyone without any evidence requirements, and then rounding up anyone supporting secession referenda.

Covertly inciting an enemy state into declaring war on the United States to unite the whole country against a common enemy.

Creating a national referendum to let the American people decide whether to keep Texas, Arizona, New Mexico and South California in the union.

Dozens of other ideas also show up on the list. In deciding next steps, President Phillipi convenes a smaller session that increases his ability to identify leakers. This session is limited to Vice President Marcia Wilt, Defense Secretary Mendoza, Attorney General Becky Cooke, Homeland Secretary Peyton and Chief of Staff Vijay Chinh.

President Phillipi starts the meeting sternly addressing Homeland Secretary Peyton.

"Before we get into problem-solving, I would like to know, Ray, how a national organization creates a four-state secession campaign with thousands of workers, and we don't know it's coming. I have serious questions about our counterterror capabilities when a group this large can plot a secession and we have no idea it's coming," the President says. "I want to know by Monday where we screwed up and how we're going to fix it. Did we hear and not believe, or not even know?"

Secretary Peyton puts his head down briefly, looking up at the President to respond: "We never viewed H2M as a threat and don't have anyone in their leadership circle. They always focused on quality of life issues for Mexican Americans. Isn't that right Xavier?"

Mendoza looks at Peyton surprised, and in renewed annoyance at a man he quietly despises: "How the hell would I know? I'm only 1/8th Mexican and I grew up in Seattle, not exactly the focus point of H2M's work."

"Oh, sorry. I thought you had connections there or knew from your leadership days at the FBI was all I was thinking. Didn't you attend the event where the kid was shot?"

Mendoza stands up and walks over to Peyton, then leans in and whispers a bit too loudly in his ear: "Are you suggesting I have anything to do with this, you S.O.B.? Still bitter I got the Defense job, General?"

Everyone can see Mendoza is angry. Even Mendoza is sure his skin color must look wind-burned. President Phillipi had put Mendoza, a retired FBI director, in the Defense job and installed Air Force General Peyton in the Homeland Security role as an attempt to drive improved intelligence cooperation across the organizations. Unfortunately, personality skirmishes between the two leaders limited any cooperation. As always in the nation's capitol, rumors circle continuously about which of them, if either, will be retained in a second term.

"Gentlemen, enough. If you can stop playing sword fight, we can get back to the nation's business," barks President Phillipi, using some of the more expressive language he reserves for closed-session, sparsely attended meetings.

Properly admonished, the two shut down the personal debate – at least for now. Peyton is pleased he has temporarily distracted the President from his agency's failings. That buys him time to find answers and report back without Mendoza around to interject his two cents of self-motivated insight.

President Phillipi starts pacing the Oval Office, circling the couches and chairs on which the others are seated. Looking at his Chief of Staff, he says, "We're going to need to understand how the American people feel about this. And I don't want instant emotional reaction. I know that reaction is going to be nuke 'em, screw 'em or who cares. I want real reaction after people think about relatives living there, the impact of shrinking as a country, the risk of Mexico being an equal in the hemisphere. That means we need to have intelligent conversations and not just ask a bunch of check-the-box questions," he says.

"Mr. President," Attorney General Cooke says. "On some of the ideas thrown out in the cabinet discussion, I don't think arresting those involved and trying them for treason will work. They were careful to word the resolutions in a way that asks voters to advise legislators. Actions seeking secession would need to be taken by elected officials. There may be other statutes we can use to shut them down, but they could easily take the calculated risk that the states will protect them, creating confrontations just like we had in the civil rights days."

The President looks at Attorney General Cooke and nods his agreement.

"I'm not sure having the federal government coming down hard on people seeking something framed as liberty won't backfire. This is a very different context than the old civil rights context. Aren't we better off seeking to explain to these people why pulling out of the U.S. would be the wrong action for them to take? I don't know that pulling out the machine gun to execute opponents should happen before we ask them to surrender and explain why they should want to do so."

Phillipi's Chief of Staff Vijay Chinh weighs in. "Marc . . ., Mr. President, you may have just been handed this election with the opportunity of the century to reestablish America as a global force. We long ago lost global economic leadership to China and India and others aren't far behind. I want to raise an option I thought about but didn't raise earlier for fear it would be leaked. Rather than allow those who want to secede from the United States to go, we should use this as our opportunity to redefine our borders. We would do well to expand our natural resource advantages by taking control of much of Canada — whether by force or by convincing them to merge. So if the Southwest states want to go, perhaps the right answer is to let the large parts of this area that are resource-free, high-cost areas go. We'll work out a deal to keep pockets of oil, gas and mining areas, and then go take control of everything in Canada except Quebec. There's no point in taking Quebec because we'll end up with more language issues."

Chinh was born to parents of Chinese Han and Indian Punjabi descent – a third-generation American and avid historian drawn to the concepts of variable national borders. Chinh recognizes that the names of those who expand territory are revered and preserved through history, while those who allow their nations to disintegrate are after-thoughts or non-existent in historical references. Chinh has no intention of being part of shrinking the United States less than 300 years after its founding.

Attorney General Cooke interjects. "I think before we even think about war, which is what you must be advocating since I don't see Canadians taking a bend-and-spread attitude to our invasion, we should take a page from President's Lincoln's playbook. The Constitution expressly allows you, Mr. President, to suspend habeas corpus, quote, when in cases of rebellion or invasion the public safety may require it, unquote. Now, I don't suggest we do this lightly and start arresting people remotely connected without due process. During the Civil War, President Lincoln didn't try doing this until riots and local militia actions were taking place. Even with a Civil War underway, Congress didn't approve suspending habeas corpus until two years into the battle."

The President asks for clarification. "Explain what suspending habeas corpus gets us."

Attorney General Cooke responds, "Well, it buys time. Treason is hard to prove, as H2M doesn't appear to openly advocate war or give aid and comfort to our enemies. I also think we'll struggle to prove anyone is engaged in espionage or even sedition – though I'm sure we could gather enough evidence to at least hold trials. While these people want to secede from the union, they are purposefully and publicly speaking out against acts of violence as part of achieving their aim. So while I'm not sure we can convict, if you suspend habeas corpus, we can remove the rabble rousers from the public and discourage all those behind them."

Homeland Secretary Peyton shakes his head. "Let's not make secession fait accompli by creating martyrs. If we imprison people doing this, especially without a fair and open trial, it will just inspire followers. Our chances of defeating the secessionists will shrink. Even worse, I think we're now in the awkward position of needing to double our efforts to protect their leaders. Failure on this will be taken as evidence the federal government is trying to kill the movement, literally. Watching what I saw today, I'm not so sure some of the leaders don't want a martyr. And there are plenty of hate groups willing to help."

President Phillipi continues to pace the room as he listens to the discussion. "Let's start with what I see as a fairly simple decision. Is there any good reason to pursue an act of war against anyone at this point? I don't see that anything good comes out of it. Any dissenting views?"

Homeland Secretary Peyton wants to be sure to head off Chief of Staff Chinh's idea at the pass. It's easy for a political type to think war is the answer. Peyton had watched too many friends die in Iraq, Afghanistan and the short, but brutal Armenia war. During that war, American forces were among the few to engage as a nuclear Iran invaded and began a genocide campaign in this small Christian country on Iran's border.

"I think its reckless and irresponsible to even consider initiating war, since there really has been nothing to provoke this response. That would just smack of desperation and I'm sure the media – not to mention your opponents – would eat us alive for starting, let me say this again, starting a war as the election gets under way. Even worse, just in case it's not clear, we would be killing our own people. Am I the only one who can't believe this is a discussion topic?" Peyton says.

Secretary Mendoza builds on his point. "Ray and I don't always agree, but even the idea seems cold and more than a bit cynical. Just imagine how it would feel if we were really doing this. That doesn't mean though, that we can't act if one of our enemies starts a war against us. Like I mentioned earlier, you know as well as anyone that the best way to unite a team is to create a common enemy. If we are at war against Iran or another terrorizing miscreant, secessionists will have a hard time arguing we should weaken the union."

"Fair point," the President responds, "but I'm not doing anything to stir up a war that will cost thousands if not millions of lives to address a political crisis – particularly when we haven't even tried to get the issue under control."

Mendoza responds: "Just one point and I'll let it go. If you study history, the critical importance of a common enemy can't be underestimated. Greek city-states fought with and even enslaved each other until the Persians came calling. Romans sustained a common army across cultures only because the fear of barbarian butchery, loss of power and enslavement was worse than Roman rule, even for some slaves. Over 2,000 years, whenever the Mongols or others weren't invading China, the Manchus, Zhuangs and others would go after the Hans or the Hans would fight among themselves and break up dynasties. Sometimes I think the only way to get the world to work together is a global calamity or a space invasion."

"Can we please be sure to not leak space invasion preparation launched to the media," the President says, making physical quote marks with his fingers around "space invasion preparation launched."

After a quick laugh, breaking what has become an increasingly tense discussion, Chief of Staff Vijay Chinh tries to draw attention back to his primary issue. "I'd like to remind you, Mr. President, that we have only a few weeks left before the first primary and while you have a plurality in the opening polls, the daily money track the others are recording isn't too much less than what's being donated to you. You need to be in campaign mode as much as possible for the next 80 days to get a chance to be the person who decides how this issue is resolved."

President Phillipi asks, "I hate to even ask this, but what do media polls tell us so far on this?"

Chinh faces the full group. "Keep in mind that we only have simple responses at this point, not the kind of what-if questioning you suggested earlier. Not surprisingly, few have hard and fast views at this point. Right now, 30 percent of the people want us to hang everyone involved in the secession effort and suspend state government in any state that even takes a vote on the initiative. Thirty percent say the majority in each state should rule and if a state wants to leave the U.S., we need to let it go. Part of this latter group says going to some of these states is like going to a foreign country anyway. Almost 10 percent want the borders kept as they are largely so their state is not on a new border. The rest really don't even know what they are being asked. In other words, no clear mandate."

The President pulls his desk chair over toward the team and sits down on its edge facing them.

"As usual, polling gives us a superficial view at best," the President says. Still circling the room, now with coffee in hand, he walks over and sits on the edge of his desk.

"So here's what I'm thinking," the President says. "Let's start with what people want from government. They want the chance to live a good, safe life where they can pursue dreams and maybe achieve some of them. They also want to be governed by people who share their values. So, if shared values matter more than a good, safe life, the easy answer is to let the people in each state determine how they will be governed. Isn't this the basis for our nation? Our founders revolted against far-away rulers who no longer shared their interests or values. I could make the case that secessionists are doing the same here, except that D.C. is now the far-away place. I certainly have felt that way countless times myself, even after moving here."

The others look at the President, wondering where he is taking this. Some fear he is leaning toward letting the states go if voters approve the referenda.

"So, if democracy is all about letting people decide who governs them through free and fair elections, the right constitutional direction is to allow the states to decide what country they want to be in."

Defense Secretary Mendoza starts to interject, but is cut off by the President as he continues to bring together the twisting paths of his thoughts.

"On the other hand, allowing the majority to rule could cut off Americans who want the blessings of our Constitution to continue. Would the secession of the states threaten domestic tranquility, something our Constitution obliges me to protect? It certainly could. Would a new government for these states necessarily provide for democracy, free speech, the right to assemble, freedom of religion and all of the other liberties we take for granted. Not necessarily, even if they promise it. And keep in mind that I have taken an oath to preserve and protect the Constitution of the United States of America, which compels me to 'secure the Blessings of Liberty to ourselves . . . and . . . our posterity.' How can I argue that I am upholding the Constitution if I allow the states to secede and no longer be governed by its tenets?"

Pausing, but holding his hand up slightly to let everyone know he wants silence as he continues to think, the President is pacing again around the Oval Office.

"As I think about this and consider my oath, I don't know I can allow this to happen. I think we need to make sure no state secedes," the President says. "Okay, now that I have a point of view, give me reasons why this line of thinking could be wrong."

The room goes silent as everyone considers their perspective.

CHAPTER 30

August 24, 2040
Detroit, Michigan

Phoenix Mining Special Projects Vice President Max Herta is back with his team to replace Rich Dore and his shift for the evening. Rich's men still out-produce the night shift by 25 percent. Though Rich occasionally tells Herta that his men deserve raises, he knows they're already well paid by industry standards.

Each night, supposedly empty salt containers return to the mine in early evening for reload. Some of Herta's men open the back wall of the mine's recreation area, then empty drug cargo from beneath the faux bottoms of these containers onto conveyors through the deep tunnel shaft.

Tonight, the conveyor runs initially in reverse. Boxes of weapons reach the salt mine, and replace drug stashes at the bottom of eight salt containers. Each of these is covered with a tarp and buried under salt to hide the real cargo from casual or satellite visibility. With weapons delivery finished three hours into the shift, Herta's men turn to loading cocaine, heroin, meth and other drugs onto the conveyor to supply Cesar Castillo's Canada operations. In addition to the weapon-laden containers, real salt-loaded containers also leave the mine by truck.

Though equipped with Ramon's logistics system, the weight and size of the salt container trucks adds risk to normal travel on side streets. The slow speed of the trucks also limits escape options should police search for them. Many of Castillo's drug distribution drivers grew lazy over the years about masking their contraband – confident they could escape any police trap. But the Herta team members who drive these salt trucks are also part of Castillo's Protection Corps. They clearly understand the limits of their evasion capabilities if discovered. They are careful to ensure that even a trained eye will spot nothing worth investigating.

Herta wonders what the weapons are for, but has learned over decades that Castillo does not always welcome curiosity. The adage that curiosity killed the cat is particularly relevant in Castillo's world except that, to Castillo, anyone with an open mouth is a lower life form than a pet.

As 4 a.m. approaches – Herta's team works hours longer than the traditional shift many nights – they have enough time to re-set the walls, sweep out any signs that point to unusual traffic and make sure nothing smells of anything other than salt before anyone from Rich's day shift comes on site.

Normal mines work three shifts a day, seven days a week to optimize returns. Herta knows a three-shift operation would put out more salt, but it would interfere with the real reason for this mine. Drugs have been flowing north unimpeded for some time now. Perhaps Castillo was working on margin gains by getting into weapons distribution. If so, Herta needs to think about the added risk of military action against the site, and how he might hide or escape.

Fortunately, the conveyor system is too small to transport tanks or missile systems. At least that makes it possible to disguise arms going out as easily as it is to disguise narcotics coming in.

Though Herta worked for Castillo through his entire adult working career, he still trembles around the man. Castillo requires Herta and everyone on his team to wear tracking devices everywhere. In addition, he also must have a child or spouse wearing a tracking device and living under Castillo's control. Someone Herta loves must always be moments away from Castillo's reach.

Castillo maintains the right to disqualify particular family members if he doesn't think his employee cares enough. After Herta joked one too many times about his expanding second wife "confusing sugar daddy's desire for candy with interest in being married to a candy factory," Castillo's security team forced Herta to move a daughter and grandchild into his hometown, not trusting that Castillo's life would be shattered if he lost his second wife without paying a settlement.

***

Washington, D.C.

Late in the evening, the President's chief advisors continue to debate. Defense Secretary Xavier Mendoza puts the secession issue into a different context: "We need to treat this the way I would treat my daughter if she tried to run away. By the time a kid is ready to run, emotions often overtake logic. She's desperate. If you try to simply block the door on the way out, she'll get violent or find another door. It doesn't matter that you can see the rape, violence and poverty she's likely to encounter. She can't stand where she is today and we need to help her figure out how to alleviate that pain, or help her to understand how she will be used without a safe home. That's our job here."

The President sees a bit of parallel here, so encourages Mendoza to continue.

"What do you do when you face a runaway child?" Mendoza continues. "You chase after her and try talking her into staying and working through problems at home. You want to just grab her and drag her home, but that physical restraint may be exactly what she's trying to escape. So you need to figure out how to get her to sit down and open up."

President Phillipi looks at Mendoza. "I like the analogy of dealing with a spoiled child trying to run away. Let's use that to think through this problem."

Mendoza feels the need to interject, "I didn't say the kid was necessarily spoiled. I just said they couldn't stand living in that home anymore. There's lot of reasons kids get to that point."

"Duly noted," President Phillipi says, "and perhaps something to consider."

Homeland Secretary Peyton comments, "Before we get into how to deal with the child, I think we have to understand how a child gets to be so entitled that they won't sacrifice their desires for the good of the family.

They get there because we don't impose discipline on them. We don't make the child be part of the family. We don't require them to sit down and talk during family meals. Do chores. Contribute to the community. Most of all, we don't make them engage in healthy conversation, where they listen and think about what they say before saying it. That's how we got in this problem in the first place. We had a large group of people come here and we not only didn't make them join the family, we may not have even invited them indoors. We let them stay off to the side, talking to each other. It's like adopting a 12-year-old who speaks only Russian and never teaching him English. How can you possibly have an effective family if you don't even know how to speak to each other?"

"I understand your point Ray, but we're dealing with the 16-year-old here who has already decided he doesn't want to be part of this family. So the question is what to do now?" the President says.

"I'm not sure that's the case," Attorney General Cooke says. "As the mother of a 16-year-old, I think what we have here is the moody teenager telling us what she thinks she wants to do and looking to see how we react. She may be bargaining to spend the weekend at a friend's house and hinting she'll run away so we are relieved she's only going away for a weekend. She may also be crying out for stronger parental control and structure. She may be enamored with independence, but scared to death of the consequences of what that means. Maybe she knows just enough that this can be a sick world where young girls have their world destroyed by disgusting old men."

"Why are you looking at me when you talk about disgusting old men?" the President asks, cracking a modest smile to let Becky know he is not really offended.

"We'll, just for clarity, I am looking at you because you're the President and this is ultimately your decision. But if you want me to look at Vijay or Ray when I talk about disgusting old men, I'll be happy to do it," Attorney General Cooke says, with Chinh and Secretary Peyton feigning indignation. "No, my point is this, and maybe Ray was alluding to this. I think the people feel isolated. For a while it seemed like isolation is what Mexican immigrants, particularly illegal immigrants, wanted."

Mendoza adds to the thought, "Staying separated is easy when people first come to this country. It's easy to speak Spanish, follow Primera teams and gather at quinceanara parties. For new immigrants, that makes it feel like home. It fits our mental frame of what life should be like. Comfortable. Familiar. My family respects the Mexican part of my heritage, but isn't bound by it. And I think that is true of a lot of Mexican heritage fa . . . ."

Cooke cuts him off before he finishes. "That's more true in some parts of the U.S. than others. It's been much easier in the Southwest for Mexican communities to stay completely isolated from the rest of America. Same goes for Cubans in south Florida. For a people to really integrate, they need to be part of the broader community. I wouldn't move to Mexico and not learn Spanish, so I don't know why it makes sense to allow immigrants here to not need to become fully functional members of the broader country – not just a local community – at least over time."

"So, what do you think we should do about it," President Phillipi says.

"I think that rather than agree to let them go, we should pursue requirements that make these people be part of the family – force them to take part," Cooke says. "And doing that means we need both sugar and straps."

"You mean carrots and sticks?" Peyton asks.

"Call it what you want, but I use my term because I don't like carrots and straps run in my family history."

"Lawyers always have to create their own language," Mendoza says.

"Can we skip the lawyer jokes? Please. It's tiresome. The sugar here is we need to provide English training – free – to any citizen or legal immigrant to learn to read, speak and write English. We can set up this training in schools all around the country and not just for Spanish speakers. We can also provide accelerated citizenship courses for illegal immigrants who need to learn the language, learn the Constitution and embrace some aspects of our way of life to become citizens," Cooke says.

"We may want to provide that to a lot of citizens too," Chinh says.

"Whatever," Attorney General Cooke responds.

"And the strap?" President Phillipi asks.

"English-only requirement for all government actions goes in place in three years," Cooke says. "Any non-citizens who don't show basic skills in English and constitutional knowledge and agreement in three years lose their work permits, with real enforcement behind it. And we make it clear that we won't allow states to secede. I can't be part of an administration that destroys America, and I agree with you Mr. Not Old, Not Disgusting President, that your Constitutional obligation requires you to preserve and protect this Union."

The President stands up and pulls his chair back over behind his desk – a move that all the participants recognize as the clear signal the meeting is ending.

"Given the arrogance of some Governors and Mayors, if we decide to let these states go, we'll have 10 others states want to become their own Belgium and dozens of major cities think they should be the next Singapore," President Phillipi says.

"I'm going to give us all 24 hours to think some more, but we'll convene the full cabinet tomorrow at 1 p.m. and address the American people at 9 p.m. We can't allow this issue to develop a bigger life than it already has. I fear the next few months will be some of the most difficult and challenging days we will face in our lives. It's clear to me now what we need to do."

CHAPTER 31

September 2, 2040
Washington, D.C.

With public debate on language and secession issues heating up, Professor Paul Stark and Congresswoman Jill Carlson find themselves routinely appearing together on television, radio and livecast shows. Often, the appearances are virtual, with Professor Stark in Chicago and Jill appearing in either D.C. or Indiana. But at least every other week for the past couple of months, some Sunday morning program asks them to appear together as part of a live debate.

Gradually, the two warm to each other. Professor Stark's visual attraction to Jill was immediate, but a deeper intellectual connection later created interest in wanting to spend time with her. As the weeks pass, they meet for breakfast before or lunch after each news media session. She enjoys the chance to debate and sees political value in being associated with Professor Stark, given his strong credibility with the public. As summer draws near a close, Professor Stark is flying home from another Sunday morning roundtable when he receives a message from Jill.

"BTW. The producer caught me just before we went on air to tell me I had spinach in my teeth from my breakfast wrap. You should have told me!"

Professor Stark is still uncertain how to think about their relationship. Colleagues? Friends? Potential romance? Could she possibly find me attractive, or I am just delusional? As certain as Professor Stark is on issues he studies, he has never had a sense of where he stands with women he finds attractive. His reserve is often taken as aloofness, even arrogance, but it stems from long-held insecurities. Seeing this as an opportunity to test the waters, he messages back.

"I'll let you choose from the following responses," he writes. "1) I thought you had taken up chew, 2) I was so mesmerized by your eyes, I didn't even see it, or 3) I'm pretty oblivious. Please tell me you have teeth?"

He waits for a response for what seems an eternity. Why isn't she responding? Ah crap, I gave away my interest, he thinks. Then, as he starts kicking himself, the response comes.

"DEFINITELY #2."

Okay, well that's better than 1 or 3, he thinks, but how good is it? It's in all caps. Does that mean something?

***

September 3, 2040
Flagstaff, Arizona

Pete settled in the hills east of town a full 36 hours early, ahead of tonight's H2M concert and rally. The first night he dug an area allowing him to remain fully camouflaged through daytime, with his biggest struggle being how to hide the fresh movement of dirt and stay out of human view. Since he does not need much energy while remaining still, he strictly limits his calorie count to save food for the return hike. He struggles to avoid leaving anything in the area that could carry dead skin or hair and become a DNA match risk even years later. "I should have taken photos of myself with a group on this spot ahead of time," he mumbles to empty space. "That way, I'd have an alibi if they find any DNA."

He goes through the shot repeatedly in his head, hoping nothing has changed about timing or stage set-up since his last discussion with JT. Sunset in early September occurs before 7 p.m. His target will likely come on stage at the beginning, too early to get the shot off without being spotted from satellite, if not also by someone on the ground. But the target also should come out at the end for a closing rally, JT told him.

Pete lies still as he has done in stretches for years in his New Rite pod; legs and torso beneath dug out ground, with a camouflage tarp, native plants and fallen trees concealing his head and arms.

In such stillness, he hears the sound and feels the pulse of his heartbeat – 52 times a minute beating, thumping, relentlessly reminding him of his mortality. His breath sounds like wisps of wind through an open window, though the steady hum of too-close highway traffic dulls the sense of calm, as does a nearby game of squirrel tag. Pete dug and covered the hole in a way that allows him to change positions during the day to keep blood flowing and prevent atrophy to his muscles. His equipment is stored inside the hole. His biggest challenge is spreading the dug out dirt to spots hidden enough to not attract attention.

For the first time in years, Pete thinks deeply about his physical family – the people who raised him as a child, but didn't understand his passion for gaming. They wanted him to create a conventional life. If he listened, he wouldn't have the opportunity to save America from the intruders who are trying to destroy it, Pete reasons.

Pete wonders what has happened to old family and friends, and questions under his breath whether they'll ever know he's a hero: "I wonder if they'd be proud of what I'm doing to save them, or would they think this is a waste too. I'm finally making it – making a career out of what I love. And I don't have any drill sergeant riding me like a bull in heat. I have a life where I decide what I do, with awesome weapons to mess with anyone messing with me."

By late afternoon, an end to the latest monotony is in sight for Pete. Teams of laborers set two stages side-by-side and connect large equipment trunks. Pete is reluctant to look too long, not wanting to risk an unusual reflection. It looks like they'll play from alternate stages to keep the show moving. Pete checks his electronic sight to be sure he has a clear shot either way. He's certain he can connect using JT's missile bullet technology, even at this multi-mile distance. Now he considers whether he's better off launching during sunset or at night. At sunset the flash from the missile gun and bullet separation launch could blend into the evening sky and possibly be missed. However, satellites could trace his location. If local police think to check, they may be able to start tracking him too soon after he starts his hike out. At night, the short separation flash will be visible, but satellites won't see where he goes.

Without the tarp in daylight tomorrow, his hole will be easy to spot, particularly since he can't stick around to fill it. Too many searchers are likely to come within view. Until morning though, the hole will look like just another pocket in the landscape, hidden in the density of the forest. By morning light, he'll be far enough away they'll have trouble tracking him and likely assume he escaped in a vehicle.

Governor Jesús Muñoz opens the concert with what must have been a rousing speech based on the cheers. Maybe I should take out this bastard, Pete thinks, but knows to stay focused on his mission. Honor to Mexico Founder Ángel Herrera doesn't appear with Juan Gonzalez and other leaders along his side until nearly 9 p.m. A standing ovation makes clear he is preaching to the converted when he advocates that Arizonans need independence. Pete is now 40 feet up a tree, tied in and ready to take his shot.

Control your heartbeat. Control your breath. Settle in.

Set target. Breathe. Breathe.

The crowd moves hands in the air back-and-forth in wave-like rhythm, looking as unified as a massive gospel choir.

Focus.

Breathe.

Shoot.

The missile adjusts its path ever so slightly as wind bursts threaten to take it off target over this extended path. Travelling at six times the speed of sound, the bullet stays with its electronic mark. Correcting course to stay on target, the missile releases with a short flash just outside the stadium. Less than a second later, Pete knows he has done the job.

Pete hears the screams of the entire stadium as the large screen picture above the crowd shows Ángel's head being shattered. Pete is already dropping down from the tree and doesn't look.

In no time, the crowd stampedes out of the stadium, fearing another massacre like Harvard. In the commotion, the police order the stadium lights fully engaged. This lights the stadium and parking lot, but outside-in lighting makes it difficult for police to search the perimeter.

Pete pulls over nearby fallen branches to cover as much of his sleep hole as possible, puts on his hat and takes off at a rapid pace, making sure to avoid visible exposure to the arena. Thirty minutes later, he has circled under cover of the forest to an area behind the stage, somewhere the shooter could not possibly have been. From there, he makes his escape north.

Police helicopters are in the air with lights scanning the area. Pete moves quickly but keeps his eye on the lights to be sure he is down and camouflaged when they pass near him. As expected, they stay in the vicinity of the arena, looking for evidence of someone who would have shot a conventional bullet.

Forensic experts enter the stadium to do pain-staking work to determine the direction of the bullet. They look at how the body fell, the entry and exit wounds and look at how the shrapnel and skull fragments embedded in the stage. In the dark, they can't see a logical location in range to fire a shot. Spectators tell police they saw a light flash at the back of the arena, and police scour the area looking for any evidence of a shot from that direction. Whether it was a light flash, or the light of a mobile device wasn't clear to them, but they look into every potential option to find the shooter.

News goes out nationally and globally within seconds of the death – with media outlets racing to air video of Ángel's head exploding, a move justified by warning viewers the video would be graphic.

MSDNC airs its immediate reaction.

"For the second time this summer, a key leader of the Honor to Mexico Hispanic Freedom movement has been shot, and this time the murderer succeeded. Ángel Herrera, a man who has dedicated his life to improving the welfare of immigrants, has been assassinated. This latest shooting is clear evidence an organized and sophisticated group has begun a war against advocates of self-determination. Speculation has already begun that the U.S. government is involved in this campaign of terror. MSDNC will fully investigate any potential connections between this shooting and the CIA, the FBI or any of the other shadow agencies in U.S. government," the MSDNC anchor says, though failing to point out that government involvement speculation came from discussions among MSDNC staff.

Police substantially restricted public release of Convention Center shooting details. They hope whoever was involved will slip and make statements only someone involved in the plot would know. Because the secrets were not shared, the general public believes Juan miraculously recovered from a vicious attack. To believers, this made him appear to be God's chosen one to lead his people from the overlords who controlled their lives, just as Moses had done thousands of years earlier.

This messianic view of Juan draws adherents from generations of Mexicans and Mexican Americans, and attracts an audience of believers well outside his traditional ethnic base. The death of his most public advocate has these believers shaken.

***

September 4, 2040

Now clearly heartbroken and fearful after seeing Ángel's head explode and being covered with some its remnants, Juan has not slept. Though still the middle of the night in Flagstaff, it is nearly 6 a.m. Eastern. National media surround the stadium room where Juan and the other speakers are sequestered under tight police protection. Everyone on stage has been initially interviewed as police seek motives for the killing.

Juan agrees to a hastily arranged press conference, with extensive security surrounding him. He works on his remarks while his mother holds him as he alternates between weeping and trying to control a rage few have ever seen.

Fist marks now pocket the wall. Juan's hand is bloodied and aching. He doesn't feel it. His mother, who drove up after work with friends to see the concert and spend time with Juan for the first time in weeks, tries to calm him.

With a media gathering that has swollen to several hundred gathered in front of the other stage, Juan walks, trembling and biting his lip, to the center of the microphone stand.

"In just the few months I have known him, Ángel had become the father figure to me that I missed for so much of my life. But, to the world, he was much more than that. He was a keeper of his people, helping to feed, clothe and house so many. He preserved our culture – teaching us that our religion, our music, and our values are worth saving and living no matter where we choose to live. He believed in our future – seeing an opportunity for all Mexicans to control our own destiny," Juan says, his face bookended by tears streaming down the outside of both eyes, framing his deep pain and anger.

"What frightens me is that some coward – perhaps the same coward who tried to kill me – is so afraid of letting us have our freedom that he would rather kill than allow us to remove the slave-like controls that dominate our lives," he says, anger starting to control his voice. Juan turns from the podium to wipe away tears and compose himself before speaking again. "We can't. . . . I can't let this stop me from pursuing Ángel's vision. Ángel has given us an opportunity, a platform from which to make a difference. Now, I see that God has chosen this day to bring him home. But he has also chosen this day to test our resolve in the pursuit of freedom."

"Those of you listening or watching – in Arizona, in California del Sur, in Texas, in New Mexico, and yes, even those of you in other states who have until now watched with disinterest – I beg you to support what from now on I will refer to as Ángel's law. Ángel is now God's in heaven, watching over us and giving us the guidance and strength we need to succeed. We cannot fall back in fear. The person who killed Ángel cannot see his death as a victory. Instead, I beg each and everyone to make Ángel's death a sacrifice that forms the base of his ultimate victory. Our independence."

Though the gathered media start yelling out questions, it's clear Juan is done speaking.

As he walks away from the podium toward the back of the room, his mother puts her arm around his waist and gently pulls his head to her shoulder. Though the back room is dimly lit, many of the cameras near the exit door capture the scene of the two of them together – mother comforting deeply pained son. That image takes over the national news.

***

Washington, D.C.

Waking early morning to news of Ángel's death, President Phillipi immediately sees the shooting as a terrible tragedy.

"The timing could not be worse," he says to Chief of Staff Chinh, as the two finish watching Juan's press conference. "I want a statement out immediately expressing deep outrage and anger at the shooting and promising any federal resources necessary to bring the guilty to justice quickly and immediately. I want this out in 10 minutes before the media twists this into a national confrontation. Cancel the cabinet meeting. We'll revamp my speech tonight to something other than our anti-secession agenda. This is an awful time to make policy statements, right in the middle of such emotional human tragedy. I'm calling Ray, Betty, Xavier and the others to tell them to keep their mouths shut. And we better get the National Guard ready to react to riots."

***

Detroit, Michigan

Limos pull up to the Detroit Salt Mine less than 18 hours after Ángel's assassination to whisk the full night team away for a week's vacation. Though not up to the production standards of Rich and his men, the second shift had been closing the gap.

Herta is one of the leading mine experts in the country, but salt mining is different than the hard-rock and deep tunnel mining that had been Herta's primary experience.

"Rich, I need your team to work 1-1/2 shifts a day for us this week so I can give my men and their families some time off without falling short on orders we've already sold. We already called your homes to let them know you'll be four hours late. I know you'll understand," Herta says.

"Hey, we're all part of a team here. I can't imagine the sacrifice you guys make so I'm sure the guys will be happy to stay and earn a little extra," Rich responds.

"We may be reassigned internationally after the week, but we should have at least a couple of guys back next week. Regardless, go back to normal single shift hours when the first guys from the second shift return," Herta adds. "We've cut back sales commitments until we can get a full second shift back here."

CHAPTER 32

September 6, 2040
Seven Cities

Morning rush hours in major U.S. metropolitan areas move at their usual steady pace. Satellite-run navigation systems in One Shot, Size Right and other similar vehicles help commuters reach work at consistent times, and allow drivers – they still call themselves drivers – to fully concentrate on activities other than driving. Most relax; eating breakfast and watching news videos, making personal connections, finishing dressing and doing all the other activities that used to lead to multiple car pile-ups. Long-haul versions of the vehicles come with urination tubes and fully reclined seats that allow the riders to only stop to refuel or for an extended restroom break. The navigation systems pull drivers into extreme proximity of each other to maximize wind-drafting – further reducing fuel consumption.

Further progress in speeding commutes was made after Congress passed President Phillipi's tax incentives for people in smog-restricted metropolitan areas to move closer to work. If new homes meet commute-reduction requirements, all taxes associated with the move are waived and banks must transfer previous loan terms at the homeowner's request to the new mortgage up to the outstanding amount of the prior loan. Eligibility is based on extensive data collected by Ramon's logistics systems.

As has been the case for days, millions more pay attention to the news than usual. Video of Ángel's head being shredded still causes a gagging reflex for many. The realistic nature of the three dimensional video allows the few who can stand the sight to rewind, zoom in and see the bullet entry in slow motion. One of those doing this is D.C. Police Sgt. Rey Moore – who immediately looks for similarities to Juan's shooting, suspecting the two are linked.

"No antidote exists for this shot," Moore says to his detective. "Somebody thinks the first message was ignored, and is stepping up the intensity of the fight." In cities with large Mexican American communities, anti-government rioting and protests started just hours after the shooting. Students continue to throw rocks through school windows. Looting in Hispanic neighborhoods targets stores run by whites, blacks, Asians and Arabs. The worst riots continue in Chicago, Denver, Kansas City, Seattle and in small minority white and black neighborhoods in Dallas, Houston, Austin, Phoenix and Los Angeles. News coverage of these riots is interrupted.

CNN Anchor Brody Maguire is first on air with the story.

"Two minutes ago, at 9:30 a.m. Eastern time, bomb explosions along major roads in at least seven major cities – Washington, New York, Chicago, Denver, Cleveland, Seattle and San Francisco – left extensive wreckage and killed countless Americans on their way to work. No one has claimed responsibility, but we believe there may be a link between the assassination two nights ago of Honor to Mexico Founder Ángel Herrera and the bombings this morning. Our recent contacts with government officials suggest several white supremacist groups have mobilized in recent weeks and may be involved in these attacks."

Forensic experts sent to the explosion sites begin meticulously GPS-tagging the location of the vehicles and body parts, and video scanning the explosion holes in each road for computer analysis.

Scans of the 14 bomb locations – each city was hit in two major road arteries – show remarkable similarities in the size and shape of the bomb holes, as well as the number of vehicles destroyed and lives lost. The bombs all hit the single commuter lanes dominated by One Shots, where vehicles travel front to back within inches of each other, and side-by-side within inches of another narrow vehicle in the same travel lane.

Mandated use of these short, narrow vehicles, aided by sophisticated navigation systems, allowed metropolitan areas to absorb continuous population growth while minimizing the need to take land for new road construction. They also made the killing impact of today's bombs that much greater.

The FBI downloads morning satellite feeds of each city, focusing on each bombsite. Searching recordings back to first light, investigators find no evidence that any bombs were embedded in the road as they look in the gaps between chains of vehicles. Over the next several hours, teams of agents work backward from the explosions in minute-by-minute reviews, trying to determine who dropped the bombs and when. At that hour, chains of vehicles were fairly long, reaching as many as hundreds of vehicles all travelling within inches of each other, their computer systems and sensors continuously communicating to avoid rear-end collisions and enabling vehicles to close gaps as others ahead of them exit or enter a highway.

Within 30 minutes, investigators identify the chains of vehicles between which no bomb is spotted on the road and when the bombs exploded. The chains are as small as 70 vehicles at some locations and as many as 500 vehicles at other sites – all travelling in tight trains.

Homeland Security Secretary Peyton calls President Phillipi immediately with the FBI's findings. "These bombs were not installed on the roads," he says to the President. "These are suicide bombers."

"What do you know about the link between these bombings and the murder of Ángel Herrera? Do we have an orchestrated attack underway?" the President asks.

"We don't actually know anything about a link. But the timing leads us to believe there's a link," Peyton says, drawing out the word "know" to make clear that the agency is a long way from anything more than speculation.

"People are frightened. We're under some sort of attack, but we don't know who's doing it. I don't need to tell you but I'll say it anyway; there is nothing more urgent than finding these terrorists and bringing them to justice. Now tell me how we know these are suicide bombers," President Phillipi says.

"We've used satellite imagery of bomb location, running backwards to see when bombs might have been planted. Reviewing this, we see no evidence roadways were disturbed in any way. There were no unusual objects sitting on the roads that could have been bombs. So that narrows us down to two options. One, the bombs were planted on 14 roads when those roads were last built and set to go off at exactly the same time, something we believe highly unlikely as some of those roads were last fixed years ago. Or two, one of the cars in each travel chain was rigged with a bomb in or under the vehicle. The depth of the pits in the road suggest aboveground detonation if our computer models are right," Peyton says.

"Next question, did all of the bombs detonate at exactly the same time? How close were they to each other?"

"Exactly at 9:30 a.m. EDT, Mr. President. No deviation, not even for a second," Peyton responds.

"What does that tell you?" the President continues.

"It tells me this group was extremely well coordinated, highly sophisticated and wants to make sure we know it," Peyton says.

"I'll agree with that, but does it necessarily mean these were suicide bombers, or people picked out from the population based on consistency of their travel times and routes?" President Phillipi asks. "Or . . . did someone figure out how to send these cars all out on their own?"

"I see where you're going, Mr. President. We haven't identified which cars had the bombs. We're contacting the head of the logistics company that provides the backbone intellect in these cars to get records of all vehicles and locations within 250 yards after each bomb and up to one-half mile ahead of each bomb. We'll use that to test for any common associations and will assign FBI and local police to speak to anyone we can find. The Justice Department is already pursuing a subpoena allowing us to track the travel history over the past year of anyone killed by the bombs, as we suspect we'll find a connection point that helps us identify the mastermind."

Peyton pauses, with time passing on the phone as he waits for the President's response.

"Good thoughts, but can we also make sure these cars were all occupied by live humans," the President requests. "It's possible an enemy with access to decent technology could send these vehicles to specific locations without needing to convince 14 people to get in. I think it's far more likely we're dealing with a sophisticated computer mastermind than 14 brainless lackeys on express rides to eternity."

As Peyton returns to the FBI operations room, he asks to see the 14 explosions displayed in simulcast against the large wall display screen. After a few minutes of manipulating the display configuration, the 14 bombs display on the wall. "Let's start at 1 minute before the explosions and track until everything is completely stopped around the bombs. Let's go through first at $1/20^{th}$ speed. Everyone pick a couple to compare across and look for commonalities," Peyton says.

Exactly 20 minutes later, the first bomb explosion visibility starts. "Hold it right there. Take it back to exactly 9:30 EDT and 0 seconds."

Sure enough, the first visual clues appear as flashes out the sides and backs of vehicles. One minute later, or three seconds into the explosions, the massive extent of the damage is visible, but Peyton notices something.

"Move back to exactly 9:30. Let's go in $1/10^{th}$ of second increments and I will tell you when to move. I want to show all 14 at the same time," Peyton states. "Go."

Less than a minute later, Peyton tells the display controller to stop.

"There's something critical here," he says. "Who can tell me what it is?" An agent in the room spots it as well. "You can see the explosion flash to the side of each car, with the width of that flash almost precise. However, the front and back views across the explosions aren't the same. That either means bombs were placed at different points in the cars or were on the roads. And in some cases, the intensity of the flash between cars is much greater."

"Let's go back and frame by frame look to the ground between the vehicles prior to the explosion and see what we can find," Peyton says. "Simultaneously."

Careful study enables the team to identify the exact time at which several bombs first showed up between cars. While difficult to see with the naked eye, given bomb coloring that matches the pavement surfaces, slight glints of sun reflection on the north-south roads in several cities provided enough clues that bombs had been dropped. After studying, the team estimated the bombs were slid out the bottom of vehicles about 12 seconds before explosion – just enough time for the drivers of these vehicles to escape the perimeter of the bomb.

"The bomb perimeters are about 100 meters, so the vehicles dropping would be outside the perimeter as long as they went 20 miles per hour. I want all the vehicles in front of each explosion checked for any evidence of a floor opening and any residue from a bomb. These aren't suicide bombings at all. This was a carefully orchestrated terrorist attack and the attackers are likely out there. I want no work to wait for resources. No one does more than takes an overnight nap and drink water until we get this settled," Peyton says. "And let's get every security camera from anywhere near a highway to see what visuals we can pull of driver faces and license plates."

An agent estimates velocity on each of the 14 highways and finds two were travelling at less than 20 miles per hour at 9:29:48. "The Golden Gate bridge bomb and the I-290 bomb in Chicago might be our best shots," the agent yells out. "Travel speeds were lower than usual with heavy rain causing flooded streets in Chicago and a suicidal pedestrian jumping into the Golden Gate traffic just seconds ahead of the bomb, causing a rapid deceleration there. The cars of the bombers were likely caught in the mix."

As additional bomb forensic expert teams are dispatched to these two sites, the headquarters team carefully replays satellite of the Golden Gate explosion and watches the aftermath. Having identified cars that likely dropped the bombs, the team watches as dozens of cars explode, sending bodies and car parts scattering and extending the range of the explosion damage out hundreds of meters. Cars they suspect as involved brake to a stop as immediately dictated by on-board computers. Once everyone is stopped, some people get out and walk toward the bomb blast to see if there's anyone to help. Two drivers who appeared to have mild wounds neither ran away nor went to help. On the Golden Gate Bridge, they zoom in and watch a man from a potential bomb drop car do something unusual – walk past the bomb blast and back toward the direction from which he had come.

Perhaps he's running home, investigators consider. But when the man makes it to the entry of the bridge, he heads off the highway and is next located by satellite history running on Conzelman Road toward the Golden Gate Recreation Area. "By now, he can be as far as Muir Woods," Secretary Peyton says. "We'll certainly lose any aerial view with the trees there. Get a description of our runner out to police and have them pick up anyone who looks like him in the area. Find him on satellite, follow him and get the police to him. I'm heading back to the White House."

CHAPTER 33

September 6, 2040
Washington, D.C.

As Homeland Secretary Peyton walks into the Oval Office for the second time today, President Phillipi finalizes a national address. "You're writing this yourself?" Peyton asks as he sees the President putting pen to paper.

"When I write, I think more clearly about what I'm saying. Besides, this is likely one of the most important speeches I'll ever make," Phillipi says. "What else have we learned?"

"Mr. President, this appears to be a coordinated, sophisticated military operation against the United States. Our early thoughts that these are suicide bombers may be wrong. The bombs were dropped out the bottom of the cars and all but two of the bombers were outside the explosion zone when the bombs went off. We're looking for every bit of video we can find to identify them, but don't have anything concrete for 12 of the bombers yet."

"What about the other two? Dead?" Phillipi asks.

"No, very much alive. We're chasing one suspect near San Francisco as we speak and have the perimeter of where we believe him to be locked down with 1,000 officers in pursuit and helicopters surrounding the perimeter in case he gets past them. We should have him in one hour or less. The other suspect we're tracking in Chicago disappeared into a crowd gathered around a bombsite. We lost him under a series of trees, and are tracking 30 people who came out from that area. He took off the hat and shirt he was wearing during the explosion while under the tree so we are scanning body types and trying to narrow down where we chase. We're also doing DNA analysis on those clothes. My fear is he made it to someone's garage or underground parking and disappeared from there."

"What else do we know?" the President asks.

"Mr. President," Peyton says as the President puts his head down, knowing that Peyton calls him Mr. President when they are alone only when he is delivering truly bad news. "If the video we gathered from the bridge is right, the Golden Gate bomber appears to be Hispanic. From the way he looks and moves, it would not surprise me if he is military."

"Are you saying it's one of our guys or are you saying another country did this?" the President says with raised voice and raised eyebrows.

"Neither, Mr. President. I'm saying we're searching for a Hispanic male running at a just over four-minute mile pace away from the Golden Gate bomb wreckage. "More than 1,000 people know that is who we're looking for, and given the Herrera shooting, the chances that this won't be all over the media are slim and none. I just want you to know so you know what speculation will start. And, of course, we can't rule out Mexican military involvement or a few other countries."

Phillipi pushes the call button on his desk for his Chief of Staff. "Ray, stay here. Vijay, I need you here now. I need to talk to President Suarez. If I find out Mexico had anything to do with these attacks, our response will be swift and severe."

Twenty minutes later, President Suarez is on the phone. A Yale-educated lawyer, Suarez is known for winning most verbal battles by choosing his words carefully, a skill that served him well in bringing relative peace to the northern regions of Mexico that now operate under Castillo's police control. With violence under its best control in generations, Suarez is riding a wave of public enthusiasm.

"President Suarez. As you know, the United States was attacked today by ruthless killers who exploded bombs on 14 of our busiest highways. These explosions have killed hundreds of Americans," Phillipi starts.

"Yes, President Phillipi, I've been following this news with great sadness. I hope you received my condolences and offer of support. This is a terrible tragedy, and coming so soon after the assassination of Ángel Herrera, I am truly concerned for you in this terrible time," Suarez says.

"I appreciate your condolences. Let me get straight to the point. There were 14 bombers in cars who set off these bombs in what appears to be an attack so coordinated and sophisticated that it appears to be achievable only under the direction of a sophisticated military. And we know it's not ours," Phillipi says.

"What? Are you? Are you saying? Are you accusing Mexico of being involved? That's absurd . . . and dangerous," Suarez says, clearly angered by what he is hearing.

"No. No. No. I'm making no such accusation. But I'm telling you we've identified the vehicles of all 14 bombers and are tracking two drivers of these bomb cars already. I expect us to have them in custody soon. If there's something you can help us learn about these men, it would be better for everyone if we cleared up any misunderstanding right now," Phillipi says.

"You're clearly under a great deal of stress Mr. President because you are spouting foolishness. There's no way the Mexican government would have anything to do with attacking the United States, particularly not when your own people are telling you that they want to leave your United States for our Estados Unidos anyway. So, Mr. President, let me ask you this. A cynic might question if the United States is willing to bomb its own citizens to create a pretense under which to attack Mexico. And the tone of your question gives me grave concern," Suarez says loudly. "I think you better get a good night's sleep before we speak again. In the meantime, I'll assume you've momentarily lost your mind."

"President Suarez, I'm threatening nothing. But we must investigate every possible explanation. I'm simply asking for cooperation should you find any news of interest as you have discussions across a broad network in your country," Phillipi says, trying his best not to respond to Suarez with the same level of anger he hears in Suarez's voice.

"Then perhaps you should look in your own backyard. If you don't know who your terror threats are at home, we'll be happy to join at your invitation in helping you figure out how to keep peace in your country," Suarez responds.

"Look, from our initial surveillance review, it looks like the perpetrators are Hispanic and the level of detailed planning that had to go into pulling this off suggests a highly sophisticated government was involved," Phillipi says, giving away more information than he intended.

"So you are accusing Mexico of attacking you. I remind you, Marc, that you have just described millions of citizens of your country so before you accuse Mexico of anything, I suggest you gather your facts. You may also want to refresh your memory of history, when your Arab enemies tried repeatedly to appear Mexican to infiltrate your country," Suarez says as he hangs up the phone.

Immediately after hanging up, both Presidents raise the military alert levels of their troops. Suarez calls the United Nations General Secretary to plead his case for U.N. troop protection.

"I probably should have thought about what I was going to accomplish before I made that call," President Phillipi says to Chief of Staff Chinh. "I didn't hear anything suggesting he is involved, but there are enough layers that act independently that it doesn't mean someone high up in Mexico isn't in the loop. We'll learn more as soon as we track down the people involved."

He paces the Oval Office and waves his hand to let Chinh know he wants him to stay.

"We need to start defusing animosity right away. If Peyton is right, then most of America will believe Mexicans or Mexican Americans have started a war against the United States. On the other side, Mexican Americans here probably believe the U.S. government or a racist group has just assassinated one of their most revered leaders. The coincidence of the timing is almost too much to believe these actions weren't either timed together, or the bombing wasn't an immediate response to the assassination," President Phillipi says.

He blows out a rapid-fire of short air breaths before continuing.

"I watched a bit of Professor Stark and the kid speaking on TV together. They seemed to get along well, even while totally disagreeing. The kid is now the de-facto leader for H2M. Professor Stark is well respected politically and has established his credentials as believing the country needs to stay united. Can we get them both here and let the media know we're pulling together an emergency summit? Who else do we need to include? I want to keep it small enough to be productive, but inclusive enough that most people will feel a connection to someone who's here. "

***

Detroit, Michigan

Rich and his team heard nothing about the explosions while in the mine for their third extended day. Rich was focused on mining in five extra hours what it normally took the second shift eight hours to do. On the ride home, his internally competitive focus was interrupted by the disturbing news of the bombs.

"Fourteen massive explosions at highways around the country killed hundreds of Americans today. An extensive manhunt is underway for a group of young males in excellent physical shape who were driving vehicles that dropped these bombs. San Francisco police have released this tape of a suspected bomber running away from the Golden Gate Bridge bombing. He is believed to be Hispanic based on eyewitness and video accounts, and appears to have been hit by shrapnel. The man was last seen running into a heavily wooded area north of San Francisco."

Hearing this, Rich told the program to capture the past five minutes, and then replayed the video, freezing the view on the subject. A foggy mist minimized the quality of the video, but police enhanced the video using data from the multiple frames in which the bomber was captured on various bridge cameras and individual mobile videos. It was difficult to see the face fully, with a Giants baseball cap, trim beard and mustache making identification tough.

As Rich hears more about the attack – carefully coordinated, all 14 drivers wearing baseball caps, bombs released and set off at identical times in seven cities – he wonders if his suspicions about Herta and his men are valid. If they are, he knows he and his family will not survive if he is caught pointing police in their direction. He also knows he can't keep concerns to himself and sleep well.

After arriving home, Rich reheats dinner.

"Hey, I'm going to the park to exercise. My back is starting to get to me and I need to get in better shape," he tells his wife.

"Glad to see you finally recognize how much you're neglecting your health," she responds. "You're not exactly young and agile anymore. But be careful."

With long summer daylight hours, Rich knows he still has a few minutes before dark sets in. The basketball courts are full and games sometimes are heated. Wearing sunglasses, a hooded sweatshirt and looking down as he approaches, he walks several miles past the courts to a pharmacy and buys a prepaid mobile phone. Rich places a call to the Detroit FBI office.

"This is the FBI. Choose your language," the recorder says, before going into a long list of languages to select from. After selecting English, Rich goes through the next list.

"Please say one if calling to report a crime, say two if calling to provide anonymous crime tips, say three. ... ."

Rich figures that even if he doesn't leave his name and number, he can still be traced. The phone number isn't his, but he presumes the FBI has a way of finding which phone numbers are sold by which retailer, and then methods to track down whoever bought it. He paid in cash and tried to hide his face, but will that be enough?

Not sure whether to leave a message or speak to a person, he hangs up the phone. When he returns home, he places the phone inside the built-in safe in his basement wall.

As Rich settles back at home at nearly 9 p.m., he grabs a beer and sits in the recliner that had been worn enough to be tossed to the street if his wife had her way. But like the 30-year-old jeans and 25-year-old steel-toed boots he wore most days, the recliner was finally molded to his body.

Several channels he flips past alert viewers that President Phillipi will speak to the nation in three minutes.

***

Washington, D.C.

"My fellow Americans, we stand today at a crossroads in our nation's history," the President begins his televised address. "This is a time that will define our generation for millennia. In the past three days, we've endured two terrible tragedies. Ángel Herrera, best known for leading a social justice movement for Mexican Americans but also initiator of a recent secession effort, was gunned down. This morning, highway bombings in seven of our cities killed hundreds of Americans and injured hundreds more. This is the deadliest attack on American soil in nearly a decade – an action we will treat as an act of war. I have issued a presidential order that all those involved in the bombing, whether foreign or domestic, be treated as enemy combatants unless we find clear evidence that no foreign government was involved. We do not yet know if the bombings have any relation to the Herrera assassination."

"In both events, the attacks were carried out with sophistication not likely and perhaps not even possible without foreign government involvement. FBI forensic experts tell me the bullet that killed Ángel was propelled by a highly sophisticated guided missile system. It takes military-grade technology to develop such a weapon, and particularly to do so without our knowledge. I've been told that many in the Mexican American community suspect U.S. government involvement in Ángel Herrera's death. I can personally assure you, and have been assured by the members of my cabinet and the Joint Chiefs of Staff, that not only did we not do this, but we would not do this, and do not today have a weapon like the one used in the killing. Just this afternoon, we identified the location from which we believe the missile bullet was launched. We are now doing everything we can to track the killer.

"The bombings this morning used equally sophisticated technology, and precise military coordination. Fourteen bombs were dropped from vehicles on busy highways in seven cities at exactly 12 seconds before 9:30 a.m. eastern time, a time that clearly was chosen to maximize carnage. The bombs exploded exactly at 9:30 a.m. eastern, neither one second earlier nor one second later. The level of precision needed to carry off this concerted effort, along with the ability to have 14 men operate these vehicles without any leak, suggests a highly trained military unit of enormous capability and sophistication.

"Because of this, we are investigating the possibility that foreign governments carried out both killings in an effort to create instability, weaken the U.S. role in world politics or hurt us economically. Should this be the case, we will take all appropriate actions to punish those involved. In the

meantime, I ask any Americans who have clues or even suspicions to contact the FBI with that information. We have assigned massive teams to
investigate these crimes, and have put our National Guard and active duty
military on full alert."

"You'll hear a great deal of speculation about the ethnicity of those
involved in these terrorist activities; speculation that I believe is reckless,
heightens racial tensions and may cause us to overlook the true criminals.
I urge you to recognize that any such speculation is just that at this time,"
the President says, voice cracking slightly with emotion but consciously
remaining strong to calm citizen nerves. "The United States is the leader
of freedom in the world and freedom sometimes comes at a heavy price.
Hundreds of Americans paid that price today. We will honor their sacrifice."

"Tomorrow, we are gathering a summit of those representing various
viewpoints in the United States, including our friends at Honor to Mexico
who have been so aggrieved at the loss of their leader. Face-to-face, we'll
work to determine our path forward with full attention to the best interests
of our people and the peaceful resolution of differences. Please join me in
praying for the families of those killed in recent days, and in dedicating
yourself to preserving our freedom. Please also be extremely vigilant. We
have no way of knowing whether more attacks are planned."

As he concludes, the President stands up and the camera follows him
into a room where he is shown meeting with his national security team.
The feed concludes as the President reaches the table around which the
team is gathered.

Chief of Staff Chinh is also in the room and talks to the President before
the hastily arranged meeting begins.

"We can either become a country united or a country divided," the
President tells Chinh. "If every American focuses on the very real possibility that outside forces may be trying to destroy our country, these incidents
could spur unification. A common enemy helps make a nation strong."

"But we don't know for certain whether these are outsiders, or disgruntled Americans, do we?" Chinh asks.

"We don't know much, but I do know any agitation to destroy America
is very likely the work of outsiders, even if it turns out that Americans carried out the directions," the President says. "Besides, we have no military

or police branch that has identified this new weapon or that can come up with likely suspects given the sophistication of the bombing attack. No U.S. satellites were used by anyone in Flagstaff or with the 14 bombs. This sounds like a foreign government has developed new weaponry and wants to show us their superiority on our turf."

"I see where you're headed," Chinh responds. "Tomorrow's summit will start at 10 a.m. We flew Air Force Two to pick up Juan Gonzalez and the H2M leadership team to help assure their safety. Given the assassination, they are wisely scared to be in a public setting right now, so we'll provide military escort for Juan to the White House from Andrews."

"Who else will be here?" President Phillipi asks.

"Professor Stark and Juan Gonzalez are joining as you requested. The Chamber is sending Chet Leach from FirstWal – you met him at several events in Chicago over the years and he's the guy FirstWal says created the English-only policy that sparked the Arizona language controversy. We've also invited Congresswoman Jill Carlson to represent congressional conservatives and Senator Manny Jones to represent congressional liberals. Larry Wallace is joining from the AFL-CIO. The last member of the group, if you agree, will be Secretary Mendoza. He has credibility with the military, the FBI and several Hispanic activist groups."

President Phillipi cups his arms behind his head and exhales audibly: "You don't think the others will see Mendoza as an effort to stack the group?"

"None of the participants are worried though you can be sure MSDNC will reach that conclusion. As long as you don't care about fringe media, I think we're fine," Chinh says. "But you will need to intervene to make sure people listen. There are a lot of talkers and advocators in the group."

CHAPTER 34

September 7, 2040
Washington, D.C.

The next morning's weather is unusually beautiful for a summer day in Washington, D.C. With temperatures in the low 80s and unusually light humidity for this former swampland, the President decides to move the day's discussion to the veranda overlooking the South Lawn. Chinh orders audio absorption screens around the discussion area. The area is set up in comfortable family room style, with side tables for beverages and snacks. Cameras can pick up visuals of the discussion, but audio is protected from pick-up by even long-range microphones.

Greeting each of the participants, President Phillipi works to ensure a personal rapport with those he is meeting for only a first or second time.

News media release video of the President and Secretary Mendoza shaking Juan's hands and appearing to express condolences at the death of Ángel. Jill is shown giving Juan an extended condolence hug, with the two whispering in each other's ears. First Wal's Chet had not previously met most of the participants. He and Juan engage in a formal handshake, but don't carry on much as the group gathers purposely within camera view to show that not only are they talking, but also they are doing so outdoors. Professor Stark is second to last to arrive, having flown commercially and been caught in two mechanical delays. Texas Senator Manny Jones whisks in just two minutes ahead of the formal start time, and 28 minutes after he was asked to arrive.

"The President has not stated his expected outcome from this Presidential Summit," CNN's news anchor says, "but several items are clear. The group wants to show it's not afraid to be outdoors, even with new technology with a multi-mile kill range. It's also clear the President wants to show that leaders of the secession movement and those who want to keep the United States together can share compassion in tragedy. How far that compassion goes in resolving this national crisis is a question we'll better understand in the coming days and weeks."

After Senator Jones finishes introducing himself to the other participants, the President invites participants to be seated.

Before sitting, Juan asks Secretary Mendoza for some assurance, "Mr. Secretary. Are you sure we're safe here? With Ángel assassinated and threats against my life, my advisors, well, my mother, asked me to be careful about putting myself at risk. "

President Phillipi overhears the question and jumps in before Mendoza can respond.

"Juan, I understand, and I can certainly empathize with your fears. I go through every day knowing someone is out there who wants to kill me. Fortunately, the Secret Service is the best in the world and I trust them to keep me, and all of you while you're with me, safe. For extra precaution, we closed the Washington Monument and shut off access to any building with any kind of sight line here. The cameras at the end of the South Lawn have all been thoroughly searched so we're perhaps safer here than almost anywhere on earth," the President responds, turning to the rest of the group as everyone finds their seats.

"Is everyone comfortable? You should find a couple of your favorite cold drinks in the buckets placed around us, if our advance team is right." Heads nod around the room. "I want to thank you all for coming here at this critical point in our nation's history. This is not a debate. I don't have time limits. So I suggest we each listen, respect everyone's right to participate and focus on understanding each other and what we're trying to accomplish."

Heads nod again.

"Juan, you've had the most personal tragedy in recent days, so I'd like to open it up to you to start if you'd like."

"Thank you, Mr. President," Juan says. "But I think it better if I listen and gather myself now and certainly will talk as we go."

"That's fine. Does anyone else want to start?"

Chet Leach starts to stand up, as he traditionally does when he wants to circle his executive room and make clear he's in charge. President Phillipi tells him to sit down and Chet quickly complies.

"I need to start with a formal apology to Juan from FirstWal, and from me personally. Juan, as you likely know, the English-only policy at FirstWal was my policy. I've been asked to repeat to you that it was not one authorized by our new corporate headquarters," Chet said. "But I want you to know this policy was not imposed out of malice. I imposed it with the idea of opening up opportunities to our employees. In my view, we could best promote and realign employees if everyone could adapt linguistically to any store."

"Linguistically?" Juan asks.

"Speaking the right language is what I mean."

"Got it."

"If we allowed regional languages to dominate, many of our top people would not have been able to work in Quebec, Florida, the Southwest or many of our urban and suburban stores – and people from those regions might not have been able to move to advancement opportunities in other locations. I never intended for the policy to discriminate against people like you, and on behalf of FirstWal, I offer my personal apology for these decisions."

On hearing Chet was invited to the White House, Jia saw an opportunity to further fix FirstWal's reputation. She ordered Chet to issue a personal apology to Juan. Her orders were so precise that Chet looked down at notes to be sure he spoke the exact wording settled between Jia and him. Jia hoped that Chet's prior political activism could actually help FirstWal now, rather than his newly assigned responsibilities simply being a way to emasculate him until he quit.

"Mr. Leach, or may I call you Chet?" Juan says. Chet nods his assent.

"Chet, I have to thank you in a way. Had it not been for your policy, I would never have become an activist. Without your policy, I would not have had the opportunity to even think about playing a role in gaining independence for my people. I also need to tell you this appreciation has reservation. Your policy led me to a life in which I was nearly killed, only to later watch my mentor be savagely butchered just feet from where I stood. So, at once, you created my hope and my tragedy. But I realize that you intended to do neither, so I accept your apology."

Chet pursed out a modest smile, even as he privately steamed at the thought he had just apologized to someone he would not even have spoken to if he had been a FirstWal employee. Being forced to backtrack on a policy he still believes is right is toxic to Chet. But his contract states clearly he can be terminated for insubordination with severe financial penalties that could limit the extravagance with which he plans to live the rest of his life. He needs to follow explicit instructions and think about how to follow his beliefs even as he bides time until he has a chance to retake his rightful place running daily operations.

With the apology and acceptance behind, a bit of the initial tension dissipates. Defense Secretary Mendoza sees an opportunity to focus on what he considers the more relevant issues today.

"I appreciate the personal issues here, and recognize the need to settle these issues, but want to be clear that what's at stake here is far more troubling than being slighted for a job. The future of our country is at stake. As Secretary of Defense, I have no higher calling than to protect this nation from all enemies foreign and domestic. As a Hispanic, I understand the desire of those in our community who want greater political control over our lives."

The sense of calm Juan started to feel after Chet's apology was replaced by a combination of anger and fear. "Secretary Mendoza, if you really believe I'm an enemy for wanting freedom for my people, you should have me arrested right now," Juan says.

"Juan, someone has you amped up for a battle that I'm not even engaging. My reference to enemies is not a personal attack. If we thought your actions were treasonous you'd be behind bars. For now, I'm working off the premise that your secession request is driven by not understanding there are other ways to get what you want," Mendoza says. "I think you're confusing desire for freedom and independence with a desire to avoid immersing yourself in a different language and culture."

Congresswoman Jill Carlson intervenes as she sees from facial expressions that Mendoza's typical condescending way of speaking is being poorly received by Juan.

"Around the nation, millions of Americans want to protect their heritage and their traditions," Jill says, looking directly at Juan. "There's nothing wrong with that. It's natural to want to preserve one's culture and language. But preserving our past can't prevent us from taking the actions we need to secure our future. One of those actions, if I hear Secretary Mendoza correctly, is to work toward a common language so any citizen can succeed anywhere within our borders."

She looks at Juan to give him an opportunity to respond. He is asking President Phillipi and Professor Stark if he can try the shrimp cocktail and mini crab cakes sitting on their respective snack tables.

"Sorry, I was listening, but I wanted to try these. I get what you're saying Congresswoman, but that means Mexicans here are second-class citizens. Our language isn't good enough to merit the same consideration. Why can't we require that everyone learn both languages? That way no one would be restricted from any opportunities," Juan retorts. "In Canada, I'm told all the signs, documents, everything has to be in English and French."

Professor Stark puts down his Mango+ DMD drink.

"Not a bad concept, Juan," Professor Stark says, "But here's the problem from a global economic perspective, which I think we need to consider. English is no longer the single dominant global business language and its relative value is shrinking every day. Spanish is also far from the dominant business language. That means that for America to succeed in the global economy, we need people who can speak English, sure, but perhaps more important to also speak Mandarin, Hindi, Arabic, German, Portuguese, Russian and all the other languages of leading business markets."

Moving to sit closer to the end of his seat and look alternately between Juan and the President, Professor Stark continues. "If we teach everyone here to focus on two languages of declining influence in the global business world, we lose the attention needed to create an America that is a hub for all languages. I think we need one common language that we can share with each other, and English makes the most sense to hold us all together as it still has more global economic prominence than Spanish and is used by more people here."

"We need to make sure not to make this just a language discussion," President Phillipi says.

"Understood," Professor Stark responds. "One more point and I'll leave it alone. Knowing only one language is leading America to relative economic and geopolitical decline. Every American needs to understand at least one other language, custom, culture besides English. We're total laggards here. We need to make America a welcoming place so trade partners can feel at home here. This will help to attract the best and brightest to get our economy moving back in the . . . ."

President Phillipi cuts off Professor Stark, "I heard you make similar comments earlier and I have to say your concept is intriguing. We're one of the least global countries in terms of language ability among leading economies. But anything we start now will take generations to impact our economy and does nothing to resolve the much more immediate crisis we face today."

"Actually," Professor Stark responds, "If we make a conscious effort, we're 50 percent of the way there in one generation if you consider that generally two generations are working at a time. More importantly, we make clear America is again becoming an amalgamation of great cultures and one in which all immigrants – new and old – have a place."

Chet jumps in. "I think we may be losing the point here. Isn't the point of this discussion to figure out how Spanish speakers and English speakers can coexist – at home, in government and in business? It seems to me that we're way off topic. Especially considering people are being killed over these differences."

"Chet, if I may," Professor Stark responds. "You're right that teaching global business languages to our children may not directly solve this issue, but it does several things. If everyone shares a common English language as a base, we can better communicate with each other, helping to reduce tension. Then, when we teach other languages, we send the message that learning other languages and cultures is something we value in our country. It teaches tolerance."

"I really don't see how that works," Chet says.

"Let me explain. Once you've tried to order fish in France and been told by the kind waitress that you've ordered poison instead, you're less likely to be disturbed when a new female employee from France runs around desperately seeking a rubber, though perhaps you are still a bit embarrassed when you find out later that what she really wanted you to give her was an eraser," Professor Stark says, getting a loud chuckle from everyone. "And I should point out, since that poison order was my own, that the waitress in fine French hospitality did offer to get poison for me if in fact that was what I wanted to order. But the point is we have to be patient with each other, understand each other, and perhaps each of us needs to swallow a bit of our own pride to get where we need to go as a country."

Chet leans forward. "Well, if it's pride-swallowing we need to do, you're running into a new skill set I've acquired. I've had to swallow so much pride of late, I could take up sword swallowing without even a throat scratch."

Over the next two and one-half hours, the group continues to talk about issues facing the country, finally spending time at the end on how to quell the violence that has started to destroy so many lives. As they conclude the session, distant cameras catch a series of handshakes and hugs that, displayed on news networks around the country, give the general population reason to believe amicable settlements can be reached.

When asked by a reporter what he concluded after the event, Juan sums it up simply, "It's clear that we all care about each other as people and no one wants to see anyone hurt. Our problem is we don't agree on who gets to tell who what to do. While this was a good use of time, I suspect H2M and I will press forward helping our people control our own destiny. But I am delighted the President has agreed not to stand in the way of our rally."

CHAPTER 35

September 7, 2040
Near Grand Canyon, Arizona

Pete is moving in the dark at slow speed back to the New Rite Utah compound and is surprised not to hear human sounds tracking him. Coyotes, elk, deer, and other animals make their presence known. But no helicopters, cars or even dog hunt parties are tracking him.

He's grateful, of course, but wonders why no one is chasing. Maybe JT is right. If no one understands the power of his weapon, they might not find his shooting spot. Certainly someone had to see the flash where the bullet separated from its missile base and understand this isn't a traditional rifle, Pete thinks. Continuing to move in isolation, Pete resists the temptation to turn on his emergency transponder. JT had cautioned Pete to avoid electronic transmissions.

Pete resists the urge to connect, but ponders nonetheless: "Was I successful? Sounded like it. What was the reaction? Would H2M fold now that leaders knew they could be taken out one-by-one? Would they think the U.S. government did this and respond with guerilla action? If this turns into a full-scale battle, could I join the Marines? Americans who fought off Mexicans are heroes even 200 years later, so maybe this is my destiny. I'm not a slacker. Everything prepared me for today. I can be the greatest military hero of my generation."

Pete starts believing he understands his purpose on earth. In his mind, everything he has done to this point has prepared him for the hero's role he's now pursuing. He moves briskly but carefully, still aided by night vision goggles that keep him in full day-like view in front and clear view of movement around him.

Pete continues to fill the time with mumbling thoughts: "My parents simply didn't understand my mission. But it all makes sense now. Video games. Connection with New Rite. Physical exhaustion that took away from homework or a part-time job. Leaving home. Moving to Colorado to train in higher altitude to improve fitness. Success in New Rite's contest. Meeting JT."

Clearly this must have been God's plan and now Pete is sure he can see it. For the first time in years, Pete considers that maybe there is a God with special plans requiring him to be on his own. Pete's self-pride expands to a level he had never reached, much greater than the pride of success in the gaming world. As he approaches the Utah camp, he hopes JT and his APB are there tonight. He's ready to sleep on a bed and get a full night's rest. And maybe, just maybe, Ally will want to disturb his sleep.

Pete arrives near the camp too late in the night to make it all the way inside a building before enough light is shining to make him visible. As anxious as he is to get to a bed, he digs in for a last day of hiding. He decides to bury his weapon as well, just in case someone sees him now. It's not worth the risk to have the launcher with him when boarding the APB. And no one will ever find it here, he convinces himself. So, for a last time, he finds a great hiding spot, wipes down the launcher for any prints, digs in to secure invisibility from satellite and sleeps.

As light builds over the camp, Pete takes a last look. Nothing unusual, but no sign of JT either. This was the day JT said he expected me back. Was he expecting me back last night or tonight? It appears tonight or JT would have been here already.

CHAPTER 36

September 10, 2040
Washington, D.C.

After burying Ángel in his small rural Mexico hometown, H2M leadership set this day for a mass demonstration. H2M called for a 10-million person march on Washington D.C. and simultaneous million-person marches in 10 other cities to celebrate the birth of the 100 millionth Hispanic in the United States. Dubbed the March for Freedom, the day is billed as a day of liberation for all Latinos and Latinas in the United States.

As the sun rises over the Capitol on rally day, tents housing tens of thousands come down peacefully. Metro stations around the area are packed at opening and full trains stop before reaching the sub-Mall area. Passengers are all forced to walk the last mile. The Mall itself is packed. Demonstrators spill over to close off the 14th Street Bridge. The crowd grows so quickly it is now expanding to cover grounds surrounding the Arlington National Cemetery. Homeland Security Secretary Peyton asks Defense Secretary Mendoza to send troops to guard the cemetery. "We can't have protestors anywhere near our veterans' graves. That'll just spark serious animosity," Peyton says in requesting military backup.

With crowds already densely covering the area and cars parked on most major roads leading to the city, bringing traffic in and around the city to complete halt, Secretary Mendoza sends helicopters to Arlington National, dropping troops to strengthen the perimeter protection.

As the helicopters and airstream boats fly up the Potomac River toward the cemetery, they spark fear. "Watch out, we're under attack," a handful of demonstrators shout from various points on the 14th Street Bridge and surrounding parks.

The quiet whir of the helicopters attracts everyone's attention within sight. Shouts to calm down dominate the crowd, but a few start pushing their way through the dense crowds to get to cover.

As helicopters near the bridge, they veer west and toward the cemetery. A noticeable exhale comes from even those who had been telling everyone to stay calm.

The size of the demonstration overwhelms the effort H2M put into logistics. Bathrooms are in large demand. With 75 minutes still to go until the start of rally activities, lines are long. Bathrooms in every building along and around the mall are opened. Still, the reflecting pool and the Potomac River receive countless unwelcome contributions.

Even more so than at the secession announcement rallies and concert fundraisers, H2M's resources are overwhelmed. Live broadcasts are displayed for those with a sight line to a stage, but half of the crowd can't see or hear from their vantage points. Fortunately, enough participants open up Lifelink screens to enable the rest to follow the action.

Sergeant Rey Moore is on duty, as is every available policeman who hasn't just finished a 16-hour shift. From his vantage point atop the Washington Monument, Sgt. Moore searches for confrontations and typical criminal predators. Moore's suggestion that everyone in the crowd be asked to film the day's activities helped. Ultimately, Homeland Secretary Peyton agreed to ask rally attendees to record everything they saw at the event, and upload anything that smacked of criminal activity. The system captured GPS data from each recording device, and visually confirmed the locations against stationary objects to find criminals quickly. Already, even before the event formally starts, more than 300 arrests have been made.

H2M organizers aren't fond of the FBI capturing records of the event. H2M leaders initially asked that no one record the events outside of the official H2M recording. Once Ángel's son, Gabriel, now the official President of H2M, was informed by the FBI that they were already able to trace nearly everyone who attended if they saw the need to do so, Gabriel announced his support for filming up to official start of the rally. He still discouraged people from filming and uploading during the actual rally, but most continued to record as they realized the official video of the event would likely be sold at a later point – and for a steep price. Everyone attending wanted a record of the day.

Houston, Dallas, Denver, San Francisco, New York, Chicago, Seattle, Miami, Atlanta and Phoenix host simulcast side rallies, each drawing crowds estimated at between 100,000 and one million. Local leaders open and close each of these events, but the bulk of content originates in Washington, D.C.

"Today, being Hispanic in America means being part of a group of 100 million people," Gabriel Herrera announces as he kicks off the event. "We are large, we are strong, but we are not in control. Thank you for extending your weekend to join us here in Washington . . ." Gabriel pauses as video of the crowd is displayed to the participants ". . . and in our sister rallies in Atlanta, Chicago . . . and Seattle." He went through each city slowly to share live video of each site. "With these rallies, and with our votes in November, we will tell America, no, we will show America, that we are 100 million people united by a culture and ready to take control of our destiny."

The roar of the crowd was deafening and so energizing it prompted Gabriel to walk around the main stage clapping for the crowd. Gabriel was angered at not being invited to the White House session, and sees this as his opportunity to establish himself as the real leader of H2M. He explains that the event is in English because H2M wants to be sure English speakers understand why independence is needed. Simulcasts in Spanish are also provided.

"I want you to know we're not just fighting for our Mexican brothers and sisters. We're pursuing this dream for all Latinos who want freedoms and economic opportunity that America used to represent. We want this to be a country where we control our government, and where our language doesn't make us second-class citizens. Even that I give this speech in English is clear sign of what is wrong with America today. Not only do we expect four states to form an independent republic, we plan to pursue an agreement with the rest of the United States to allow those of you who want to join us to trade homes and jobs with those who want to leave our new country."

That statement made the millions attending the rallies in D.C. and states outside the planned Alta Texas territory realize that the dream of secession and independence is for everyone who wants to be part of the new country. In the weeks since the ballot proposals were first introduced with mass rallies, the number of whites, blacks, Asians and Arabs moving out of the four states increased 80 percent from the prior year, but an offsetting number was racing to move in.

As Juan Gonzalez is introduced to the crowd, it takes nearly three minutes for the celebratory atmosphere to die down enough for Juan to be heard.

"In eight weeks, four of our states will vote whether we want to become an independent nation – friendly with the United States, but independent, Spanish-speaking and in control of our own destiny. We will no longer be the people whose hard work props up the incomes and status of people whose only advantage over us is that their ancestors came to the United States before our ancestors – or whose ancestors simply took land and resources from our ancestors."

Juan covered his thin, defined frame in blue jeans, a button-down shirt, bolo tie and sport coat – his most formal public look outside of the formal suit he felt compelled to wear giving Congressional testimony. Knowing now that people judge appearances as much as deeds and words, Juan decided on a look to earn respect and honor tradition.

"There was a time when we came to the United States to pursue a better life, to escape poverty, to seek opportunity. Even today, with 100 million Latinos here, we don't earn the respect to be treated as equals. I was told face-to-face that the reason I could not work was because of my language, my heritage. How many of us have been denied work, denied promotions, and never told?" Juan tells the crowd, with intermittent interruptions for cheers, applause. "How many of us worry every day that we will be forced to leave children behind? How many of us never pursue lives we know we cannot have simply because of our heritage?"

Dozens of other speakers mix their versions of the pro-secession story into speeches bridged by musicians and comedians over the next two hours.

A comedian entertains last, as organizers decided humor at the end would help calm emotions. However, as he concludes his set, skirmishes break out in Lafayette Square across the street from the White House. Protestors angered by the march had also descended from all over the East Coast, though in much smaller numbers. With anti-secession protestors nearly 100,000 strong, D.C. police push them into Lafayette Square and surrounding streets. They hoped to use the White House and Treasury Building as buffers between the anti-rally protestors and the Freedom March rally attendees.

That buffer of several hundred police, including 20 mounted police, is collapsing east of the Treasury Building. Barricades set between the groups are slowly being pushed in on both sides. Police yell at both sides to get away from the barricades, which have closed to only 40 feet apart.

With the loud amplification of the rally now over, both sides can hear insults.

"Slither on home, hombre."

"Get a job whitey."

Anti-secession demonstrators shout a variety of chants – many growing in volume in unison as mobile messages tell the still-growing anti-rally crowd what to yell.

"Who invited you?"

"Don't like it. Leave it."

"Here's your bus pass."

Freedom rally attendees alternate chants between English and Spanish.

"Secede. Succeed. Secede. Succeed."

"Mi casa. Mi país."

Over time, the chants shift to more vulgar expressions.

Insults grow louder, until rocks are thrown from well behind the barricade into the anti-rally demonstrators. Within seconds, demonstrators from both sides push through the remaining barriers and attack each other with all of the vigor of a full-fledged street war.

"We have an all-out battle at 15th and F breaking out," Sergeant Moore calls out from his spotting position. "We need back-up ASAP. Get tear gas into the crowd. Police at Station F-15, put on gas masks immediately."

While the uniformed police on the ground circle to protect themselves, fighters on both sides see the mounted police pulling on gas masks and immediately know what is coming.

"Tear gas," shout several demonstrators as canisters are shot in by nearby SWAT teams. Recognizing their horses are not masked, mounted police try to move out of tear gas range, using batons, rubber bullet guns and electric pulse weapons to knock groups of fighters out of the way. Seeing children and women on the ground, some already bloodied from rocks, Sergeant Moore calls for more support. "We'll need all available officers to F-15 immediately. Hundreds already down. Medical and crowd control STAT."

Seeing police groups running toward the area, rally attendees in the Mall realize from on-line feeds that the loud noises and shouting they hear are turning violent. For tens of thousands in the Mall, the opportunity to witness or jump into the action is too much to ignore. Soon police running to 15th and F are being followed by groups of largely young and middle-aged men looking for a chance to get in on the fight.

While anti-rally demonstrators back away from the tear gas, the constant message communication they receive tells them that a broad attack from rally attendees is on the way. Crowds in and around Lafayette Square prepare for a mass fistfight, with many breaking past security in government buildings to try to get wives and children to safety. Police, who had been letting lines of people use first floor restrooms, are quickly overcome by those seeking to escape the violence.

Watching the events unfold from Camp David, President Phillipi and family see the White House threatened. From all angles, people try scaling White House fences. Secret Service officers ask for permission to shoot.

Knowing that shooting demonstrators from the White House could be the trigger that turns this battle into a full-scale civil war, Phillipi refuses to approve lethal shooting as demonstrators climb the fence.

"Seal everyone into the White House and only shoot to protect the White House from entry," the President orders. Several Secret Service members make runs for White House entrances, standing outside with guns drawn to keep demonstrators away. Human pyramids help hundreds of people jump the White House fence. Desire to join them shrinks as dozens writhe in pain on the grounds from broken legs, ankles and backs from bad landings.

From outside, many believe the wounded have been shot, and start throwing rocks at agents who are arresting and quickly cuffing dozens.

"The White House is under attack," Sergeant Moore reports. "People are being shot and knifed all around the White House. We need military back-up and we need it now."

Within minutes, three-dozen military helicopters on alert at Fort McNair are on site dropping 12 soldiers each by rope into the middle of the fray at 15th and F. Minutes later, troops from Andrews Air Force Base descend onto the South Lawn of the White House. Thirty of the troops join the Secret Service in protecting White House entrances. Already a dozen protestors trying to get to the White House have been shot in the leg.

Sitting behind the main stage area resting after the end of the rally, Juan watches his Lifelink display the terror unfolding. His hopes for peaceful creation of an independent country are being eclipsed. He asks the stage crew to restart the broadcast equipment and goes back on stage.

"Those of you fighting and attacking, I beg you, I beg you to walk away. You're doing exactly what we must not do if we want to prove we're ready to lead our own country. Please walk away now. Get your families and go home, please," he says. As he repeats the message in Spanish, Gabriel joins him on the stage, having raced back from a meet-and-greet with H2M's largest contributors.

Gabriel puts his arm around Juan in a brotherly way, motions for the cameras to focus on him, and as he starts to talk, he tightens his grip on Juan and pulls him around and away from the camera.

"Supporters of the rally, I ask you to restrain yourselves and walk away from the government paid antagonists who are searching for any reason to start a war against our people. We will not fight and cannot win a war where our people are all gathered in a slaughtering field for the military to mow us down. We have already heard of our people being shot and killed by White House security. This is the time to go home, yes to retreat, and to live to fight another day. Next time, we will fight on our terms," Gabriel says.

Upset at the powerful grip still holding his shoulder, Juan pushes Gabriel away. The two start a physical battle caught briefly on camera before the transmission is stopped.

"What's wrong with you?" Juan yells. *"We can't win a war. This must be peaceful. I didn't sign up to fight a war, and never would have supported even your father if he had asked me to go to war against America."*

"You stupid kid. This was always going to be a war. My father knew it all along. You're just a pawn to help us get to the battle on our terms. Your service to H2M is no longer needed. Get the hell out of here before we shoot you again," Gabriel yells at Juan as the two are now behind the stage curtains.

Juan is startled. He wonders if he really was duped. Was Ángel in on this? Wait, did Gabriel say they'll shoot him . . . again?

Gabriel and Juan realize at nearly the same time that Gabriel said something he should never have said. Gabriel starts to chase after Juan, who is already bolting out from behind the curtain. Gabriel orders his men to chase down, restrain and gag Juan. He runs back onto the stage and yells in the direction he sees Juan running.

"You're a traitor. A traitor," Gabriel yells at Juan from the front of the stage, grabbing a microphone to be sure the largest number of people hear him. "You're an agent of the White House, just as I suspected. Someone stop him."

People who can hear Gabriel are too stunned by his accusation to do anything to stop Juan. Juan is a hero. He won the Spanish-only requirement in Arizona, an important victory that led to the effort to secede. He brought one of the largest corporations in the world to its knees with a protest that forced them to change policies or lose money. He is clearly advocating for secession. How can he now be a traitor?

Juan grabs a baseball cap, crosses Maryland Avenue and runs toward the Federal Center Metro station. Ducking underneath the overhang of the HHS facility on Second Street, he trades hats with a girl in the area and kisses her hand in thanks while pulling her Lifelink unnoticed from her purse. *Juan messages his mother: "Get out of there now. Hide from Gabriel and his people. I'm running. Get someone you trust to take you and hide. Don't tell anyone where you are. Don't connect again for exactly 15 hours."*

As Juan enters a Metro train travelling east from the Federal Center Station, he checks a number, throws away his own Lifelink and pulls out the one he had just taken. He quickly sends a message to Professor Stark. "Gabriel said he'd shoot me. Again! Life in danger. Don't know who to trust. Running. Can you help me and mama? Going silent. I'll be where we last spoke in exactly 14 hours. Please, please, please help."

CHAPTER 37

September 10, 2040
Chicago

On the same day as the March for Freedom Rally, the fall quarter at the University of Chicago opens. Professor Stark's two-quarter master's level course, "The Integration of Religion, Culture, Business and Government" attracts several students who last spring finished their undergraduate studies in Professor Stark's undergraduate Culture and Government course.

Professor Stark's protégés often fared well since the reforms proposed in his Pulitzer Prize winning book, "The Bastardization of Acquired Democracy" took national hold and led to the Political Freedom Amendment. Since then, Professor Stark has had the ability to select students from the large number seeking entry to his class. He makes selections only partially based on proven academic success. Work and volunteer experience influences his selections, as does ensuring students come from all ends of the political spectrum. For his master's level course, he adds religious background diversity to consideration.

Almost eight years after the purchased democracy limelight had passed, Professor Stark is back consistently in the national news. He is a regular interviewee on language mandates propping up in numerous states in addition to nationally. Adding to this wave of media coverage, Professor Stark attracted widespread interest in a book released three weeks ago called *The Elements of National Destruction*. The latest Professor Stark book is already known popularly as *The END* following on his 10-year earlier

The Bastardization of Acquired Democracy book that is popularly called *The BAD*. Substantial portions of it provide the academic support for Professor Stark's views that the United States risked becoming a failed nation. Many failings of a democratic America remain even after the political system reforms he helped champion. *The END* postulated that democratic process reforms removed some impediments to better government policy, but did not eliminate the potential for cycles of policy failure exacerbated by leadership failures.

In his book, Professor Stark used various analogies to compare political system failures with elements of failure from other areas of life. Most of the students entering Professor Stark's classes know they better understand his vantage point to prepare for his rapid-fire Socratic system. Since Professor Stark's public debate sessions often attract media attention, more is at stake for the students than just poor grades if they are unprepared for his class. Early political reputations can be made and destroyed in single debate sessions.

Professor Stark's comments on financial market failures discussed lessons from the extreme crashes of 2008 and 2029 that created intense blocks of poverty worsened by political system failures that kept core issues from being quickly fixed.

"Just as investment markets move based on constantly evolving blends of rational data and emotional interpretation that must be considered before making a bet," he wrote in *The END*, "government solutions to societal problems must contemplate the mix of short-term impacts driven by political motivations and the long-term behavioral adjustments people make in response to government-induced incentives. Presumptions that people will not shift behavior to maximize the benefits of, or minimize the consequences of, various government programs created many of our worst public policies."

Professor Stark's comments on the relationships between failure-based motivations in business and government drew media attention, and substantial Wall Street backlash.

"Investing and government intertwine in other manners. Politicians do not all benefit from the success of the enterprise for which they are responsible, just as investors no longer all benefit from business condition and market improvement. Investment firms have always had an interest in outperforming the competition to help attract the next wave of capital, but for many generations, investors almost all preferred to see the general economy improving."

"The development of options, particularly the rapid increase in the use of short strategies, has created an investment environment in which economic failure of some or many can be the direct outcome sought by an investor. For decades following the Great Depression, most investors benefitted when the economy moved forward. Through this time, our sins of envy were confined to jealousies around relative wealth creation. Collectively, we believed in the idea that a rising tide lifts all boats. That axiom is no longer true in our business environment, and perhaps never has been true in our political world.

"Today, your poverty can be my prosperity due to the creation of financial products that increasingly dominate America's investing philosophy. It is not surprising that our investment world has increasingly become a win-lose environment, as our political world has too often been win-lose. There were periods of time in American history when political parties were comfortable remaining in the minority in the House and/or Senate as long as the overall United States was moving in the right direction and the right policies were being adopted.

"The 1989 election of then Georgia Congressman Newt Gingrich to Republican Minority Whip over Illinois Congressman Ed Madigan triggered the latest ascendance of the politics of destruction. Statesmanship and bipartisan resolutions were tossed aside for generations in favor of seek-and-destroy political gamesmanship. Democrats thought the lesson of Republicans winning control of the U.S. House in 1994 was that they were not extreme enough in their liberalism. When Republicans later lost control of the House back in 2006, they thought it was their failure to push conservatism aggressively. Democrats interpreted the same results as a directive from voters to destroy conservatism. When Republicans again took control in 2010, Democratic leaders reacted like they had again not been strident enough, ignoring that their losses were largely amongst centrist and conservative Democrats. As control continued to see-saw over subsequent decades, extremism and negativity were practiced in equal measure by both major political parties at the expense of the American people," he wrote in *The END*.

In his first class of the quarter this morning, Professor Stark welcomes North Californian Rachel Cruz, Chicago native Tamika and fellow Midwesterner Jeremy from his winter/spring course. Students from a wide variety of ethnic, religious and cultural backgrounds introduce themselves to him and each other simultaneous with the start of the Freedom March rallies. No one skipped class to attend the Chicago part of the event.

"I'm going to load you up early and keep you loaded until class ends," Professor Stark says to open this quarter's class. "We're at a critical time in U.S. history, and the topics we debate in this course are as relevant as ever. So, for our next class, I need each of you prepared to deliver orally a 100-word – and not one word more – description of the critical role or roles that religion should play in governing a people. Along with it, I want posted for review a 2,000-word essay explaining your position. The essays must be posted by midnight Wednesday, which gives you 11 hours to come up with your condensed version for Thursday discussion."

Looking at student jaws dropped around the class, a few of whom didn't realize this is standard operating procedure, Professor Stark sees he will likely achieve his goal of getting the uncommitted out of his sight before he ever wastes a moment grading their work.

Jeremy isn't about to take it without a comeback. "I'm glad to see your efforts to get a tan this summer didn't soften you up Professor. I was worried when I saw you that between your tan and Sunday morning talk shows you might be distracted with other pursuits this fall."

"I'm not sure what pursuits you have in mind Jeremy, but when you're the kind of person who can see tan lines in your neck fat, you have to take your profession seriously. And Jeremy, while we're on the topic, I suggest you take your academics seriously," Professor Stark says, to substantial giggling from Rachel, Tamika and a few others who already know Jeremy.

"I don't know why you're all still sitting here. You have a busy 47 hours, 1 minute and . . . 15 seconds before I see you next," he says as he dismisses class.

Jeremy, Rachel and Tamika are happy to see each other again. After the bombings and Harvard shootings, they had only had one more class and a final before heading off to internships and summer jobs.

"Well, I guess Professor Stark wants to make sure he gets his shots in," Jeremy says, prompting a disgruntled look from both women. "I mean, figuratively," he adds as they walk outside to a pleasant and peaceful day in Hyde Park. "I have my Lifelink with me. Does anyone want to go sit at the Lake and get started? We can talk on the way."

Rachel and Tamika agree that sitting at Lake Michigan will make the exercise less painful than heading back indoors on this sunny, warm day. Walking under the decrepit train overpass, Rachel and Tamika look at each other, remembering the last time they passed this way, including the uncertainty and panic that swept over them and thousands of others.

Mosquitos are out in full force around the Osaka Garden lagoons, so they pick up the pace walking past the 59th Street Harbor and under Lake Shore Drive. Once by the water, they drop their small totes and roam out to the pier jutting into Lake Michigan to dictate their papers. Jeremy lays out facing the sun to maximize exposure. There is enough Irish in him that tanning often seems more like reddening, but he hates being pale.

"I feel like I've been kissed by an angel to be out on such a beautiful day with two beautiful women," Jeremy says.

"Did your angel also give you that hickey?" Tamika responds, pointing to the back of his neck. "Please tell me the girls you're dating are at least legal."

After laughing for several minutes, Rachel has to pull her cheeks down to relieve the soreness.

"I guess I deserve that," Jeremy finally admits.

"It's a good thing we like you already," Rachel says.

Rachel is also happy to get a little sun, but Tamika sits with her back to the sun, simply enjoying the warmth and the occasional freshwater mist as waves hit the nearby barriers.

"It's interesting that we're taking a course on the role of religion in government and culture when, if there really was a God, the horrible things we've been enduring would never happen," Tamika says.

"I know what you mean," Rachel adds. "I'd like to think there's a God out there who cares, but I find it hard to make sense of this."

Jeremy sits up partway, not using his arms at first, but then putting his arms to the ground to hold him as his stomach muscles tighten. After a summer of work and play with little workout in between, the cramping in his gut comes before he finishes the second sentence.

"Here's my thought, and I'd be interested in any arguments if you think I'm wrong. I think people need religion to control our base instincts. Most people, or at least most guys, think of success as dominating other people. We wrestle to find a winner. When we fight, we don't care if the other person thinks we're right as long as they do what we want them to do. When we win, we do a little dance or flex our muscles or say something to be sure the other guy knows we own him," Jeremy says.

"If you're looking for us to argue guys aren't creeps or are intellectually superior to women, you have the wrong audience," Tamika says. "Ninety percent of the time, you use your small brain to do your thinking. I don't know that religion changes that."

"Maybe. Men like to compete," Jeremy says. "We want to prove superiority to attract women. But what's the ultimate way to prove superiority. You kill the other person, and you take what they have, not necessarily in that order. Religion is a tool to convince us that our instinct for domination has to be controlled; that there's a higher victory we can achieve only by suppressing our instinct."

"Most religions tell you not to rape, steal, kill or cheat on your girl-friend, but a lot of guys don't seem to get the message," Rachel says, adding cheating to the list as an indication of a recent personal sore spot.

Jeremy considers how to pull his paper together.

"Logic would tell us that when we make the world better, we benefit from that better environment. But if you read *The END* already, it's pretty clear there are lots of ways for people to see the failure of others as their success. The belief in an after-life sometimes helps us restrain from seeking our success through your failure because we worry about the consequences on our eternity. It's easy to see how if two of us play a game, your loss is my victory. It's much harder to figure out ways to change the game so we all win."

Tamika looks up from her notes. She outlines her paper while listening to Jeremy.

"First, I'm astounded and actually impressed that you think that deeply. Second, I can think of dozens of ways your philosophy is wrong. My mom got a promotion at work beating out a guy. When my high school team won a basketball game, the other team lost and we won. If I went after a guy that another girl wanted to go out with, when I won I was happy and she was pissed," Tamika says.

"I get it. I get it," Jeremy says, "but here's my point. We need religion to provide a reason to take joy from our success, and not from someone else's failure. Did your mom get promoted by being successful, or by unfairly attacking her competitor? There's nothing wrong with seeking success through honest, hard work and gaining recognition for what we accomplish. But, to many people, success means just making sure the other alternative or alternatives are worse. This seems to be what's happening in politics," Jeremy says, turning his head toward Rachel and Tamika. "Okay, I think I know what I'm writing. What's the concept of your papers?"

A wave crashes into the pier just 10 feet away, sending a sizable spray that hits all three and causes Jeremy to stand up and start running back toward the shore line. Both women laugh at him.

"What did you think was going to happen sitting here?" Tamika says.

With Jeremy already gone, Rachel and Tamika also walk back off the pier and sit and lay on the grass nearer to Lake Shore Drive. As they settle into their spots, Rachel explains her concept. "My thesis is simple. Religion and politics are tools that can be used to serve a people or to rule them, and both can be badly misused by those who care more about power than service."

Tamika nods her head. "There are plenty of examples of that through history. The Crusades. Jihadists. The Holocaust. You can probably get your 2,000 words with just a list of some of the abuses in world history," she says. "Heck, you could get there just with a list of jailed Illinois politicians."

Rachel shakes her head. "You know, that's an interesting idea – the world one. I wonder if I could just categorize the tragedies behind their common link. Uhh, I don't know. What about you?"

"I'm still struggling," Tamika says. "Religion to me is a philosophy of right and wrong – and government's job is to take society's definitions of right and wrong and embed them into enforceable laws. I think government's role is to protect society from criminals who ignore society's rules to their personal advantage. So religion's role is to help society define right and wrong and provide an aspiration beyond what we can see. Part of the trouble in American society today is we have so many religions with contradictory versions of what's right and wrong. Some Baptists believe singing and dancing is the work of the devil, while in many religions song and dance are ways to praise God."

"That's an interesting perspective," Jeremy says. "So the problem we have in America today is based on the basic principle that we have different definitions of right and wrong? Is that what you're saying?"

Rachel's leg bounces up and down at a rapid pace. Noticing this and stopping it, she says, "I don't know whether the fundamental differences are that great. I don't know of any mass religion that says it's right to kill others, even if some men who run religions seek power by saying it's okay to kill people who don't share their views."

"That's right Rachel. It's men's fault," Jeremy says. "No bad women have ever killed anyone."

"But men are usually the problem is all I'm saying. In our hearts, I think we all know no real God would ever say we should kill innocent people, ever. We don't believe in stealing, rape, lying, beating others. But government seems unable to synthesize the common views of various religions, and turn that into enforceable policy. Oh shoot. I don't know where I'm going with this. I just know I have to go wherever I'm going fast."

Waves from Lake Michigan splash up along the barrier, creating a mist that helps cool Rachel as she is again walking up and down the jutted pier trying to figure out what to write. Clouds alternately hide and release the sun. Rachel shoots and watches video of herself as she pulls her hair back into a ponytail, deeming the mess that tops her head unfit for others to see. She turns back toward the grass to dictate her thoughts.

Rachel starts outlining her concepts, talking through her thoughts and capturing them directly on her Lifelink. "Religion's a unifying force for a people, giving them a shared sense of purpose and expectations," she starts.

Looking out over Lake Michigan, seeing water as far as she can see and a glimpse to her right of the industrial remnants that make up Northwest Indiana, she rattles out her ideas. "When religious principles are embedded into law, they help to maintain order in society for the good of all . . ., as long as the laws are based on protecting people from each other. . . .

"Religion frequently provides a logical reason, like avoiding eternal damnation, to not pursue actions I think we all know intuitively are wrong but might pursue if left to our base instincts. Often, though, religion provides a context for destroying people different from us: the Crusades, Jihad, the wars between Protestants and Catholics in Ireland, the Baltics, Sudan, Syria, Sunnis vs. Shiites. Too many examples to go through," Rachel continues.

"Religion is often used as cover for a power grab. What role did Constantine play in today's gospels, and how did his focus on ruling his empire impact what gospels we read? Are religious leaders consciously focused on the need for followers to procreate continuously as a means of growing their following, their wealth and their power? Is the need to expand followers through large families the driving force behind anti-gay church policies? When religion is used to justify government overthrows, how often is the real motivation service to God and how often is it political power? How do we tell where one stops and the other starts? Why do some governments embrace religious diversity and others try to crush it, with nations seemingly able to survive either way? Is there a parallel between forcing a single language and forcing a single religion in order to control a population? Maybe this is the topic to focus on. Underline last sentence."

All three were nearly finished outlining their papers when Rachel's MSDNC news alert tore away her attention.

"10 million person rally erupts into violent brawl and attack on White House. Thousands injured and killed in largest government slaughter of citizens since Kent State. Juan Gonzalez branded by H2M leadership as a traitor. Gonzalez now fleeing on foot."

"You have to read this," Rachel says to Tamika and Jeremy.

CHAPTER 38

September 10, 2040
Chicago

Professor Stark's news alert came only seconds after the message from Juan startled him. So much for a quieter quarter, he thinks to himself.

Immediately scanning video uploads from the event, he searches for main stage video. He doesn't see anything from the program that concerns him, so starts searching news networks for the latest update.

H2M president Gabriel Herrera is holding a press conference as Professor Stark switches on.

"I am saddened to tell my friends and family that a young man I thought was the greatest hope of our generation has turned on us. Juan Gonzalez is a traitor to the cause of freedom for Latinos. He was caught conspiring with President Phillipi and the U.S. military to secure the destruction of H2M and our leadership. We were able to stop him just before he could set off what appears to have been a massive bomb underneath the H2M stage, which you can see in the picture on the screen behind me. We believe the fighting between rally participants and the anti-H2M mob was a diversion orchestrated by Juan and the U.S. government to give him time and reason to blow up our leadership team," Gabriel announces with a clear fury to his voice.

"Juan escaped before we were able to restrain him, but I hope you'll help track him down and hold him for us to deal with. When you find him, please do not turn him over to his co-conspirators. We will get him back to our states and deal with him there."

One of the reporters broadcasting the feed raises his hand and shouts his question simultaneously. "Are you saying you're asking everyone who attended the rally today to help you kidnap Juan Gonzalez and deliver him to you for you to administer justice. That is not the way this country works," the reporter says.

"Your question is a forceful argument for why we need independence for our states as a nation," Gabriel responds. "Thank you for pointing out one of the many failings of this country, in which we are prevented from making decisions that are in our best interest as a people."

Hearing Gabriel speak, Professor Stark understands now why Juan thinks he is in trouble. He also realizes that Gabriel will characterize government help to protect Juan as proving Gabriel's point that Juan is a traitor. He feels comfortable he can get through to President Phillipi through several channels – the most direct being Jill.

"Stop thinking about her," he chides himself as he thinks through what to do. If you want a date, ask her on a date. Don't get her involved in this just so you can see her again. But maybe she can be useful. There aren't many people in Washington I can trust to help me. Okay, use your brain. Juan is wrong about secession and knows I completely disagree with him, but he reached out to me. Why would he do that? Surely, if he wants to prove he isn't a traitor to the cause, he won't want to be associated with people who argue his views are wrong. So he's not worried about image right now. He must really believe he's in danger.

Juan doesn't have a father, at least as far as Professor Stark knows. Professor Stark met his mother and knows she would give her life to save him, but it's also clear Juan won't save himself if it puts her life at risk. Ángel was like a father figure to him, but really the only strong male in his life, and now Ángel's son is the man who seems to want to destroy him. Juan doesn't have any close connections in Washington. He could call friends in Arizona, but what could his high school buddies do for him? Wow, the kid must believe Gabriel really wants to kill him. He's desperate.

Professor Stark knows now he has to get to Washington, D.C. to meet Juan and help him get to safety. He checks and quickly finds air transport is all booked up. High-speed rail could get him as far as Cleveland, but then what.

Professor Stark considers his next steps: How long will it take me to drive? I can't take my One Shot. That will tell everyone where I'm at and it could shut down as I approach the Capitol. If someone figures out I went to get him, they'll be able to track me if they have any contacts in a police force, which they surely must. D.C. police are really good at capturing people with out-of-regulation vehicles. The pollution sensors at all the major entrances to the Metropolitan area are certain to go off if I take out my mini-Cooper. I can barely get away with driving it in Chicago, he thinks.

After considering all the potential channels, he decides high-speed to Cleveland is his first step and he'll figure it out from there. He can pick up the 4 p.m. train in Gary and be in Cleveland at 6:30 eastern, giving him 10 more hours to make it to D.C.

"Jill, Paul here," Professor Stark says as his One Shot takes him to the Gary high-speed stop. "I hate to call you for a non-social reason, but I desperately need your help."

"What do you mean by non-social reason?" Congresswoman Jill Carlson inquires, with Professor Stark's call being one of many events today she had not anticipated.

"To cut to the chase, I would have liked to call you for a good reason, but I'm afraid that's not why I'm calling," he says.

"Okay, I'm curious," she responds, picking up a brush off the counter and brushing her hair as they speak.

"You've been following the rally today?" he asks.

"Of course, hard not to when the entire city is at a standstill with the mass of people and violence here," she says.

"No names please, but there's a person you and I both have met and talked with that we, I think, both think highly of even though he's wrong on a particular issue," Professor Stark says.

"Why are you talking in code? What's going on," she says.

"I think that person is afraid he may be wrong about topics we can't even imagine," Professor Stark says.

"I'm lost."

"I don't want to say much here. I don't know who listens. I'm on my way, but will show up at your door by no later than 4:30," Professor Stark tells Jill.

"In 45 minutes?"

"No, I mean 4:30 in the morning."

"If this is the professor's way of inviting himself over for breakfast, you should know that I don't cook, especially when I'm not awake," she responds, still thinking this might be his awkward sense of flirting. "Other than to catch a flight, I haven't been up at that hour since I left the farm."

"I'm turning my mobile off and won't turn it on again until after I see you. I'll explain when I get there," he says, hanging up.

Jill is deeply perplexed. A few minutes later, she tries calling back, but his Lifelink is off. She turns on the news to see if she can find an explanation.

Ten minutes into catching up on the violent outbreak and the accusations of Juan as a traitor, she thinks she understands: "I better go get some coffee. I have a feeling I'm going to need it."

***

Washington, D.C.

As the Metro train pulls out of Federal Center and makes its way past Capitol South, Juan realizes he has no idea where he's going, or where to hide. On the subway, he slips to the corner and tucks his head down like he's napping. Even with the vagrant's coat and hat he now wears after another trade, he can't risk anyone seeing him. As he listens to reports from people getting updates around him, he realizes the risk to his life grows by the minute.

Exiting at the Stadium/Armory stop, he walks down to the Anacostia River banks, careful to build a bit of limp into his step to fit the vagrant look he hopes will keep him from being visible to anyone around. Along the river, he stays hidden until dark, then makes his way to the National Arboretum. Climbing inside the arboretum he and his mother had visited during a break in a trip to D.C., he hides in the conifer collection. Underneath the branches, he catches two hours of sleep before his racing mind and some wind bursts wake him.

I hope he comes, Juan thinks, and knows where I meant to send him. He estimates he's almost five miles away from the White House, so needs to leave by 2:30 to be within sight of where Professor Stark would hopefully meet him. He's already decided to not risk a cab. He'll walk slowly and stay out of traffic view until in range of White House cameras. With cameras near the White House certain to be active, he's hopeful Gabriel won't make an attempt on him there.

Once in Cleveland by high-speed train, Professor Stark pays cash at a mom-and-pop store that rents old style cars for people who enjoy the thrill of driving themselves. Driving is a skill the young have lost, but Professor Stark is old enough to remember the freedom of deciding how fast to drive to get wherever he wants to go.

Though tired as midnight approaches in the mountains of Western Maryland, his mind races on the threats ahead. Fortunately, traffic is almost non-existent at this hour or the automatic override even these rental cars are required to maintain would take over the driving. Getting to D.C. before 4 a.m. allows Professor Stark to avoid the emission detectors that help minimize smog creation on warm days.

***

September 11, 2040

As he pulls in front of the small townhouse where Jill maintains a basement apartment, he still hasn't quite figured out what to say. Jill also hasn't slept much and is dressed in jogging gear when he pulls up on the street. When she sees Professor Stark get out of the car, she comes out to greet him — extending her hand and then giving him a light, partial hug.

"Men are always confusing, but you have me both confused and intrigued. What's going on?" she says.

"Where can we talk to be sure no one is listening?"

"This is as good a place as any, though this isn't the best time to hang around outdoors and avoid suspicion. Why don't you come in," she says.

"Great. Do you have a car? We'll need to leave in 30 minutes for our pick-up," he says as they walk down to the basement apartment.

"Coffee?"

"You read my mind."

"Well that may be the only mind-reading I'm doing these days, but let me tell you why I think you're here and then you correct me," she says. "The H2M crew accused Juan of being a traitor and he's concerned his reputation is being destroyed and wants your help protecting it. And you called me because you know I like the kid and can be cajoled into helping him, even if I think his actions are destroying our country. How close am I?"

"Actually, pretty good given the little I said, but it's far more serious than that. Juan is convinced Gabriel Herrera, Ángel's son, is trying to kill him or have him killed. Apparently during the fight we saw starting before they were pulled off-stage, Gabriel said something about shooting him . . . again," Professor Stark says.

"Again? That means Gabriel was in on Juan's shooting?" Jill asks. "That doesn't even make sense. Why would they want to take out the kid who renewed life in their movement?"

"I don't get the motive, other than the possibility of a power grab. For now, I think Juan doesn't have any idea who to trust and is afraid for his life. He told me to meet him near the White House gate, at least that's what I think he meant, at 5:30 a.m. this morning. It'll be just dark enough that we should be able to walk away without being seen."

"Why do you think he wants to meet there?" Jill asks.

"I think he wanted to avoid naming an explicit site, assuming his or my messaging traffic is being watched and fearing he will be caught or shot whenever he is seen. So his message said to meet where I last saw him. I last saw him as we said goodbye at the White House gate after the White House summit."

"That's mostly right," Jill says, "but if you recall we actually said goodbye by the horse statue in the Park. So how do we hang out at Lafayette Square before dawn and not look suspicious the day after a violent outbreak around the White House. That area's bound to be blocked, with police and military protection in a broad perimeter."

"I hadn't thought about that," Professor Stark says. "And I didn't think about how to meet up with him."

"I've got an idea. Fortunately, I bought you a gift so it fits in," she says, looking down toward his feet. "I didn't get socks though, so you'll have to be the goofy old man jogging in running shoes and black socks. I figured you had raced to get here so likely didn't think about what you'd be wearing today. I would have gone with something more formal, but I wasn't sure what size to get."

"You're thoughtful on top of everything else," he says to her.

"When this is over, I want to hear what you mean by everything else," she responds, smiling.

"And you'll have to tell me why you think I'm a goofy old man," he says.

"That was a reference to the black socks. Sensitive about your age, are you?"

"Not usually."

"I guess we have a couple of topics to cover when this is over," she says.

"I certainly hope 'when' is the right word," Professor Stark responds. "You need to drive, and assuming we find Juan, I suggest you tell your staff that you decided at the last minute to speak to my Thursday class on religion in government and politics. I've already notified my students we would have a special guest speaker that day."

"If I do that, I could miss votes today and tomorrow. My opponent in the next election will ridicule me for not taking my job seriously," she says.

"A, I don't think the votes you were planning to take are going to happen in light of yesterday's violence. B, I'd be surprised if the Capitol Police didn't beg Congress to take the week off until some calm can be restored. And C, we need a way to get Juan somewhere safe. I'm worried about putting him in any public transportation. I'm worried about staying in my rental car and being tracked. I think it's best to leave it somewhere where the license is tough to spot in case someone comes looking for me," Professor Stark says.

"Quite convenient of you to make me your chauffeur," Jill says.

"Frankly, there is some added security being in the company of a member of Congress should anything go wrong," Professor Stark adds.

"Sure, that's what I was thinking."

After pulling his rental into a spot in a seedy neighborhood several blocks away – a spot that may get the car pulled apart before the police find it – Professor Stark gets into Jill's car. Together, they take the short drive over to a K Street parking garage, then get out and start slowly jogging toward the Lafayette Square area. Jill wears a hat to obscure her identity, but Professor Stark keeps his face open so Juan can recognize him.

As Jill suspects, the streets around the White House are closed. The nearest they can get is the north edge of the Veterans Affairs headquarters building.

"I guess the best we can do is circle the area," she says as the two start to make a looping semi-circle jog.

"You move pretty quickly for an old man," Jill says, smiling, after about 10 minutes of jogging around the area.

"You're killing me with the old man cracks," he says, glad he had gotten back in shape over the summer, part of his continuous cycle of gaining 10 pounds every fall and winter quarter and taking most of it off at Christmas and in the summer.

As they approach a building corner, Professor Stark suddenly stops jogging. He's frozen physically. Jill looks to see what is startling him. Seeing nothing, she looks at him. His eyes are frozen on an object she can't see.

"Paul," she says. "Paul. Paul."

After a few seconds, Professor Stark responds. "Sorry. This is a bad place for me."

"Why?"

"I got beat here," he says.

"Oh, here. I didn't know this is where it happened. I was supposed to interview you the next day, you know."

"Really?"

"Yes, when I worked for the Republican News channel. I was supposed to see if I could poke holes in you or your theories."

"Maybe there was some good in it then. I'll never believe they were random robberies, you know."

"Four times in four cities in two years seems unlikely to me too," Jill says. "Are you okay to keep going? We need to find Juan."

"Yeah, let's go."

As they reach 17th and H, a vagrant gets up from the grates and whispers out, "Professor."

Professor Stark and Jill are both startled and start to turn when Juan whispers, "Look at me like you're telling me you won't give me money."

Professor Stark stops and motions like he's dismissing a request for money. Jill tips her hat up so Juan can recognize her.

"We're parked two blocks away, on K Street. Walk toward 16th and K. We'll meet you there. We won't lose sight of you," Professor Stark says as he and Jill start jogging forward and backward like the backward jog is part of their exercise program.

As the three reach the parking garage nearly simultaneously, Juan follows them down to Jill's car and they get in. Jill's privileges as a Member of Congress allow her to drive an over-sized vehicle, even in the highly restrictive D.C. area. This waiver means neither Professor Stark nor Juan need to be identified in the car.

Once inside, Juan starts to break down, and struggles to gather himself.

"I haven't been in contact with Mama since yesterday. Do you know if she's safe?" he asks.

"I haven't heard anything about her not being safe. But I can't say I know she's okay," Professor Stark says.

"Well, that'll have to do, for about 52 more minutes. I told her I would call her exactly then to find out where she is," Juan says.

"In 52 minutes? It will be lighter outside then. People could see inside my car," Jill says.

"Thank you Congresswoman, for helping. Am I safe here?" Juan asks.

"You're safe as far as I'm concerned, but we still don't know what kind of trouble you're in," she responds. "I've heard nothing about the police or anyone else issuing warrants for you."

"I didn't even have any idea until yesterday that Gabriel was in on the attempt to kill me earlier. It all makes sense now. I'm not sure they really wanted me dead before, but now that I know that the 'assassination' was a set-up, they need to get rid of me before I tell anyone," Juan says.

"So the best way to make sure your mother is safe is to keep you safe until we can get you a platform to talk to the media and tell your story. Once the facts are out there, it will be counterproductive for them to come after you or her," Jill says.

"That's what I have in mind in Chicago," Professor Stark says. "I have media coming in to hear a surprise guest speaker from Washington speak to my class on religion in government and how that changes with the brawl yesterday. The topic is important enough that we should get a substantial media presence, which will cascade nationally once the media see you are both there."

"That's a great idea Paul," she says, "but what do we do about Juan's mother."

"We need to have Juan call from somewhere extremely busy and keep the call to less than one minute. Then we need to throw that Lifelink away and get the hell out of there before anyone catches us. Agreed."

"Agreed."

After finding that his mother had safely made it with an old friend into a safe location, and hearing she would stay tucked away until he could get to her, Juan hangs up and tosses the girl's Lifelink he had taken into a shopping mall parking lot garbage can. Jill sets the car directions for Professor Stark's home in Chicago and the car takes off. Thirty minutes later, all three doze off.

CHAPTER 39

September 11, 2020
New Rite Headquarters, Colorado

September 11 marks the 20-year anniversary of the overdose death of Luke Alton. Luke started a daily weed habit as a 12-year-old seventh grader. Slowing down his brain helped Luke deal with the boredom of class work so dumbed down that he performed well while half-listening, drugged up and never studying. To Luke, the in-class boredom was palpable, a feeling older brother JT could sympathize with. JT had survived by spending the bulk of his time pursuing an intense interest in weaponry and electronics. He was a freak to his classmates, and was constantly watched as potentially dangerous by school social workers, but JT's childhood fascination was in the mechanics of making the weapons work rather than in the outcome of using the weapons.

Luke's effort to have a purpose came from delivering drugs, collecting cash, and testing his body against an increasingly dangerous mix of narcotics, alcohol and painkillers. He kept track of what he took, the impact on his body and recovery time as he tested to find the perfect concoction. The fatal concoction noted in his tracker pad included a mix of heroine, alcohol, hallucinogens, painkillers and a blend drug called HD.

Eleven years Luke's elder, JT left his mom's house less than one hour after finishing high school and only rarely returned to check on his little brother. JT struggled to deal with a younger brother taking attention away from him after years as an only child. With Luke taking any attention, JT's obsession with weapons deepened and provided a ready excuse to withdraw from his family. JT's anger grew exponentially when his father took off to start another family and forgot about the one he already had. JT couldn't decide then whether he was angrier with his father, the two-year-old Luke or the house-wrecker his father left to be with.

JT's survival and gaming company was already showing success in his early twenties. Luke started to play the New Rite games, though JT sensed Luke's real interest was mainly in connecting with him. They talked from time-to-time as Luke grew older, and sometimes JT would ask Luke to tell him how kids would react to new weapons or scenarios he and his fast-growing company created. They talked every couple of months, enough for JT to tell Luke was struggling, but not enough for him to understand the destructive impact Luke's addictions were taking on his life.

JT knew something was wrong when his mother and father showed up together at his company headquarters. He hadn't seen them together since his dad had walked out on the family. It made him wish for days when he had a real family, but he could see from the pain in their eyes and faces that this wasn't a happy visit.

"Mom. Dad? What are you doing here?" he said at the time.

"Luke's dead," she said, sobbing and starting to collapse to the ground. JT's dad pulled a chair over and sat her down.

"What?"

"Drug overdose. I thought I should tell you in person, but I just couldn't bear the thought of telling you alone," JT's mom said.

JT walked over to close the screens on his office and sat down as well, biting his lip, pulling his fingers in tight to his palms and upper body shaking as he struggled for control. "What the hell happened? How do you die from lighting up?" he asked.

"It wasn't just the weed. Luke was a mess. We both tried everything we could to get him straightened out," his mom said.

"Why didn't you tell me this before, when I could have done something," he said angrily, glaring at them.

His mom gathered enough strength to stand up and walk over to JT. "He was a smart kid like you. I thought this was a phase," she said.

"I want you to have this," she added, handing Luke's Lifelink to JT. "This was still open when I found Luke. I put it away before the police got to the house, but I saw that he had drug experiments on it before the screen locked up. I want you to have it and see if you can find out something that helps us understand this."

Using code-breaking technology he acquired to help build and protect his gaming systems, JT quickly unlocked Luke's pad. The password was a heartbreaker to JT. "JTmybro11" was the code that opened the pad.

For a drug addict, the pad's contents were surprisingly orderly.

Scanning through the contents, JT saw day-by-day narcotic mixes, each with notes that described physical sensation, emotional feeling, after-effects and Luke's overall rating. The mixes include the who's who of body and brain killers. The list ran nearly a full year, making clear to JT that Luke's troubles had been deep.

Looking through the rest of the pad's contents, he found something else – a password-encrypted note he knew he had to bust. Hooking up his software, he quickly broke the code to file "Dream2020" and found names, phone numbers and other information that told him that Luke had been actively delivering and picking up cash for a local drug gang. JT called in his security director and asked him to identify Luke's dealers, without leaving evidence of a connection.

"Mom. Dad. I'll be home tomorrow. You go ahead. But know this. I won't forget the people who did this to Luke. I won't forgive either," he told them then.

Days later, on returning to his company headquarters outside of Denver, JT's security director let him know what he had found. The gangs were believed by the FBI to have been supplied by a fast-rising Mexican drug cartel leader known as Caskillo.

JT had not been there for his younger brother when he was alive. He was not about to abandon him in death.

Twenty years later, he is ready to take his revenge.

CHAPTER 40

September 12, 2040
Chicago

An hour before his Wednesday class starts, and with campus police protecting his guests, Professor Stark sends a class alert on who is speaking, lets them know the larger room that has been secured to hold the class, and sends a media alert. Campus police realize Juan has received death threats and set a full security perimeter around the building.

Though better rested, Juan is nervous when he arrives in front of the class. Jill is comfortable speaking in front of any group, and knows the discussion on government and religion will be an afterthought to Juan's announcement.

Professor Stark and Jill had helped Juan with his scripted opening statement, which he veers from at times as he provides his description of what happened.

Dressed in slightly oversized clothes Professor Stark had picked up for him, Juan found himself entirely surrounded by uncomfortable environment. Not his clothes. Not his city. Not his people. So he takes a deep breath.

"I've been accused by Gabriel Herrera of being a traitor to the cause of liberation for Latinos in America. His accusation came after a heated argument on whether we should encourage the violence occurring in Washington Tuesday. I strongly argued that conflict will not bring the freedom we seek, and that truth in our message will win if we give it energy and time. What followed this argument was a threat made by Gabriel that he would shoot me. What's more, Gabriel said he would, and I quote, 'shoot me again.' I took this statement as meaning Gabriel either knew about or spearheaded the convention center shooting. From the look in Gabriel's eye, I knew to take his threat seriously, and ran to avoid physical harm."

Several reporters start sending out rapid-fire alerts as the press conference unfolds: "H2M power grab may be involved in Juan Gonzalez shooting. Juan Gonzalez escaped second murder attempt." Other alerts follow in succession as Juan continues.

As soon as the gravity of Juan's charges becomes clear, national news networks switch to live coverage.

"Not knowing who I can trust to help and feeling betrayed by someone who had become like family, I asked Professor Stark for help getting to safety. I would like to thank Professor Stark and Congresswoman Carlson, who put their own lives at risk to get me here. Though we disagree on some issues, I met them in debates and found them to be good people. I was hopeful the H2M security team, which is far more capable than I think anyone would suspect, would not think to follow Professor Stark in their efforts to find me before I could speak in public and save my life and that of my Mother."

As Juan sits back on a chair behind, Professor Stark steps to the podium next. "Congresswoman Carlson and I each have a short statement to make. We'll take 10 minutes of questions, and then my class and I will walk down the hall to hold our actual class session today with Mr. Gonzalez and the Congresswoman as our special guests. That session will be livecast, so you will have access to our discussion, but the questions there will be questions from my students."

Professor Stark twitches at his sport coat and tie he has donned for the media gathering as he starts his review of the last two days.

"Juan left an urgent voice message for me Tuesday telling me he felt physically threatened. In my interactions with Juan, I found him to be a decent and thoughtful young man whose primary failing is he doesn't have enough experience to understand the implications of his views. That aside, I like Juan and am honored he trusts me to help. I'm also grateful to Jill, Congresswoman Carlson, for the extraordinary risks she took to get us here safely. It's clear to me that Juan's life is threatened. Once we were secured in this building this morning, I phoned an aide to President Phillipi to ask that they retrieve Juan's mother from the location she has been hiding in. Because of concern that H2M's security team would be able to track Juan and his mother electronically, both had not used any traceable devices, save for a one-minute exchange between the two yesterday morning using a device that didn't belong to any of us.

"Oh yeah," Juan says, walking back to the microphone panel. "I forgot I need to apologize to the girl who I kissed her hand for taking her Lifelink when we traded hats. I hope she can forgive me and I will pay her back for whatever I owe. I hope she will understand."

Professor Stark looks at Juan. "If she didn't understand before, I'm sure she understands now."

"Sorry, I needed to say that."

Seeing that Juan was done, Professor Stark continues.

"I'm pleased to tell you that Mrs. Gonzalez was found safe and sound by the Secret Service holed up in a National Art Gallery janitor's closet, where she had retreated when violence started on the Mall."

Jill walks over to the center of the stage to speak next.

"Normally, when a man calls you and says he wants to come over in the middle of the night, his intentions are pretty clear," she says, looking at Professor Stark and gaining an unusual amount of laughter from the gathered media.

"When Professor Stark called to tell me he would show up at my door in the middle of the night, I did not suspect we would be jogging before dawn, picking up a young man disguised as a vagrant near Lafayette Square and getting in my car to drive all day to Chicago. I also would have thought you crazy if you told me I would empty moving boxes in Paul's garage, climb in the box and be rolled with Juan by Paul, uh Professor Stark, into his house to avoid any indication we were there. Only later did I contemplate that it was my car in his garage. Like Professor Stark, I had the opportunity to get to know Juan during several debates and find him a decent young man thrust into the national spotlight by a group that now appears to have just been using his love for his people. With those comments, we'll open up to your questions."

Media members try to outshout each other to get the first question.

"Mr. Gonzalez, you've accused the President of H2M of threatening to kill you and of having been involved in your shooting earlier this year. By doing this, don't you believe you're dooming the chances of securing independence for the Southwest, for your people? Doesn't the simple act of reporting this internal disagreement show that you will sacrifice your cause for your own personal advantage?" a reporter from MSDNC asks.

Juan looks at the reporter, checks a translation and shakes his head.

"Wow, that's an interesting spin on me objecting to being killed. Let me ask you, if someone in this group told you they were going to shoot you and you knew in your heart they intended to do it, would you not report it to avoid harming the image of the media? That's loco. Clearly, if I was not willing to risk my own life for this cause, I would have gone away after the first murder attempt. But there's a big difference between knowing generically that some people might want you dead and knowing specifically that someone close to you is trying to kill you. I have no reason to believe this extends in H2M beyond one evil individual. That the security team chased me after Gabriel accused me of being a traitor is their job, given what they have been told."

"So you had nothing to do with the bomb attempt?" came the follow-up question.

"Of course not. They don't teach bomb-making in high school chemistry," Juan responds. "At least not in West Nogales."

Another reporter asks the next question. "Do you fear for your safety right now?"

"Now that I have had the chance to explain what happened, I think the H2M security team, and those who might have been inspired by Gabriel's attacks in the media against me, will now back down and wait for the facts. I feel as safe now as I did before the rally, particularly now that I know my mother is safe."

From the side of the room, a younger reporter asks, "Gabriel accused you of being a collaborator with the White House, and now you have turned to the President and the Secret Service to protect your mother. Doesn't this suggest that you are, in fact, comfortable collaborating with the White House and might indeed be working against the interests of the secession cause?"

Professor Stark can see Juan is a bit shaken. He's struggling himself to keep from going after the reporter.

Leaning over, he pulls Juan away from the sound system. "This is what they do, Juan. Focus on what you want to say, not the questions they ask," he whispers lightly.

After Juan bites his lip briefly to remind himself to maintain composure, he responds.

"I've been clear since I got involved in these public debates – first on language and then on secession – that we need to pursue our goals without violence. The lessons of Mahatma, Mandela and Martin are ones we must not lose. I learned that in school, but heard this even more from Ángel Herrera, who in a short time became as close to a father for me as I have had. All three knew their causes were born of truth, and I feel the same about this cause. Truth might require patience to succeed, but it ultimately wins," he tells the media and student audience.

After Juan clarifies for a few who aren't sure that he is referring to Mahatma Gandhi, Nelson Mandela and Martin Luther King, Jr., another young reporter who Juan recognizes as working for TMZ.com asks the next question.

"Professor, it sounds like the Congresswoman is saying she thought you were making a booty call. Does this mean the two of you are hooking up?" he asks.

Before Professor Stark can respond, Jill holds her hand up and pushes him away.

"I did not say that I thought Professor Stark was making a booty call because I would tell any man to buy himself a blow-up doll if I thought that was his intent. And that's when I'm in a good mood. I was mystified though at what he intended to do when he made it to my home. Anyone who knows Professor Stark knows it had to be something serious. I simply joked that the intent of most men who want to visit in the middle of the night isn't tough to figure out," Jill responds.

"Does that mean you aren't interested in getting together with the Professor?" the TMZ reporter asks as a follow up.

"I don't see how that matters when we're talking about subjects as serious as those exposed today," Jill says.

"So that's a yes?"

Professor Stark moves to the podium. "Clearly we've allowed one too many questions and lost focus on the seriousness of the issues raised today. Now if my students can follow me with your Lifelink in hand, we'll proceed to class."

As they walk toward class, he turns to Jill. "Remind me never to let that reporter in anywhere again."

CHAPTER 41

September 12, 2040
Chicago

"You've been exposed directly to what is likely one of the most troubling, lurid stories of the year," Professor Stark says as he opens the class. "But you're all here to learn more than criminal behavior, so I've invited Mr. Gonzalez and Congresswoman Carlson to take part in our discussion. Who wants to start the discussion of the connection between religion and government?"

Jeremy volunteers to kick off the discussion.

"Professor, given the events of the last several days, it's hard for me to focus. We just witnessed some of the largest and deadliest conflicts between Americans since the 1960s and 1970s, and while government is involved, it's hard to really see the role religion has played in the debate. So I stepped back to something you wrote in *The END* and this is where my 100 words starts," Jeremy says.

"So, just to be clear Jeremy, I shouldn't count the 50-plus words you used to introduce your 100-word statement against you. Is that your plan?" Professor Stark says.

Nodding his head, Jeremy proceeds.

"You wrote that, 'effective government controls citizens' rights and money only to keep them from being controlled or harmed by others, to meet basic needs of those incapable of self-help, and to provide essential infrastructure no private organization or lower government could effectively provide.' Religion, in my view, is about enabling people to believe whatever they must to control their base instincts, which I support as long as those beliefs aren't turned into tools to control society. So, government keeps religion from infringing on the rights of the people, and religion keeps governments from infringing on fundamental rights of humanity," Jeremy says.

"Interesting start, Jeremy, we'll take several more before we ask Juan and the Congresswoman to comment."

After another student comments on how organized religion helps people rationalize societal institutionalization, Rachel discusses her perspective.

"Religion can play a role in society in three ways. First, it can, as Jeremy said, provide internal reasons to control our bad behavior. Second, it provides the basis on which a society can establish order – the ground rules of working with each other. Third, when religion is misused, in my view, it creates justifications for those who want to control others. Governments and religions interact in each of these: enforcing laws set by the community, and managing the military and police forces needed to control others who would take advantage of us," Rachel says.

"Interesting ideas, some of which we may explore further. Next," Professor Stark says.

Tamika takes her chance to expound her views.

"Religion is primarily a tool to aid the weak, undisciplined and ungoverned. Most religions describe in detail actions that are acceptable and unacceptable. Given that men write these rules, just as men write government rules – no offense Congresswoman – I see religion and secular government as an either-or proposition. Good religions, and they aren't all good, help people to place long-term collective success ahead of short-term individual gratification. When governments are strong, they have clear, enforced rules. When this happens, religions fade to minimal roles. When governments are weak, religions must gain strength to help control society's worst impulses," Tamika says.

Next up is Jun Chen, the son of a Chinese government official who is studying at Chicago to better understand Americans before entering Chinese government ranks.

"I hope you don't mind if I speak from my perspective on an American issue," Jun says to Professor Stark, who nods his assent.

"I would argue that government's job is to facilitate hope and enable opportunity, while ensuring that individuals act with a full sense of responsibility and accountability. I think government's role is to provide access to the tools we need to achieve our greatest collective success and contribution. That greatest success does not necessarily mean the right to pursue happiness – as your Constitution states – particularly if your pursuit of happiness comes at the expense of others. We have a greater obligation than happiness. So to me, I agree with Tamika, with strong government, religion becomes unnecessary," Jun says, well aware his father's business enemies track his words.

Professor Stark is impressed that the students seem to have largely recalled his direction.

"Several interesting viewpoints and thank you for sticking to the 100-word requirement, but let me stop at this point to ask Jill and Juan if they have something they want to add to the discussion," Professor Stark says as he looks toward the pair.

Jill finds herself also uncomfortable wearing clothes that Professor Stark thought were today's style. At least he got the sizes right, following her written instructions. "I think an interesting viewpoint has been expressed by this gentleman," she says, motioning toward Jun. "However, I do not see government and religion as duplicative, but rather as interdependent. For those of you raised in religious households, you know that church services, sermons, readings can provide the back story that helps us to understand why we follow rules in a free and fair society. To his and the first speaker's point, I see the role of Congress as passing those rules and regulations – and only those rules and regulations – necessary to create a well-functioning society that properly balances opportunity and responsibility, while protecting our fundamental rights as human beings," she says.

With a glint of a smile, she turns to Professor Stark: "I hope you don't mind if I continue here, because I'm sure I'm sailing past your 100-word requirement."

Professor Stark chuckles lightly and nods.

"Great. I was hoping I could get more than 100 words in return for joining you in a life-threatening endeavor, being woken in the middle of the night and being boxed up like a piece of furniture to be carted into your house," she adds, with the class laughing, welcome relief to the high level of tension they all continue to feel.

"So, my point," Jill continues. "My point is that people are driven in equal measures by fear and hope. Governments largely operate to implement rules that create a tangible fear in our lives. Fear of being jailed, fined, taken from or taxed, government rules are focused on protecting us from others and protecting others from needing to fear us. Religions also can operate on fears. The fear of eternal damnation is a mighty motivator to believers, but is more intangible than government-imposed fears and requires a higher level of understanding to follow."

"Both can create fear, but I believe religions are far better suited than government to provide hope. Religion can provide us a reason to keep moving forward when every ounce of our being wants to give up in the face of the obstacles life throws at us. Life is not always fair. In fact, it is almost never fair. But religion reminds us to be grateful for who we are and what we have, because we can always find people facing even greater challenges that God decided not to put in our path. When government gets too far into the business of trying to mandate fairness, it almost always fails to ensure that hope and opportunity are matched with responsibility and accountability, to the gentleman's point, which only creates a different type of inequity and muzzles the human spirit. Juan?"

From the corner of her eye, Jill sees Juan stand up and start pacing around the room, trying to fight off a wave of exhaustion creeping over his body as the enormity of the last two day's events subsides.

"Well, thank you for the opportunity to take part in this discussion. I haven't even started college yet, so forgive me for being nervous," Juan says. "If I hadn't taken the year off to get the independence initiatives passed, I might have been here on Monday instead of being chased around D.C. I just hope I don't bomb, uhm, uh, I mean suck."

He walks up and down the aisles as he talks.

"When I got involved in getting passage of the Spanish-only requirement in Arizona, I did it because a giant company tried to destroy my opportunities as an individual to achieve success I believe I should be able to pursue. When that happened, it was clear to me that pursuing religion as the solution wouldn't work. I pray every week for the opportunity to honor the sacrifices my mother made, but I didn't see God intervening to choose Spanish over English. As a Catholic, my God accepts prayers in any language. So I saw this as a government role, to ensure fair opportunity. I see the same with the independence movement. In the Southwest states, we had the unusual situation of having our majority populations governed by rules established by people who don't share the same land, the same language or the same values."

Rachel instinctively raises her arm to ask a question and gets the nod from Professor Stark to go ahead.

"Juan, is it okay if I call you Juan?" she says. After seeing him nod his approval, she continues.

"Juan, I was born and raised at the south end of North California. Today, the primary language spoken there is English, but if you go just a bit south, you're in South California. California del Sur has largely operated in Spanish since its creation and my friends there see themselves as more aligned with Mexico than with those of us in North California and the rest of the United States. If you succeed in your ballot initiative to form an independent, Spanish-speaking country, isn't the logical next step that people near me will want to secede, and that Nevada and parts of Chicago and New York will want to secede, and southern Florida will want to become part of Cuba. At what point do the people who move to or live in a country have an obligation to ensure the success of that nation?" she asks.

Professor Stark interjects, "Rachel that's a fair and reasonable question if this were still the press conference, but please explain what that has to do with the role of religion and government?"

"Not much really, but given that people are dying now over this issue, and that almost any rational religion objects to murder except in self-defense, the philosophical battle over the right of a race or ethnicity to control its destiny is now mixed with moral issues over whether killing people is justified to let them control their destiny," Rachel says. "Juan was shot, the leader of H2M was killed, we had bombings on the roads and at colleges, and hundreds of people were killed at the supposed freedom rally. Now you, and Juan and the Congresswoman have been running for your lives – fearing someone might want to kill you – and I'm totally freaking out."

Professor Stark looks around a while, delaying his response as he thinks through whether to let the class go off on this topic. He peers over at Juan and Jill and both shrug their shoulders as if to say why not.

"Okay, this is a bit off topic, but since we likely have more than our share of people watching this livecast and I can't think of any subject more critical for our nation to consider and understand, let's go ahead and have this discussion," Professor Stark says.

Jill offers her thoughts, "I understand and sympathize with Juan and those who live in areas where a language other than English is the predominant language. Over the centuries, we had large groups of immigrants enter the country to pursue freedom or economic opportunity. For most of our nation's history, the primary social services for these immigrants were provided through churches – through religious institutions. When a large group of Poles moved to Chicago, the Catholic Church and others provided social services in Polish, but government actions remained in English. Immigrants could get help with the basics of life – food, shelter, housing, entry-level work – without learning English. But to fully succeed in society, to be educated and to participate in government, you had to learn the language," she said.

"Throughout that time, it was not unusual for first generation immigrants to stay closely connected to their heritage and language, and to be comfortable with the limitations on success that came with that isolation. They made those sacrifices so subsequent generations educated in public or private church schools could become substantially more integrated into society. Often, for the parents, it was difficult to foresee what that integration meant. Over time, marriage between ethnicities, religions and backgrounds helped to breed understanding across racial and religious lines of the common elements between us as people, and we became an increasingly tolerant, though clearly highly imperfect society. As we moved in the past 50 years toward a society in which some immigrants were no longer expected to integrate into the mainstream, and no longer needed to integrate to get access to every opportunity, we created a nation of separation. That is a mistake."

As she finishes, Juan looks to Professor Stark to ask permission to speak. "It's your floor, Mr. Gonzalez."

"I believe countries need to change as the people inside its borders change. It's human nature for us to want to be governed by people who are as much like us as possible and, no disrespect to the Congresswoman whom I greatly admire, but the people in Washington are not very much like me and certainly live in circumstances very different from the way I live and were raised in situations completely different from how I was raised."

"That's true for most of us here," Tamika interrupts, with heads nodding around the room.

"I understand they live differently, there," Juan says. "But we don't even think they care about what's going on in our part of the country or with our people."

Tamika stands up. "Juan, if I may, I would like to invite you to go home with me for dinner, and see if maybe you won't see there are a lot of us who feel disconnected from our government, and think they don't care very much."

"If it's possible to do this, perhaps the three of us could all join you," Juan says, motioning to Professor Stark and Jill.

"I'm sure it's okay, but let me call my mom to check," Tamika says.

"Juan, if you don't mind," Jill says. "I understand what it's like to feel isolated and abandoned. You see other kids out there who have it easy. They have two parents. They get to go have fun at night instead of working to make enough to eat and heat the house. They drive a car to school instead of spending two hours on the bus every day. There's two ways to respond. You can either spend your time trying to destroy people who have it easy and think that after thousands of years of life being unfair, that you can magically make it fair for everyone. Or you can do the hard work it takes to create a better life for yourself and your family, take pride in overcoming more than everyone else around you, and then be blessed with the ability to make life a little fairer for people like you with the actions you take and contributions you make."

"I agree. I think it's my responsibility to make life a little fairer for people like me," Juan replies.

A second later, Tamika's Lifelink vibrates and she looks down at the screen.

"My mom says it's okay," she announces. Professor Stark sends a quick message to campus police asking them to protect them on their visit.

"We can continue this discussion at your house," Juan says, "I see class time is about to end, so here's my final comment. Well I hope not my final comment, but my final comment for this class."

A bit of nervous laughter echoes in the room.

"Whether a society rebels against rulers who try to take their country from them, or whether immigrants to a country gradually take control of positions of power, change is inevitable for any nation. Change that occurs by force, through the use of power and fear, does not last. Change that occurs because it's clear it's in the best interests of all involved can last for millennia. If you look at the history of China, something I studied as I worked on Mandarin, you see military-like crusades that expanded and shrunk the size of China over thousands of years. But when military force was the dominant means of controlling a society, and when Chinese of different ethnicities were excluded from the ruling class, the environment for rebellion grew and the central part of China eventually shrank," he tells Professor Stark's class.

"It's hard to argue Latinos aren't part of the ruling class in the United States. We have governors, senators, representatives and even Supreme Court justices of Latino descent. But all of these people have to speak English to do anything. For those Latinos without the ability to speak English, they endure isolation from government and, often, economic isolation as well. By separating the Southwest into a separate country, more of us will be able to participate in running our government, and without interference from people who don't really know us."

"Juan," Jill says, "I think it's clear we agree on the problem – the isolation of parts of the nation from the rest of the country. It is terrible government policy to allow this, and your effort to impose a Spanish-language government requirement in Arizona tacitly acknowledges that everyone should speak a common language for a government to truly serve its people."

"You'll have to explain 'tacitly' to me later," Juan says.

"Certainly, given your skill with English, I forget English isn't your native language, or even just your second language. Perhaps Professor Stark was right when we first debated this topic. Perhaps you're on the right solution if the problem is defined as Arizona. I define the problem as encompassing the United States, and with that as the area of interest, perhaps the right step is an English-only requirement for government, with full services to help everyone learn the language," Jill says.

Rachel raises her hand, asking for a chance to ask another question.

"Since I didn't really get into the role of religion and government earlier, I wanted to redeem myself raising a topic that directly deals with the topic. In the Christian Bible, the story about the Tower of Babel suggests that God wanted to keep people from sharing a common language to prevent them from building a tower that reached him in the skies. If this story is right that God created diversity of languages and does not want everyone in the world to speak one language, how does that perspective fit with any single-language requirement?" Rachel asks.

"That's certainly an interesting question," Professor Stark says, "and one we need to spend a lot more than the two minutes we have left discussing. We still haven't covered much of the content I originally intended for today. Good news is we'll continue to cover the papers you prepared for today at our next session. The bad news is I expect you to post 1,000-word summaries on two additional topics. The topics: One, from the perspective of the religion of your choice, what actions would the texts that govern that religion suggest be taken on language requirements in Arizona and the United States? Two, what conflicts, if any, would implementing that perspective create for maintaining appropriate separation of church and state under the U.S. Constitution?"

"Juan, to conclude, I think you should consider the University of Chicago next year. I would start you with an A on your first test in my class, since you have done so well here," Professor Stark says, "even though I don't agree with your conclusions."

On the way to Tamika's home later that day, Juan travels by car with Jill and Professor Stark. Tamika invites Rachel to also join, with both traveling by train.

The conversation is relaxed, certainly more so than it had been the last two days. Juan changes that as he asks Jill and Professor Stark a question.

"If we had been killed this week, would either of you have had any regrets?" he asks.

"Regrets. Besides being dead," Jill says.

"I mean, like not being married, and not having kids," he says.

"Actually, it probably would have been easier not having kids. As bad as it hurt to lose my mom, I can't imagine how painful it was for her to leave her girls," Jill says. "I never want to know what that feels like."

"What about being married?" Juan asks.

"Boy, you don't back away from the tough questions do you?" Jill says.

"It's alright if you don't want to answer. I'm just trying to figure out if everything you get from a career is worth it. I've been questioning whether any of this is worth it if I die," Juan says.

"A career didn't keep me from finding the right husband," Jill says. "I just wasn't lucky enough to find someone I wanted to be with for all of what's left of my life. What about you Paul?"

"I was hoping you'd leave me out of this," Professor Stark says.

"I think we've gone through enough together in the last few days that a few personal questions are appropriate," Jill says.

"Well, if I'm being honest, I would have liked to have settled down and had a family 15 years ago. I kept hoping God had a plan for me. Now, I'm just hoping he's done testing my patience," Professor Stark says.

"You mean she's done, don't you," Jill says.

"Sure, I can go with that. But you don't need to rush into anything at your age Juan. I'm sure you'll know when you've found the right time and the right person."

"I hope I have that chance," Juan says.

CHAPTER 42

September 12, 2040
New Rite Compound, Utah

The underground tunnel from a small shed on the edge of the New Rite Utah property opens up. Pete is relieved to find the cargo door open and the APB sealed to the tunnel entrance. Deeply exhausted, he's barely settled inside before falling asleep. JT walks toward the APB thirty minutes later after completing his site leadership team review.

Hearing a light snore, he stops early to say goodbye to the camp director. "You left the noisemaker on," he says quietly, pretending he's talking to himself, and making mental note that he now needs to develop a human sound noisemaker.

JT jumps in, turns on the engine to cover the snore, checks back to be sure it is Pete, closes the cargo door and takes off.

Though Pete awakens on lift-off, JT and Pete discuss nothing on the flight to Colorado, fearing voice scans will pick up Pete over the quiet whoosh of the APB. Any physical or electronic communication before Pete returns to where computers say he has been will compromise several weeks of cover. Law enforcement focus on New Rite after the Juan Gonzalez shooting has both men on heightened alert.

The flight back is quick. A crisp, early fall day displays the full beauty of this part of the United States. Colors have not yet fully come to the area, but the combination of trees, mountain lakes and rivers, barren sandstone and sprawling subdivisions create enough visual diversity to make the trip interesting even after dozens of such trips for JT. Pete sees nothing but the interior of the APB from his spot, which JT has stocked with non-dehydrated fresh fruit, vegetables and clean water that Pete had gone so long without. Once landed at the Colorado camp, Pete waits for the cargo hold to seal before climbing down into the underground tunnel that runs to JT's mountain home.

JT prepares all New Rite sites with these tunnels, telling those who build them they assure his luggage and electronic equipment stay safe when he lands in wet weather. In reality, JT wants to maximize freedom of movement – for himself and the weaponry he and his team develop.

Meeting with Pete inside the Colorado camp home, JT is anxious to update Pete on the success of his mission and subsequent events but gives Pete 30 minutes to shower and change, having endured enough strong body odor in the APB.

JT meets Pete on the outdoor deck of his guest home area, this time carrying a blackened filet, bacon-wrapped scallops, pecan-crusted sweet potato gratin, grilled leeks and apple crisp – all prepared by Ally who had earlier asked Pete about his food favorites. Ally was surprised at how long Pete had been holed up in the guest cabin without asking for anything or coming to see her, so she enjoyed the chance to make what she recalled was his dream meal, particularly after finding out he hadn't actually been there.

"The world has changed since you left, Pete, and I can't thank you enough for what you've done," JT says from the comfort of the guest home that was carefully built to prevent sound monitoring.

"More than that, since Ángel's death, H2M has held a rally that turned violent, led to thousands of demonstrators being killed, shot and arrested trying to break into the White House, and caused a media firestorm when Ángel's son, who had quickly taken over H2M, threatened to shoot Juan Gonzalez – the kid – and get this, 'again.'"

"What do you mean 'again'?" Pete asks.

"Well, if yesterday's press conference is to be believed, it appears Gabriel Herrera and perhaps others in H2M arranged the assassination attempt on Juan – the one you and many others in New Rite were questioned about," JT says. "Even better, the media are speculating that if Gabriel was involved in the kid's shooting, it's quite possible Ángel's shooting was arranged by

H2M as well – either as a coup attempt by Gabriel or a desire by Ángel to be martyred," JT says, walking over to grab a glass of melted mountain snow from the cabin refrigerator. "They're even saying now the shot may have been remote controlled."

"From our perspective, this couldn't have worked any better. Not only did you accomplish what we needed, but you also didn't draw any suspicion. And, because only a couple of people in my organization – including now you – know we have this missile rifle technology, the White House thinks a foreign government or a certain hated Mexican drug lord must have arranged the attack," JT says.

Pete nods his head and relaxes a bit more comfortably in his seat, still eating in small bites. His stomach has shrunk over the past several weeks.

"So," JT says, "the key question now is how do you feel?"

Pete looks at JT, trying to get a sense of what JT means by "feel."

"I'm just tired," Pete says. After several seconds of silence, he adds, "But I don't feel any remorse, if that's what you mean – not after what you told me he has been doing. I feel like I saved a lot of lives. The weapons you provided all worked. No way I could have pulled this off on my own," Pete says.

"They have video of it everywhere if you want to see," JT says. "Personally, I recommend it's better not to watch. You don't need the image in your head."

"Yeah, I'll think about it," Pete responds.

As JT stands up to leave Pete alone, Pete asks a question he has thought about since getting to the Utah compound.

"You know, the smartest thing for you to do is to kill me here. I realize I don't stay in touch with my family. I'm the only one who knows about your connection. You can go through the rest of your life knowing no one alive knows anything. I know I would never tell anyone, but how could you know what's in my mind," Pete says, with JT looking at him quizzically.

"Pete, I tested you 100 times to make sure you were the right person before I brought you in. I trust you. You can trust me. This partnership is far from behind us. America may be on the brink of civil war. Would you get rid of your best soldier with war looming," JT says, and smiles.

"I guess the next question is, what happens if I'm caught," Pete says.

"Very simple," JT responds. "There's no prison in the United States I can't get you out of. It might not be the first day you're there, but if you get caught, your interest in freedom depends on me being outside to free you. You trust me, and I'll take care of you."

JT leaves and heads back through the tunnel to his main home on the other side of the mountain. As he does, Pete decompresses a bit, lays down on the bed, and falls into a deep sleep where he remains for the next 14 hours.

As he awakes the next morning to the aroma of coffee, bacon, scrambled eggs with green pepper and onion, and a cup of yogurt with fresh berries and granola, he feels a gentle shoulder massage, which he hopes is not from JT. Seeing Ally smiling and patting his shoulder as she now knows he is awake, Pete concludes that JT must have changed his mind, because he somehow ended up in heaven. His heaven ends quickly when Ally rubs the top of his head, tells him where his training clothes are and gives him his training regimen for the day.

"JT needs your help with another project and you need to start training today to be ready," she says, walking away in what Pete sees looks like military gear.

Too stunned to respond, Pete just sits up and stares past the door as Ally walks away.

CHAPTER 43

September 13, 2040
Washington, D.C.

The last of the presidential open primaries is just days away. With most of the state primaries concluded, it's almost certain that President Phillipi will fall short of the 50 percent of national vote needed to avoid a November run-off. Now back to and stuck in the White House because of the ongoing national crisis, Phillipi knows the nation is on the brink of disastrous, potentially violent protests.

Juan's press conference alleging Gabriel's involvement in his shooting gives the President a chance to position H2M as a national interloper and he isn't going to waste this opportunity. Choosing the Lincoln Memorial for a national address, Phillipi ignores advice to condemn his almost certain run-off opponent for her tepid response to violence at the Freedom March rally. Phillipi is startled Democratic candidate Sue Appling had so quickly called for a national day of mourning for the H2M rally attendees who died in the violent confrontation with no mention of the anti-rally protesters who were killed, including dozens of women and children on both sides. But with the violence occurring so close to the open primary, he assumes the Democratic contender is appealing to the large Hispanic vote and pro-secession supporters to ensure making the run-off. Once in, he expects her to move to a more centrist position for November.

Set up so video feeds will show the contoured marble sculpture of President Lincoln behind him, President Phillipi again argues the future of the nation is at stake, with a more animated, impassioned speech than is his norm.

"The last time a group of U.S. citizens thought they deserved the right to run a country under their own rules, with their own leadership, and without the interference of people with whom they disagreed, 625,000 Americans lost their lives. During the Civil War, nearly two percent of the U.S. population was killed – more people than in World Wars 1 and 2 combined. To put that in perspective, if the same percent of people are killed today, eight million of our friends and family die," Phillipi starts, pausing to let the severity of a civil war sink in to those listening. "I hope we all agree violent conflict is an unacceptable outcome. Efforts to incite such violence cannot be tolerated."

"So tonight, I stand before you, in the shadow of a President who sacrificed everything to secure the united future of our union, asking that we honor the sacrifices of our forefathers, as well as the generations before us who fought for our freedoms. Those who seek to secede from our union may tell you they will guarantee the same rights and freedoms under their leadership, but we all know no such guarantee can be trusted. The referenda proposed in Texas, New Mexico, Arizona and South California are carefully written to express support for secession, without expressly creating an act of treason. As a group of Americans created the initiative, we could initially find no link to our enemies. Without such link, it is our obligation to protect First Amendment free speech and assembly rights. It would set a dangerous precedent to take away what our founders correctly deemed inalienable rights.

"Tonight, though, I asked the Justice Department to begin a rapid and full-scale investigation into links between Honor to Mexico and the Castillo drug cartel – one of our largest and most sophisticated foreign enemies. Should we find these proposals were initiated, supported or otherwise enabled by Castillo or elements of the Mexican national government associated with the Castillo organization, we will find Americans who took part in this and prosecute them for treason. We also initiated an investigation into the involvement of Gabriel Herrera and others elements of the H2M leadership into the shooting of Juan Gonzalez and the assassination of Ángel Herrera. The method used in the attempted assassination of Mr.

Gonzalez is unusual. We traced a component used to a company owned, we believe, by Cesar Castillo. If the accusation by Mr. Gonzalez that Gabriel was involved in his shooting turns out to be true, the direct link between that shooting and the Castillo organization creates grave concerns for our national security."

Even before President Phillipi began his speech, Gabriel and several other H2M officers departed Washington D.C. by private jet, travelling to Arizona. Prior to and during the course of their flight, they negotiate with Governor Jesús Muñoz to provide secure protection, and land at a large Arizona National Guard base the governor established near the Mexico border just a few years earlier.

After landing, Gabriel releases a video statement he carefully scripted with his team during the flight.

"It is shameful that the U.S. President is seeking to use lies and manipulations to defeat a freedom initiative that allows Latinos to gain control of their future through an independent Republic," Gabriel says in the statement.

"I fully and firmly deny accusations of any involvement in the shooting of Juan Gonzalez, find it contemptible that anyone would accuse me of complicity in the death of my father, and absolutely deny any association with the Castillo cartel."

As the President arrives at the White House, having walked back over the objection of the Secret Service with cameras covering him, Chief of Staff Vijay Chinh greets him with a hard copy of Gabriel's remarks. "What do you make of this?" the President asks Chinh after he finishes reading.

"I don't know that there's anything else to say, though I do find it curious that he left D.C. before you spoke," Chinh says. "I'd like your permission to ask the FBI to investigate Governor Muñoz for evidence of links to Castillo as well."

"Why?"

"Because of his connections to H2M," Chinh says.

"We're getting into questionable territory when we track any U.S. citizen without a specific crime in mind; more so when we're talking about a Governor who opposes us. Any reason to believe the FBI can't get a judge to authorize this?" the President asks, trying to avoid imposing a presidential order.

"I think there's enough reason to grant it based on what I know, but I'm not an expert. I'll contact Betty and ask her to do it and let us know if there's a hiccup," Chinh says.

"It's better that way. If I really thought the Governor was a national security threat, I'd take the risk, but we certainly should have learned a lesson from Nixon. Every President thinks his reelection is a national imperative, and anything that challenges that goal is a threat to security. I don't like how this looks if I order it," the President says.

"One more question, Marc," Chinh says. "I hadn't heard of links to Castillo before. Is this something strong we have from the FBI?"

"The evidence is from D.C. police. We don't have proof, but we have enough to warrant an investigation," the President says. "The Attorney General looked at what we know, and she thinks the coincidences and circumstantial evidence add up to too much to be ignored."

"A bit risky to go right at H2M as in bed with Castillo," Chinh half says, half asks.

"Not really. The government has known for many years about an old relationship between Ángel Herrera and Castillo, though we've never had proof of anything illicit. The CIA has tracked Castillo and Ángel as in the same general area on opposite borders over the years, but we've never caught them together. We've also tracked links between companies we believe are owned by Castillo and people we think do Castillo's wet work. Either something's there or someone has masterfully set them up."

CHAPTER 44

October 15, 2040
Denver, Colorado

With so many Hispanic politicians expressing support for separating the Southwest as an independent Republic, and many more initiating proposals to separate their states or cities into independent Republics, many Mexican Americans around the country are internally torn between pride in their ethnicity and pride in their adopted country. For generations, too many politicians fostered an "us versus them" political agenda from the cocoons of court-mandated majority-minority districts.

Majority-minority districts established through race-based mapmaking are intended to ensure congressional membership mirrors the general public's racial diversity. The unintended consequence of the separate legislative districts is political leaders have learned over generations to be less sensitive to populations outside their race, encouraging politics of confrontation over politics of collaboration. In a number of Hispanic and African American districts, elected officials often focus on race-based policies as a source of political power. Whites and Asians often are targets of this animosity, and as white populations lost majority status in many states, race-based hate crimes against whites and Asians increased. In some all-white districts, racial insensitivity went unchecked as well.

With the November referenda and national presidential elections just weeks away, these days are particularly troubling for mixed race families with a strong Mexican heritage – particularly families where Spanish is a secondary or dropped language. Added to the mix, immigrants from Mexico make up an increasingly large part of the U.S. military force. For many in their third, fourth or even 10th generation in the United States, Mexico is the place they are from. They left Mexico in many cases not because they wanted to leave home, but because the freedoms and economic opportunities of the United States promised a better life. Now they question whether a new Republic will be more like the United States of old, when merit and hard work enabled people to escape tough starts, or more like the U.S. and Mexico today, when extensive government involvement in every aspect of life means political connections often determine winners and losers.

While Mexico has important natural resources, those resources have long been controlled by the political elite, and often misused by government-run entities. Violence in prior generations created by drug runners destroyed far too many families, and many who came to the United States for non-economic reasons came to escape the violence. Some, however, came to build the drug trade in the United States, maintaining connections to Castillo and the few related drug organizations that Castillo allows to flourish.

Some Americans watch the referenda battle as an aside to choosing between President Phillipi and Democratic opponent Sue Appling, who finished second in the September open primaries. For most, the contemplated break-up of the nation is the primary issue influencing their presidential vote.

H2M movement leaders, including Gabriel, routinely label those protesting against secession as racist. Gabriel has worked assiduously in the past month to reconcile with Juan, convincing Juan that everything was a misunderstanding. Gabriel shows Juan evidence that U.S. military material was used to create the bomb that Juan was accused of planting. Gabriel says he now realizes others had duped him in an effort to destroy their relationship and their shared mission. More out of sharing an objective than true trust, Juan has decided to give Gabriel another chance. Still, he only meets with Gabriel in public settings. No formal charges have been issued against Gabriel, a fact that Gabriel tells Juan is evidence of his complete innocence in the Convention Center shooting.

Presidential candidate Appling is not above playing the race card consistently through the campaign. Appling goes into the general election knowing Phillipi secured 39 percent of the primary vote and several Republican candidates split 31 percent of the vote. Fifteen percent of this Republican vote went to a candidate favoring immediate military action to stop any effort to secede. Appling finished second to Phillipi, gaining 25 percent of the vote, with only one other Democrat taking more than one percent of the vote in the open primaries.

With freedom marches and protest responses cropping up around the country, violent confrontations continue, though none are as large, or as deadly, as the post-Labor Day rally. Families stop bringing children to most rallies – fearing injury or worse.

Denver hosts perhaps the next-worst violence. White supremacist groups established a national call-to-action alert to get every member of these resurging organizations to meet in Denver, a majority Hispanic metropolitan area with nearly 60 percent of the population of at least partial Mexican heritage. Rather than diffusing their impact across multiple sites, the leadership of these hate groups decided to make a big splash in a visible community to show no one is safe. Most importantly, they coordinated carefully to ensure members arrive in downtown Denver just as a local demonstration in favor of Denver's separation from Colorado and alignment with the Southwest states is launched by Denver's Mayor and a local congressman.

White supremacist national leadership had long preached against using satellite-traceable vehicles, fearing government's ability to control their mobility. Without Easy Ride software on board their vehicles, the descent of these groups causes a spike in accidents. Denver's Mayor asks for National Guard support as verbal exchanges incite violence. Violent confrontations promise to climax at a downtown rally, where the expected 10,000 secession supporters now face attack from more than 50,000 Aryan Nation, KKK and neo-Nazi demonstrators.

Seeking to avoid a repeat of the D.C. violence, President Phillipi orders the immediate relocation of 25,000 troops to the Denver area. Hours later, the first relocated troops arrive from Laughlin, Holloman and

Davis-Monthan Air Force bases, followed quickly by soldiers from Fort Bliss and Fort Huachuca and Marines from Camp Pendleton.

With racial tensions exacerbated by a wave of murders across the country over control of the drug trade in many areas, national tensions are as high as they have been since 2001.

***

Detroit, Michigan

At the Detroit Salt Mine, Rich Dore announces to the first shift team that the second shift will only be four men for the next several months, as more experienced members of the second shift team have been permanently redeployed to a precious metals find overseas. Rich and his men return to single-shift operations.

Rich decides he can no longer keep his suspicions to himself. Later that night, he calls from a prepaid phone he purchases after driving to Windsor, Ontario.

CHAPTER 45

October 22, 2040
New York City

Inside the secure United Nations compound in New York City, protected from the impositions of a city as diverse as U.N. delegates themselves, Secretary-General Sudarto Suryasumantri receives an unexpected visit from outside official U.S. diplomatic channels. Given the turmoil in U.S. politics, he decides to let the surprise visitor come to his office.

As Texas Senator Manny Jones walks in the door, he strides confidently to shake hands and slightly bow before the Secretary General, unsure of the appropriate show of respect for the former Finance Minister from Indonesia who leads the global organization. Sudarto, named after Siddhartha, the birth name of the founder of Buddhism, sees his role as a servant of the world's people.

"Mr. Secretary, I'm U.S. Senator Manuel Jones, from the current U.S. State of Texas. It's a pleasure to see you again. I'm not sure if you recall we met at a reception in your honor in D.C. not long after your installment. We also spoke earlier this year in a session on solving the water crisis. I found your view that people have the right to govern themselves and provide for their future, free from the impositions of global corporations, to be compelling and visionary."

The Secretary-General, a thin yet commanding presence, thanks the Senator for his kind comments as he takes tea from his assistant and points to the tray to offer tea to the Senator. Waving his hand, Senator Jones declines.

"I appreciate the kind comments Senator, and certainly look forward to your support of our water rights mission, but you didn't come to New York to discuss water, I presume. How may I assist you?" he says.

Secretary-General Sudarto gets back up from his chair and walks over to pull a chair up next to the Senator.

"As you know, four U.S. states will vote soon on whether to secede and form an independent republic. I know the U.S. Ambassador has briefed you on these votes, and assured you that the votes will result in no changes. While that could happen, the polling we have been doing shows these votes will pass overwhelmingly. You and I both know that once the people have spoken, action is not far behind," Senator Jones says.

"That certainly has been the history of the world, even if that action sometimes has been brash," Secretary-General Sudarto agrees. "Once a repressed population clearly obtains majority status in a country or even in a large region, there's inevitable pressure to escape repression. More new countries have been formed in my lifetime than the number of years I have lived, all as populations have shifted and fear-based power has been out-lasted by the resilience of people's demands for freedom. I suspect this may be part of the reason for your visit, though I have no idea how I can help other than to continue to express my belief that people must be able to control their own governments."

Senator Jones looks at the Secretary-General and asks, "Is there some-place secure we can talk?"

"You're in as good of a place as any," Sudarto says. "We sweep for bugs daily, and the walls and windows are sound-proofed."

"Mr. Secretary, I need to be clear. If what I'm saying to you does not happen, this conversation can't have happened," the Senator says. "Do we understand each other?"

"Perfectly well, Senator. I realize you reached out to me outside your normal protocol, so expect there is a reason for this approach. I don't know how you knew I would even be here," Sudarto says.

"One of the benefits of running the Foreign Relations committee is building a network of friends who know what's going on around the world.

A former aide of mine is married to an aide for our U.N. Ambassador, so is able to pay attention to your comings, goings and doings," Senator Jones says. "But let me get to the point."

"Yes, the point, Senator."

"I believe the referenda will pass overwhelmingly. Beyond wanting to be governed by our own people, we also want to escape Washington. So when these referenda pass, the Governors of all four states will at the right time demand that the United States agree to our secession as an independent Republic."

Sudarto stares in stunned silence.

"When this demand is issued, or perhaps sooner, the current U.S. government can react in two ways," Senator Jones says. "They could find an acceptable timetable for our independence. Or they could react violently, and begin taking political prisoners and perhaps even killing thousands or millions of our people. Clearly, we want a non-violent separation, but believe the chances of this happening will dramatically improve if the United Nations will send troops to protect our new Republic."

"You and I both know the United States veto in the Security Council will prevent such an action," Sudarto says as he walks over to stare out the window over the East River, eyes fixating on Roosevelt Island.

"Sure, if the issue is voted on. But the U.N. can provide a forum for members to act. And if you can let me know what day and time you're prepared to address the issue, I can assure you the U.S. Ambassador will be unavailable to participate."

"I can't be party to detaining our delegates, Senator," Sudarto says in response to his interpretation of Senator Jones' comments.

"You're misunderstanding my intentions. I share your revulsion at violence, which is why I'm asking for U.N. protection. I was only telling you that the Oversight Subcommittee I chair will hold a very special hearing on the day and time you choose to raise issues that will certainly occupy the Ambassador," Senator Jones says. "All we're asking is that the United Nations commit to protecting the people of our states – I mean our Republic – should the United States turn on its former people. Certainly, for many members, this will be an opportunity to side against repression. It may even be a chance to repay the U.S. government for interfering in their countries in a show of force so strong as to discourage actual conflict."

Secretary-General Sudarto pulls up his cup, downing the last sips of now lukewarm tea.

"I'll think about this. Making such a request will define my time as Secretary-General and is almost certain to put at risk the funding we receive from the United States. I'll need to be sure our other countries understand they'll have to carry an extra load until normal relations are resumed. I presume the new Republic will support the United Nations if we help protect you in your infancy," Sudarto says.

"A safe and accurate assumption," Senator Jones says.

"If I decide to proceed, you'll receive a note from a messenger with the date and time for the meeting. It will be hand delivered. It was an interesting moment speaking to you, one I'm sure I will not soon forget. I presume we shall not come into contact again unless through official channels with your new nation," Sudarto says, standing to end the conversation.

"I agree that would be wise," the Senator says as he reaches his hand out with a more formal handshake.

CHAPTER 46

October 29, 2040
Washington, D.C.

With the general election rapidly approaching, a young woman stops Senator Jones to ask for his autograph. As he reaches for a pen, she pulls out a piece of paper and a green Sharpie marker. On top of the autograph paper is a smaller note, which she places under the Senator's thumb. He looks at it, signs the autograph paper and puts his left hand in his pants pocket with the small note. Certain later that no one is watching, he pulls it out and reads: "2/11 14:00"

At first puzzled, he quickly remembers most countries put the date first, followed by the month. Military time is more universal – 2 p.m. in the afternoon is the same as 14:00. He presumes it's safe to plan for Eastern Time since both New York and Washington are in that time zone.

Senator Jones drops in on his Foreign Relations Committee staff director. The staff director is working on a sense of Congress bill that will likely have little effect on the Central Africa violence it chastises, even if passed in the post-election lame duck session.

"Good morning Senator. I'm surprised to see you here," he says, "so close to elections for many of your colleagues."

"I didn't expect to be here, but we have a real issue. Our U.N. Ambassador is involved in a compromising relationship with Brazil's U.N. Ambassador. I want to discuss this issue with him on November 2 at 2 p.m. – privately if he agrees or in a public hearing if he prefers. I'm certain he'll agree to the private meeting, since his wife won't take kindly to his infidelities becoming a national news story. Call the Ambassador and offer a meeting between the three of us. If he agrees, make clear it's best he not tell anyone where he's going if he doesn't want to lead the media to me. If I get any media questions, I won't lie, so the only way to keep this quiet is if the Ambassador can keep his mouth shut and we can be assured no national harm can come from him," Senator Jones says.

"Do you believe it best that I make the call and not you?" the staff director asks.

"Yes. I want him to know two of us know about his indiscretions, just to stomp out any idea he may have about trying to discredit me," Senator Jones says. "He's smart enough to know it won't pass the smell test to go after both of us given what we can independently say triggered the response."

"So" the staff director says, "why don't we just out him publicly and be done with it. With the election coming up, this will help Sue in the presidential race."

"We all make mistakes. I hate when personal attacks are used to try discrediting me. The date and time are firm though. I want to be sure he understands he isn't going to jerk me around on this or any other issue."

Later that afternoon, Senator Jones gets confirmation from the staff director.

"Ambassador meeting is set," says the note.

***

November 2, 2040

As the sun rises over the East River, Secretary-General Sudarto knows this will be a monumental day. At 1:50 p.m., he calls an emergency Security Council meeting.

With the U.S. Ambassador to the United Nations in D.C., there is no way for him to get back to New York, even if he skips his meeting with Senator Jones. Secretary General Sudarto ensures the meeting is limited to Ambassadors only.

Secretary-General Sudarto is certain Senator Jones is a highly motivated man interested in giving him time to make his pitch. Mexico's President quietly joins the Secretary-General in presenting to the remainder of the Security Council.

After merciless questioning on his relationship with the Brazilian Ambassador, U.S. Ambassador Hugh Brent steps out of the admonishment meeting with Senator Jones at 4 p.m. His Lifelink connections have been turned off all day to avoid tracking risk. With the good news that Senator Jones will not mention his relationship as long as he resigns before starting a second term, he quickly recognizes today still will be a horrible day as he turns on his Lifelink and catches up on messages. "Security Council approved sending U.N. troops to U.S. for peacekeeping. Release in 30 minutes," is the first note he opens from his chief of staff.

"What the hell?" he shouts, gaining the attention of several in the hall.

Faced now with choosing between his job and his marriage, he calls his chief of staff. "I'm stuck in D.C. today on a confidential meeting. I'm heading over to the White House to get my hide handed to me. How was a security council meeting called without me?" he asks.

"We approved the meeting sir. We thought you were here. You had open space for a private lunch on your calendar. I thought you'd be able to cancel that, uh, that meeting," his chief of staff says.

"What have I said to you about making assumptions about issues on which you have no damn understanding. You have killed my job and perhaps even our national security," he yells. "I have to get to the White House right now and need to see the President. Make it happen, you ignorant, stupid . . . ."

Angry as she was at being mistreated, Ambassador Brent's chief of staff calls White House Chief of Staff Vijay Chinh with the news. After working through three layers of filters to reach Chinh, she is patched through just before Ambassador Brent arrives at the White House.

"Have you gone nuts?" Chinh says to Ambassador Brent as he meets him. "Creating risk of war just days before the election. What's wrong with you?"

After Brent relays the events of the past hour, Chinh visibly shakes when entering the Oval Office.

"What?" President Phillipi says loudly. "Spit it out."

The Ambassador looks at Chinh, who looks right back at Brent with a stare that makes clear he isn't sharing this foxhole with him.

"The UN Security Council passed a resolution offering full U.N. protection to the referenda states – quote – should the United States consider attacking its own people – unquote," the Ambassador says. "A release to this effect will be out in now three minutes."

"Where were you when this happened to exercise our veto? How do you skip a meeting, not to mention not even inform me of the topic, on a subject so critical to our nation? This is an abject failure with dire consequences for our country. Where were you?" the President screams, as loudly as any had heard him yell in years.

"I was called to a private meeting with Chairman Jones to explain . . ." the Ambassador starts to drift off to think about the wide range of painful consequences heading his way.

"To explain what, damn it."

"To explain what impact my affair with the Ambassador from Brazil would have on the national security interests of the United States."

"I've met homeless drunks with more common sense than you, you disastrous S.O.B. You sacrificed the security of our country to protect yourself from your wife. I hope she will impart punishment more cruel and unusual than what I'm allowed to do and I guarantee I'll pardon her if she does. Now get out of my sight and find a spot to sign your resignation letter. I'm announcing your resignation as soon as I head down to the media brief," President Phillipi says.

Seeing the life sucked out of the Ambassador's face doesn't do anything to control Chinh's rage, but he very quickly moves to damage control mode.

"Before he goes, Mr. President, I have one question."

"Talk to him out of my sight. I'm so angry, I'll knock him senseless if he stays one minute longer," the President yells.

As they walk out the door, Chinh looks at the Ambassador. "I have questions. When did you set your meeting with Senator Jones? Who knew you would be here for the meeting? And when was the Security Council meeting announced."

"The Security Council meeting was announced at 1:50 p.m. today to start 10 minutes later. I had turned off my Lifelink so I could not be tracked. My staff director had agreed to the Security Council meeting, I believe assuming that my out of office meeting was with Brazil's Ambassador. I didn't know she knew about the affair. We had always been very discrete. As for the meeting with Senator Jones, that was set up late last week. To my knowledge, the only people who knew the meeting was happening were Senator Jones, his staff director and me."

"So let me get this straight," Chinh says. "You arranged a meeting with Senator Jones here at 2 p.m. and no one except you, Senator Jones and his staff director knew about the meeting. By some stroke of luck, the U.N. Security Council meeting to vote on whether to invade the U.S. is at the same time as that meeting and you can't possibly be two places at once. And your Chief of Staff is married to who, Hugh?"

"You're not saying that Senator Jones set this all up. Oh, my God. You are. I'm a moron," he says with the painful aura of recognition.

Stepping back into the Oval Office, Chinh asks for the President's approval.

"Based on what I just heard, I believe Senator Jones has conspired with the United Nations to bring troops to our border. I want your permission to ask the AG and FBI to investigate and see if treason charges can be brought?"

"Do it. Fast. And quietly. No leaks until I decide what to do with anything we learn," the President says. "I need to get to the briefing room before everyone gets anxious."

"What will you say about the U.N. action?"

"I'll make clear that a U.N. presence on our border or in our territory will not be necessary and will not be tolerated. I will also announce the resignation of Ambassador Brent, and call for the resignation of the U.N. Secretary General," Phillipi says. "Has the U.N. announcement gone out?"

"Not yet. I would not ask for Sudarto's resignation. I would simply say that if this isn't fixed, we will stop U.N. funding. Calling for his resignation won't change anything, but withdrawing our funding will get his attention."

"Call the foreign policy and defense teams together. We need to work through our response."

As part of Secretary-General Sudarto's negotiations, he secures agreement from Mexico to allow U.N. troops to set up inside Mexico's borders, with troops under the command of the Mexican military. Mexico's President remains concerned with potential U.S. aggression after the highway bombings. Mexico also allows the Chinese, Russian and other navies to conduct offshore exercises in Mexican waters south of Los Cabos and near Cancun. Near enough to the U.S. to cause concern, but not on the border.

CHAPTER 47

November 6, 2040

On Election Day, the pro-secession referenda gain between 55 and 62 percent approval in all four states. Even so, President Marc Phillipi is reelected with 59 percent of the national vote. In the weeks after the election, the President promises to bring all sides together post-inauguration to determine how to improve state-federal relations to provide people in the Southwest states with more day-to-day control over their government. He also announces plans to make English the primary language for all national government activities, though promises to make multi-language content available to new immigrants. With Congress focused on organizing and the President restocking his Administration, discussions on a more complete response to the referenda votes are delayed.

Gabriel Herrera and Juan Gonzalez co-lead victory celebrations with Texas Senator Manny Jones and other political dignitaries in the four secession state capitols.

Investigations into Gabriel's role in the shooting death of his father and shooting attempt on Juan still have not turned up enough evidence to support an indictment. Juan and Gabriel continue to slowly mend their relationship.

***

December 23
Sinaloa Province, Mexico

As Christmas Eve approaches, Pete Roote finalizes preparations for his next assignment. Pete's close bond with JT is the closest connection he has had with another person in nearly a decade. Pete is determined to prove he can meet any objective JT sets out for him.

Pete parachutes out the bottom of one of JT's APBs at just before midnight. With no moonlight and unusually thick cloud cover, he avoids visual detection.

Parachuting clothed in a thin layer of radar absorption clothing and a parachute made of similar material, he hopes to evade the detection technology surrounding his target's compound. Thanks to a close relationship with the Mexican military, making a strike on Cesar Castillo's home compound is as difficult as raiding an army base. Doing so covertly, without the full backing of the U.S. military, is practically suicidal. Still, Pete sees the importance of the mission.

As Ally guides the APB to his drop spot, Pete has only five hours to create cover from the time he lands. If he misses his mark by too much, he'll have to move too quickly and likely will leave tracks making him easy to hunt.

Pete jumps from 30,000 feet and descends in a steep dive. He and Ally practiced this maneuver at 30 different sites in the months since he returned from his Flagstaff venture. The first trip out, he thought Ally was starting the APB for JT to come fly. As she pulled up from the Colorado camp, she told Pete, "Now you'll see what I really do."

JT's APB is largely undetectable, though JT rarely runs with anti-detection countermeasures deployed. Since the APB is visible to the naked eye, it's important to avoid being physically seen by someone who could notice his absence in digital tracking. Though darker that night than during almost all of his practice jumps, the night vision capabilities in his goggles give Pete as clear a view as possible of the desert below. After releasing his parachute at 3,000 feet, he fights a few wind gusts but lands just 500 feet from his target. Still, that's 500 feet of using his elevation walking gear and carefully brushing away evidence of his presence.

After landing, Pete's elevation shoes keep him three inches off the ground, requiring incredible balance when he hits rock with any of the ant-hole-diameter spikes. Pete practiced using these shoes in training. He falls fully just once on the way to his target location, but a few stumbles leave him with extra sand grooming.

At 2 a.m., Pete finally prepares his hole. He'll hide out here for seven days before getting a chance to take a shot, getting settled before Castillo arrives and security measures increase. Forced to dig to deepen his planned hiding hole, he needs to displace enough sand, rock and soil that someone familiar with the area could notice. Since military forces do a 15-mile radius sweep daily of the compound area, Pete is cautious. The elevation of the chosen hiding spot gives him some cover from ground detection. As long as he moves the sand sideways or down, his chances of going undiscovered improve.

In seven days, muscles can atrophy enough to threaten the mission, so Pete spends the second night expanding his hole. His parachute drapes over pop-up sticks to cover the hole. Once Pete settles in the hole, he leaves an opening on top only large enough for a small extendable brush and camera to reach out to cover the last part of the parachute tarp. The hole also lets air in. Pete tries to sleep several hours each day. Since there is no nearby water source, Pete uses a urination bottle to filter out his next day's water. His body absorbs much of the water he drinks each day, so Pete carefully adds freshwater he brought to his cleansed urine to get through each day. Food isn't any better. His 10-day store of calories is designed to maximize nutrients with the least possible weight and size. Taste is clearly not part of the objective, though at least the food is bland rather than bad.

Whether this mission has any value is yet to be seen. For it to work: Pete has to be elevated enough to see the compound, Castillo has to show up, Pete has to live undetected for a week in the perimeter of one of the most secure facilities in all of Mexico, and then Pete has to hit his target. Getting out was another element of success to Pete, though that is the least practiced part of the plan.

"If you hit your target, I'll get you home," Ally had assured him while teaching Pete how to align his parachute and spread out the connecting ropes for easy pickup. The APB has a hoist on board that allows Pete, once connected, to be rolled up. If that works, all they have to do is make it to the U.S. border before Mexican military jets track them, and hope the U.S. military stops Mexico from following them into the United States.

"Do you know how difficult it is to trust someone with your life?" Pete said to Ally during a training exercise when she first ran a hoist pickup run with Pete. "I do it every day," Ally told him. "JT has technology I didn't have in Air Force Special Ops, and that gives us an advantage. He's careful to not disclose his capabilities and his researchers are extremely loyal. It's not like the military doesn't know that New Rite has military capabilities. JT sells some of what we develop to help fund our operations. But he's selective about keeping a few things to just us. I would never have this discussion with you if you hadn't already seen for yourself."

"How many people are we talking?" Pete asked.

"Doing what you have done, just you," Ally told him, making it clear she would not provide a real answer to his question even if she knew.

Enough with the past, Pete decides as the final night approaches. He rechecks his equipment for what must be the 30th time. If the base guards have sites as long as his, he knows he'll be in their view tonight. That they didn't see him land by parachute is a good sign. It's a good thing their technology isn't as good as our technology, he mutters.

On New Year's Eve, Pete sets up for his shot. It crosses his mind that the rest of the United States is celebrating with champagne, hors d'oeuvres and a midnight kiss at least. Not my issue tonight. Those will be waiting when I get back. When. Yeah, when.

Using the same missile rifle launch and bullet technology he used on Ángel, Pete sets up. From this extended distance, the larger lens and launch equipment has to be put together while Pete sits in his hole. If he doesn't do it correctly, it could explode on him. As midnight approaches, he looks out and zeros in on a figure moving in the compound with a machine gun. That looks like him, he mutters, and conducts a facial recognition search to confirm: Castillo.

"JT's right again," he whispers to himself as Castillo walks over to a shooting range and blasts away with his machine gun. It is Castillo's annual New Years Eve celebration ritual. JT has tracked him long enough to know he would be there.

Taking 10 deep breaths, Pete fires the launcher and sends the missile bullet screaming toward the compound.

The flicker of light behind it is visible to Pete, but all eyes in the compound have turned to Castillo for self-preservation should his shooting eye wander. Pete sets his tracer right on Castillo's heart, locking on. Once locked onto the target, it doesn't matter if the target moves, but Castillo is too busy blasting targets to move.

When it hits, the bullet tears through Castillo's chest, leaving a massive exit wound. Less than a second later, Castillo collapses to the ground, finally releasing his finger from the machine gun trigger. When his guards see him go down, they rush from behind cover to see what happened.

"*Ricochet. Castillo is down,*" one of them yells. That initial assessment gives Pete some time. Pete turns on his satellite mobile and orders steak and eggs for 12:30 room service.

"Set" is the immediate reply.

Pete has only moments to hump down behind the elevated hill he is perched on and out of visual sight. He'll leave footprints for sure, so if Ally doesn't get him, the next day's military sweep will. He doesn't have enough weapons to fight off more than a couple, so this is a one or done attempt.

Pete sticks the extendable poles in his equipment bag up, puts on the harness and laces the parachute over the poles with a thin metal rope. As instructed, Pete turns on his satellite tracker at 12:28, allowing Ally to get his precise position. His poles are set directly east/west. This allows Ally to come from the south, latch him in and head straight north.

12:30 hits, and there's no sign. 12:31. 12:32.

"I'm screwed," he says out loud, looking down at his mobile again. Lights are now being used to search outside the Castillo compound walls.

12:38. "Ugh," he gasps out as he is propelled up at a much faster pace than any of their training pickups. He's rolled up to an APB different than the one used in the training exercise. Once on board and told hurriedly to strap in, he realizes why, as this one has an extra speed.

"What's this?" he tries yelling toward Ally, but with audio off and the engine pushing them at full speed, she can't hear him.

With 30 miles left to reach the border, Ally takes the new APB up sharply and Pete realizes why as Mexican military jets close in. She stops.

The new APB is essentially standing still in thin clouds, holding exactly in place.

He'd love to ask Ally what is happening, but he thinks he knows. Besides, she needs to concentrate on making it to the border.

Fighter planes take shots where they think she went, but can't see her. Radar isn't picking up their signal. Jet roars dwarf the APB's propulsion noise.

Mexican jet fighters move toward the border to protect the perimeter and keep the intruder in Mexico. Another 50 jets are scrambled to take down the invader. Several United Nation fighter jets join Mexico's force in the scramble.

Ally wants to eliminate any chance of being seen. She turns off navigation assistance and uses her night vision helmet – just like the one Pete has been using. Vision software has trouble adapting sight lines as quickly as she is moving, but is good enough to get her to the spot, albeit with a hard landing. The truck bed they land on moves quickly, pulling them inside a manufacturing plant. With the engine off now and the truck and APB dropping deep below ground, Ally fills Pete in.

"We're taking one of Castillo's tunnels back to the U.S.," Ally says. "Our team has known about this tunnel for a while, but we took control of both sides while you were on the mission. We lost a little time fighting with a guard station halfway through that we didn't expect. That's why I was late."

"A little late, I can live with. Besides, I wasn't expecting you to be on time. Women always make you wait for a date," Pete says, breathing fully for the first time tonight.

"Is that what this is? I can think of better things to do on a date than get shot at," she responds. "And if this was a date, you would pick me up."

"What are you doing tomorrow night?" he asks.

"Keep focused," she replies. "We're not safe yet."

CHAPTER 48

January 1, 2041
Dallas, Texas

The wealthy founder of Perfect Logistics and creator of the nationally used Easy Ride vehicle operating software, Ramon Mantle indulges the perks of wealth with increasing frequency. After attending an exclusive New Year's Eve celebration, he is just getting to bed when an alert from Castillo startles him.

"I have to call in," he tells his date, whose name he can't quite remember.

"Call in. You're the boss. Come on baby, we're just getting started."

"I know. I know. After this, I'm all yours."

"This better not be another woman," she says.

"What woman could take me from you?" Ramon slurs. "This is a work crisis. I have to take it outside."

"Don't you have people who handle things for you?" she says. "Can't it just wait?"

"Not this."

Ramon leaves the room searching for an empty area to call from. Forgetting his suite has multiple rooms, he stumbles to the elevator and rides to the lobby. Walking outside, he calls in. "You called."

"He's dead," says the voice on the other end.

"Who's dead," Ramon says.

"The one you call."

"He's dead. How?"

"They got him."

"They? Who?" Ramon asks.

"Your government. Destroy everything," the voice says, hanging up.

Ramon keeps walking to his security car.

"Take me home now."

"What about the girl?"

"Who cares about the girl?" Ramon responds.

Shaken to near sobriety, he wakes his parents in their wing of the house from a sound sleep as soon as he arrives home. His father is home on a rare weekend pass from Castillo, a gift to Ramon for his loyalty.

"Get Celia now and get away from the house. Don't come back 'til I tell you."

"What's going on?" his dad pleads.

"No questions. Go now."

"What about you?"

"I said no questions. Go. Now."

***

January 2, 2041
Detroit, Michigan

As Max Herta and almost all of the second shift return to the Detroit Salt Mine, Herta feels good about being back in familiar surroundings.

Max shakes hands with Rich Dore, exchanging New Year's pleasantries during the first full shift change in many months. Rich and his team head home after a long exhausting day, rushing out to beat the worst of a winter storm.

After they leave, that day's salt containers are returned from the depot, filled with the mine's real source of profit. Checking to be sure the last of the first shift miners are gone, Max and his team prepare to send another full drug load to Canada for burial under commodity grains and then national distribution.

As Herta's men open the break room hatch leading to the deep tunnel, FBI agents storm out with weapons drawn. As noise from that encounter alerts them, another team of FBI agents emerges from beneath salt container tarps. Herta and team are fully surrounded.

While being cuffed, the FBI agent in charge yells out, "Which one of you is Max Herta?"

His head down, Herta looks up. "That's me."

"Mr. Herta, you and your men are under arrest for murder, gun-running, drug trafficking, bomb making, and a long list of other charges. Most importantly, you are charged with 134 counts of murder in the Harvard massacre, more than 200 counts of murder in the highway bombings, one count of attempted murder in the shooting of Juan Gonzalez and one count of murder in the shooting of Ángel Herrera. You have the right to remain silent. Anything you say can and will be used against you in a court of law . . .," the agent says. "In case it's not clear, your lives as you know them are over."

"I think you're mistaken," Max says.

"About what," the agent says.

"Our lives are not over. If anything, you've just made a mistake we'll sue you for and take your money for the rest of our lives. We had nothing to do with any of this, the bombings, the poisoning of Juan Gonzalez, shooting Ángel Herrera, none of it," Max says.

"I wonder if you feel the same way after I tell you that Cesar Castillo was killed early yesterday. And I must thank you for just having admitted to one of these crimes."

"I admitted to no such thing."

"Sure you did, but you're so deep in it, you probably don't even know what you said."

Max looks at the agent. His pupils expand. Mouth drops. Shoulders slump.

"Anything else you want to say," the agent says.

CHAPTER 49

January 5, 2041
Fresno, California

"What do you think about the secession votes, Papa," Rachel Cruz says as they drive to Pelosi International Airport. Rachel is returning for winter quarter of graduate school at the University of Chicago.

"That's a tough question. I'm really torn. Proud to see Mexicans doing well and taking control. Concerned because the reason we came to this country was for a better life that I now have earned with a family I love . . . and a daughter who makes me proud," he says.

She reaches over to hug her father, a moment she encountered too infrequently the past 10 years.

"I see what you can become in this country and it makes me question why I would want to change this," Papa Cruz says to his daughter. "Still, I know the struggle to make it here without knowing the right people or being from the right background. So maybe it would have been easier if we had lived in South California or been part of an independent country."

"What do you think Rachel?" he asks.

"You heard what I said in class," she says. "How many students get the joy of having parents critique their classroom speeches when they're away at college?"

"Yes, but what do you think today? You're smart enough to know that you should change your mind when you learn new facts."

"I guess I like the idea of Spanish and English being equally important – regardless of where we go. But that's because those are my languages. I don't know what's solved splitting up the country. Even in countries with little diversity, success still depends on who you know and who you find a way to meet as much as what you know. Not everyone gets the same opportunities," Rachel says.

"Do you know the right people?" Papa Cruz asks.

"I don't know if I know the right people, but I'm learning how to do my job when I get a chance," Rachel says. "And that never would have happened without you and Mom."

"My greatest joy is seeing you succeed at something you worked hard to accomplish. When I see you work hard, and have success from it, it makes me know that your life will be good. No parent can feel any greater joy," he says.

"Is that why you push me so hard?" Rachel asks.

"Life isn't easy. It isn't fair. Most of the time, it isn't fun. But if you set goals that fit your talents and work hard, you can obtain what you need to have real happiness," he says as the car approaches the airport. "As a parent, my job is getting you to do the things you don't want to do so you can achieve what you want to achieve. Most people don't realize how much short-term sacrifice is needed to earn the true satisfaction that comes from long-term achievement."

"I never thought of it that way. I guess that makes sense."

"You know what the hard part is?"

"What's that Papa?"

"The hard part is sometimes you won't know it's worth the effort for years, maybe even decades."

"So why would anyone take that risk?"

"Because the payoff is so big. Like watching your child graduate from a great university. I was even clapping my hands walking to the bathroom when you got your degree last spring. I'm so proud of you."

"You are so weird," Rachel says.

CHAPTER 50

January 20, 2041
Washington, D.C

At his inauguration, President Phillipi pledges a national year of healing. Professor Stark and Congresswoman Jill Carlson sit together for the ceremony, creating gossip media frenzy. Their relationship is moving slowly; victimized by a lame-duck session that forced Jill to be in D.C. and by Professor Stark's commitment to his students. With media appearances absorbing much of their time outside the classroom, they've had little time for each other.

Tonight, at President Phillipi's second inaugural ball, Professor Stark and Jill are determined to escape early to get some rare time alone. At least the bit of time they need to stay and dance is time together. If the paparazzi get their shots of the pair at the ball, perhaps they'll let them leave without following.

Soon after the President and First Lady open the dancing, Professor Stark, Jill and hundreds of others join in.

Right hand on waist. Left hand clasped with her right. Chests pulled tightly together. Step by step in his mind he goes over the dance steps he had studied with his virtual dance trainer for the past three weeks. He practiced every day, hoping to be less mechanical in his dancing and work off a bit of his middle-age, end-of-quarter gut. At least part of the effort worked. Tonight, he carries eight pounds less than on Christmas Day.

As they move around the dance floor, Professor Stark and Jill watch cameras follow them. Professor Stark concentrates on making sure he doesn't get caught looking down at the too-low-cut-to-not-attract-his eyes evening gown Jill is wearing tonight.

"Just relax, Paul. Don't worry about the cameras," she says. "Just focus on me, and everything will be all right."

"I'm not worried about the cameras," he responds with a sheepish laugh. "Although I guess I'm worried about getting caught looking at something other than your deep, thoughtful eyes and radiant smile."

"You boys never grow up, do you," she responds.

"Not when we are stunned, as I am every time I look at you," he responds.

"If we were in a bar, I'd give you a B- for that line. But a B- line from an A+ man is good enough for me. Let's get out of here," she says.

As Professor Stark and Jill say goodnight to the President and First Lady, New Rite Founder JT Alton walks up and waits to the side for a chance to have a word with President Phillipi.

Exchanging pleasantries a few minutes later, it's clear to others around that they've met before. Despite founding one of the most successful on-line gaming systems in the world and building a rapidly growing weapons empire, JT has purposely kept a physically low profile so he's an unknown to most.

"Mr. President. I haven't seen you since your reelection and I want to congratulate you on your victory," JT says. "It's wonderful to know that America has seen the wisdom of giving you another four years to lead us and, perhaps just as importantly, to provide you and the First Lady the chance to continue making this a better world for our children."

"Thank you so much for your support," the President says. Putting his arm around JT and speaking softly, the President asks JT to join him in a side room set up for confidential Presidential discussions.

After both arrive in the side room, President Phillipi says to JT, "I hear from Secretary Mendoza that you're responsible for getting the year off to an explosive start. I wish you would've cleared this in advance to avoid the panic we had thinking we were being attacked. Still, the world is a better place for the work you and your team did and I will not leave you hanging if others discover your involvement."

"I can't really say anything, Mr. President, not while my team is being held inside one of my camps against their will," JT says.

"That's for their own protection, from what I understand," the President says.

"We'd feel safer if there wasn't an unusual military presence drawing attention to our people."

While the two men continue to talk, the Secret Service interrupts the President and yells at him to run. In less than a second, he joins the First Lady in jogging toward exits with a full Secret Service contingent. Seeing the President and First Lady whisked away by the Secret Service, guests in the room panic.

Professor Stark and Jill aren't yet outside the building when they hear the commotion and see the President and his team heading underground to their caravan.

"What's going on?" Professor Stark says to Jill, with both displaying startled looks. Pulling Lifelinks out of his tuxedo pocket and her inside dress pocket, they quickly find out.

"Secession formally declared. Former U.S. Senator Manny Jones declared interim President of Alta Texas. United Nations troops entering Alta Texas and surrounding former U.S. border military bases to provide protection. Several U.S. generals and key military leaders defect."

As they read further into the announcements, they learn more about what transpired over the last several hours.

Troops from China, Russia, Iran, Pakistan, Mexico, France, Germany and dozens of other countries are sweeping into the Alta Texas states. U.S. military bases in those states are surrounded and issued an ultimatum in a highly coordinated attack that includes the cooperation of several U.S. Generals and other high-ranking military leaders, many of whom had been involved in decisions to relocate troops to Denver and other cities facing racial tensions.

United Nations Secretary General Sudarto announces from Switzerland that the United Nations has dropped the United States from membership and that its member countries are all dedicated to securing the safety of Alta Texas citizens. Senator Jones, or now interim President Jones, announces that the Alta Texas leadership hopes to resolve border and resource reallocation amicably and to allow 12 months for individuals to exchange homes and citizenship with a counterpart.

A few generals had carefully worked in recent days to ensure armament would be locked at bases in the Southwest states. Whether the U.S. pursues a military response is now in the hands of the President. President Phillipi quickly realizes that any battles will not only lead to massive casualties in the Southwest and surrounding border states, but could also invite full-scale war against several of the world's superpowers.

The New Year's death of Castillo means his Protection Corps are aligned with a Mexican general and an unknown replacement for Castillo. Within hours, substantial resignations of U.S. House and Senate members from the four states make clear this is not just the power-grab of a single Senator.

Jill decides to call Juan Gonzalez.

"Juan, have you heard what's happening? Did you know about the U.N. troops attacking our bases?" she asks.

"Good evening Congresswoman. It's good to hear you're safe and sound. Have you heard from the Professor? Is he okay as well," Juan says.

"Yes, yes, he's fine. He's right here. I'll put you on speaker," she says. "So are you part of this Juan?"

"I haven't decided, but I've been asked, in a way, to join President Jones' administration as ambassador to the United States," Juan says. "I want this secession to be non-violent and President Jones doesn't believe there's any way to guarantee our safety without U.N. protection."

"I can't believe what I'm hearing," Jill says. "This is treason."

"No, this is helping my people find the freedom and self-control they deserve. We have the right as an independent Republic to invite foreigners to join us as we . . . as our President deems appropriate," Juan says, in loud and tense voice.

"I can't even begin to tell you how disappointed and angry I am with you," Jill says. Professor Stark adds, "I'm afraid Juan, that you're being used. It's only a matter of time before those who understand the true elements of power will sacrifice you and your life to their aims."

"I thought about that. President Jones assured me that his first act of goodwill will be to turn over Gabriel Herrera to the U.S. FBI if I ask him to do this, particularly after today," Juan says. "I hope I will be able to talk more soon, but I have to ensure our people are protected and decide what I need to do. Goodbye Congresswoman. Goodbye Professor."

Professor Stark tries to jump in on the call. "Juan, Juan, Juan."

"Yes, Professor."

"You say you want to create freedom and safety for your people as your primary objective," Professor Stark says.

"That's what I've been saying all year. I'm glad you understand," Juan says.

"As you decide what to do, just think about what the nations who have come to supposedly protect you will expect of you and your people to repay that debt," Professor Stark says. "If you think through this carefully, I think you'll see you're making the greatest mistake of your life. Please think about it. They'll demand to set up military bases on your land and it will get worse from there."

"How's that any different from the U.S. paying down debt by giving away land? Oh, no, I need to go," Juan says as he hangs up the phone.

Jill heads to her congressional office, assuming a vote on a Declaration of War can't be too many hours away. She asks Professor Stark to join her.

***

Chicago

Rachel Cruz, the University of Chicago graduate student, calls home.

"Mom, I just heard. I'm scared. You're too close to the new border. You all need to get out of there," she says, voice trembling.

"Rachel, talk to your father. He's packing up his weapons and says he's heading to the border to fight," her mother says.

"To fight? On which side."

"I don't know, I didn't ask. I'm trying to get him to stay here."

"Let me talk to him."

As the Lifelink is handed to Papa Cruz, he says hello to his daughter, a young woman he had dropped at the airport only two weeks earlier to return for the winter quarter of graduate school.

"What are you doing Dad?" Rachel says.

"I'm going to make sure nothing happens to my family."

"How can you do that?"

"By making sure no one gets past the border."

"How will you know who's on your side? How will they know you're on theirs?"

"I haven't figured that out, yet," he says. "But I will. I love you. If something happens, be good to your mother."

As he hangs up, Rachel hears the most haunting, terrifying silence of her life. She collapses to the floor.

***

Washington, D.C.

Arriving in her office, Congresswoman Jill Carlson and Professor Stark listen to President Phillipi's national address, one of few midnight addresses in the nation's history.

"For generations we have failed to create a unified nation; one that respects and values our differences, but does so off a core, common foundation. We have not solidified shared basic common beliefs in freedom, values and a desire to maintain the integrity of our nation and our Constitution. Tonight, with the cavalier invasion of our borders by countries acting under the name of the United Nations, we see our people and our land being stolen. We all understand that the people of Texas, New Mexico, Arizona and South California want more freedom to control their own destiny. The votes expressing a sense of the people in November told us this.

"I had planned at the State of the Union to announce a new agenda to turn back many responsibilities usurped by the federal government over the last 250 years back to the states – moving government closer to the people where it belongs. Rather than patiently wait to resolve the critical issues we are debating, power-hungry politicians have seen their chance to seize control. What's worse, they are enslaving our people to foreign governments who do not share any interest in the survival and prosperity of our nation, let alone its people," the President says.

"I am offering these treasonous politicians and the military officials backing them a one-time deal. If, in the next 72 hours, they demand that foreign troops withdraw from their invasion of the United States and fully abandon efforts to have our states secede, I will offer full presidential pardons and allow them to live out the remainder of their lives comfortably at an enclave of the choosing of the President of Mexico. If, in 72 hours from this moment, this deal is not accepted, we will bring the wrath of the United States military down on all involved and I am afraid far too many innocent people in a terror I am frightened to even imagine.

"Please pray with me and please pray that our enemies will gain wisdom. Lord help us all in the next 72 hours and, God willing, beyond."

***

As the speech concludes, Professor Stark walks to the window of Jill's congressional office. Staring past the Metro entrance to the dark streets beyond, he shakes his head back and forth, slowly, methodically: "I thought we had more time."

CPSIA information can be obtained at www.ICGtesting.com
Printed in the USA
LVOW12s2319041213

363960LV00010B/293/P